Do Me

"Literature—creative literature—unconcerned with sex, is inconceivable."

Gertrude Stein

Do Me

Tales of Sex and Love from *Tin House*

Tin House Books

Published by Tin House Books, Portland, Oregon, and New York, New York

Distributed to the trade by Publishers Group West, 1700 Fourth St., Berkeley, CA 94710, www.pgw.com

ISBN 10: 0-9794198-0-8
ISBN 13: 978-0-9794198-0-5

First U.S. edition 2007
Interior design by Laura Shaw Design, Inc.

www.tinhouse.com

Printed in the United States of America

TABLE OF CONTENTS

TOUCH AND GO

:::

Carol Anshaw

ALICE'S MOTHER is not going without a fight, or at least a small scuffle. In her living will, Loretta checked the box saying she wants all those extreme and heroic measures, the ones everyone else forgoes. She does not, she has made clear, want her plug pulled.

And so Alice has used connections and spent a little money to give her a death that is state-of-the-art. She has her mother hooked up with the best oncology department in the city. She has three specialists and is on a protocol so experimental that, so far, it has only been tried on mice and Loretta. Something like that. In the hospital, she has a private room with mahogany furniture, indirect lighting, maroon drapes, a window seat striped like a rep tie, the window itself affording a view of the lake.

In a quiet, discreet way, a lot goes on in the room. Bags of thick, transparent plastic hang above the bed, also dangle beneath it. There's an industrial cast to this, as though Loretta is part of some manufacturing process, filtering the plentiful clear and pastel fluids dripping from the above bags into the more meager, viscous yellow and dark green liquids filling the bags below. While she is at work in this way, resisting the firm pull of death, her progress and regress are chronicled by the orange readout numbers on one small black screen next to her bed, the blipping green line on another accompanied by a thin, high-pitched beeping. Alice and her brother, Nick, watch the numbers and the lines, listen to the beeps. They are waiting this out together.

When Loretta surfaces a little from the fog of drugs, she begins singing, softly but with jazzy, piano-bar inflections, *Do you know the way to San Jose?*

This prompts Nick to his feet to inspect today's IV bags, which are different from yesterday's.

"Excellent upgrade. Self-regulated morphine drip," he reports. Then taps the control clutched in Loretta's hand. "A person could get a little trigger-happy."

Nick is a connoisseur of narcotics.

:::

"How's she doing?" Alice asks when Dr. Pryzbicki comes into the room, pulls the folder out of the slot at the foot of the bed, and reads its latest notes.

"It's touch and go at this point," the doctor says.

Dr. Pryzbicki then checks the sacks and the orange readout, and peers at the green line, and listens to their mother's breathing with a stethoscope, and takes her blood pressure with a cuff dangling from a wall unit. In conclusion, she writes something impressively detailed on a fresh page, then by way of leaving, pats Loretta's hand and tells them all, "Just hang in there."

She turns in the doorway to say to Alice, "Of course, if you have any other questions . . ."

Alice unfolds herself from one of the visitor armchairs, leaves behind the book she was reading, and follows the doctor out of the room. They don't talk the rest of the way down the hall to the small room where Dr. Pryzbicki—Diane—who is the resident on this floor on the overnight shift, sleeps when she gets any free patch of time at all. They don't talk once they are inside the room, which is over-air-conditioned and contains only a single cot. So far they haven't used this. So far they only make out pressed hard against the door, which does not have a lock.

Technically, Alice isn't even attracted to Dr. Pryzbicki, who is too young, also overweight, but not in any interesting way, and whose doctor coat is cheap and shiny and pilled, its pockets stuffed with pens, note pads, the black tubing of the stethoscope coiling out. If this were a fantasy, Dr. Pryzbicki would be a little older and more sophisticated, tall and lean and dark and brooding. But even just the fact of her being a doctor, specifically the doctor in charge of these long nights of Loretta's death, eroticizes her and impels Alice to follow her to the little staff sleep room for these rushed assignations. She was disappointed to find out that Dr. Pryzbicki has a first name, although of course she would have to. Since that revelation, Alice has been trying to keep further confessions at bay. If she finds out that Diane has a hobby or a vacation time-share, the fantasy will collapse in on itself; it is not a weight-bearing structure.

"You are so hot," Dr. Pryzbicki says, dragging her lips down Alice's neck.

"Oh, I know," Alice says. She's not arrogant about this; it's simply a fact that has sometimes worked to her advantage. Other times, it has sent her through harrowing and ultimately pointless detours for a year here, two there. It's ridiculous, really, how much time she has lost on this sort of thing.

When Alice comes back, Nick doesn't appear to notice that she has been gone. She takes this to mean he used her absence to pop a small fistful of painkillers. After a long time on the straight and narrow, Nick has started using again. He has been cadging money from Loretta, who has always been a soft touch for him. The money goes for pills—Vicodin, Xanax, and a muscle relaxant called Soma. His dealer is a wheelchair-bound Vietnam vet he connected with through an Alcoholics Anonymous outreach program. At first Nick dropped by as he was supposed to, bringing videos, playing gin rummy with the guy. Then he started buying up half of his prescriptions. The VA, Nick says, hands out hearty scrips. (This Alice has come to see as one of the little pitfalls of twelve-step programs—that they bring one in contact with people who are on their best behavior. And sometimes this is a very temporary state, and then when they revert to their worst behavior, they're still hanging around nearby, full of bad ideas and excellent connections.)

"I got caught up in a medical discussion with the doctor," she lies, although she knows it doesn't matter to him where she was. "I lost track of time."

Nick waves off her excuse. "You can lose track of it all you want. No problem. It turns out time may not even be a true dimension. It may just be a human construct, a way we have of ordering events. Some guys—some of the important guys—think everything in the billions of years of the life of the universe may actually be happening simultaneously. We may just have put in time ourselves, so we don't get confused."

In a previous life, when he was a fully functioning adult, Nick was a physicist. This is hard to imagine now.

"Well," Alice says to him. "Good thing we have the construct then. And day planners."

He doesn't smile. He's in a serious mood. He wants to talk about his romantic life. In addition to throwing his money at drugs, he has also been throwing some at a couple of tough hookers, both named Mandy. He tells Alice he has fallen in love with one of them.

"I'm just guessing," Alice says. "It's Mandy, isn't it?"

He has just bought Mandy a car—a used car, he is quick to point out.

He pulls a folded snapshot from his wallet and hands it to Alice. "What do you think?"

"She wears an awful lot of makeup for someone in her underwear."

The hookers are really just part of the drug thing. At this point, Nick only keeps bad company. The better company has dropped away.

Loretta's illness has brought Alice and Nick closer, as though they are sitting inside one of the rainy-day card-table tents of their childhood. Once they start shuffling through their memories, though, they find they have quite different versions. Tonight, Nick goes into a long rhapsody about his days on a Little League team called the Boilermakers, playing shortstop in games to which their father never came. Apparently it was their sister, Carmen, who helped Nick out, tossing sock balls to teach him to catch without fear.

"Honestly," Alice says, "I can't even remember any baseball. I remember you blasting off all those bottle rockets, and lying out all night behind the cottage with your telescope. But baseball . . ."

She is surprised at not being able to retrieve this memory. Back in those days, she kept a close watch on both her siblings. The three of them were partners in a buddy system critical to getting through the despotic reign of their father, Horace, who ruled by proclamation and edict and by maintaining a low level of terror among his subjects. Loretta's part in this was more passive; it only required her to sacrifice her children to her marriage.

What they have held on to from the long days before they were allowed to leave their bad childhoods is different for each of them.

Alice's own indelible moment doesn't even belong to her. It was watching Horace cuff Nick, who was maybe seven or eight, on the side of the head, hard but under the guise of genial roughhousing.

"That's for nothing," he said. "Wait until you see what happens when you actually *do* something." The smooth way he said this made Alice sure he had heard the line somewhere and was trying out the joke at home, for a little extra fun. Like when he would suggest to one or the other of them, "Why don't you go out and play in traffic?"

The cuffing moment still comes to mind from time to time. A few weeks ago she read a terrible news item about hunting resorts stocked with bears drugged to make them slower, goofier, easier to shoot. And the story, of course, made her think about the bears, but it also made her think about that capricious whack, and the moment immediately following when Nick stood cupping his reddening ear with one hand, his fear stained with confusion. (He had yet to understand that he had already been designated by Horace as the family fuckup. He didn't yet know that he would never be able to win for losing.) She can also see clearly the next moment, in which Loretta looked up vaguely from the fat paperback she'd been reading, and chastened Nick, "You listen to your father now. Next time there's going to be real trouble."

By now the three of them—Alice and Carmen and Nick—have had long years of adulthood to put their slightly tragic stories behind them. Long years plus Horace's short, steep decline into dementia. He now sits most of the day in a chair in the activity room of a nursing home on Fullerton, soiling himself and demanding Oreos. He confuses the shows on TV with the commercials. He recognizes no one. He has moved beyond the reach of their revenge.

Their mother they have forgiven more or less—Alice more, Nick a little less. Carmen not at all. Carmen thinks there is a point to not forgiving. Alice is more romantic. Her belief system includes changes of heart, overdue apologies, dramatic reconciliations, resolved misunderstandings. This philosophy also has room for profound treacheries and unequivocal abandonments, bitter and lasting fallings-out. On any given day, Alice awakens ready for large and dramatic event. Hanging out at the hospital is mostly waiting for her mother to come up with something last-minute and significant, something that will explain her distracted, casually irresponsible version of parenting and reveal a secret devotion to her children, particularly to Alice. Carmen would not allow herself this sort of cheesy fantasy. She gave up on Loretta long ago, has absolutely no expectations of her anymore. If she comes to visit, she will do so purely to fill one of her requirements for being a decent human. Alice wonders what it must be like to live like her sister, to travel always on firm, flat ground, breathing the fresh, gusting air of certainty.

:::

"I was thinking of asking Mandy to come here to the hospital with me," Nick says to Alice after a long while of silent consideration. "To kind of bring her more into my life."

Alice doesn't bother to address this.

:::

Nick and Alice are alone in the hospital room only at night. During the day, Loretta has a brisk traffic of visitors. In these past few years of being no longer really a wife, but not actually widowed either, Loretta has blossomed in unexpected ways and acquired a surprising new circle of acquaintances. Since Horace, a devout atheist, is no longer available to be withering about her religious impulses, she has joined a Presbyterian congregation, which has turned out to be a high-yield community in terms of corporal works of mercy. These women take "visit the sick" seriously. They show up with soft pillowcases and verbena water they mist around Loretta's head. They read to her from religious novels, books she would have ridiculed at any previous point in her life.

Another surprise: despite all the years spent as the wife of an artist at the center of a hipster crowd, Loretta had belatedly taken up the corniest possible interest—ballroom dancing. Two dapper guys—one old, one disconcertingly only in his late forties—have turned up as frequent bedside visitors these past days, and from them Alice and Nick have learned of their mother's reputation on the dance floor, particularly in the areas of tango and West Coast swing. It annoys Alice to think of Loretta having moved on, not to an old age filled with regret, but rather to catching a second wind—twirling and dipping in God's grace, and a little limelight.

:::

Alice has come with Diane to her apartment. What is she doing here? Diane is naked on a creamy leather sofa, where she has been quite commanding and masterful for the past hour or so. Alice had hoped to keep this affair semiclothed, but everything has moved quickly in an unexpected direction. She has no understanding of her attraction to Dr. Pryzbicki. It seems, by this late-ish point in her life—Alice has just turned fifty—she should have a "type" or at least some guidelines for whom she will get into bed with. Instead, she will wind up in situations like this one. Not as often as when she was younger, but still.

"I'd better get back to the hospital," she says, pulling herself up against the arm of the sofa, dragging Diane, who is on top, along with her, the air around them thick with sex and sofa leather. "How do you think my mother's doing?"

Diane cocks her head.

"Oh boy. I'd say at this point your mother is kind of beyond *doing*. We've taken her off the protocol. How can I put this? You know those old doctor-patient jokes? Like the patient asks his doctor, 'How am I doing?' and the doctor says, 'Well, I'm sorry but you only have ten to live.' And the patient says, 'Ten *what*?' And the doctor says, 'Nine. Eight. Seven . . .'" Diane looks at Alice with a large measure of sincerity and says, "I hope I'm not speaking too frankly."

:::

Loretta slips in and out of consciousness. She eddies between the uninteresting world of this hospital room and a pageant of scenes from her earliest years. She calls out to her own mother, dead now for decades. It's not a cry of distress, rather a joyous shout, as though she's asking for attention to how high she can make herself go on a swing set.

"She's way back there," Alice says to her sister.

Carmen has finally come to the hospital. Through the discipline of Jungian analysis and by studying the texts of her dreams, Carmen has dispatched her mother to a place where she doesn't have to expend energy hating her. Her way of talking about Loretta now is to damn her lightly with faint praise. "Well, she didn't drown us in the bathtub. She didn't leave us on the median strip on the highway," she will say, or, "She didn't sell us on the black market for parts like that Russian woman with her grandson."

"She looks so harmless. Imagine that," Carmen says now, as they watch Loretta wave across the backyard of her girlhood.

:::

Alice is in the shower with Diane. They've been here awhile, since Alice followed Diane home in the morning when her shift was over. The water has run down from hot to lukewarm. They're well beyond frolicsome lathering and rinsing.

"Don't stop," Alice says.

"I might have to, though," Diane says. "Stopping might be the best thing for you."

"No," Alice says in a voice so small and distant she can hear it echo vaguely off the shower tiles. Alice is falling into something soft-focus and emotion-bearing with Dr. Pryzbicki, something she could not have predicted. She has been toppled by kindness. Outside of bed, or the shower, where Diane withholds to put a little spin on things, she is generous in a bounding way. It has only been two weeks, but already there have been small presents—unusual cut flowers from a Japanese shop on Belmont, a book of good poetry. But also a whole new category of sideswiping gesture. Like yesterday, on her day off, she asked to borrow Alice's car and brought it back washed, waxed, oil changed, tires rotated.

Diane isn't any sort of person Alice ever thought she'd be interested in. Alice has spent most of her adulthood falling for and recovering from adventures with good-looking, lightly cruel, mercurial women, all of whom seemed initially different from one another, movies in a darkened theater, opening against the backdrop of one or another exotic locale, stories so filled with potential she would become euphoric imagining herself into them. By their endings, though, these stories turned out to just be slightly different versions of the same story—an essentially dull tale pumped up with bursts of emotional squandering. And yet, all along this bumpy way, the idea of Diane never occurred to Alice. She hadn't considered someone serious and constant, someone who wouldn't make her nervous.

Diane isn't an oncologist; she is only rotating through on her way to becoming an emergency room doctor. She likes the front-line aspect of doing good. She also wants to take care of Alice. If you'd asked Alice a couple of weeks ago, this wouldn't have sounded appealing. Now, she's not so sure.

:::

After all their vigil keeping, when Loretta dies, no one is there. Alice, who has gone home to get a night of something better than chair sleep, gets a call at three thirty in the morning from Diane, who is on duty and has just signed the death certificate. Alice calls Nick, but there's no answer, then tries Carmen, but just gets voice mail. Carmen battles insomnia with a white-noise machine set to tropical rain forest; once the machine is on, it's raining like crazy and you can't reach her. And so Alice heads down to the hospital alone. On the way, she hops a little ahead of herself into what she expects to find: Loretta in some grim basement morgue, slid by an attendant from a wall cabinet on a steel body tray, her skin gray fading to blue.

But when Alice actually arrives, her mother is still in her deluxe room, in the bed with the mahogany headboard. The machines and bags of fluids are gone, though, there being nothing left to monitor or measure. Her face holds no expression at all. She doesn't look peaceful or angelic, only as though she is off somewhere else and has left herself behind.

Alice takes her mother's cooling hand and waits for something significant and terrifying to open up around them. What she sees instead is that death isn't going to offer much of anything, that her mother will now merely move down the metaphorical block a bit and take up residence in Alice's dreams.

:::

She goes over to Nick's apartment, buzzes twice, then lets herself in with a key she keeps for when he needs to be rescued from himself.

A berry aroma fills the place, from a large candle on the counter that separates the living room from the kitchen. The ceiling above what must be the designated candle-burning spot is black.

Nick is sitting on the sofa in front of his TV, which is huge. She notices a scattering of porn magazines on the coffee table. The top one is *Vinyl Pals*. The two blondes on the cover wear shiny, brightly colored lingerie. They appear to be not so much sexually involved as stuck to each other. He looks up at Alice from a vast painless place.

"This is a great movie," he says, nodding toward the TV, although the video—she recognizes it as *Bound*—is on pause, flipping up like a flash card, an endless repeat of Gina Gershon, smoldering. Her lips, magnified on the large screen, are nearly the size of throw pillows.

"Listen. Mom died."

He nods for such a long time Alice begins to think he is preparing to offer something important. But when he finally speaks, it is to say, "Do you want an ice cream treat? I have lots in the freezer."

She gets a Nutty Buddy and takes the chair across from him. "I love these," she says when she is halfway through.

:::

Loretta wanted to be sent off from a funeral chapel in her neighborhood. She left instructions about everything. She wanted to be laid out in an open casket, which is disturbing to Carmen.

"Who does this anymore?" she says to Alice as they sit in Chapel Number Two. "I mean outside of Sicily?"

"Who cares, though, really?" Alice counters. "All her chums can see her one last time. And she looks pretty good. I mean, they did a nice job. The makeup and all."

"What are you even saying?" Carmen says. "She looks *dead*. I don't even know what to say about her now." And then all of a sudden, Carmen is weeping, then grabbing tissues from one of the many boxes set out all around the room to manage exactly this sort of flaring and unbidden emotion. She has clearly surprised herself.

"I know," Alice says. "What *can* you say?"

"Well," Carmen says, taking her time while she pulls herself together, "I guess we could say she didn't lock us in the cellar and make us eat dirt."

They look around the room, which is set up to resemble a small church.

"Where's Nick?" Carmen says. His absence has just occurred to her.

"Indisposed."

"You couldn't get him to come over?"

"I tried. You can try if you want. Go over there. I don't think he'll straighten out, but you can have an ice cream treat."

"He called me a while back," Carmen says. "He wanted to go looking at apartments. This was when he was living in the lovely motel. He had the Sunday *Trib* with a bunch of open houses circled, and I fell for it. I thought, maybe he's pulling himself together and he's saved up enough for a security deposit and a month's rent, or I thought maybe you or Mom had helped him out a little. Anyway, we went to, like, five apartments before I figured out that he was going through medicine cabinets in the bathrooms. His pockets were jammed with pill bottles; he clicked when he walked. Like he was accompanying himself on castanets."

:::

The funeral home asked for photos of the deceased, which have been slipped into frames and now cozily clutter the tables in the foyer of the chapel. The one printed on the prayer cards is a shot of Loretta in her fifties, her deep-tanning years. Her teeth and the whites of her eyes pop out, as though electrically illuminated.

The first of the mourners begin to drift in. The Old Town bohemian crowd from the early days of her marriage is present in faint outline—a guy in a beret and a wispy ponytail, a woman in black chaps and black bolero jacket, and a wide hat with a heavy veil. Alice recognizes her; it's Cindy Beecham. Larry and Giselle Zorn have come, natty and stylish, although the style is thirty years out of date; their glasses are huge. Others of the old gang are absent because of illness, or due to being already dead themselves. Horace wasn't invited, as he no longer recalls being acquainted with Loretta. The largest contingent of those in attendance is her replacement friends—women from her church as well as the snappy dance partners. Behind them Alice spots an aunt and windbag uncle she would just as soon duck.

"Look," Carmen says, putting a hand on Alice's arm, directing her attention to the other entrance. "Isn't that Mom's doctor? From the hospital? She must just be so dedicated, to follow through like this."

:::

At the funeral the next morning, the sisters sit in the front pew with Nick between them. Carmen went over to his apartment, got him to put on a sports jacket, and drove him over. He looks as though he is about to come out of his skin. He mutters something bogus about having to leave for an appointment. Carmen clamps a hand on his thigh.

"I'm sorry," she tells him. "You're going to have to do this. We're all doing this and then we'll be done."

He nods and simmers down a little. Carmen is a powerful person. With the right moral lighting, she can be fearsome.

:::

On the weekend, Alice invites Dr. Pryzbicki over. She fixes a little dinner, or rather, gets a carton of tortilla soup from the storefront restaurant across the street and pours it into a pot, then chops up an avocado and leaves the chunks out on a cutting board so they'll look like a last step she hasn't taken yet. Alice is an inspired faux cook. She has a small repertoire of these tricks up her sleeve. For potlucks, which used to be such a cornerstone of lesbian social life, she would line an old pie plate with waxed paper (her touch of genius), then arrange a boxful of KFC pieces inside, and then cover the whole thing with a checkered napkin.

Diane takes off her coat.

"Mmm. Smells good in here," she says. She probably needs to be put into the girlfriend category. Alice is being forced to abandon the initial plan (perfect in a small way) to just have a totally cheesy affair with her.

Diane has brought along Larry, a short black dog she found foraging in a dumpster behind her building and has been keeping in a temporary way that seems to be turning into permanent. The dog is a blender special with a luxurious coat, big, sweet Lab head, a stocky body set on spaniel legs.

A purely wonderful moment is gathering up, Alice can see it forming—the new dog and Diane, Etta James on the stereo, the avocado chunks vibrantly green on the counter, ready to garnish—everything full of small promise and beginning. She tries to dampen her expectations, tries to stare hard past all this, down the road, to how it will end badly—the exact ways they will wound each other, the betrayals that will do them in, the irretrievable words that will be spoken. But the view to all this is obscured by hope and distance, and by the mist that lies over the new. They will get there, though, Alice tries to reassure herself. They just need a little time.

"Watch out," Diane says. "Here he comes."

Larry the dog is high on his new life out of the trash can. Set loose in Alice's loft, he immediately disappeared into the shadows of her studio. Now he has reappeared and is trying to work up some speed despite his shortness of leg. He runs in a rocking horse canter across the vast old wood floor of the loft, puts on the brakes as he skids to a stop in front of Alice and Diane, then looks up at them, super-ready for whatever comes next.

SANDMAN

:::

Sarah Shun-lien Bynum

IT WAS THE ANNUAL All-School Safety assembly. The police officer looked short and lonely in the middle of the stage as he rattled off the possible threats: flashers in raincoats; razor blades in apples; strangers in cars.

Ms. Hempel wanted to raise her hand. Wasn't he forgetting something? He hadn't even mentioned the predators she dreaded most. And wasn't it all supposed to sound more cautionary, more scary?

The grisly details that the officer omitted, Ms. Hempel's imagination generously supplied. The black and shining van, the malevolent clowns, their wigs in sherbet colors. The dim interior, the stains on the carpet. Doors that shut with a rattling slam.

Ms. Hempel clenched her muscles. Terror flowered darkly inside her.

In the very back row of the auditorium, the eighth grade sat and squirmed. Zander, upon completing a drum solo, crashed an invisible cymbal. Elias drew a picture of a small, slouching boy on the back of Julianne's binder. Jonathan, with the toe of his sneaker, battered the chair of the seventh-grader sitting in front of him. Here they were, arrayed before her: restless, oblivious, vulnerable, all of them.

"Come on, guys." Mr. Peele, microphone in hand, glowered at the eighth grade. "This is serious."

An assertion that prompted the entire back row to explode into laughter. The eighth-graders were banished to their homerooms. As they exited the auditorium, banging into everything they touched, Mr. Peele, his palm clamped over the microphone, instructed the homeroom teachers to finish off the job. "And don't forget to remind them about Safe Haven," he said, but the homeroom teachers were already walking out the door, rolling their eyes at each other. They had inherited yet another mess, like the teaching of sex education, the chaperoning of Trip Days, the organizing of canned-food drives and danceathons.

Ms. Hempel's class, jostling their way back into the homeroom, looked decidedly pleased with themselves. "We're missing French!" Sasha announced. Victoriously, they slammed their backpacks down onto the desk-chairs. "How many more periods until lunch?" Geoffrey asked.

They had no idea of the danger. "Don't you realize," Ms. Hempel cried, shutting the door behind her, "all the terrible things that could happen to you?"

The class regarded her coolly. The whole assembly, they explained, was not for their benefit. They weren't small or cute enough anymore. They were too wised-up. "Want some candy, little girl?" Elias said in a cooing voice. Who would fall for such a stupid trick? Probably even the fifth- and sixth-graders knew better.

"I mean," Sasha said, "we're not exactly the ones to worry about."

"I know!" A chorus of agreement. And then, the cherished complaint: no one seemed to have noticed the fact that they were, virtually, in high school and thus fully capable of handling their own affairs.

"Haven't you heard," persisted Ms. Hempel, "about the clowns? Who kidnap you? Who drive around in vans!"

"Oh, Ms. Hempel," Julianne sighed. "We're fine. Really."

"Can you imagine," Sasha asked, "a clown taking off with Jonathan Hamish?"

The class turned and looked at Jonathan, who had peeled the sole off his sneaker and was now trying to insert it down the back of Toby's shirt. The logic went: in the unlikely chance that Jonathan could be swayed by the promise of bottle rockets and lured into the back of a dark and fusty van, he would exhaust the clowns before anything creepy might happen. The kids chuckled at the thought: the clowns slumped over, wigs askew, wearing the same dazed, disbelieving expression they sometimes saw on the faces of Jonathan's teachers.

Meanwhile, Toby wriggled valorously.

Ms. Hempel confiscated the sole.

"What is Jonathan, or any of you, going to do when the clowns sneak up behind you and clobber you over the head with a tire iron?" she asked. "Or stuff a chloroform-soaked towel underneath your nose, and you pass out, dead to the world? What are you going to do then?"

"They do that?" Geoffrey asked.

"For real?" Julianne asked.

"Yes!" Ms. Hempel said. "I read it in the newspaper."

The eighth grade looked appalled. Ms. Hempel felt appalled, at the enormity of her lie. Generally speaking, her lying was of the mildest sort, only because she couldn't do it very well. A genetic failing. Her father was a terrible liar. "Did you get in touch with the insurance man?" her mother would ask, and he would answer, "Yes!" in a confident way that made it quite clear he had not. Once, when he picked her up from school, more than forty-five minutes late, he had glared at the dashboard and growled, "Emergency at the hospital," even though his damp tennis shorts in the backseat were letting off a most powerful reek.

But he was scrupulously honest about important things. When faced with a difficult question, he never lied or dodged or even faltered. "Toxic shock syndrome," he had once explained to her, "occurs when a woman leaves a tampon or an IUD inside her vagina for too long, allowing bacteria to gather. The bacteria then causes an infection that enters her bloodstream and can, but not always, result in her immediate death." Mastectomy and herpes were described just as clearly.

It was a model she admired. "Sodomy," Ms. Hempel now said to her class, "is what's happening in the back of those vans. And though *sodomy* is a word that can be used in reference to any sort of sexual intercourse, it most commonly refers to anal sex."

They seemed to have a good understanding of what that was. Roderick made a joke about taking a shower and having to pick up a bar of soap off the floor. The class laughed warily. They shifted in their desk-chairs.

"The clowns do this to you while you're unconscious?" Toby asked.

"Exactly," Ms. Hempel said, and the kids fell silent. The other clowns, the ridiculous ones, wearing wigs and clutching candy, had been replaced: these new ones marched through the homeroom swinging their tire irons, waving their towels, unbuckling their pants.

"So do you see why we're scared? Why we want you to be careful?"

The kids nodded. They seemed to have gone suddenly limp. Ms. Hempel felt horrible.

"But don't worry!" she said. "There are stickers everywhere. You've seen them. The blue ones? With the little lighthouse on them."

"Safe Haven," said Sasha dully.

"Right!" Ms. Hempel said. "If you see that sticker in a store window, you know that you can walk inside and they'll take care of you and call the police and call your parents."

"You mean if the clowns try to clobber us," Zander clarified.

"Or if anyone strange approaches you," she said. "Anyone who makes you feel uncomfortable."

"But Safe Haven doesn't work!" Gloria said. "When this gross guy was following me home from the bus stop, I went into Video Connection, and the girl there didn't even know what I was talking about."

"A gross guy followed you home?" Ms. Hempel asked.

"He kept singing 'You are the sun, you are the rain,' really quietly, just so I could hear. You know that song?"

The other girls squealed softly in disgust.

"When did this happen?" Ms. Hempel asked.

"It happens all the time!" the girls cried out, and like a flock of startled pigeons they all seemed to rise up at once. Didn't Ms. Hempel know? Weirdness was lurking everywhere: behind the bank, holding a broom; on the subway, grazing your butt; at the park, asking if he could maybe touch your hair. *What book are you reading? What grade are you in?* The girls bounced up and down in their chairs, seething, commiserating, trying to outdo each other. When I was walking to school. When I was visiting my cousin. No, wait! Listen: When I was, like, twelve . . .

Homeroom discussions always seemed to end this way. The girls in a glorious fury; the boys gazing dumbly at the carpet. What would possess a clown, Ms. Hempel wondered, to kidnap one of these beautiful girls? So lively, and smart, and suspicious. Such strong legs, from kicking soccer balls and making jump shots. So full of outrage.

The boys, though: brash and bewildered, oddly proportioned. Some of them were finally beginning to grow tall. They wore voluminous pants that hung precariously on their hips. They grinned readily. During the winter, when it was very cold, they refused to wear their coats in the yard: We get hot when we run around! they said. Their T-shirts flapped against their thin arms; their chests heaved. The ball rarely made it into the net, but they didn't seem to mind. It was all about the hurling, and the frenzied grasping, and the thundering down to the other end of the court. And even though the girls were always plucking at Ms. Hempel's sleeve, demanding that she listen, it was the boys who tugged at her heart, who seemed to her the ripest for abduction.

:::

Ms. Hempel wondered if her story of that morning could be true, or if it were, factually speaking, impossible. The detail about chloroform bothered her; it struck her as transparently dramatic, like a woman who dashes about with a long, fragile scarf fluttering behind her. It was an anachronism; something from the days of white slavery, and opium smuggling, and jewel heists. Where had she learned about chloroform, anyway? Probably Tintin.

"If you wanted to kidnap someone, what would you use?" she asked Jack. They were lying in bed, with the lights off. "To knock them unconscious. So that you could drag them into the back of your van."

"Chloroform, I guess."

"Really?" She brightened. It made her happy that the person she was marrying would commit crimes in the same way as she would. "There isn't anything more modern you might use? Aren't there all sorts of new chemicals?"

"No, I think chloroform would do the trick," he said.

"Good," she said. "That's what I thought, too."

"Are you planning on kidnapping anyone?" he asked.

"Maybe."

Then, "Of course not!" she said, and laughed, and slapped him on the arm. They settled into each other.

She had gone to the same high school as Jack, even graduated the same year, but they had barely spoken then. She remembered him as black-haired and elfin and somewhat aloof: in an innocent, not a superior, way. His one distinguishing trait had been his devotion to cross-country running. Sometimes her car pool passed him on the road, and she would lean her forehead against the cool glass, wondering how many miles he had already covered and feeling glad that she was splayed across the backseat of a station wagon. She never once saw him panting; it seemed as if he could bound along interminably. Both of her best friends had seen his penis. As part of a short-lived weight-loss regimen, they had joined the cross-country team, and as they straddled the lawn, stretching their muscles, they had glimpsed the head of his penis, appearing from beneath the edge of his delicate, shimmering shorts.

When she saw him again, years later, this detail reared up before her as soon as she sat down beside him. It was an alumni event, an idea that embarrassed her, but her school had reserved seats at a French-Canadian circus that she badly wanted to see. Jack was there, he said, for exactly the same reason. They discovered many other things in common: warm feelings for Mrs. Kravatz, the biology teacher; a passion for the novels of Thomas Hardy; regret that they hadn't joined a circus themselves. They admitted to each other that even though, as students, they had regarded their high school as detestable and oppressive, they now sometimes caught themselves yearning for it.

The circus, too, filled her with longing. As soon as the lights fell, and the audience hushed, and the circus master appeared barking out his welcome, and the acrobats came tumbling into the ring, and the quaint little orchestra struck up its tinkling song, and the lovely women pranced about with thin velvet ribbons tied around their necks, as soon as all this began, she felt herself missing the circus even as it unfolded before her. Folded and unfolded—this circus was famous for its contortionists. But what they did seemed like the most normal thing in the world; their bodies, glittering in the blue light, appeared enormously relieved, as if they had been permitted, finally, to relax into their most natural states. Clearly she saw how the feet longed to roost behind the ears, how the spine was as stretchy as chewing gum. It made her feel sorry for her own creaking vessel, shuffling along dimly, made to stand upright on two feet. No, not vessel—because if this circus, so full of secrets, revealed anything, it was that the body does not contain, but is contained; rather than comb through the jungles of Asia and Africa and bring back, in shackles, the wildlife found there, this circus had coaxed out of hiding a strange beast, the body.

"Oh, those Canadians!" she murmured, and Jack nodded ardently, as if he understood precisely what she wasn't able to say.

It was the circus, she felt sure, that had made possible all that followed. Where else but in the company of acrobats could she imagine her own body fitting with his? Watching him from the station wagon, his black hair, his small frame skimming along the road, she could not have imagined it. Her imagination would have balked, recoiled: why, she wasn't sure. But it was subdued, now, compliant; she sat beside him at the circus and the unimaginable became suddenly, forcefully possible. Everything else seemed easy: the long correspondence, the breaking off with his girlfriend, the bringing together of their two libraries.

And his penis she forgot all about, even after she had herself encountered it. Her two best friends had to remind her of the story.

:::

Her best friends, Greta and Kate, had their hearts set on a bridal shower. It was held at a Victorian tearoom, with mismatched china and plates of watercress sandwiches. Only the three of them were invited.

In a wobbly rattan chair, her legs firmly planted, sat Kate. "Don't sit there," she said to Greta. "Floral chintz is for Beatrice. The Angel in the House."

Greta tucked herself into a wing chair. With a great show of ceremony, she unclipped her beeper and stuffed it deep inside her purse. "No interruptions!" she declared. The symmetry was pleasing: a doctor, a lawyer, a teacher, the professions you aspire to when you're a child, before you learn about all the other possibilities.

"Ooooh, look at you!" Greta said to Beatrice, who had removed her sweater.

Beatrice looked down at her breasts. "Do you think it's too much?"

"No!" they said at once.

"You wore that to school?" Greta asked, and Beatrice nodded.

"Those poor boys," said Kate, reaching for the sugar cubes.

"Pup tent!" Greta cried, and though Beatrice tried to protest, tried to explain that her students didn't look at her that way, that they were inflamed by other teachers, like Ms. Burke, who taught science, and Madame Planchon, who wore seamed stockings, her two best friends were already slapping hands above the teapot.

"Your breasts are *lovely*." Greta leaned over and squeezed Beatrice's leg. "You *should* show them off."

"Absolutely," Kate said.

This type of flattery—excessive, heartfelt, slightly barbed—was their favorite activity. They served as each other's most passionate advocates: no one, in Beatrice's mind, was as intelligent and beautiful and kind and brave and talented as Kate and Greta. And Kate and Greta, in turn, would insist the same of Beatrice. It was puzzling, then, that together they had managed to collect such a number of men who seemed less alert to these qualities. Jack was a departure in this regard. And Beatrice wondered if she might be a disappointment to her friends, not because she was getting married, but because she had stopped falling in love with men who were childlike, or ill-tempered, or flat-footed, or unkind. Or maybe simply indifferent.

Which was not at all what they had planned when they were in high school. These plans had imagined graceful men, with slim hips and luminous skin. At least that was what Greta described. The fact that he might be gay to begin with would only make his conversion all the more remarkable. Kate wanted a looming, overpowering man, one who could make her feel petite (for once), and envelop her entirely. And then? A nighttime wedding, with Japanese lanterns. Quails and asparagus. A honeymoon in Prague. Nearly every lunch period was spent in this fashion. Pushing their trays to one side, they huddled over the table and spangled their futures with intrigues and travels and children and accolades. For the sake of realism, they threw in obstacles: a callous lover for Kate (she eventually comes to her senses); Beatrice's close call with pharmaceuticals (from which she emerges chastened, but stronger). Then they liked to skip far ahead, and picture themselves on a porch, widowed, delighting in one another's company once again.

Now, having arrived at the future, they liked nothing better than to recall their days around the lunch table. They exclaimed over their miscalculations. Holding up their tearoom selves and measuring them against their lunchroom selves, they tried to account for the discrepancies. How did wild-eyed Beatrice become a teacher? How did she succeed in getting engaged before anyone else? The trajectory was not at all what they had predicted.

"Who would have thought," Greta asked, loosening a strawberry from its stem, "that you would marry Jack Curtis?"

"Can you imagine," Kate said, "sitting there in practice and knowing, 'That penis, one day, is going to penetrate our beloved Bea.'"

"I bet he never would have dreamt it," Greta said.

"Did he?" Kate asked, excited. "Did he notice you then?"

Beatrice had asked him that very question, even though she felt it vain and somewhat despicable to do so.

"Oh no, not in that way. He was scared of me."

"He was?" Kate and Greta laughed.

"Yes!" Beatrice said. "I can see why."

Her infected nose piercing. Her scarlet bra straps. Her eagerness to take off her clothes: for the spring play, for the advanced photography class, for any tedious game of Truth or Dare. Her fits of weeping. Her steel-toed boots. Her term papers on "Edie Sedgwick: Little Girl Lost" and "Get Your Motors Running: The Rise and Fall of the Hells Angels." A quote on her yearbook page from the Marquis de Sade.

"But who could be scared of Ms. Hempel?" Kate asked cheerfully.

"Speaking of which—we have a present for you!" Greta said and dove beneath the tea table.

Kate cleared a space in front in Beatrice: "Whenever you wear it, you must think of us."

Greta resurfaced, beaming, and brandishing a box.

"Open it!"

Carefully, Beatrice tugged at the bow, lifted the lid, burrowed through the crackling tissue paper.

"What is it?" she asked.

"Keep going," Kate said. "It's in there somewhere."

She felt something slippery and grabbed it.

"What can it be?" she asked, as she imagined, very clearly, a silk nightgown. She pulled her present from its box.

Greta and Kate shrieked. "Do you love them?"

Beatrice nodded.

"Crotchless panties!" they cried and clapped their hands, as if applauding all the stunts she would perform while wearing them.

They weren't at all silky. Beatrice brushed her cheek against them: 100 percent polyester. And smelling of something sweetly, sickly rubbery.

The saucers rattled. Greta leaned forward, dunking her lovely beads into her cup. "Do you like them? Really?"

Beatrice smiled bravely. "They're perfect," she said, though they absolutely weren't. They were woefully inadequate. Not up to the task.

"I hope they won't shock Jack," Greta said as Beatrice gently returned them to their box. She looked up from the present at her two best friends, her two talented, brilliant, unintuitive friends. They had no idea.

If someone had asked, Beatrice might have described her notion of sex thus: warm bodies in the dark, sighing and rustling, then arcing up in perfect tandem, like synchronized swimmers. Jack's concept involved something much more strenuous and well lit and out of the ordinary. His requests often alarmed her. She knew the crotchless panties would strike him as silly, or simply beside the point. This thought made her feel sad, both sad and spooked.

Even worse, she felt duplicitous, as though she had worked on him an unforgivable deception. He now carried about with him a baffled, slightly disappointed air. But she couldn't help it: how her body clenched, how the alarm was raised, how her every muscle responded with a panicked shout of *sodomy!* He had mistaken her for something else entirely, and who could blame him? The scarlet bra straps, the Marquis de Sade. The fondness for acrobats.

She wondered at what point his appetite had turned. As far as she understood, an interest in anal sex was not something one was born with. She imagined an early, unsuccessful coupling; flickering film-strips; a summer spent in Europe. All it took were some crooked signposts, some conspiracy of events and influences. Because he couldn't have always wanted this. Why hadn't she stopped the car? Why hadn't she sprung out of the station wagon and loved him then? When a kiss was a surprise, the introduction of tongue an astonishment. When a small, black-haired boy would have swooned at the thought of her underwear. Would have died, nearly, at the touch of her hands, her chewing gum breath, her permission to enter. It would have been enough; it would have been the whole world then.

So much more was asked of her now. Stamina, flexibility, imagination (or, perhaps, a quieting of her imagination). A willingness to endure, and to enjoy, what she feared would be a rupturing pain. It all made her feel exhausted and very far away from him, as if he were standing atop a flight of stairs and she were stranded at the bottom, too breathless to climb up. Even though he waited there, full of love, full of patience, full of expectancy, she wondered how long it would be before he stretched out his hamstrings, took a deep breath, and bounded off.

But maybe she was remembering it all wrong; maybe there was never a time when a kiss could stun and astonish. Maybe, if she aligned the years correctly, she would discover that while Jack was devoting himself to cross-country running, Greta was contorted (the true contortionist) over the stick shift in her mother's car, offering an illustration of how to manage a penis inside one's mouth, and Beatrice was sitting in the backseat, watching very closely. Greta, who now leaned across the tea table and grasped Beatrice's hand and said, suddenly, "We love you so much, Bea."

:::

To Beatrice's surprise, Jack liked the crotchless panties. He wore them on his head and danced around the apartment. "All of me," he sang. "Why not take all of me?"

He sang and danced with his eyes closed. He snatched her up, and held her close, and with a snap of his wrist, unfurled her. She dangled out in space, teetering on her tiptoes, ready to crash into the television set—but then he spooled her back in again. Together, they danced wildly. They dipped and spun and almost knocked over a lamp. He tried to lift her off the floor, but he wasn't quite tall enough, so she gave a little push and folded up her legs, and it was nearly the same as being swept off her feet.

"Can't you see," he sang. "I'm no good without you."

She hung on to his neck and they waltzed over her pop quizzes. And into the bookcase, where he stumbled, and books toppled, and he pulled away from her, doubled over. She stooped down to help and suddenly he shot up, taking her with him, slung over his shoulder like a squalling child. She flailed and shrieked. Staggering about the room, Jack huffed, "You took the part that once was my heart."

With a thump, he deposited her onto the sofa. "So why not take all of me?"

He then twirled around and lurched down the hallway and out the door. To buy them two bottles of ginger ale.

Beatrice lolled on the sofa and hummed a coda to his song. What luck! What fortune! A thousand blessings had been bestowed upon her. A springy sofa, a clean apartment. A pile of pop quizzes that could wait until morning. A dancing fiancé. An airborne Beatrice. A pair of best friends, and a beautiful bridal shower.

Abruptly, she stiffened. For where was her present? Still perched atop her fiancé's head. Preening itself. And ruffling its polyester feathers.

And where was her fiancé? Walking down the avenue, with a small lilt, a small stutter, in his step.

Beatrice retrieved her shoes from beneath the sofa and ran out into the street. She looked both ways. She saw a dumpster, a dark alley, and a brand-new van with a voluptuous woman painted on its side. She didn't see Jack. She didn't see anyone on the street, as if she had rushed out of their apartment and into her own bad dream.

Her nightmares took a truly frightening turn when she was about eleven, and her father began to appear in them, to save her. But she always knew, through the inevitable logic of nightmares, that her father would be destroyed, that he would struggle valiantly but to no avail, and that his knees would crumble and his eyes would dim and he might try to speak a few loving, gurgling words to her before he expired. She knew it with an awful, churning certainty. It didn't matter what shape the menace took: sometimes it was a sticky pink substance that came bubbling under the door; sometimes it was an infernal drug lord, disguised as her principal, who was trying to bring her school under his narcotic control. These terrors were acute, yet relatively benign, as long as she was battling them by herself. Once her father got involved, the nightmares would escalate: for what was more paralyzing than the sight of your father, corroding in acid, pinned down by a pitchfork, drooling and drug-addled? In one dream, she sat in the back of his car and watched his eyes in the rearview mirror as he slowly melted into his seat.

Beatrice hurried down the street. She passed a ladder, a trash can, a pool of broken glass.

In her dreams, death always took her father by surprise. Even up until the very end, he'd remained convinced of his immunity. With this same conviction he would, in real life, pick fights with fellow motorists, climb up onto the roof rather than call the handyman, and disappear into the wilderness for whole days at a time. Beatrice found these weekend excursions particularly infuriating. What better way to court calamity than canoeing? She had seen movies; she knew about the dangers. The willful rapids, the bears snuffling about the campsite, the invisible parasites infesting the water. Not to mention the belligerent, banjo-picking locals who would immediately recognize her father for the city-slicking, fancy-pants doctor that he was. She would try to tempt him with alluring alternatives: "We could go to the mall," she'd say, "get some of those soft pretzels that you like." Or she would volunteer to help him load up the car, and then tell him mournful stories about a girl in her class whose grades—due to her father's death in a tragic canoeing accident—had experienced a precipitous decline. But these tactics rarely worked.

Her mother didn't want him to leave either. She would not make him sandwiches to eat on the road; she would not smile; sometimes she wouldn't even appear in the driveway to say goodbye. On the weekends that Beatrice's father went away, she and her mother would catch glimpses of each other as they stalked about the house in an undisturbed rage. But when the telephone rang, her mother, answering it, would say gaily, "Oscar? He's off canoeing!" And somehow, the way she said it—in a bright, emphatic tone that left no room for further questions—made it seem as if Beatrice's father were right there with them, uttering the words himself. She spoke in the voice he always used when asserting what was most obviously untrue. The effect was strange—hearing this voice come out of her mother. Then, with a slight shrug, she would return to herself, her face slackening, her pen circling the telephone pad, and Beatrice, confronted with the mystery of her father, the mystery of her mother, could only write repeatedly, in ever tinier cursive, *Canoeing is a perilous outdoor sport*. She wrote it five times on the last page of her science notebook, stopped, remembered herself, and neatly tore out the page; at the end of every two weeks you had to turn in your notebook for a grade.

By Monday morning he would be back again, in time to make Beatrice breakfast and deliver her to school. She softened at the sight of him standing there in the kitchen, flushed and rumpled and stubbled, placing her favorite antique spoon on the table. The wilderness had released him, had given him back. And just like that, all her fury would be snuffed out. Any irritation was now redirected at her mother, who upon his return had camped out in her bathtub, listening to NPR at a deafening volume. She should come downstairs! Beatrice would silently fume. She should come fluttering in, full of kisses and gratitude and relief!

Disaster had been held off once again. Wasn't that cause for rejoicing?

For there Jack was, waiting in the checkout line, his small black head shining above the magazine racks. No crotchless panties in sight. Beatrice stood on the sidewalk and watched him pay for the two bottles of ginger ale. What luck, she felt. What extraordinary fortune.

:::

The eighth-graders were less fortunate. The next morning dawned drearily, with assurances from the weatherwoman that the sky would remain overcast. The sky was always overcast on Trip Day, the one day out of the whole year when the eighth grade took a very long bus ride to a rather grimy beach. They showed no signs of discouragement, however. Even at the stoplights, the school bus rocked back and forth crazily.

"Rule Number One!" Ms. Hempel hollered, before she let them disembark. "Don't go in past your waist. There's only one lifeguard on duty. And don't forget to wear sunscreen. Those ultraviolet rays will burn you up, even though it's cloudy!"

"And don't talk to clowns," someone shouted from the back.

"Right," Ms. Hempel said.

The eighth grade clattered off the bus and without awaiting further orders stormed the beach. Ms. Hempel and the three other homeroom teachers trudged grimly behind, trying to balance between them the poles for a volleyball net. Yelps could already be heard from the water.

As they cleared the boardwalk, Ms. Hempel saw her students frisking bravely in the surf. It was still very cold out. Some girls wore cheeky little two-pieces flecked with polka dots and daisies; others skulked about in their fathers' T-shirts. The boys were already immersed up to their necks, their sleek heads bobbing atop the waves. "It's freezing!" the girls wailed. "Ms. Hempel! It's freezing!"

Ms. Hempel held their towels in her outstretched arms and rubbed their backs when they scrambled, dripping, up from the water. The girls clustered about her, reaching out their trembling hands and pressing them against her cheek: "See?" they asked. "See how cold I am!"

"Brrrrrr!" Ms. Hempel said, and rubbed them harder.

The girls then arranged their towels into a beautiful mosaic on the sand. Dropping down upon their knees, they dug into their beach bags, emerging with plastic containers and painted tins and shoe boxes lined with waxed paper. These they gravely placed in the middle of the mosaic. Julianne circled about them, distributing paper plates, while Keisha handed out Dixie cups half filled with soda. One by one the lids were removed, revealing jerked chicken, fruit salad, crumbling banana bread, couscous, fried plantains, sesame noodles, sticky little rice balls. The girls fell upon the food. "We organized a potluck," Sasha explained, forking a pineapple wedge and making room for Ms. Hempel. "Please help yourself."

Meanwhile the boys had straggled up onto the beach and were now huddled around the school cooler, peering down into sodden paper bags. They consoled themselves by clapping their sacks of school-issued potato chips and making them explode.

"They thought a potluck was stupid," Alice said with profound satisfaction.

A family of seagulls and the three other homeroom teachers patrolled the area. Ms. Hempel shouted out, "Everything's okay over here!" and accepted a lemon square, reminding herself that her presence was required. She would make sure that no paper plates were left in the sand. She would apply sunscreen to the girls' shoulders, and provide an adult perspective on their discussions. Drowsily, she gazed out at the ocean. "I can't believe you went in," she murmured.

The morning passed slowly. Swimming and lunch had already taken place, and it wasn't even eleven yet. No one dared return to the water; common sense had set in. And the volleyball net kept collapsing. The girls wrapped themselves in their towels and asked Ms. Hempel personal questions. Was she wearing, underneath her sweater, a one-piece or a two-piece? Did she propose or did he? But everything she said seemed only to remind them of something more urgent that they needed to say. Each one of her answers was interrupted, and then abandoned, as the girls hurried from one new topic to the next: discriminatory gym teachers; open-minded parents; plus-size models. The animated nature of the discussion kept them warm. When they wanted to make a point, they threw off their towels, baring themselves like superheroes.

Ms. Hempel found herself noticing a group of boys off in the distance, bending themselves to a task with a suspicious degree of concentration. "What do you think they're doing?" she asked.

"Who knows?" Gloria sighed.

"Maybe I should go check on them," Ms. Hempel said.

"They're fine," Julianne said, a bit sternly.

But they didn't look fine. They were crouching over something. Maybe they had found a stash of hypodermic needles, washed up by the tide.

"I had better go see," Ms. Hempel said.

"Ms. Hempel . . ." the girls called, but she was already on her feet and walking away from them.

Upon closer inspection, she saw that the boys were absorbed in a fairly harmless activity. It involved one boy lying down on his back, the other boys heaping sand on top of him, patting it down, and then the boy heaving himself up and lumbering to his feet. The boys took great care to smooth out the sand so that when the body began to stir, the grave would crack and fissure in a dramatic fashion. She wasn't sure where the pleasure lay: in burying a classmate, or in freeing oneself from the sand. They attacked both roles with equal gusto. She stood to one side and watched them.

When it was Jonathan Hamish's turn, the boys began to add, at his behest, anatomy to his burial mound. As they shaped two sandy breasts, they glanced over at Ms. Hempel, to see what she would do. Their glance both defied and invited reproach, a look with which she was very familiar. She smiled at them permissively, then rolled her eyes to show how unflappable she was. An argument arose as to the size of the outcroppings: some boys, among them Elias and Toby, felt they should be round and realistic, while others, like Roderick, wanted to keep building the breasts until they sat high and pointy on Jonathan's chest. "That's not what they do," Elias muttered, but sand was an imprecise medium to begin with. Jonathan grinned down at his protrusions.

The breasts turned out so well the boys decided to add a penis. They glanced over, again, in Ms. Hempel's direction. They even cleared a little space for her so she could stump over to the penis and object. But didn't they know? She was the young teacher. It was her job to indulge them, to be impervious to shock, to watch all the same television shows that they did. She laughed when they made off-color jokes. She allowed them to use curse words in their creative writing. She taught sex education with unheard-of candor. Of course, they were constantly testing her. When she asked her homeroom to anonymously submit any question, any question at all, regarding puberty or sex or contraception, she received some very graphic queries. She stood at the front of the class and read each question aloud. Competently, intrepidly, she described the consistency of semen, what purpose lubricant served, why a woman might enjoy receiving oral sex.

Jonathan Hamish, who didn't even try to disguise his handwriting, had submitted a question of a more challenging sort. He grinned at her when he saw that she had pulled his crumpled paper from the pile. *Whose the best lover you've ever had?* Jonathan watched her closely, waiting for her to discard it, frown at him, send him downstairs to Mr. Peele's office. But she found herself mysteriously touched, felt herself blushing in a pleasurable way. Another word, surely, would have been the more obvious choice: What's the best sex you've ever had? Who's the best fuck? But even in his efforts to provoke her, he had selected a word that was exceedingly charming. Full of solicitous, gentlemanly concern. And he grinned at her—not devilishly, not leeringly—but sweetly almost, sweetly and frankly. As if he really wanted to know. As if he were asking only because all aspects of her life were of interest to him. As if the thought of her embroiled in sweaty sex were unimaginable. In Jonathan Hamish's view of the world, Ms. Hempel would make love.

When she read the question aloud, the homeroom swiveled in their seats and glared at Jonathan. They knew that only he would ask such a question.

"Well," Ms. Hempel said, displaying her ring finger. "Shouldn't the answer be obvious?"

:::

The penis, having a more slender base, proved more difficult than the breasts. It kept on toppling over. After a few frustrated attempts, the boys settled on a suggestive hillock (a pup tent, Ms. Hempel realized). They stepped back and admired their handiwork.

"Keep going," Jonathan commanded, waggling his hands and feet. "I'm not completely covered."

They heaped more sand upon him, making it necessary that he remain absolutely still, for even the smallest twitch of his fingers could disrupt their progress. Jonathan, as Ms. Hempel well knew, was a child unable to stop moving. And perhaps it was a relief to him, this stillness, this weight pressing down on him.

But he still was not satisfied with the effect. "Try putting more sand on my neck, and up around my ears," he instructed.

The other boys squatted down beside his head and carefully shaped the sand. "More," Jonathan said. "It doesn't feel right."

He couldn't move his head anymore, but his eyes darted back and forth, monitoring their efforts. "You can put more on my forehead, and my chin," he said. "Get as much on my face as you can."

His voice kept getting quieter and quieter. Ms. Hempel peered down at him anxiously. "Are you all right in there?" she asked. "Jonathan, do you want them to stop?"

Finally, in a very small voice, he said, "Enough."

The boys were proud of what they had done. "Picture!" Roderick yelled. "We have to take a picture!" None of the boys had brought a camera. Only the girls had thought to do that. So off they went, thundering down the beach. "Don't move!" they shouted back at Jonathan.

"Okay," he whispered.

Ms. Hempel knelt down beside him. "Jonathan," she said. "Are you really okay?"

"I'm okay," he whispered. His mouth had turned a funny dark color, as if he had just finished eating a grape Popsicle.

"Promise me."

"I'm just resting," he said, and closed his eyes.

"Jonathan?" she asked. "Do you want me to get you anything? Do you want some water?"

"No," he sighed, his eyes still closed.

Then he asked, "Do you see them?"

"They'll be back any minute now," she said. "It's not very far."

"This sand is heavy," he whispered.

"Do you want to get up?" she asked. "Jonathan?"

"I'm okay. It's just a little hard to breathe."

"Oh, sweetheart," she said. "That doesn't sound good."

"It's okay," he whispered. "Are they back yet?"

But only Ms. DeWitt appeared on the horizon: teacher of advanced math, coach of girls' basketball. When she called out, Ms. Hempel waved back at her and smiled.

"Everything's fine!" she shouted, despairingly.

Another teacher would have intervened, she knew, would have brought it all to a halt. *Stand up*, she imagined Ms. DeWitt barking. *Right now. This is dangerous.*

Words that Ms. Hempel should have said from the very beginning.

"Can you see them?" Jonathan whispered.

"Yes," she told him, though it wasn't true. "They're running straight at us."

:::

The boys returned, eventually, and the picture was taken. Jonathan had become quite blue by that point. He wasn't able to burst forth from the sand as the others had. It was much more of a struggle for him, and when he pulled himself to his feet, he was shivering violently. The other boys draped him in their towels. "Let's go back to the bus," Ms. Hempel said. "We can ask the bus driver to turn on the heater."

Together they climbed up the beach toward the parking lot. The boys ran ahead and tripped each other and kicked sand, but Jonathan walked behind them, still trembling, a towel thrown over his head like a hood. Ms. Hempel made him stop.

"Come here," she said, and she held him.

A FOREST PATH

. . .
. . .

Bill Gaston

> The cougar was waiting for me part way up
> a maple tree in which it was uncomfortably
> balanced . . .
> —Malcolm Lowry, "The Forest Path to the Spring"

UNLIKE THE ABOVE EPIGRAPH, this is not a fiction. I have a distrust, a fear, a hatred of fiction, and I have my reasons. You might find these reasons colorful. The first example I'll give should suffice: my middle name is Lava, this the result of having had an eccentric and literary lush for a mother.

I have things to say on other subjects, but this has primarily to do with Malcolm Lowry, Dollarton's most famous man. You'll find I can speak with authority here, one of my credentials being that I grew up not more than one hundred yards from Dollarton Beach, the very place Lowry had his shack, wrote *Under the Volcano*, lived with M—, drank himself cat-eyed, and all the rest. As concerning all famous people, one hears contradictory "facts."

The first "fact" is this. It is said that Lowry's first shack, containing his only complete draft of *Volcano*, all his possessions, et cetera, was accidentally consumed by fire. It is said he was consequently overcome with despair but proceeded, using his vast reserves of memory and imagination, to write an improved draft. None of this is correct.

The true facts are that, one, in a drunken rage, his feet bandaged, Lowry burned his shack on purpose, having cut his feet too many times on the broken glass that glittered all around it. He was in the habit of disposing of his empty gin bottles out a window with but a flick of the wrist and, you see, it was time to relocate. (If you want proof, bus fare to Dollarton will give you proof. The glass is still there, and children still cut their feet.) And, fact two: while a draft of *Volcano* was destroyed, it was a draft that embarrassed him. The three other drafts were scattered around the parlors of Dollarton's sparse literati. My mother had one.

I will push on with my account now, confident that I need supply no further proof. But I should add that not only do I abstain from alcohol as resolutely as I eschew spinning fictions, I hold no tolerance for those who indulge in either. It amazes me that men like Malcolm Lowry are ever believed, let alone admired, at all. When, head in hands, he announced that morning to the various fishermen, neighbors, and squatters, "My God, my home is gone! My book is burned! But at least M— and I are alive!" he no doubt looked wretched and despairing. To be fair, how could his audience have known the truth? It was easy for Lowry to look wretched and despairing when he was in fact hungover and ashamed. But I have to ask, why would anyone ever believe one whose profession was to weave yarns on paper? One who tried to lie and lie well? One whose voice all day was but a dry run for grander lies spawned with purple ink later that night in the name of art? Add to that his drinking. Lowry was incapable of telling the truth. Perhaps I should feel sorry for him. I don't.

While living in Dollarton, Lowry wrote a story, "The Forest Path to the Spring." It was published posthumously, by M—. The story is a rather long, rambling affair, and while some of it is a lie, much of it is not, and so I recommend it to those who must read. In fact, it is perhaps the closest Lowry came to not lying, for the mistruths found in it are not so much lies per se as they are drunken inaccuracies. I'd like to rectify some of them.

The story involves his life in Dollarton, his life on the beach with the inlet fronting him and the dripping coastal forest pressing at his back. I find it a very nostalgic experience each time I read it, and I have read it many times. (Again, I have my reasons.) Lowry describes the unfurling of sword ferns, the damp promise of a forest at sunrise. The dutiful tides of Indian Arm, the rich, fish-rank croaks of gulls and herons, the smell of shattered cedar, the sacred light in a dewdrop reflecting the sun, the mysterious light in a dewdrop reflecting the moon. He describes creeks and trails I myself know well. He dived off rocks that I and my friends once used for the same purpose. And, more, he mentions in passing the elementary school I attended as a child (where no one knew my middle name); he describes the tiny café where I bought greasy lunchtime fries for a dime after having thrown away one of my mother's inedible eccentric sandwiches.

Again, it is a rambling story, its focus hard to find. Love, perhaps. He tells of his love for midnight walks through the forest, his love for fetching crystal mountain water from the spring, his love of dawn plunges off his porch, his love of M—, his love of life. We know that last one is a bald lie. He hated life, which is why he drank and why he created a lying life on paper. In any case, the story's climax of sorts occurs one fateful day in the woods when a cougar leaps out of a tree across his path. He is startled, awestruck, petrified. And in what amounts to a none other than cosmic revelation he learns that his Eden, his forest-haven-of-a-life, has on its outer edges forces of amorality and destruction. He discovers, it seems for the first time, that a rose has thorns. Critics cluck like sympathetic hens and suggest that what we have here is a classic hidden theme, one that reveals no less than a genius admitting to a suicidal battle with the bottle.

The cougar! What a bitter laugh! All of it!

Before I explain why I am laughing, I want to discuss my mom. Rather, memories of my late mother. Her name was Lucy, and she was unmarried. If there are two kinds of eccentric—one who doesn't try to be eccentric, and one who does—my mother was the latter. People tend to dislike her kind, withdrawing from their reek of fakery. And since my mother's kind choose their eccentricities, their choices tend to be exaggerations of qualities they admire. Mom, for instance, wanted to be a mad poet. At the start, she was neither, and by the end she was only mad.

In Dollarton in the forties it was most unattractive to dress up in flour sacks, mauve scarves, bangles, and canary yellow hats. To spout bad poetry in public was abhorrent. This was Mom's choice. Dollarton was at the time a huddled collection of sulking fishermen and poor squatters, and though my mother had a captive audience, she had few fans. Perhaps they could smell her self-consciousness; perhaps they noticed her eyes lacked that electrified blankness of the true eccentric.

And while you may think what you want of her, she was but the tactless extrovert, a bucolic extension of the loud woman in the turquoise caftan, and harmless. The harm set in when she began drinking. I see one cause of her drinking to be identical to that of that man who lived one hundred yards down the beach from her: an overactive imagination and no appreciative fans. For Lowry was at that time in no way famous.

I gather these facts from years of researching my personal history. My sources are the aforementioned fishermen and squatters. When they speak of my mother, they speak kindly but apologetically. They hadn't liked her, and I can see in their faces their embarrassment. I am tempted to ease their pain and tell them I not only didn't like her much either, I detested her. And loved her, in the intense and awful way reserved for only sons. To illustrate: Not long after she died I tried to read her poetry, and while I read for only ten minutes, I hyperventilated for twenty. It was dreadful poetry, revealing an embarrassing mind. But only I who loved her so much have the right to hate her so much.

I don't know if Lowry liked my mother or not. I have gathered that it was she who took to him first, if he took to her at all. She must have seen him there on Dollarton Beach, looking slyly Slavic-eyed, yet burping and twitching like a lunatic in the hot noon sun. He would have been as naked as legally possible, for in the early days he was proud of his build. Mother would have known he was a writer. She must have thought: At last! Another sparkling mind! I believe she first tried to attract his attention in the local bar, where it's reported she attempted (successfully) to buy him drinks. I don't know what M—, secure in her childlike love for him, must have made of that. And it's said she would sometimes flag him down in the streets, on the trails, on the beach. Perhaps she'd borrow a canoe and arrange to accidentally bump bows out on the inlet. I can picture her trying to impress him. My spine creeps as I envision her passing a lime green scarf over her unblinking Mata Hari gaze. Having caught his eye, my mother now goes for his mind and, with that flaccid flare of spontaneity-rehearsed-for-days, she points to the sun and cries laughing, "The moon! The moon!" (I believe my mother was capable of little more than cheap paradox. I also believe she was the last person of this century who held alliteration to be somehow profound. Not long before she died she said to me, in that awesome hoarse whisper of hers, "Meeting Malcolm melted my mind.")

I suspect that you share my embarrassment. But I would also hope you are coming to understand my loathing for imagination, and writers, and fiction, and drink. If not, keep an open mind. My sole purpose here is to free the steel blade of truth about Lowry from the paste-jeweled scabbard of fable that now hides it. I can assure you I'm not denigrating Mom here for pleasure.

So I doubt that Lowry liked my mother much, unless he was a bigger fool than I imagine. His writing demands that I admit he, unlike my mother, at least possessed subtlety. Perhaps fleeting genius, clarity in bursts (burps). Whatever the case, how my mother got hold of his manuscript is unclear. It could be that, like an adult relenting at last and giving candy to a brat, Lowry handed over a copy so she would go away. He likely thought it would take a woman like Lucy a full year to sift through such a book as *Volcano*, but he was wrong. No, in Mom's words, she "communed with his mind for twenty-three hours straight," and finished it. And her "communion" with him proved to be the beginning of her end. For my mother, whose mind's sole ambition was to snap colorfully, Lowry's fiction, his obsessive flowery pain-packed verbiage, was the necessary nudge. It was on the day following Mom's twenty-three-hour binge that the Event—and my reason for writing this—took place.

The Event has to do with the story "The Forest Path to the Spring," specifically with the cougar the narrator saw. As I mentioned, he was out collecting water from the spring, looked up, and there was the cougar. He describes the encounter at great length. Again, it was "uncomfortably balanced" in the tree. It was "caught off guard or off balance," and then "jumped down clumsily." But it was "sobered and humiliated by my calm voice" and it "slunk away guiltily into the bushes." There is more, much more. Page upon page about the cougar, Lowry's fear of it, his thoughts about his fear, his thoughts about these thoughts, his clinging passionately to M— all through the ensuing night, shaking and having tremulous sex together in the knowledge that Danger Lurks.

That cougar made quite an impression on him. However, I'd like to draw your attention to his summation of the encounter, which was that it was so weird an apparition that "an instant later it was impossible to believe he'd ever been there at all." Having done so, I'll simply come out with it: That was no cougar. That was my mom.

:::

I sometimes wonder just how drunk a man can get. I think about that as I try year by year to understand the man Malcolm Lowry.

Wandering Dollarton Beach (or Cates Park, as it's come to be called) again this week, along the path that is now proclaimed by sign to be Malcolm Lowry Walk, I took a good, steady look. A sober look. I studied hard this plot of land and sea so described by Lowry to be "everywhere an intimation of Paradise." He found "delicate light and greenness everywhere, the beauty of light on the feminine leaves of vine-leaved maples and the young leaves of the alders shining in sunlight like stars." Oh, he goes on and on and on. Unadulterated opulence, with four adjectives per noun. But here is the one I can't help but smile grimly at: "The wonderful cold clean fresh salt smell of the dawn air, and then the pure gold blare of light from behind the mountain pines, and the two morning herons, then the two blazing eyes of the sun over the foothills." Did you get that? *Two* suns? The words *blaring* and *blazing* to describe light? This is a description not of nature but of a raging dawn double-vision hangover. I have lived here by the beach all my life and I have never seen herons travel in pairs. This passage would have been different had the man had a palm pressed to one eye.

While walking the identical path, I saw beauty too, certainly, but not Lowry's bombastic brand. I, too, saw rustling dainty foliage of one hundred shades of green. I saw sturdy stoic trees, and mountains with their awesome noble mysterious élan. (It's easy to be Lowry.) Boats on the oh-so-wonderful water, King Neptune's refreshing wavelets tickle-slapping the angel-white hulls, et cetera.

But what else did I see? I saw slugs midpath, dry pine needles stuck to their dragging guts, their bellies torn open by the sensible shoes of strolling ladies. I saw dull clouds muffling mountains logged off and scarred for ever; clouds muting the high notes of birds; clouds reflected better in the oil slicks than in the patches of clear water. I saw rotten stumps, diseased leaves, at least as much death as life. In short, I saw reality. I had no need of hiding from the truth. I didn't have the need of a man ashamed, the need of a vision hungover and in constant pain. Lowry donned his rose-colored glasses and painted the shuffling gray world with the glad shades of Eden in order to stay sane. Art was his excuse as much as it was his tool. He probably believed what he wrote.

On to my mother, and the Event. I should add that I heard all of this straight from Mom's mouth, and the disturbing mix of anguish and ecstasy in her eyes as she spoke makes me doubt not a word of it. She told me several times, and the story didn't vary.

Her words:

"I just finished reading *Volcano*. In twenty-three hours. Oh, I was in rapture. I was under a spell. He had called out to me and I wanted to answer. And I had to answer in a worthy way. I decided to go to him dressed to celebrate the Day of the Dead. In the book this was the first thing mentioned—the Day of the Dead, the costumes, the skulls, and all of those things that so horrified poor Geoffrey Firmin. In the end, Death is the last thing Geoffrey sees. It is the book's heart: Death. It was important that Malcolm knew I understood, as he knew I would. So I made the skeleton costume. The material should have been black, of course, but I had no time, and all I had was a brown one, a rabbit costume left from a bygone Halloween dance. I cut off the ears and painted on the bones. It wasn't a good job, I'm afraid. My word, I had just read *Under the Volcano* and naturally my hands were shaking."

I was scared as my mother told me this part, because each time she told me, even though the Event was years past, even though Lowry was dead and Mother was in her hospital ward, only obliquely aware of me, her hands would begin to shake.

"But the idea itself was enough. My plan was to show up at his door, because I knew M— was back East. She hadn't taken to me, you see, and I can't say as I blame her, of course. Malcolm would act positively fidgety around me, a torn man. But anyway, I happened upon a better plan. I felt it was important that he *look up* to see me, to see Death, just as Geoffrey did at the end, from under his horse. So I climbed a tree and waited. I knew he'd be along soon. I had spied on poor Malc and I knew his habits. Englishmen, especially Englishmen who drink, have strict habits."

Here Mother would stare coyly down at her feet, pretending naughtiness, and laugh like a girl. The final time I head this story, Mom looked very old, her fingers were ochre from cigarettes, she was dressed as always (the staff let her keep her stash of scarves and hats under her bed), and yet she could giggle as pure and free as a little girl. I felt like crying. I felt like looking up and shouting: You may be dead, Mr. Lowry, but *look what you are doing*.

"So I found a nice tree and waited. And my Lord, don't you know I fell asleep. All that reading and no sleep. Also, I confess to having sipped some."

That is, had a lot to drink. But I admit I love to picture her up that tree, and I perversely enjoy Lowry's version, that of "a lion uncomfortably balanced." What a nobly optimistic euphemism for a snoring drunk crazy lady hanging there like a noodle on a chopstick.

"But I knew Malcolm would understand. When he gave me the book he said, in that marvelous Oxonian of his, 'This is a tome best read drunk, for so its best bits were thunk.' Ah, Malc, a lad so boyish. A boyish genius."

Here Mom might drift off. If I felt like hearing more, I'd prod.

"There I was asleep, eight feet up. The next thing I knew, I heard a scream. Yes, a scream. My Lord, don't you know I thought it was a woman. I must have startled, for I fell. And considering I could have met Death myself right then and there, I wasn't hurt much. A broken rib and a cut on my back, and thank the Lord for having sipped some. When I looked up, there was Malcolm running with his clattering empty water pails back in the way of his cabin. He was making the most curious noises in his throat. I was concerned. I think he'd been sipping rather heavily that week, what with you-know-who gone."

My mother's story would go on one segment longer. She would gaze searchingly through the smudged windows of years until, seeing what she wanted to see, her eyes would close and she'd say, "And I followed Malcolm Lowry home. In I walked, dressed as Death, bleeding from my back, and I told him I loved him. He rose slowly from his bed, stood ramrod straight, and told me in a whisper that he loved me too."

Once, and only once, she added: "And we . . . communed." Perhaps realizing for the first time who her audience was, Mom went instantly shy and changed the subject. My mother may have been extroverted and insane, but she was conservative when it came to certain subjects.

:::

I saw Malcolm Lowry only twice that I remember. I was eight or nine, and it was just before he returned to England for good. The first time, my mother had sent me to his cabin with a letter, sealed in a black envelope and smelling—good God—of perfume. Lowry bellowed "Come!" at my knock, and there he was, sitting at his writing table. He had erect posture and a barrel chest, but a big and flabby stomach. A deeply proud bearing. His eyes looked almost oriental. He just sat there, sober I think, and he seemed to know who I was. He didn't look pleased to see me. I gather from my probings that he'd during those years been spending considerable energy avoiding my mother. I gave him the letter and fled.

The second time, mere weeks later, I was again a messenger boy. I knocked at the same door, and hearing only the oddest whoops and titters but no invitation to enter, I peered in at a window. There sat the same man, but hardly. This time he was naked. (I have heard he sometimes wrote that way.) He looked dark and crude, a greasy feline-eyed peasant. His table was littered with papers and books, and crumpled balls of foolscap covered his cabin floor like a spill of giant's popcorn. He was hunched over and rolls of pale fat lay on his lap. He began to make noises again, noises that are unforgettable but hard to describe: a high-pitched kind of squealing, but with a deep bass undertone at the same time. As he squealed he swung his head back and forth in arcs. His lips were clamped open, showing teeth, and his scrunched eyes looked on the verge of tears—like he was trying for tears. Swinging his head faster and faster, he finally stopped and took several glugs from a bottle he had at hand's reach on the floor. I recognized the brand: Bols, the same English gin my mother drank. I stared, fascinated, with the avid hollowness of car accidents when a cop with a flashlight stands over a puddle of someone's blood. What made me run in the end was this: Lowry finally managed to get his pipe lit after missing the bowl with several matches. He took a long draw and settled back and sighed as if in satisfaction. But instead he grew dizzy from the smoke. He began to sway in his chair. And suddenly he shot up, threw back his head, and howled. In the middle of howling—I swear this is true—he accidentally shit himself. I *think* it was an accident. In any case, it was an explosion of diarrhea, expelled in a one-second burst. Much of it sprayed his buttocks and legs, and, snarling now, Lowry began to twirl and slap at the wetness, stumbling as he did so. I ran then.

I realize I am more or less trampling on the reputation of a man a good many readers respect and admire. And I don't mean to rub it in further—no, I only mean to establish thoroughly my reasons for writing this—when I tell you it was on the same afternoon that I first heard Malcolm Lowry was a famous man. Handing me her latest note, Mother had told me, "Be careful with this, dear, you are taking it to a very special person. He is a writer, and his book is in all the bookstores of the world." Well, I had just seen my first writer, my first famous man, and now fame and fiction had a face.

You have already guessed a number of things. First, the reason for my bitterness—namely, that Lowry and my mother had sex after she fell from the tree. My feelings stem not so much from the act itself but rather because what meant so much to my mother meant so little to Lowry. I believe it was his utter rejection of her after the Event that shoved her down insanity's slide.

Mother never told me about it herself, this I admit, but the evidence pointing to their carnal union is overwhelming and I don't for a moment doubt it took place. One, she told me she followed him back. Two, M— was away. Three, as she told me but once, they "communed." And my research has given me these clues as well: There was a two-week period during M—'s absence when Lowry was purportedly most upset. "Crazy," my sources put it. On a nonstop gin binge, he raved to all who'd listen that he'd met Death in the flesh, that he'd met Death and defeated it. One barfly heard him distinctly say, "I rogered Death from behind like a dog." (I don't like to picture this.) During that period of time, he would laugh and rave, rave and cry. What ended his raving was news of a cougar in the area. Hearing this news seemed to cheer him up. He took to saying he, too, had seen the cat, and so his run-in with Death went the way of bad dreams. It takes no detective to sort out the self-serving machinations of this drunken man's mind. For sanity's sake, for relief from devils, he made himself believe he'd seen a cougar, not my mother, not Death.

I hate but can't help picturing the scene. Lowry, drunk and whimpering, finds that Death has not only leapt at him from a tree but has followed him to his door. My mother, ludicrous in a rabbit's costume with a skeleton etched on it, with a broken rib and bleeding from the back, tells him she loves him. She embraces him and, scared, Lowry can't deny Death its desire. My mother instigates the unthinkable. And two hideously incongruous dream worlds unite there in a shack on Dollarton Beach: My mother believing she has won over her aloof treasure, her boyish genius. Lowry believing he is copulating with Death.

On Lowry's behalf, I like to assume that at some point in his passion he reached that minimal level of awareness where he realized it was in fact a mortal woman in his bed. Someone who was not M—. Though in "The Forest Path to the Spring" he writes that after his brush with the cougar he and M— "embraced all the night long," I should restate that during this time M— was gone for three months, and I doubt that even a gin-riddled Lowry could stay unaware of that. So did he know it was my mother? Did he make himself believe it was M—? What shaped pretzel of logic did he construct in order to stay sane? Lowry was by all accounts a monogamous husband, and so perhaps it was his horror at this odd adultery that made him go mad for a while. We'll never know.

For years, my mother assumed he'd known it was her. But when she first learned of his death—she did not read newspapers and it was me who told her—she said, "I thought he'd send word. *Something.*" Then she laughed, and lapsed back into what was now her world, a state of waking dream. And when "The Forest Path to the Spring" came out in 1960, and after Mother read certain parts over and over, she closed the book at last and—cried.

I could go on and on about Lowry's life, Lowry's lies to himself. Indeed, I could water my prose with imagination and assault the man with a decadently flowery language he would well have recognized. It is tempting. I see now how the taking up of a pen and the posture of writing itself seem to abet some kind of exaggeration. Once begun, words find their own momentum in the direction of color, veneer, dream. Lie. I can only hope that by now you understand that my loathing for fiction is so resolute it has allowed me during this account to tell you nothing but the granite truth. However much I am tempted to sink into venom, attach the leash of speculation to Lowry's name and drag it through any number of cesspools, I won't.

Nor will I go on to describe his final fall, for to do so would be to ennoble it. His tawdry death. Myth be damned: his death was nothing but tawdry, as tawdry as my mother's. I'll draw no cheap conclusion from this, but the equation is there for all to see: two people, lashed by self-doubt, forced by life's grinning skull to turn to dreams and poetry and imagination, poisoned yet further by alcohol—two people die a false and tawdry death. My point is made. I give it to you and leave it; I ask only that you refrain from embellishing either their lives or their deaths with yet more poetry. I have the right to ask this.

I'll likely never discover whether Lowry knew he was my father. He may have known; he may only have guessed. Perhaps Mom told him. Perhaps she pestered. But, not being the kind to ask for money or seek a scandal, my mother would have preferred cherishing me in secret, me her precious relic of a single sacred meeting.

Not knowing has been hard on me. Harder, in fact, than having had no taste of fatherhood, save for a singular image of a naked man squealing, stumbling, slapping at glistening legs. It's been hardest of all to admit to myself that, in the booze-blurred moment of my conception, not only was I not planned, not sought for, but was in fact the result of a man's lust for a woman other than my mother. To be blunt, Lowry's sperm was meant for M— (or perhaps for Death!), but was waylaid, like a manuscript, by a lonely woman in a bid for a bit of attention. Such was the flavor of my beginning, and such remains the flavor of my life.

Proof that I'm his son? It took no wizardry to ascertain the year and month of the cougar event, add to it nine months and, lo and behold, arrive at my birthday. My mother had no boyfriends and was not known to have affairs. Lucy was a remarkable woman in many ways, not the least of which being that she knew a man's nakedness but once, and this while wearing a rabbit costume.

As I mentioned when I began, my middle name is Lava. "The Forest Path to the Spring," and the later stories—and, according to my mother, all his work to come—were to be part of a magnum opus he would call *Mount Appetite*, a renaming of Mount Seymour, the mountain at whose foot Dollarton squats. Why rename a mountain? For poetry's manipulative sake, of course. For metaphor's aggrandizements. According to Mom, Lowry raved about his project endlessly and famously, to all who would listen. People here talk of it still. *Mount Appetite* was to catalog and sanctify the many kinds of human desire. A portrait of passions, a rainbow of hungers. (Gamut of gluttonies. I can't help but picture a troupe of pained eccentrics, driven by desires feral, pungent, twisted, and hidden. Equipped with ropes and spiked boots and clenched jaws, they eternally scale the Sisyphean heights of their sticky needs.)

My mother's inspiration for "Lava" was equally metaphoric, if sillier. In this case, I know the meaning. In her way of speaking to me as though I weren't there, staring up into space and talking over my head both literally and figuratively, Mother more than once intoned grandly, "Lava. You are my Lava. My dear little man. You are the emission of a volcano."

She doubtless imagined I'd be as wordproud as my father. No. But I'll travel that road as long as I can stomach and extend her metaphor for her: hot lava is upchucked dumbly into the world, soon cools, and resents having been spewed there. Lava is nothing like the fiery bowels of its father. If lava could feel, it would feel like effluent, like scum. Not art but puke. It would feel carelessly and wrongfully ejaculated—I cannot resist—under the volcano.

As I've been writing this history, I've often stopped and asked myself: Is this the voice of bitterness? Malc and Lucy's bitter bastard boy? If not, why do I smear both a mother and a father? I seek neither notoriety nor a noble name, neither a paternity suit nor a share of his estate, if he left one. So why do I expose? Whose voice is this?

I like to think it is my father's voice—his voice had he lived, his voice had he learned to stop lying, had he learned to lift his head high and breathe, for good and all, the pure cold air of objectivity. If children inherit one thing from their parents, it is the claustrophobic fear of their parents' faults. I thank mine for helping me, through revulsion, toward clarity. My mind's best food has been the flesh of their faulty lives. Neither of my parents understood that appetite is mostly about the art of control.

I've been drunk but once in my life. I was seventeen. My mother had just died. That it happened to be my high school graduation party didn't matter to me—this wasn't a celebration but an exorcism. We drank under the stars in—where else?—Dollarton Beach. Under Mount Appetite. In paradise. A body had been found here in a burned-out car earlier that week, a murder, so added to the evening was an air of danger lurking. And I drank gin, my parents' brand. I slept with neither cougar, ghost, nor woman, but still I had a wondrous time. I cried about my mother and raged about my father, pounding a driftwood club into the beach fire, sending showers of glowing amber skyward. None of the other kids noticed me really, for many were first-drunk as well, and flailed about in their own style and for their own reasons.

PHONE SEX IN MILWAUKEE

:::

Alison Grillo

MY ROOM IS DARK except for the television, where ESPN shows a rerun of a college hoops game. I'm holed up tonight at the Milwaukee Marriott. Last night I was in Atlanta. I forget where I'll be tomorrow night.

"Our windchill factor here in the city of bratwurst and beer is a brutal five below zero," I tell Val. "I'm glad you could join me tonight. As we speak, I'm snuggled under the covers, wearing a woman's wool nightshirt purchased recently at forty percent off."

Val has a quick, blaring laugh that always sounds worst over the phone.

"I'm serious about the gender-bending attire."

"I know. You just surprised me."

"I'm not a transvestite or anything, but simply a crackerjack beat writer with a very feminine side. Wearing this exquisite woolly garment makes me feel less lonely. Okay, so in my fantasy we're living together, preferably in Boston—aka the Hub of the Universe. I get very lonely when you're away at an academic conference. Let's say you're at one now, in a certain warm and sunny city on the Gulf Coast of Texas. You're delivering a paper on feminist literary theory. Something very radical and empowering. Something that will get you juiced up."

"Sounds like the Lacan symposium."

"Right. One of those Frenchmen. You're at your symposium, and I get lonely and put on your nightgown, which you've given me permission to wear when I am really, really lonely."

"You're lost without me."

"Like a player without his agent."

"Remember the old TV commercial for Brut aftershave, where a woman puts on her husband's oxford shirt and his tie and of course dabs on a little aftershave? I deconstructed it as an undergraduate."

"Commodification raises its ugly head again, eh, professor?"

"I bet you look cute in your nightgown."

"I do. It matches my eyes: Celtics green. Okay, so I'm wearing this nightgown, which smells like you and is shaped like you, and its woolly female essence is rubbing against me."

I picture Val sitting up in bed. She is dark and compact and big-boned, with cunning black eyes and swimmer's shoulders and a mole over her left breast. Age thirty-eight, marital status divorced. Your typist is forty-one and never married. We met on December 30 in Chicago, where she had come for the annual Modern Language Association powwow. Who knew our "relationship" would last past New Year's, past MLK Day, past Valentine's Day? Who knew we would be having phone sex twice a week as she teaches literary theory and sits on committees and jockeys for fellowships and course-load reductions, and I chase the Celtics from one end of this great land to the other?

"After your silly basketball season is over, I want you to come to Houston and be my houseboy."

"Will do."

"You'll keep my house nice and clean?"

"Immaculate."

"Water my plants?"

"Flood them."

"Wash out my undies?"

"Dutifully."

"Pick up my skirts at the cleaners? And my gorgeous woolly dresses?"

"Anything with a hem."

"I need someone to be waiting for me when I get home from school. You'll be on your knees, waiting for instructions. I want you to be either naked, or if it's very cold, in your nightgown. I want you alert, attentive, and kneeling."

And so on.

The next afternoon the Celtics beat the Bucks by fourteen points. We hop a quick flight to Chicago and check into the Palmer House.

Too jacked up to sleep, I go down to the cocktail lounge for a beer, sitting on the very same bar stool where Val had sat the afternoon I met her. Soon I am joined by Hammy Loomis of the *Herald*. Hammy is thirty-something, tall and stoop-shouldered and thick-waisted, with a hawk nose, black thinning hair that he wears combed back, and a fleshy, kindly face. We're the only two customers.

"I met a lady in December, right here where we're sitting," I tell Hammy. On the television behind the bar, *SportsCenter* shows highlights of the same Celtics-Bucks game we covered hours ago.

"Yeah?"

"She teaches English at a college in Houston. She asked me to visit her. Spend a couple of weeks down in the land of oil wells and long-necks."

Hammy nods, his eyes scanning the basketball scores that flash on the television. "That sounds fun."

"You're saying I should do it, then?"

"Of course. If you like her."

"I do. But I hardly know her. The chemistry could change by the time we get together again. You know—the karma? The holiday karma that we enjoyed in December could languish in the Texas heat."

"Well, that's life. You know what they say: 'Nothing ventured . . .'"

"I did a long weekend with a woman in North Carolina once, right in the middle of a July heat wave. It was the longest weekend of my life."

"I'm sure your professor friend has air-conditioning. Too bad we're not scheduled for any more trips down there." Hammy looks at his watch. "It's late."

"I'm not sleepy."

"Why don't you call your friend?"

"She has an early class tomorrow. What room are you in?"

"Six eighteen."

"I'm in six forty. Do you want to come by? I've got *Das Boot* on DVD. The mother of all submarine pictures."

"No thanks. What is it with you and that movie, anyway?"

"I don't know. The male bonding? The claustrophobia? How 'bout it, Hamster?"

"Some other time."

He finishes his beer, shaking his head when the bartender points to the empty glass. I sense a bout with insomnia coming up. In a few hours I'll be wide awake and watching a rerun of this same *SportsCenter.*

"I think my father was claustrophobic."

"Yeah?"

"He freaked out on a bus that was supposed to go to Fenway Park. We were waiting for the bus to load. It was a humid summer morning. The kind of weather Houston probably gets all year round." The bartender takes Hammy's empty glass and sweeps his change off the bar. Hammy looks at me. The bags under his eyes suggest a big droopy-faced hound dog who just wants to go to sleep. "He started shaking, and then he made this kind of blubbering sound. We got off the bus. I was ten years old. The Sox were in a pennant race."

"Do you think it had anything to do with his drinking?"

"I don't know. I'm pretty sure he was cold sober that morning."

"Maybe he just didn't like buses. Did the bus have a toilet?"

"No. It was just an old school bus."

"Well there you go: long bus rides without a toilet are bad news." He stands up. "Good night, kid. Get some sleep."

In my room I watch some of *Das Boot* on my laptop. Dad would have liked the movie. He was a bomber mechanic during World War II and a history buff all his life. He would tell me war stories, those he lived and those he read about in volumes from the Military Book Club. I would shrug, roll my eyes, or otherwise act uninterested in his tales. I was not an easy kid to talk to. Aloof—at least from him. With Mom I was different. Mom and I were (are) simpatico. She took me shopping, she took me to *Mary Poppins* when it came out in the sixties. Now she sends me care packages of socks and underwear, and candy on Halloween and Easter. I try to make it home (Worcester, Mass.) as often as possible. You could say I'm a momma's boy, but so are Larry Bird and a lot of other sports greats.

:::

The Cs lose to the Bulls and we fly back to Boston for a four-game home stand. It's 3 AM by the time I open the door of my Beacon Street apartment. There are no signs of break-in. No letters from the IRS. The message machine contains only a routine greeting from Mom.

Even my Toyota Camry, parked on the street, still has its radio. I go to bed and fantasize about being the only male sailor on a U-boat full of women. I help out with the navigation and with the torpedoes and do the girls' hair and iron their clothes and cook for them. Val is the captain. Somewhere in the North Atlantic we encounter a convoy. Alarms sound, orders are shouted, bearings taken. Torpedoes shoot into the black water. "Down periscope," Val says. She orders me to her cabin. She needs to decompress. Meanwhile, the hull of a fifty-thousand-ton British freighter splits into two.

Benefiting from home cooking and a scrappy guard purchased from Cleveland, the Cs play tough defense, crash the offensive boards, and trash-talk their opponents. They beat the Lakers and the Pistons on successive nights at the Fleet Center, where the Hub's genteel fans clap politely and discuss vacations plans. On a rare day off I get my hair cut. I go to bed just as my favorite Lacanian calls:

"How long is this basketball season of yours going to last? My house needs cleaning."

"The NBA finals are slated to end June 12, should the series go a full seven games."

"I'll be abroad by then, teaching in the school's summer program. Remember?"

"Damn."

"Get out of your playoff commitment. Tell the editor about your domestic responsibilities." Her tone is both sexy and frightening. Maybe it's good ours is a long-distance relationship.

"No can do. I'm their hoops guy. It's like being on a submarine. You're on board for the whole voyage. You have to stick around for everything—the torpedoes, the depth charges, the male bonding. You get off early, the awesome weight of the ocean will crush you."

"You're not making any sense, dear. But you're cute when you're incoherent. And I have an idea. You can come to England when I'm there. I'll arrange dormitory space right in London."

"Dormitory? At a college?"

"Yes. Chelsea College."

"Will I have to have a roommate?"

"Yes! Me!"

"I see. Coed housing, then." I rise from bed and pace about with my portable phone, sensing a decision to make, a moment of truth.

My stomach tightens the way it did twenty-odd years ago, when my parents moved me into my dormitory on my first day as a college freshman. The residence director gave me a key that opened a door to an impossibly small space, with beds not five feet apart. I was supposed to *share* this space? With someone I hadn't even *met*?

"So, what do you think?"

"An exciting offer. Your typist will be happy to mull it. But once basketball season is over the *Globe* might want me to cover the World Cup. You know, soccer? It's getting more popular here in the U.S."

"Don't be ridiculous. No one cares about soccer. I miss you."

"Okay. We'll see." That's what my father would say: *We'll see*. It didn't necessarily mean no. He said, *We'll see* when I asked if we could go on the Fenway Park bus trip. Was he already worried about the lack of toilet? In any event I got him on that bus and then he had his anxiety attack. We sure saw, all right!

:::

In April we embark on our last West Coast trip of the season. What can I say about the trip? The Cs lose in LA, where it's sunny, and win in Seattle, where it rains. In Oakland they beat the Warriors in overtime. After the game, one of the local writers asks the Warriors coach a question he doesn't like, and the coach glares at him. The moment reminds me of the scene in *Das Boot* where the navigator asks the captain when the hell they're going to surface, as the crew is suffocating from stale air. The captain responds, "We'll surface when I give the order to surface, Herr Navigator." Crazy, but the movie makes me want to go and cover a submarine voyage. I'd chronicle arguments on the bridge and heart-to-heart talks in the torpedo room. I'd make morbid jokes about water pressure, and pad my stories with stats on tons sunk and number of consecutive hours underwater.

On a cold, rainy night we fly to Denver, where my hotel room is warm and redolent of Lemon Pledge. There is a refrigerator with snacks and beverages. From my window I watch a taxi pull up to the hotel and a man in an overcoat clamber into the taxi with an overnight bag and an umbrella. I watch the taxi drive off, following the vehicle's taillights down a long empty street. Poor guy, whoever he is, to have to schlep off somewhere on such a night.

The phone rings.

"The switchboard says you just checked in," Val says. "Were you sleeping?"

"Not yet."

"I couldn't sleep, thinking about you." She sounds like she has a cold.

"I was thinking about you, too."

"Really? What were you thinking?"

"I was picturing myself doing your nails."

"Oooh! That would be nice. I need a manicure."

"I was doing your nails as you sat pampered and decadent, talking on the phone to one of your Vassar classmates."

"I went to Mount Holyoke, remember? But I catch your drift."

Our dialogue continues. Rain pelts the window. After Denver the Celtics contingent will fly home, where the high temperature tomorrow is expected to reach sixty degrees. Summer is coming no matter how long basketball season continues. In summer a well-heated hotel room will not be so great. In summer you want to get out, you want to wear less clothing and have more fun. Summer, in the sweet days before puberty, meant plenty of time for both reading and television, and fierce games of Wiffle ball and Monopoly with my best friend, and long bike rides to nowhere, and finally a week at Cape Cod with my parents. Cape Code was as far as my father ever wanted to travel. My mom always wanted to go to Europe. The worst thing about the beach was the teenagers strutting around in noisy cliques. I was old enough to feel self-conscious, to imagine the teenagers looking down on me—a nerd still trapped with his parents.

"Are you still there?"

"I'm here."

"So, what about London?"

"Nice town. I almost went there once to cover Wimbledon."

"Do you want to come?"

"You mean to visit you?"

"Yes!"

I remember Val in Chicago. She fretted over whether she would catch her flight back to Houston. The shuttle bus was late. She kept making a fluttering motion with her hand—the kind of habit that will seem charming when you first know a person and then grown tiresome. But I'm only contemplating a two-week visit. How tiresome can any habit grow in just two weeks?

"Okay. I do."

:::

In the first round of the playoffs the Celtics eliminate the Knicks in five games. I arrange for a Delta flight to London and promise to send Val money for my share of a Brit-Rail pass. She talks of weekend trips to Scotland, Ireland, Paris, Amsterdam. She sends me a copy of *Frommer's England* and a book of essays about travel by Alain de Botton. We discuss my father's alcoholism and her own youthful abuse of drugs. She is becoming less an object of my fantasies and more a real person. Scary. I feel married to her, and am less inclined to initiate phone sex.

Second round: Celts vs. Bulls. The games are close and physical. The Cs steal the first game after the Bulls' center gets ejected for throwing a punch. Chicago wins the next game, Boston takes one in overtime. Eventually we're tied three-three. My fantasies have become wilder with each passing game. I was initially Val's houseboy, then her maid. Now, at the start of game seven, as the teams warm up and I stare at a blank laptop screen, I can think of nothing but wearing pumps and hose and a pleated skirt, and being Val's secretary in the English department, where my gender-bending bondage is public and protracted, stretched over forty hours a week, a nine-to-five grind, something I've avoided all my life, unlike my father, poor sap, who did the nine-to-five grind most of his life because he had to, because he had a wife and kid to support. His best days were during the Big One. He wasn't on a submarine, he didn't see combat. He served at a variety of stateside army air corps bases. He got to see the West, he did some boxing, he rigged his car to run on bomber fuel. His worst horror story was getting lice.

The Bulls win. It is May 19. I'll have a few days off and then cover the Eastern finals and then the NBA finals, and finally the season will be over and I'll be with Val, nowhere to run, no cozy hotel room to hide in. Goodbye phone sex, hello real sex. I'm not sure which one is better. Both leave much to be desired. You reach a point where you and the woman have shared all these intimacies and fantasies, and talked each other into long-distance orgasms, and you want to say, That's fine, thank you, I'll do it by myself from now on, and I'll be thinking of you.

:::

My bags are checked in, my boarding pass is tucked away in my waist pouch, and my flight doesn't leave for another two hours. There is a noisy little pub next to the security area. I pace back and forth before this pub, waiting for Hammy. He shows up tanned, wearing a crisp white golf shirt and beige Dockers.

"You look poised for a solid eighteen holes, Hamster!"

"Try a birthday party for six-year-olds. Are you okay, kid?"

"I'm fine. I'm going to get on that plane."

"You sounded kind of worked up when you called."

"Preflight jitters. Thanks for rushing over here. I just needed some company."

"You said you felt walls were closing in."

"You know me and my metaphors. I was still waiting to check my bags. A little kid behind me was shrieking."

In the pub we both go nonalcoholic with Diet Cokes. The bartender keeps filling up our glasses, which will only make me pee more. On the television, ESPN shows stock-car racing somewhere in the South. My insides feel like jelly. The thing to do, perhaps, is start shrieking like the kid in the check-in line.

"It didn't take you long to get here."

"No. I live right by the interstate."

"Is there any way you can meet my return flight? On July 2?"

"I'll be at the World Cup."

"No one cares about soccer."

"Wait until they read my copy. Anyway, I can't help you, kid. Call a shuttle service."

"A shuttle is not the same as my good buddy and rival from Boston's other newspaper."

"Please, kid."

"Okay, okay. Be that way. I'll still bring you a souvenir when I get back. *If* I get back."

"You'll get back."

"Can you imagine: two weeks with a woman. The same woman. It'll be a personal best for the kid if he can do it."

"You can do it."

"She has an annoying habit of fluttering her hand."

"You'll get used to it, kid."

"Right. I'll take things one day at a time. I'll reach down for something extra. I'll screw my courage to the sticking place."

Hammy finishes his soda and stands up. "I have a bunch of kids waiting for me. Everything's going to be all right."

Everything is going to be all right, I keep telling myself over the next two hours. The Hamster's words resonate all the way onto the plane and into the air, and eventually our jet stabilizes and your typist gets all the Diet Coke and nervousness out of his system, and the worst problem is the passenger in the next seat, an old chatterbox who insists he was at Ted Williams's last game. I study my guidebook, I stare out the window. Stretches of the Atlantic Ocean are visible between cloud patches. Down there, somewhere, is the wreckage of the U-boats, their torn hulls encrusted with algae, their crews' bones scattered. The subs are now iron coffins. The men down there could tell war stories more compelling than my father's. They could tell stories of jarring explosions, explosions that would paralyze their boat and send it sinking deep. Too deep. Rivets would pop like firecrackers, water would seep in everywhere. The lights would go. The ceiling and the walls and the floor all converged on you, and your space became violated by water and iron and the flailing limbs of your mates. There was no space even to scream. Or maybe it wasn't like this at all. How would I know? Nothing like this happens in the movie. In the movie the sub makes it back. As I've said, my father would have loved the movie but hated submarine service. He would have felt the walls closing in. I, on the other hand, am claustrophobic only in the figurative sense. I don't like to have my space invaded or to share it. As lonely as hotel rooms are, they never get crushed by water pressure. Anyway, goodbye to loneliness for the next two weeks. Val will meet me at Heathrow. We'll be together for what will seem forever. I can imagine the two of us going to plays in the West End, eating fish and chips, strolling through Hyde Park. Beyond that is hard to imagine.

XMAS IN LAS VEGAS

∴
∴

Denis Johnson

CARLO HAD ALWAYS WANTED to visit Las Vegas during Christmas. The place wouldn't be as crowded as in other seasons. Hotels would offer bargain rates. Lenore's kids were long gone—they didn't want to come home for Christmas. This seemed the time. Lenore didn't voice any enthusiasm for the idea, but she went along with it in the absence of a better plan. But she didn't feel altogether okay on the streets of Las Vegas at Christmastime. "I feel virtual," she said.

"What does that mean?"

"It's something the kids say. Whatever it means, it means the opposite of virtual. It means on the bogus or phony side of the spectrum."

"Well, if it means you don't feel down-to-earth, I don't feel down-to-earth, either. This isn't a place to feel down-to-earth. Vegas is another planet. The planet of glitz and giggles."

"Glitz and giggles," she said. She seemed delighted with this expression.

"I don't want to gamble," she said. "I hope we're not going to."

"I haven't gambled except for four times, and that was during my very first tour in the service," Carlo said. "Twenty-two years ago." Carlo had the numbers ready because this was a conversation they'd already had many times in consideration of this trip.

That first night, the twenty-third, they had a very good and very inexpensive dinner downstairs at the Sands Hotel and turned in early, and he and Lenore watched a movie on the big-screen TV. Lenore ate two small packs of M&M's while the film played. She'd brought them all the way from Cincinnati. Her innocent joy in the taste of

M&M's was one of the things that made Carlo feel sentimental about his wife.

On the twenty-fourth, they woke to blue skies over Las Vegas. They'd had blue skies since the day before the trip began. The whole country was on a break from winter. They'd had an easy flight over, literally "clear sailing"—Carlo had taken the window seat and had not counted one cloud in the air between Ohio and Nevada.

They searched in the paper for a good show. They didn't find one. The big names were all on vacation. They'd expected that. It went with the discount prices and the sparse crowds of the Christmas season.

"Choose one for yourself," Lenore said. "Choose one with plenty of titties and rumps. They'll make me feel like dieting."

She and Carlo didn't have to go farther than right downstairs again, where they sat through a skateboarding extravaganza, a dozen helmeted and padded athletes jumping around impressively to the canned music of *Star Wars*, plus a small parade of extraneous undressed females. The drinks were cheap, and Lenore got halfway wrecked. She wasn't entirely serious, but she didn't let up: "What are we doing here? What are we doing here? We might as well gamble. I guess if we went broke, we could go home."

"Do you really want to go home?"

"Not really. I'm just looking for a reason why we're here. We came a long way, and it's not all free."

Later, Carlo woke briefly in the middle of the night. Beside him Lenore slept propped up on pillows, one hand resting on her stomach and holding the TV's remote control device. Beyond the foot of the bed the TV played without sound, and a readout in the screen's corner read 12:17 AM, which meant Christmas had come. Lying there in the silent room, Carlo watched a scene from, he guessed, a movie, in which a young woman hung white laundry on a clothesline. Suddenly a look of utter shock transfixed the woman's features. She let go of a white shirt. A man walked into view, dressed in sooty rags. Meanwhile, the white shirt blew down a hill. The man and the woman embraced. A brief kiss—then lovingly they studied each other's faces. A long view now: the man laughed as he bounded down the hill, chasing the white shirt. Carlo took the remote control device from his wife's fingers.

He had to pee. He wanted a bite of cold fruit. He wanted to smoke a cigarette. He didn't want to get sick, or have accidents, or be dead. He turned the television off. Holding the control device in his fingers, he fell asleep.

Christmas morning they woke up absolutely without any plans. Carlo felt apologetic about that, but he didn't apologize. He waited to see what Lenore had to say. What she had to say about it was nothing. Completely unconcerned. A day like any day: he woke up, and there was his wife beside him, watching the all-news channel with the sound off.

"Well," he said, "Merry Christmas."

"Same to you."

In a minute he asked her, "Do they ever say 'Xmas' anymore?"

"'Xmas?' I don't know."

"They used to abbreviate it down to 'Xmas.'"

"Hmm—you know what? I don't think I've seen a lot of that lately. I think they stopped. I think they decided it was offensive."

Carlo showered and stepped out and dried off with a white, fluffy towel. There were side-by-side sinks in the bathroom, with fixtures of gold plating, or fake gold plating—whichever, the gesture was appreciated. He turned on both faucets. Both gave out identical streams of water. He turned one off and brushed his teeth at the other. The toothpaste was something new Lenore had gotten. He'd never heard of this brand. Very pleasant, it was alive, it gave him a fantastic tingling sensation in his mouth. He rinsed and finished with some mouthwash, also new. It was horrible, like gargling gasoline. It jammed in his throat. He spat it out and rinsed his mouth, croaking, "Yuck! Ptooey! Ridiculous!"

Lenore must have heard him suffering, because she called from the bedroom, "Carlo? Hon?"

He found her sitting up, wearing a complimentary bathrobe, reading the hotel's bedside literature. "What is this crap?" he said, holding the jug in his hand. "This stuff is poisonous."

"I just grabbed it," she said.

"Well, do you mind if I throw it out?"

"Sure," she said. "It's just something I grabbed."

"Good. I don't want it around. I don't want to make the same mistake twice. There oughta be a law against this one. God!" he said. "I thought there were regulations." He replaced the cap tightly and threw it in the bathroom wastebasket. And he felt good thinking that in two or three hours, somebody paid to do it would come and take it away. He was crazy about this hotel. He got dressed and told her, "I need coffee."

He headed downstairs, still swallowing a bit of unpleasant taste. He sat at the lunch counter overlooking the main casino. He washed away the bad flavor with a cup of coffee poured for him by a redheaded waitress.

The main casino wasn't hosting much action currently—nobody at the craps or the roulette, only a couple of lone blackjack players at separate tables, and several diehards giving the slots a workout. One of the blackjack dealers, a young woman, sported a red elf's hat with the white ball on its peak. The casino seemed to be snubbing the holiday—maybe from spite, because it cut into their trade. Carlo saw no seasonal décor around the place. The elf's cap was perhaps the result of a personal decision.

Wow, he thought, forget about Christmas—they don't even have Xmas here.

Meanwhile, he wasn't sure the coffee tasted quite right. The horrible mouthwash must have maimed his taste buds.

He couldn't really blame Lenore for just grabbing things off the supermarket shelves and hurrying off on more important errands. Neither of them had time to do any serious shopping. They both worked eight-hour days, and in fact Lenore worked a bit more than that, also did a fair amount of traveling. When it came to the home front, they both contributed what they could.

They'd been married six years, and they got along fine with each other. He'd been single until he was forty years old, and now he liked being married. You hate the mouthwash, and there's somebody beside you to register the complaint. You don't go with it into the darkness of the grave.

Lenore had a good job, and she was an intelligent woman. She trained new employees for the Illinois-Indiana-Ohio region of Kinko's, the nationwide photo-duplication outfit, a quite sizable corporation. Carlo worked for Motor Vehicles.

What Carlo knew but hadn't told her, what he sensed about himself, was that on this trip at some point he was going to have sex with someone he wasn't supposed to.

He'd messed around in the service, he'd had a few experiences in foreign ports, enough to know that this was going to be dreary and it wouldn't turn out the way anybody expected it to, the way it advertised itself inside your mind. It wasn't going to be glitz and giggles.

The redhead poured and was already turning away when he asked her, "What's your name?"

She turned back. She wore a small name tag on her yellow uniform that said, CHARLENE.

"I'm sorry," she said, "what did you say?"

"Nothing."

"More coffee?"

"No, thanks. Not yet."

"Oh," she said, "I just gave you some, didn't I?"

"It's great stuff," he assured her.

The café's Muzak, at least, gave a nod to the nature of the season, faintly playing selections in the Christmas spirit. "I'll Be Home for Christmas" . . . the original "Rudolph," sung by Gene Autry . . . familiar carols done in every style—rockabilly, big band, the bland pop of the early 1960s. Right in the middle of this collection, they played "Papa Was a Rolling Stone."

"How about now?" the waitress said.

"Pour away," he told her. "And let me see that pack of Philip Morris—just to look at."

"You want to see it? Look at it?"

"Yeah."

"You just want to look at it?"

"Yeah. I'm just interested."

He hadn't handled a cigarette pack in years. He examined it. It was Christmasy, red and green, shiny, with an actual hologram on the front of it: the original Philip Morris bellboy, his hand cupped beside his mouth as he called out for Philip Morris. The friendly image floated right up toward your face. It turned this way and that, absolutely three-dimensional, not phony 3-D—not at all "virtual."

"I've never seen anything like it," he said.

"It's a promotional thing. It's a final farewell gesture. They're changing their name. No more Philip Morris. They're getting out of the business. No more coffin nails. Cancer. Death. It's all bad business."

"Do you remember the ads where this little man right here would say, 'Caaa-aall for Philip Mooooor-ris?'"

"No," she said, "I don't. I got no idea who that little head is supposed to belong to."

Carlo paid her for the pack, and she laid it out on the counter in front of him along with a book of the casino's matches. "Thank you," he said.

She poured him another cup of coffee while saying, "Hello and good morning," to a man who joined them at the counter now, sitting in the stool right next to Carlo's.

"So—is that a wedding ring?" the man said to Carlo first thing.

Carlo held his hand out before him and looked at the back of it, fingers spread, peering at the gold band on his left ring finger, and didn't exactly make an answer, not because he didn't know what to say about the ring, but because the man had made only one remark, and this was already an eerie conversation.

The man was gray-headed, but thickly so, and had a young, smooth, dark face. The man said nothing further—got his coffee—but after a while held up his own left hand exactly as Carlo had done. He wore no ring on any of his fingers. Carlo sensed that something was coming.

"Spent five hours yesterday in a car with my ex-wife. We had to drive to Laughlin in this van I rented, get the stuff at her sister's house where it was stored—stuff from when we last lived together—had to get it over here to Vegas." He was quite earnest in his speech, almost urgent about it, but soft-toned, and polite. "So we're tooling along in this rented van. Half our old stuff goes to my place, half goes to her place, et cetera. Spending a good bit of time together on this thing. And we got along fine. I wish I could've been that comfortable with her when we were married. Not that it would've made any difference, because from the first day we had no compatibility in the sack—but that's how it goes. Anyway, it was like two old friends. She asked me about some infidelities of mine that she had heard about. Repeatedly heard about. Rumors. I admitted I had an affair for eleven years with a woman in Boulder City, all during the time we were married. She asked me who, but I refused to tell her. I wouldn't involve another person. At that point—bam, flat tire. I lost it. Swearing, yelling, screaming. But I got over it in less than ten minutes, and I was calm again, and I dealt with the situation. After that we didn't talk at all for the last fifty miles. She was sort of crying. Well . . . she was hurt. People have their pride."

"Yeah . . ." Carlo lit up a cigarette for the first time in seven years.

"I got home, and my girlfriend is pissed because I just spent all that time in the car with my ex. I said fine, whatever you want, move out, whatever—but if you move out, you ain't coming back . . . Who was it who originally said . . ." There was a long silence during which Carlo was only in love with his cigarette. "Said . . . Damn. Damn it, I can't remember the famous old saying I was going to say."

"Much less who originally said it," Carlo said.

The man laughed. He, like Carlo, seemed to have no reason for sitting at this counter.

The waitress came back with the glass pot and said, "Let me touch that up for you." As she poured, Carlo noticed she wore a diamond wedding and engagement set.

While the waitress busied herself busing tables, out of earshot, Carlo told the man, "I've got a curiosity about something. Don't be embarrassed."

"Hey. This is Las Vegas."

Carlo took that as some kind of reassurance. "When somebody goes to a massage parlor looking for more than just a massage—" Carlo stubbed out his cigarette in his coffee cup. "You know what I mean, right?"

"You're looking for a happy ending."

"I'm looking for a happy ending."

"You can get a massage anywhere. Right here at the hotel, probably. But not," the man said, "with the happy ending."

"But at a massage parlor—"

"Yes. At a massage parlor."

"I ask for a happy ending?"

"No," the man said. "To be completely sure, you gotta ask the girl for the erotic massage. With full release. Say to her, 'Do you perform erotic massage with full release?'"

"Wow," said Carlo. This phrasing felt very distant from anything he'd ever experienced. It seemed to come from so far away he could barely make sense of it. He said, "These girls—what time do they crank up?"

"Crank up?"

"You know."

"It's a twenty-four-hour town. There's no cranking up. It's always open."

"Aha, right," Carlo said, "I get it."

"But," the man said, "a massage parlor? I don't even know where you'd find one of those in this town. What you'll find around here is about a million call girls. Call one up. Call one up. They sell magazines full of their phone numbers—give them away free, actually, full of ads, and their pictures, and every other damn thing. Slip them under your door at your hotel!"

"Well, it was just a crazy impulse," Carlo said.

"That's what life consists of. Crazy impulses."

"Yeah."

"Go visit the old folks' home. Pry open some old guy's eyelid and look in there to his brain. Guy's ninety-nine years old, he's in a coma. And you know what you're gonna see? He's thinking about the elusive female."

Carlo laughed. Their waitress had returned, and she told the man, "No more coffee for you! You need a cold shower!"

"Long as you're alive, brother," the man said, "and that's the simple truth. I used to say to myself, 'The car's not going to Boulder City tonight. No way. The car's not taking the Boulder exit. Not tonight . . .'"

"Is that the same gal you ended up with?" Carlo asked.

"No. This one's a new one—if she comes back. I told her, 'No way, don't come back,' but you know what *that's* worth. I'd love to say I'm done with her, but come on—this is a moment of truth, I just dropped all but three dollars at the blackjack table. Sure, you say to hell with her, but you'll be back sniffin'. You'll be back for a sniff. Very few can stand the boredom of a certain kind of night, when you're just hanging around alone. Then—wham, you pick up the phone. You hop in the car. You head on over. And that goes on for years. Yeah . . . that pattern really stretches out on you.

"You meet a couple, they're like seventy-seven years old, you say, 'How'd you two work it all out—about life, and love, et cetera—now that you've hit your fiftieth anniversary?' Guy says, 'Work it out? No way! I'm gonna leave that bitch! She never has respected me!' And that's pretty much me. The nice lady doesn't respect me, but I'll go back and eat what she's dishing out just to keep from smelling my own stink. So: Now you've heard the truth. If I hadn't just lost fourteen hundred dollars at the tables, I'd probably have the strength to keep it up with my usual lies, but now you've heard the simple truth."

Carlo said, "Fourteen hundred dollars?"

"Yep, fourteen hundred. I'd call it a major reaming."

"Wow," Carlo said, "that's a lot of money."

"Welcome to Las Vegas," their waitress said, adding, "viva Las Vegas!"

"I shouldn't mention it," the man said. "It's bad luck to mention bad luck."

"They comped you good, I hope," the waitress said.

"They comped me. I'm comped. I'm comped two nights and six meals. I'm comped half the way up my large intestine."

Carlo and the waitress fell silent. Carlo believed they were watching a man fall apart right before their eyes. But he also felt as if Las Vegas was, suddenly, holding out its arms in a wide welcome.

He paid and excused himself and went to the building's main entrance, where he'd seen a rack holding just the kind of ad sheet the man had talked about. Carlo stood before it for at least three minutes.

Lenore. She was dumpy, and she was pasty, and she was flouncy. Eight years back he'd been stationed at the naval recruiter's office in Cincinnati, working in a clerical capacity. He'd rented a duplex apartment Lenore owned, and for a couple of years she'd been his landlady and had lived next door. Now they were man and wife, and they lived together in her half of the duplex and rented the other half to a retired military man, a quiet, dependable widower and an excellent tenant.

He looked at the ad sheet clamped firmly in its receptacle. Where to go to study this thing? Where to hide, that was the question. They had restrooms down here in the casino. But he pictured himself locked in one of the stalls with this confidential material laid out on his thighs, turning its pages, and that was enough. He bent close, squinting at the sheet as a person might who had no idea what on earth it was, reading the banner ads on the front page. One advertised a Christmas special. A Christmas special! The image described itself: ACTUAL PHOTOGRAPH. Another showed a shapely woman in a negligee, with abundant brown curls and a face completely shadowed, thanks to a very poor printing job. She was saluting. Maybe she had a military background, like Carlo. Her phone number was printed large enough that he could read it easily, and it included a lot of sevens—a sign of good luck? "Actual Photograph." Was this blurry person the same one you met, if you arranged a meeting? Carlo couldn't guess her age. Blurred or not, he couldn't judge the ages of women under thirty. To him they all just looked amazingly young.

He memorized the phone number, stepped over to the check-in counter, and wrote the number down in his appointment book. He warned himself that somewhere not too far down the line he'd better blot this number from the page, because it was evidence. He didn't trust himself to get away with things.

Upstairs he was surprised to find Lenore exactly as he'd left her, sitting up in bed in her nightgown.

"What have you been doing?" he said.

"Calling everybody I know," she said.

"Calling? Really?"

Lenore was delighted. "Since you left, I've been on the phone nonstop. You wouldn't believe it! There's a special deal the phone company's offering through the hotel—ten-cent long-distance phone calls all day Christmas day. I mean *ten cents* per call! It's fantastic! I've talked to just about everybody I know."

"How are they doing?" Carlo asked. "How's everybody doing?"

"Good."

"Are they having a merry Christmas?"

"Everybody's having a good one," she said, punching another number.

He looked out at their view from the fourth floor, which he judged to be a drop of about forty-eight feet down to a wide avenue lined with huge multicolored signs doing the best they could, in the bright daytime, to pulse with garish light. Suddenly he started laughing.

"Where's the comedy?" Lenore said.

He shook his head. She went back to the phone. He'd only been laughing to remember something.

The morning they'd left, at breakfast, he'd found himself staring at the box Lenore had just poured her cereal from. The messages there on the back of it struck him as strange, or faintly silly. CHEERIOS—SHARING MEMORIES, one heading said. Another—SHARING 60 YEARS TOGETHER. And a third: SHARING 60 YEARS OF CHEERIOS MEMORIES . . . Was he supposed to feel sentimental about a substance you dumped milk over and ate without thinking? He had told Lenore he thought it was ridiculous, and she'd said, "You know what's funny?—I like Cheerios now a lot better than I did when I was a kid."

He brought himself back to the situation at hand, and got his wife's partial attention as she talked to somebody. "I'm going out."

"No gambling!"

"Just a few well-placed bets."

He was kidding. She didn't hear him. "Great," she said, either to him or to the other party.

"Ten four," he said as the door shut itself behind him.

At a payphone downstairs he got out his notebook and thirty-five cents.

The first thing he did when someone answered was to ascertain he'd rung the right number and had the right girl on the other end. He listened carefully to her voice. She sounded fairly nice, but she also sounded as if she'd just woken up. He said, "I hope it's not too early. And especially—you know—today."

"That's never a problem," the woman said. "Any day, all day."

"And you'd be available . . . around now?"

"Yes, I sure would be. Why don't we make it a date?"

"Uh, just to be sure—we're talking about a massage?"

"That's right. The works."

"I feel stupid saying this, but I guess I'm looking for—'a happy ending.'"

"That comes with the works. Satisfaction guaranteed."

"Okay—I just felt I had to ask, or I should ask."

"What hotel are you in?"

"The Sands," he said. "Why? Where are you? Are you far away?"

"No. I can be there in twenty-five minutes."

"Oh, no—you can't come here," he said. "That wouldn't be good."

"Do you have someplace in mind?"

"No. No, ma'am," he said. "No, miss."

"Bummer! All right, well, I'm at the Claymore. I'll meet you in the bar off the lobby of the Claymore. We'll sit down, and we'll have a drink. If you look okay, you can come up. If you don't look okay—you don't come up."

"How will I know you?"

"Just sit at the bar. My name's Jeannie. I'll find you."

"Should I tell you my name?"

"Whenever you want to. Don't worry, we're gonna get to know each other real well."

"Okay," he said, "well—my name's Carl."

"Have you done this before, Carl? Made a date on the phone like this?"

"Not recently," he said, "if ever."

"Then can I ask you a couple favors? Will you do me a favor and take a shower first?"

"Okay. Of course."

"And we're talking about cash."

"Cash, cash, yes. A cash transaction." But this idea of a shower—that was throwing him. "Does it count if I just showered about thirty minutes ago?"

"Thirty minutes?" She laughed. "I'll allow it."

"And, so—anything else? What else?"

"Most people are usually interested in the rate."

"Oh. Oh. Oh."

"If you're a rookie, I'd better let you know it's three hundred for an hour."

"Three hundred?"

"Three hundred, up front. Cash only."

"You got it," he said.

"See? I'm as easy as pie," she said.

He took a cab to the Claymore. It looked not quite as fancy as the Sands. Inside, the colors were different, but it was the same. He headed through the casino toward the bar without looking left or right. He understood that people labored day and night designing these places just to guide his feet toward a table or a machine and get him to make a bet. But they wouldn't have any luck with Carlo. He'd lost several paychecks in the service, playing blackjack, and just the thought of those old disasters still nauseated him.

He sat at the bar and said nothing. The bartender, an older man, seemed not to notice him at first. Carlo figured if it came to it, he'd ask for club soda. Or a Virgin Mary. He was nervous—even the tomato juice in a Virgin Mary might be hard on his stomach.

"You the guy looking for Jeannie?" the bartender asked.

"That's me."

"I'll call her room." The bartender got on the phone at the other end of the bar. He came back and said, "Two minutes."

And in just about two minutes a woman came in and said, "Who's looking for Jeannie?"

"I'm always looking for Jeannie," the bartender said, brightening at her entrance. She smiled at Carlo—he was the only other person here, after all—and he smiled back at the sight of her. She had short blond hair and a pretty, girlish face, with big eyes and a small nose and a small mouth. She was well made-up, and her hair was brushed, but she wore red sweatpants and a green parka and—as he glanced down—bright yellow house slippers.

"Here's Jeannie—reporting for duty," she said, and saluted.

He held out his hand. She accepted it, gave it a shake, leaned close, and kissed him very lightly on the cheek.

"Let's sit over here a sec," she said, and he joined her at a table. She folded her hands in front of her. "Welcome to my office, sir."

"Do you want a drink or something? While you size me up?"

"Not necessary. I can tell a mile away you're a sweetheart."

"Well," he said.

"If you've got the three hundred, you can fork it over now, and we'll head on up to my little crib. Not everybody gets to do that," she added, "only the sweethearts."

"So—pay you right now? Here?"

"That'd be the way," she agreed. "I owe this guy some money." She cocked her head toward the bartender, who didn't seem aware, any longer, of either of them.

Carlo gave her three hundreds. She went immediately to the bartender and spoke to him and handed him the money and kissed his cheek.

"On with the show!" she told Carlo, and he stood up, and she hooked her arm in his and guided him off toward the elevators. Carlo noticed a lot of people around—desk clerk, patrons, a janitor in a gray uniform standing right at the elevators beside a large, heavy floor-cleaning machine—but nobody seemed the least bit aware of Carlo and Jeannie as they waited for transportation upstairs.

"Excuse the getup. Soon as we get to the room I'll make some improvements."

"You look nice," he said.

"What a dude! Just for that, I'll be gentle."

The janitor didn't look at them, and when the elevator opened he made no attempt to join them on board.

Carlo was used to feeling awkward in elevators. Jeannie was still talking as they stepped between the doors. "In town for long?"

"No, just a couple days. Just for Christmas."

"Terrific," Jeannie said. The doors parted. She stepped out saying, "This way," and, "When's that?"

They started trudging down a long hall, perhaps as long as a city block, although, because of the tunnel effect, it looked even longer. "What?" he said.

"I said, 'This way.'"

"But you said, 'When's that?' When's what?"

"When's Christmas?"

"This is Christmas," he said. "Today. Today is Christmas."

"Well, hey. Merry Christmas," she said.

"Merry Christmas." Carlo was aware of the numbers mounting as they passed, 315 . . . 317 . . . 319 . . . They were deep into the 350s before she called a halt.

He heard voices coming from inside her room, from the TV. It sounded like an old movie. Jeannie opened the door onto a room mostly pale olive green and orange, or salmon—also very pale and soothing. The movie on TV was in brilliant color with cheery yellow subtitles. She took the tag off the door and hung out the sign: PRIVACY PLEASE. The door shut behind them, and that was that. Here he was.

His young hostess smiled graciously—"One sec!"—and headed for the toilet.

Carlo read the bright yellow words of a man and a woman talking on TV. They weren't speaking French. He'd watched and enjoyed quite a few French movies, and to his American ears this was even more garbled than French. Maybe Russian. Polish.

"When I'm happy, I laugh! I dance! Nothing gets me down! And when I'm sad, I crash downward, my heart breaks, and I'm sure that God is a criminal."

He stood by the television with his head cocked, taking this in. He picked up the remote and found the mute button.

He was standing there foolishly when she came back in wearing a pink bra and pink bikini panties under a flimsy see-through negligee. Bare feet. No stockings.

She spread her arms and sang, "Ta-daa!"

He applauded softly with his hands.

"This way, please."

She guided him toward the bed and sat close beside him in a cloud of blossomy cologne. Carlo asked, "Do you come from a large family, Jeannie?"

"What?"

"I mean—is that why you like to keep the TV on, maybe? Are you used to a lot of voices?"

"I leave it on all the time. It fools the burglars."

"It fools them that you're French."

She laughed. "And now I have to be a boob and ask you your name again, because I'm sort of a boob with names."

"Carl," he said. "People call me Carlo, and don't ask me why. I've never figured it out."

"It's because people like you," she declared.

"Really?"

"When people give you a nickname, it's because they like you."

He stared at the tube. The yellow subtitle said, *"I want to weep. But I feel like I've wept already."*

She picked up the remote. "Do you mind if I leave it on very softly?"

"No. Go ahead. How come?"

"I don't know. It's too quiet in here," she said.

She brought the voices up slightly.

"When it comes to subtitles," Carlo said, "I like white lettering better than yellow, even if it's harder to see. It seems to go better with the atmosphere."

"Well. I don't think there's a button for that, Carl."

This girl was funny! "What about some Christmas music?" He pointed to the radio on her nightstand.

But she shook her head. "That old Taiwanese clock radio? It sounds more like an insect."

The people on the tube went on softly and incomprehensibly. "So," Carlo said. "Was that actually you in the Actual Photograph?"

"That's me in the picture—before the recent fiasco at the hairdresser's. I've never been to the same one twice. They always murder me."

Now they stared at the movie. Nobody was saying anything at the moment. The man and the woman were exploring a sort of garden at night.

Housekeeping hadn't come yet. Maybe they wouldn't come today. After all, it was Christmas, although nobody in this town seemed to have been told. There were towels bunched on the floor, drooping from a chair. One of the sheets had gotten away and lay twisted like a rope. Jeannie had pulled the bedspread up over one pillow. The other was propped against the wall for sitting up in bed while watching television. Nothing in sight said, "Welcome to the whorehouse."

He noticed an ashtray or two, and smelled the stink of previous cigarettes. "Do you mind if I smoke?"

"No," she said. "Do you mind if *I* smoke?"

"No."

"Well, gosh darn it," she said, "let's smoke!"

He laughed, and offered her one of his.

So far she'd shown high spirits, but dark circles around her eyes made her look soulful and mysterious.

"I think I got you up too early, didn't I?"

"No way, Carl. I'm up and down at all hours. Circumstances make the schedule."

They smoked. It was delicious. He could feel the nicotine gurgling in his fingertips.

"This is the scariest cigarette pack I've ever seen," she said. "Where'd you come from, Carl? The distant future?"

"Well, I don't know," he said.

She took a good puff, and exhaled, and appeared thoughtful before saying, "Why don't you strip down, and I'll relax you with a little back-rub? Then we'll take it from there."

"Let me think about this," he said.

"Would a little rubdown help you think better?"

"You're very attractive," he said.

"Thank you! One sec." She went to the closet and hung on to the door frame with one hand and stuck her feet, first one and then the other, into the darkness. She came back to the bed looking quite a bit more statuesque in bright blue pumps with tall spike heels. "I just got these beauties! Might as well put some mileage on."

"Great legs," he said.

"Thanks," she said. "They're all yours."

"All mine! Well," he admitted, "that's the most terrifying thing any-body ever said to me."

Great legs, definitely, and a pleasing shape, an ample, sweet-look-ing body. She was maybe a little flabby around the middle. Not that he minded in the least, but that's where she strayed from perfection.

He didn't feel particularly out of place, or confused, not even a tiny bit embarrassed. He just didn't know what he was doing here. He'd forgotten, more or less, where this moment had come from. He was trying to get back some sense of why he'd just given this nice woman slightly less than a week's salary after taxes, and then joined her here in her place of residence.

He was used to seeing luscious women in movies and magazines—standing there. He wasn't used to seeing them sit down, watching the flesh of their thighs widen as they sat on a bed beside him, or smelling the toothpaste on their breath.

"Carlo," she said.

"Yeah?"

"What's going on in that head of yours?"

"That's a mystery," he said. "Especially to me, sometimes."

"I hope you're not a nut!"

"I don't think so. Not the extreme kind, anyway. But can I just sit here a minute and sort of take it all under consideration?"

"You paid for an hour. It's your hour."

"It's just . . . I don't think I want to do this."

"Well, you paid for an hour," she said again. "Do you want a massage or something? Just a plain massage?"

"No," he said, "I—don't think I want a plain massage."

"Well, do you want to just go? I mean, listen. Whatever is your idea of a happy ending—I'm here for that."

"I appreciate it," he said.

"But no refunds!"

He didn't want to leave, at least not for a minute or two. It occurred to him maybe they could talk a little. What subject would come up between two people in a situation like this? It was like a private lesson of some kind. "I could ask you a couple things," he said.

"What?"

"Could I ask you," he said, "a couple things?"

"You mean you want to talk dirty?"

"I don't think I want to talk dirty," he said.

"Do you want to take a poll? Are you a pollster?"

"Nope."

"Well then, what do you want to ask me?"

"Okay, let's see. Well, for one thing—what does 'Las Vegas' mean?"

"What do you mean?"

He shrugged.

"It means here."

"No, think about it—do you know what 'Las Vegas' means? Think about it."

"I never thought about it."

"Well, it's a foreign phrase, probably Spanish. A lot of our names mean something in a foreign language, and we hardly ever think about it. For all we know, 'Las Vegas' could mean 'The Idiots.'"

"Then they might as well come right out and say so in English," she said. "In the case of this town, that would be a good, appropriate name."

"How long have you been living here?"

"In Vegas? I'm back and forth. I'm off and on. Reno, San Francisco. I live in hotels. Sacramento . . . Up and down the line."

"But I just want to know how long—if you never thought about it—how *long* you haven't ever thought about it. How long have you been *around* Las Vegas, not thinking about what 'Las Vegas' means?"

"Four or five years, at least."

The idea of this young person living in a series of rooms like this one, embracing a wild style of life and getting along without disaster, astonished Carlo.

"Do I sound like a regular nut?"

"No. No. No. Not really."

"These are the kinds of things that pass through your mind at the Department of Motor Vehicles."

"Well, they should let you out to run around once in a while, Carlo. You need air!"

"So I *am* losing my mind."

"Hey, come on—so what? Whatever. It's nice to meet somebody who wonders what it's all about."

"Sorry."

"Or at least what 'Las Vegas' means."

"Do you think anybody ever thinks about these things?"

"Well, you do, obviously."

"I'd like to know if anybody else ever thought about them, or if I'm the only one. I'll give you another example." He dragged a pillow onto his lap. "Colors. I point to this pillow, and I say it's—what color would I say?"

"Blue. I don't know. Light blue?"

"Some form of blue. But 'blue' is only a *word* we've been taught to say when I point to that color. Maybe—inside my head—what I see would be red to you, and what you see would be—I don't know—purple, to me, or gray, to me, or any color at all. What we *say* is the same, but what we *see* could be completely different. Have you ever thought about that?"

"No."

"Am I way off in left field someplace? Or am I making sense?"

"You're making sense, but I think red is red and blue is blue. Otherwise we wouldn't call it 'red,' and we wouldn't call it 'blue.'"

"Jeannie, wait. Do you see what I mean? I could say, 'Blue, green, orange,' but what I see would be *your* idea of purple, black, yellow. We could be living in two completely different-colored worlds. And so could every other person on this planet. Same words, different colors."

He offered her a smoke. They lit up. Carlo said, "You know, I haven't smoked in seven years, until this morning. I should feel bad, but I don't."

"I know," she said. "I've tried everything, and this is the best stuff there is."

"I wish I'd never stopped."

"I know! I don't care how high they raise the taxes, I'll never quit."

"Okay," he said, "how about this one—taking the same idea a little further. Maybe inside, when I say I'm sad, what I'm feeling is the same emotion you feel when you say you're happy. We *act* sad, we *say* sad, but who knows what we're actually feeling on the inside?"

"Same words, different feelings. Why not?"

"I realize it's a silly thing to bring up, more or less," he said, "but do you get it?"

"Same words, different colors." She was laughing at him. "Have you been to college?"

"A little bit," he said. "Just a couple courses in the service."

"I have," she said, "I've been to college. I went to college for almost two years."

"A college girl."

"Yeah."

"Do they talk about these things in college?"

"No," she said. "I really don't know what they talk about. That's why I left. What do you do?" she said.

"I work for the Ohio Department of Motor Vehicles," he said. "I administer the driving-license exams, among other things like that."

"You mean the actual—" She lightly gripped an imaginary steering wheel.

"No, a cop does that. I do the other part, the written part. And various things. I'm an administrative assistant."

"How long have you been doing that?"

"I don't know," he said.

"You don't know?"

"I never counted it up," he was a little surprised to admit. He thought about it and said, "Seven years."

"Wow," she said.

"Before that I was in the navy," he said, "long-term."

"Did you count?"

"Uh. Yeah. Fifteen years," he said. "I quit re-upping after I got engaged. I don't think a married man should leave his wife and go to sea."

The direction of the conversation was making him sweat. He didn't like hanging around in this hotel room and thinking about Lenore, about the length of time they'd been together, about the decisions he'd made in his life.

The effect of being here was beyond that of a simple one-on-one conversation—he was perched on the peak of Mount Fuji with this stranger, and nobody within miles of them. He was stranded on a Japanese mountaintop with this attractive person who didn't know or care when Christmas came.

"Let me check out a couple of other things with you, see if you ever thought about them."

"I can pretty much guarantee you I didn't!"

"Do you ever feel like everybody knows something, and you don't?"

"More or less constantly!"

"Like there's one small, important fact, and you're the only person on earth who doesn't know it?"

"No. I feel that way at *parties*—around hip people, beautiful people, but not otherwise . . ."

"*Is* there such a fact?"

"What fact?"

"Is there a fact," he said very carefully, "that you know, and everybody else knows, but I don't know it?"

She didn't answer right away. He was relieved to see her giving it some serious consideration. She thought a long time. He began to feel terrified.

"Well," she said, "if you don't know it, I don't know it, either."

"Think," he said. "Maybe it's so small, and to you so insignificant, that you don't even realize it. But to me it would be incredibly important."

"I know. But nothing comes to mind," Jeannie said.

"All right, good, fair enough, but, now, just bear with me here. Just go along with the gag. Another question: Did you ever think that we're really living our whole lives backwards? That we start out as dust in the grave, that we form ourselves out of dust in our coffins, then we're unearthed, we're dug up, and then we start living as old people, and get younger and younger and younger, until we're children? And then babies? And then we crawl up inside our mothers, exactly in reverse of what we think? Wouldn't that explain why we see what happened to us as young people?—because it's actually the future, it's ahead of us, we can see it coming. And what we call the future is actually the past, it's behind us, and that's why we can't see it—because you can't see what's behind you."

Jeannie only cleared her throat—"Hm-mh . . ."

"As far as the direction of time is concerned, what we call backwards is forwards, and what we call forwards is backwards. You can't see behind you—do you see what I mean?"

"I never thought about that."

"No? You never thought about any of this?"

"No. I'm still back at the part about the colors."

"But what do you think of it, as an idea? Am I wacky? Or do you think it could be possible?"

"That everything's backwards, but we think it's forwards? Sure. And upside down, and all of that. I mean left, and right . . . sure. But—I'm sorry, what was your name again? I forgot!"

"Carlo."

"I forgot! Sorry, Carlo."

"What were you going to say, Jeannie?"

"We just go on acting like up is up and red is red, no matter *what* we *think*. None of it matters."

"It matters to me."

"You're not kidding. I can see that."

"It winds up like this," he said to her. "It gets pretty horrible. It comes down to this: Imagine a person whose heart is actually full of love, spending every day joyously, ecstatically married to somebody whose heart is absolutely filled with *hate*, and they both use the same word for completely opposite emotions."

Carlo had expected the unexpected, but he'd certainly failed to anticipate this. You head off into the morning, and you go here and there, and you find someone finally, and you talk, and you talk, and you talk.

And what does the other person say? She says nothing. She's completely silent, as Jeannie was right now. He wondered how long she'd be quiet if he stayed quiet.

Carlo wondered if she had ideas like this inside her. These might not be the circumstances, but in the right situation, what would surface? Given an opportunity to hold forth, what would she like to say?

"Cigarette?" he said.

"Thanks very much."

"Darn, I forgot I was going to stay quiet."

"Quiet? I'll definitely allow that!" she said.

He lit both their Philip Morris cigarettes with a match from the Sands Hotel and dropped the match into the ashtray beside her Taiwanese clock radio.

"Okay. Your turn," he said. "I've got twenty minutes here. You want to say anything?"

"Say what?"

"Anything. I was just taking all this in, this unusual get-together, reflecting on it, and thinking maybe when the usual thing happens, you don't get much of a chance to talk. You yourself. Jeannie. So . . ."

"This isn't that unusual," Jeannie said.

"It isn't unusual?"

"Every once in a while the usual doesn't happen. Every once in a while. You'd be surprised. And it turns out the guy just wants to talk. Really. It's true."

"About what?"

"Well, nothing. I don't remember. Personal stuff. Not the stuff you just talked about—not college stuff! . . . I mean, I get a real wide range of people in here. The entire gamut of modern civilization."

"Like who? What do they say?"

"The only one I remember right now was a guy who said he couldn't feel an ejaculation. He was numb."

"I see—numb," Carlo said.

"He was in a motorcycle wreck that did something to his spine. Everything was fine about him, except that he couldn't feel certain nerve endings, and he couldn't experience the pleasure of ejaculation."

Carlo said, "I see."

"And he ended up not wanting to do it, and we ended up—not doing it. Instead, he told me about how much he loved motorcycles, and how much he loved women, and how, by that time, he'd lost the power to be pleased by a woman, and he was scared to death of motorcycles. And, also, scared to death of women . . . I mean, I get 'em all. But, okay . . ."

She put her cigarette out and placed her hand gently on Carlo's knee as if to keep him still and continued. "Okay. Have you ever thought that there's a reason for everything?"

"I've never thought about it," he said.

"Have you ever felt that maybe you have a purpose, a reason for being just exactly you? That you were here to be listening, like the reverse of a newspaper, almost—you're here to receive the news that a person has found out. You're here to get the discoveries communicated to you. I mean, I just bounce around. I don't own much stuff . . . I don't live anywhere, I don't have anything, I don't *know* anybody, really—not very well—I hardly even *am* anybody, when you think about it . . .

"Have you ever felt like you were almost just nobody? But it didn't matter, because you have this purpose, which is to be with other people? Have you ever kind of suspected that we almost don't exist, practically, except face-to-face with another person? Have you ever suspected that?"

"No, I've never exactly . . . suspected that," Carlo heard himself saying. Trying to follow all this just confused him. His thoughts were fuzzy, his head felt stuffed with cotton, with lint.

"Time's not quite over," she said.

"I just have one more thing to ask you about."

She laughed. "I think a shrink would be a lot cheaper. Or would it? Do they charge you a lot?"

"Just one more thing," he repeated, "and it's this: What if nothing exists? What if you're imagining all of this? I know you aren't, of course, because I know *I* exist. But *you* can't be sure. No one person can ever be sure about any of the others."

"Like, 'Life is but a dream.'"

"Exactly."

"Sometimes, it is."

"It is?"

"It sure was last night. While I was asleep. Everything that happened was a dream."

She struck him as quite a special kind of girl—steady, good-humored, generous of heart. He had an impulse to tell her this, to celebrate her qualities, but he knew he shouldn't start out saying something that could only lead to the question of how such a nice person ended up working as a prostitute.

Jeannie cleared her throat just as she had before, "Hm-*mm* . . ."

"*Did* you grow up in a large family?" Carlo asked.

"Well, no, I grew up with my mom. A single mom. In pretty much the same places I hang around now—Sacramento, Reno, Vegas . . ."

"And what did your mom do? I mean, that sounds rude. What was she like? Or . . ."

"Oh," Jeannie said, "she was a gal pretty much along the same lines as me."

"Really? And what did she do?"

"For a living? She did pretty much the same thing I do."

"Wow. Really. No kidding," Carlo said.

Jeannie said, "*Now* I remember my dream . . . I was at a fast-food joint. I had a cup in my hand, but I couldn't find the right spigot to shoot the cream into my coffee. I was almost in tears. I was sort of whimpering. And there was somebody right beside me trying to do the same thing, and we both started laughing. We kept turning spigots and pushing buttons, and we were both laughing. And I said, 'God! This is so hard!'"

Carlo saw that his time was up. He didn't know if he was still allowed to talk. "They say we get messages from the unconscious mind," he said anyway, "via our dreams."

"I know."

"There are books about it."

"I know. But I'm not about to read a thousand-page book just to figure out the message."

"You're fun to be with," he said.

"I've always said so!"

"One more question? Last one?"

"Cross your heart," she said. "What's the question?"

"Well, suppose we went for another hour? Suppose, this time, we went for the works?"

"What fun!"

"Would that be another three hundred?"

"Let's talk about a discount," she said.

They worked it out. The two hours finished up at a total cost to Carlo of $400, and compared to what he'd always imagined of sex-for-pay in the tough town of Las Vegas, he felt he got the full value, and then some.

It started off awkward in a way that was funny, then it became all right for a while, and then it was awkward in a way that would have to be called, actually, awkward. And at one point it was getting so uncomfortable he had to stop. "What is it?" she said, and he didn't know what to say. And so he just continued again, feeling his elbows and knees on her sheets, his belly against hers, his chin pressing maybe too hard against the top of her head. He remembered his baldness. He felt like apologizing to someone who might be watching. He just continued, but this time, while he was making love to Jeannie, he thought about someone else, a fantasy woman who didn't exist.

But he got what he'd ached for, which was to touch her, or anyone like her. Her skin was smooth, very uniform, almost like rubber, but warm and living . . . not dark, but not pale, either—almost bright. He'd been so hungry to press against such skin, to kiss it and taste it, that even a few minutes of this—to say nothing of an entire hour spent naked with Jeannie—felt like lying down at last after an endless, pointless, exhausting day.

For a while afterward neither of them said a word. Carlo lay there bathed in sweat, lighting a Philip Morris cigarette and thinking, I'm so glad I started smoking again in time for this.

He couldn't help it now, his eyes were drawn to the tube, where a man hung upside down by his ankles from the strut of a small plane.

A woman sat on a stump going thirstily at a slice of watermelon. She looked up. The strange dangling man flew past and grabbed her snack with one hand.

A longer view: the plane rammed a cliff face and exploded in a compact fireball.

Still longer view: a plume of smoke in an empty blue sky.

Carlo blew out smoke himself and thought once more: Just in time, I'm so glad, what a blessing.

These people on television looked familiar. Yes, he recognized them. He'd watched part of this same film last night, and here it was again the very next day. Perhaps they ran it repeatedly because it was a Christmas story—no way to tell, unless someone like Santa Claus or Jesus made an appearance. And now the next events were the very ones he'd already witnessed—the woman hanging laundry, the man approaching dressed in burnt rags, the two embracing, the white shirt tumbling on the wind down a hill.

When he left, Jeannie kissed him goodbye, and when the kiss was over, she yanked him back for one more, then shoved him away. "No more discounts. Call me."

"I probably won't," he said. "I leave town tomorrow."

"In that case, here's a freebie!" She pulled his hand to her breast and squeezed. Then she pushed him out the door, laughing at him.

"Ten four," he said as the door closed.

He hiked down the long hallway and boarded an elevator. After he'd punched the button and it began to move he had one of the crazier moments in his life, when he had no idea where this thing was taking him, whether up or down, right or left, maybe under and over like a Ferris wheel.

But how would he see it all later, looking back—assuming time ran forwards, and the past was really behind us . . . Would he feel sorry for his deeds today? He couldn't guess. He guessed this much, however: This was no piddling little thing he'd done.

Twenty minutes later Carlo was back at the Sands. He looked around himself carefully as he made his way through the casino. He did not see one sprig of mistletoe. He didn't see any jingle bells, not one holly wreath, no tinsel, no candy canes, not the tiniest indication that Christmas had arrived. As a matter of fact he saw no way of figuring out whether it was day or night—no windows, no clocks. On the Muzak a rendition of "The Lonely Bull," originally made popular by Herb Alpert and the Tijuana Brass, was just finishing. Then came a vocal, Trini Lopez doing "If I Had a Hammer."

Back in the room, Lenore was dressed now, propped on the bed with the phone to her ear. As Carlo came through the door, she waved with her fingers and gave him a happy smile. He thought to himself: People are almost always cheerful around me.

"Back from outer space," he joked.

Lenore was watching the Weather Channel with the sound off. He stood beside the television and looked. The map was unblemished. At the moment, no snow fell anywhere in the continental United States. That didn't mean there wasn't plenty on the ground already, in places like Minnesota, North Dakota, Michigan . . . but right now the determination seemed to be that there just wasn't any weather.

Lenore was sitting up on the bed with her legs out straight in front of her, her shoes kicked off and her ankles crossed. She covered the phone's mouthpiece with the palm of her hand, and though the person on the other end therefore couldn't hear, still only mouthed the words *Hi, hon.*

THE MOVES

:::

Miranda July

BEFORE HE DIED my father taught me his finger moves. They were movements for getting a woman off. He said he didn't know if they'd be of use to me, seeing as how I was a woman myself, but it was all he had in the way of a dowry. I knew what he meant; he meant inheritance, or legacy, not dowry. There were twelve moves in all. He did them on my hand like sign language. They were mostly about speed and pressure in different combinations. There were some flourishes that I never would have thought of; I imagined he'd learned them when he was overseas. A sudden reversal in both speed and direction. Still fingers held like silence, for a beat, and then long quick strokes that he called "skinning." I kept wanting to write things down and he would scoff, asking me if I would take out my notes when the time came. You'll remember, he said, and he repeated skinning on my palm with his dry fingers. It felt like a hand massage. He was incredibly confident. I could not imagine using these movements alone, with such confidence. You're going to make some woman very, very happy, he said. But I knew I had never made anyone very, very happy and I could only imagine bringing in my dad when the time came to do this. But he would be dead and I suppose she would be a lesbian and wouldn't want him to touch her. I would have to do the finger moves myself. I would have to decide when she was ready for Six and for Seven. Could she handle the intensity of the still beat and give in to the rapid pleasures of skinning? I would have to listen to find out. *Not just to her breath*, my dad said, *but to moisture on the skin in the small of her back. That moisture is your secret emissary. One moment she'll be dry as a cat and in the next moment—Cape*

Town is flooding! Don't wait to be sure or you'll miss the boat, hop on and move, move, move. Each morning when I try to motivate toward something positive I think of him saying this and it is a great comfort. I know that one day I'll meet someone special and we'll have a daughter and I'll teach her what he taught me. Don't wait to be sure. Move, move, move.

JAZZ

. . .
. . .

Dylan Landis

IT IS NOT TRUE that if a girl squeezes her legs together she cannot be raped.

Not that Rainey is being raped. She doubts it, though she is not sure. Either way, it is true that the thirty-nine-year-old male knee, blind and hardheaded, has it all over the thirteen-year-old female thigh, however toned that thigh by God and dodgeball. You may as well shove Bethesda Fountain into the lake as try to dislodge the male knee.

That's where she is: on her back, on the grass near Bethesda Fountain in Central Park. Angels darken in the dusk on the fountain's dry tiers, and Rainey watches through the slats of a bench. She had started to walk the lip of the muted fountain but Richard wanted to inspect the thin silty edge of the lake.

Not far, he said. A constitutional.

How far is far, that's what Rainey wanted to know. She didn't care what a constitutional was.

The lake edge quivered and Rainey saw that the water was breathing. Richard dipped his hand in Rainey's hair and said, "You could turn the fountain on."

Richard plays French horn, and Rainey's dad says all horn players are a little strange. Rainey likes to court this strangeness because Richard is three-quarters safe, he is appreciative in ways that do not register on the social meter, he responds invisibly, immeasurably. She has tasted the scotch in Richard's glass. Her dad's attention was elsewhere. Her dad was riffing on the piano in their living room, spine straight and hands prancing, head shaking *no no no it's too good*, the man up to his shoulders in sound. Her first taste had burned and she looked at Richard *why don't you just drink bleach* and he smiled *try growing up first*, and she was good at this kind of talking, eye dialogue, with nuances from the angle of the head. Then she swallowed without wincing and looked at Richard for affirmation and he raised his eyebrows *are you sure you want to go farther* and she arched her neck so his gaze would have something to slide down *I want to go far*, and she drank the entire rest of his glass.

At the lake near Bethesda Fountain, Richard extended two fingers with broad white moons under the nails. He tilted her chin so she stared at his big face against the bruised sky. "You generate energy," he said. "You could turn on a city of fountains."

The eighth-grade boys do not have pores.

Richard said, "You radiate power and light," and he led her, electric, to the grass.

Rainey has tea-rose oil between her toes, because one day a man might smell it there and be driven genuinely out of his mind, and she has a wedding band on her left forefinger because her ring finger is too small. Both of these things, the rose oil and the ring, she claimed from the medicine cabinet after her mother got into the cab. She looked for the plastic compact with its squashy white dome, but that was gone.

And it is true, and only partly because of the oil and the loaded ring, that Rainey radiates power and light. And it is true that she loves making Richard say these things. She loves that he is a grown-up and yet he seems to have no choice. This fascinates her, just as it fascinates her that mothers look at her strangely. They are like mirrors, these mothers, the way they register the heat disturbances that emanate from under her skin.

It could be true, but it could also be a lie, that a teenage boy can get an erection just by brushing against a woman's arm on the bus. Mr. Martin in sex ed was very specific about the circumstances: boy, woman, arm, bus. As Rainey interprets this, it is the Broadway bus, an old green 104 lumbering uptown at rush hour, and the woman is eighteen, no, she is twenty-one, and carrying a white shopping bag with violets on it and wearing a lavender cardigan. The top three buttons are open, no, the top four, but it is her slender sweatered arm as she squeezes toward the back of the bus that engenders the event.

It is a lie that if a girl doesn't do something about the erection, it will hurt so badly that some injury will be caused. Mr. Martin said this too.

Rainey ran the tip of her tongue along the rim of Richard's glass and said, "When I'm sixteen, will you date me?"

"Only with your father's permission," Richard said. She waited for him to glance toward the piano, but he didn't.

It is a lie that Rainey will be allowed to live with her mother in Phoenix when she is sixteen, because her mother belongs to an ashram now, and Rainey understands that by "belongs to" her mother means belongs to the way lipstick or leotards belong to a person. It is also a lie that her father and Janet are just friends. Rainey has plastered herself to the wall outside Howard's bedroom and listened to the strange symphony of sex—the oboe of a groan, the violin singing *Oh my God*, the cello that is her father murmuring into some part of the body that is bent or curved.

"I take it back," Richard said. "When you're sixteen I'll marry you."

Rainey is under Richard on the grass now and she gasps from his weight, and it is true that it sounds like desire, and it is true that she likes hearing herself make the sound.

It is not true that there are boulders mashing her wrists. The boulders are Richard's hands. His hands have hair on the back. Andy Sakellarios, who might or might not be her boyfriend, has smooth hands. The boulders, like the knee, are forces she accepts for the moment. She accepts them because they are fires she has lit, and men are flammable, and Rainey believes it is her born talent, the one she sees reflected in the mothers' eyes, to set the kind of flickering orange fire that licks along the ground. Rainey accepts the pressure of the knee and the boulders like she might accept and intercept the force of a river before she lies down on its current. In Phoenix the river had been colder than cracked ice on her back teeth. Rainey let the water swirl her hair, let the cold polish her bones. She loved how surrender felt like a flower opening and she loved having the power to choose it. She ended up nearly a quarter mile downstream, where her mother found her at a campsite with boys, bikini dripping, drinking Miller from a can.

It was a lie that she had taken just one sip.

The soft grunts that squeeze from inside her are hers, but not hers. They are a lie and they are not a lie. Her toes smell delirious but Richard is crushing her lungs. Her lungs look like the fetal pigs in jars in the science room, and maybe gray like them too, because she loves to smoke. Smoking is one of the best things that ever happened to her.

"Give me that," her mother had said, and snapped the Miller can away from her, and drank deep.

The man with his knee between her legs and the heels of his palms bearing into her wrists says, "Jesus God, Rainey." He says, "I want to eat your hair."

It is a lie that he actually eats her hair, but it is true that he chews on it for a while. Her hair sounds crunchy between his teeth, like sand. She does not mind him chewing on it. She thinks how this is one more interesting thing a man can be reduced to. She wonders if sex is like math, like if you make a man want to eat your hair or go too far, does it follow that you balance the equation by letting him. And she exhales a sharp sigh whenever Richard moves, and it sounds like yes, when what she really means is *Let's go hear John Coltrane.*

Rainey is on her back on the grass near Bethesda Fountain. There could be dog shit in the grass next to her, and Rainey wants Richard to roll off so she can wrestle herself up, but then he might end up lying in dog shit, and this seems like terrible damage to inflict, especially on her father's best friend, who is supposed to be taking her to hear John Coltrane in the park because her father had to play in the Village and couldn't go. John Coltrane plays three kinds of sax and he even plays jazz flute. She loves jazz flute, the way it rises hotly through the leaves of trees, then curls and rubs along the roots. Jazz flute lives about two stories off the ground. It is a reedy ache in a place she cannot name. How will Richard get her to the concert if there is dog shit on his back?

"Jesus," says Richard. "Somebody make me stop."

He releases one wrist and pushes her peasant blouse, with the scarlet and blue embroidery, up under her armpits. Rainey pounds on his back but her freed fist is soft as clay.

At school, where they are doing *Oedipus Rex*, Rainey has to hang herself from the climbing rope in the gym. She clutches the rope to her neck with both hands, and when she dies, Oedipus unfastens a pin from her toga. This always takes a few seconds too long because Oedipus, who is shorter than her and chubby, trembles in the face of her power and light and her breasts being so incredibly present, like an electrified fence he has to fix without touching. And then he pokes his eyes out. It is just like that Doors song where the killer puts his boots on and then he pays a visit to his mother's room, and then Jim Morrison's throat releases this unholy cry.

Through the ground, Rainey feels the crowd gathering, she feels blankets unfolding on grass, she feels tuna fish sandwiches nestling in wrinkled tinfoil. She feels John Coltrane place his fingers on the soprano sax like it is her own spine. She feels how a concert swells before it starts and she wants to be there, she wants to lie on a blanket while Richard smells her toes and is driven insane, and she wants to feel the exact moment when the sound of the sax shimmies over the Transverse and toward the sky, changing the course of the East River and starting every fountain in the city.

In Phoenix her mother had yanked the cold-sweating Miller can away, splashing beer on the red dirt that powdered her wet feet, and said: "This is what I flew you here for? This is what your life is about?"

It is probably true that all men want to go all the way, all the time.

It is true that when Rainey has her French notebook open she is designing bikinis and maxicoats and bridal gowns, including bridal miniskirts with trains and go-go boots, using agonizingly neat strokes with a pale pink Magic Marker. She makes the bridal gowns pink because there is no white. Is this what her life is about? It is true that she plays classical flute, and it is true that she lies and says it is jazz. She is good at drawing clothes and being Jocasta. She is good at having a disturbing and emanating body.

Richard is eating her ear now. He does it like kissing. She turns her head away but that presents the ear more centrally. Rainey wonders when he will want to get up.

She tries to talk but all she gets out is the word "What." She wants to say, "What time is it?" so Richard will leap up, wiping grass off his knees, and say, "Oh, shit, let's go." But darkness has spilled into Central

Park and if she talks too loud, gangs of boys might rustle toward them carrying moonlight on their knives.

In Phoenix the boys at the campsite had been older. She had told them she was fifteen and a half, that she played jazz flute and was dying for a smoke.

The boys smirked at the ground when her mother showed up. "Howard warned me to keep an eye on you," her mother said, and took a long, angry drink from the Miller can. Then she looked across the ring of stones where the fire belonged and said, "Thank you, gentlemen, for giving my daughter a beer. Did she happen to mention she's only twelve?"

"Not for long," said Rainey.

One of the boys had opened his mouth into the shape of a shocked twelve, and the blond boy with the gold earring and the cross had looked straight at her mother and said: "Sorry, we didn't know." The cross made Rainey want to find the badness in this boy. She wanted to ignite him with a brush of her arm. She wanted to steal this boy from God.

"You didn't know," said her mother. She had finished the Miller and crumpled the can and tossed it into the ring of stones. Rainey's mother had that ripe thing going on. Her legs were tennis-hard from another life. The boy's eyes had flickered, or maybe it was his mouth, and Rainey looked over in time to see her mother smile back, sardonic and acknowledging and quick.

Richard is licking her armpit, which she shaved on Monday with Janet's razor. Today is Thursday. She has stubble but her toes smell like tea rose. Richard raises himself so she can breathe and licks along the underwire of her Warner's Miss Debutante bra.

"Richard," says Rainey, "get OFF."

Richard says, "I'm not doing anything. I swear I won't do anything."

"You ARE doing something," says Rainey. He releases her wrists and she pushes on his shoulders. She wants to set fires and she wants to control how they burn. She likes going pretty far with Andy Sak, who is rendered both desperate and respectful by her power and light.

"I want to go to the concert," says Rainey. "Would you get OFF?"

She has known Richard since she was a toddler. She doesn't have to be polite.

"Five minutes," says Richard. He has freed a breast with his teeth. Rainey, propped on her elbows, sees how her breast lights up in the dark. It pumps out its resplendence like the sun. When Richard sucks on the nipple, the water roils up through the pipes in Bethesda Fountain and rains on the heads of the angels.

Rainey punches him on the head.

"Five minutes," he says. "In five minutes you'll be thirty-nine and I'll be fourteen and then we can go."

Rainey says, "Goddammit, Richard," and she is half crying. She is not getting raped but he won't get up. She still wants to go too far but she is not sure how far is far.

"You think I just want that one thing," says Richard. "You think there's only one part of you that's special." He kisses her mouth again, and she lets him, even though he has a beard and his mouth does not have that boy sweetness; it tastes of tobacco and steak.

Richard runs his tongue over her bare stomach.

"Thirteen," Rainey says, but there is clay in her mouth.

"I want to inhale you," Richard says. "I want to absorb you through my skin."

The current had been so strong. When she lay down on the river it had held her up and swirled her like a big liquid hand, and she lay on it, releasing energy to the sky, letting the river be the stronger thing.

"You taste like music," Richard says. "You taste like jazz."

It might be true or it might be a lie that there is only one part of her that is special.

"Jesus God," says Richard. His tongue is in her navel and she has stopped punching his head because she is thinking, she is in the hand of the burning river, she is rising hotly through the leaves, and she hears him make the long sliding moan of the trombone.

CLASS TRIP

:::

Victor LaValle

—HOOKERS, Willy said. You know them. You love them.

He was trying to get us interested. What do you think? He was talking to three tenth-grade boys. Fifteen years old. Among all four we didn't have half a brain. Willy, bullet-shaped head and all, was good at convincing and he wasn't even working hard.

—We are hopping on that train, he continued, heading out to Manhattan, and everyone here is getting his dick sucked. No arguments.

—Who's going to put up a fight? I asked. We were each calculating how best to get some money, which parent often left a purse or wallet unguarded.

Carter asked, —How much'll we need? He stood his tall ass up in front of me. When he stretched his arms over his head Carter could run his fingers around the lip of the visible universe.

Our building was budding with age groups, men and boys. Soon someone had beer; eventually it made the rounds from the eighteen-and-ups to us and after we'd taken our pulls from the tall brown bottles there were the boys we'd once been, ten or eleven, anticipating a first taste. We could all afford such open drinking until eight or nine at night because our adults were dying at jobs. Willy never left shit to settle, so before we went off he grabbed Carter, James, and me, said, —This Friday. Get like thirty dollars.

Carter and I walked, no destination, just anywhere away from home. He was chattering about where he'd get his loot, not his mother or father, but that older brother who left his cash in his old shell-toed Adidas up on a shelf in his closet. Then he asked, —So what's that woman of yours going to say about you checking out these hos?

I had forgotten about her. —Guess I won't tell, I said. He laughed, —Man, you know you can't keep no secrets when you get drunk.

—I've never been drunk around Trisha.

Carter nodded. —Well then, maybe. He began telling me something else, he was almost whispering so it seemed like a secret. I was distracted but absently swore I heard my girl's name. I wasn't listening. It was evening in Flushing, Queens, and the buildings got glowing in that setting-sun red.

Friday, man, the whole day was full of explosive energy. During precalc a girl beside me dropped her book and in my head it sounded like a squad of soldiers battering through the door. When I saw any of the other guys we nodded conspiratorially. My girl made it easier on my conscience when she bowed out of school after third period. She clutched her belly and told me she was going home early, cramps were tearing up her insides. She had a big bag, full, and when I asked she reminded me of the trip she was taking to see her aunt, who lived in Massachusetts, some town near Boston. She'd be gone for days.

Then, in the evening, we rode the 7 out toward Manhattan. It was strange traveling with them, since about thirteen I had been coming out to wander alone. Most times I'd get off at Times Square, where my ass would trip around for blocks trying to find something to kill me or make me laugh.

On the subway James scratched his balls, looked at an old asleep man, tortured in his wrinkled suit. He asked us, —What if I just punch that kid in the face? He pointed to the man. But we weren't really like that. None of us. Talk shit, that was our game. Run fast, that was our game.

—Don't start nothing, Willy said.

James sucked his teeth; the way his eyes were shaking in their sockets he seemed amped enough to hit this guy, but Willy talked him down until James sat back, sprawled out like he couldn't on his mother's couch. A year before, James had got into it with an off-duty cop who was quick to show his badge and gun to James and me. The pistol was under his coat, outside his shirt, hanging on the rim of his jeans, the snubbed nose looking like a challenge. —So you're a cop, James had said. So what?

The cop was black, so I was especially scared.

—You should watch your mouth, son, the cop said, though he wasn't very old himself. James laughed that way he does, showing all his teeth; an expression that says, And? Black Cop pressed the yellow strip to ring for his stop. In the back stairwell he said to me, —Your friend's going to get you into trouble someday.

I wasn't speaking; I nodded, but my neck was soft with liquor, so I only managed a weak wobble of my head. He had made the mistake most people did, thought that because I was the quiet kid I was the one who should be saved.

At Times Square we discussed getting off, enjoying the flickering pleasures of video booths, but Willy was sure of his mission. He said, —Y'all will thank me when you have a mouth all on your knob.

We got off at Twenty-eighth Street, walked so quickly to the West Side Highway you'd have thought we were on wheels. A few blocks up, the Intrepid Museum was docked. I had been there three years before, with my mother and baby sister; I rode in the cockpit of a flight simulator imagining I could join the air force and float somewhere above the planet. James found sourballs in his jacket and sucked one.

You keep making noises like that and some dude's going to think you're advertising, Carter said. We laughed, but then he pointed and silenced us all. There, forty feet away, was a hooker dressed all in tight silver. You can't underestimate what this meant to us; imagine Plymouth Rock.

—You suck dick? James asked. She didn't need to look up to know she should ignore us.

—Break out, she said, going through her tiny purse.

She looked down the street, lit a cigarette, saw we had not left, said again, —Break out.

Carter tried to make it clear. —My boy asked if you suck dick.

She whipped her red hair, real or fake, backward, elegantly. I frowned. Silver said, —You tell your boy I don't fuck with little kids. The way she switched her weight from foot one to foot two made us forget any indignation and check out her lovely hips.

—I'm saying, James charmed. —I got the loot and you got the mouth, right?

Silver lost her temper, cursed at us, screamed a man's name. Then there he was, behind a rotten chain-link fence, amid these half-built homes of scavenged wood and sheets of plastic, all big shoulders and blond hair, like some *Übermensch*, a fucking super-Nazi in an off-white overcoat. Carter stayed behind to unload some more words at her; the rest of us were on the move. The expression on that guy, clearing the fence, crossing the street, was like he loved hurting people. Finally Carter appeared, stretching those long legs as he caught up to us. I looked over my shoulder, and the guy was still coming. My legs went faster. Soon I was whipping his Aryan ass like I was Jesse Owens.

The first time I held my girl's hand I was shaking so deep I couldn't control it. She looked at me. —You're shaking.

It was a strange second and I didn't say shit. This was six months before the night out with James, Willy, and Carter.

Trisha said, —I think it's sweet.

We were outside school, by the library. She and I had walked out, into the October cool, because I wouldn't hold her hand in front of a crowd. —Are you that nervous? she asked.

Her hand wrapped around mine. I thought I should kiss her, touch her face, find that spot that works—opening her mouth, closing her eyes. I said, —Yeah, a little.

—Why? She was older than me. Sixteen.

—Just am.

We sat on the cold steps. She smiled. She had braces.

They were shimmering and comely, there in her mouth. I had cuts across the backs of my hands. Trisha rubbed them with an open palm.

—How did these happen?

—I don't know.

—No, seriously, you can tell me these things.

I really didn't remember what had scarred them. She laughed; usually I got that reaction, laughter, from her only on the phone, where I could loosen up; in person I was always overcome by my goddamn emotions. When the cold air hit us harder, I thought of her, asked if she wanted to go in.

Trisha nodded. —It is cold. But we can stay. I was quiet so long I forgot we were supposed to say anything.

Trisha stared to her right, to the wall where I had played handball at nine or ten. I was very tired all the time. It didn't seem strange that I was fifteen and already feeling ancient.

She had been attached when I met her. Dating someone older, a freshman at some upstate college. He still sent her things, like bus tickets. This guy promised that if she went to him he'd give her the thing she liked most: perfume. Nice stuff I couldn't afford; all she had to do was visit. Working in my favor was distance, with its power to break bonds.

—You're quiet, I said.

She squeezed my palm. —Your hand's stopped shaking.

—You want to go to a movie? I asked quickly. We weren't dating yet, that day, just the early affection. Her laugh came out slow so, at first, I thought she was considering it. I let go of her, asked, —What's funny?

—You should have heard yourself, she said. She squeezed her nose between two short, thin fingers, talked all nasal, —You want to go to a movie?

—I sounded like that?

She touched the back of my head. —You should get a fade.

—You think so?

—I think you'd look so good with one. And, sitting like that, it was on her to lean in for the kiss. I was surprised, uncomfortable.

Then Trisha stood; I still sat, touched her feet.

—They're so small.

She said, —My feet are perfect. Even the toes are nice.

I stood, laughed, liked that she was arrogant about the stupidest things.

When the four of us stopped running, Carter was the first to catch his breath, said, —Man, we could have fucked that dude up.

I punched him in the chest when I could stand straight. James and Willy heaved a minute more. We had no speed left, but we were safe. Not for the first time in our lives we were lucky.

Until a year ago none of these fellas had been my boy, but here we were looking out for one another. I went through friends quickly. That was the best thing about guys—trust comes quick and no one cries when it's over.

We walked to Twenty-seventh, where the hookers were a populace. This was their beauty: almost nothing worn, skin. We stood at a corner to watch these women move. The worst-looking one was more gorgeous than the rest of the world.

Here in the land of ass aplenty, we were being ignored. Four black kids on foot spelled little cash and lots of hassles. These workers had no time for games.

Station wagons sped through with single passengers acting alternately calm and surprised, as though they'd found this block by accident. Husbands, fiancés, and boyfriends. Newer cars bursting with twenty-year-olds eased down the street, their systems pumping heavy.

—These girls are not going to take care of us, said Willy, the pragmatist. The rest of us dreamed ideally, waved twenties at the high heels thumping past. A woman with her glorious brown chest mostly exposed saw us, said, —Go down to Twenty-fifth.

—What's there? Willy asked.

—Crackheads. She kept walking, moving in that extra-hips way that paid her bills. The backs of her thighs were right there, platformed and performing. Exposed. It is not an exaggeration to say I would have married her that night.

We made that move. Stopped at a car, the guy inside getting a blow job. His friends were waiting, herded around a telephone, laughing. The top of a woman's head worked furiously, faster than I'd have imagined possible. I craned my neck to try and see more.

—That's Nicky! one of his friends screamed. The car window was down and Nicky inside smiled back. We rejoiced with them, but only a little, any longer and a fight might break out. They were muscle guys in zebra-print pants, leather coats; their skin looked so tough I doubted anything short of a shotgun would pierce their shells.

On Twenty-fifth the market crashed, both customers and workers. Women here wore jeans and T-shirts like someone's fucked-up neighbor out for a stroll. This block looked like our school's auditorium had belched out its worst; there were slight variations on us, in groups, canvassing the street. Truly ugly men rode through in cars that rattled and died while waiting at a red light, crackheads hopped into their cars two at a time. Some rubbed close on all us boys. We tried to act calm.

James was tired and bored. A woman appeared from a shadowed doorway; he asked her, almost absently, —How much for you to suck my dick?

—Fifteen.

All of us but Willy bolted upright, so sure we were going to leave Manhattan unfulfilled. Willy stayed shrewd. —Yeah right. He'll give you five and so will the rest of us.

She brightened, scanned the crew. —All of you? Willy nodded; she agreed. That was the benefit of going to a crackhead, you could haggle.

Finally it was my turn. Carter and Willy leaned against a building while James, lust done, rubbed his stomach. Trucks were parked on this block. Police cars seemed to have become extinct. Occasionally you heard their sirens bleating a few blocks up, but they seemed to have left everything on this block for dead. Charlene ushered me down the alley she'd made into her workplace. She was about my height and twice as old. We were well hidden but she took me farther, behind a green dumpster, lid shut.

—You know why I wanted you last, right?

I smiled. Her scalp was hidden under a blue scarf with white dots, the haphazard folds making them look as random as the salt spread out on the sidewalk after it has snowed. She kicked away the cardboard she'd laid out when taking care of my friends. I wasn't thinking of Trisha.

—I wanted the good stuff from you, she said. She brought herself close; I was not going to fuck her, no way. Get my dick sucked and move on. Then came her punches, two of them: one in the face that didn't hurt, but the second got me in the throat and I went down, on my hands and knees. This little crackhead had taken me out. The concrete was cold and one palm rested on an empty bag of chips. She was in my pockets, but found nothing. Then she gave me the real one, something popping against my head like a fucking brick. It was a gun.

—Get up, she said. Stand. It was the shittiest piece you'll ever see; a rusting .22, one inch above a zip gun. She was in control. —Now give me that money. No games, I got it for her. She counted out all thirty dollars, slowly, in front of me, like she was trying to rub it in. You could say I was scared, but it was delayed, didn't go off in my stomach until the four of us were catching the train an hour later and I couldn't ease my token into the slot; Carter took it from my palsied hand and pushed me through.

—You robbed them all? I asked.

—Nope. Just you.

—Why me?

She put the money away, scratched at her pussy from outside her jeans. My head was bleeding. I saw that she was peeing her pants before I smelled it; the stain spread in her crotch and soon the thin yellow slacks were loosing droplets that fell to the ground between her and me. She answered my question. —I don't like your face, she said. You just don't look good.

The whole next week in school I was hoping for my girl's return, but Trisha was out for five days. I'd call her at home. One of her older sisters would only take a message, firmly say she'd call me, but the next night I dialed the number. I felt guilty, spent hours considering how much better life would be if I'd stayed out of the alley, if I'd been a better man.

Finally Trisha appeared. We went out to dinner. She sat at the table warm in her jacket and a turtleneck. She held my hand when we walked, but swatted me off when I tried to kiss her neck. This diner was good: the seats squeaked when you slid into a booth and a small cup of coleslaw came with every meal. —Tonight, she said, I'm paying.

—I won't argue with that.

She laughed. —You never have a problem with spending my money.

—I was going to buy you something, I told her.

She sipped her water. We were quiet until a waiter came trolling for orders.

She asked, —Where is it?

—I didn't have enough, I admitted.

—Yeah, I know you. You spent that money on nonsense.

I smiled. —You got that right, beautiful.

—So what was it?

A group came into the diner and in the wonderful anonymity of the American family, I thought they'd just left. —Look. I pointed. Trisha peeped at them but wasn't into laughing at stability. —I was going to get you this bear.

—A teddy bear?

The food arrived. —Don't say it like that, I protested. —It was a nice one. Had a smoking jacket and a pipe. He looked like me. Don't you think he would be cute?

She ate. Dinner done, she paid the bill. We got up and out. Flushing at night was like Flushing during the day, just darker. Together we walked to her building.

—Anyone ever ask why you're dating a younger man?

—Maybe.

She wore a new good smell applied to her skin, but I ignored it, busy instead rubbing my nose, my chin, my neck, learning my face's true dimensions.

—And what did you tell him?

She shrugged. —What should I have said?

We walked fast. Soon her building stood before us. It wasn't so big but tonight it seemed majestic. Trisha's two older sisters were outside.

—Hey, Anthony, Gloria said, looking to the others. The secrets this bunch held among them were enough to destroy one thousand ex-boyfriends. Trisha smiled, waited.

—What? I asked.

—You aren't going to thank me for paying?

—You're right. Thank you so much. The food was delicious.

—I know. She touched my side.

—Am I ugly? I asked her.

—You? She put her face against my neck. She tried to tickle me but neither of us was laughing. On the street, traffic was still a thriving business; the sky was purple and lost.

HANG THE MOON

:::
:::

Jim Lewis

I PAID THEM special and they opened up the fairgrounds for us at three o'clock in the morning. It was a hot night in August and there wasn't anyone else out: just her and me. I didn't tell anyone else about it.

This was in '56: we were still living on Audubon, but every day was huge, and every dollar was a kiss on the mouth. That was right after "Heartbreak Hotel" went gold. I'd been to Hollywood, I was twenty-one. It was true, what they said, that each man and woman in the world carried a divine spark within. When someone asked me how it felt, I said, Like a dream. Like a beautiful dream.

I'd just bought that brand-new Lincoln Premiere, with the purple body and the white top; it had a great big steering wheel, such a light touch that I could run all the way down Lamar Avenue, guiding the car with my knees, my hands clasped behind my head like I was getting ready to fall asleep. She said, Honey, you're going to kill us both, but I could tell she wasn't really scared. I felt her glance over at me, run me up and down, and then go back to looking out the front.

The entrance to the park came up in my headlights and there was a man waiting there. He nodded when we pulled up, and he swung the gate back for us and came over to say hello. He was tired, we must have woken him up, and he was wearing a big black pistol in a holster on his belt. I guess he wanted to be ready for anything. I felt bad for him, having to get out of bed in the middle of the night, so I gave him ten dollars when he let us in. He said, Thank you, sir.

I said, You call me sir again and I'm going to take that money back. You call me Jim, all right?

Yes, sir, he said. —Sorry. Yes, Jim, and he shut the gate behind us.

That parking lot could have held a thousand cars, but it was empty except for two or three sedans down there in the dark by the main building. She raised herself up a little with excitement, and I heard her holding her breath. What are we going to do in here? she said at last. It's pitch-dark and there's no one around. —And just then someone flipped a switch somewhere, and the whole place lit up: the merry-go-round, the Ferris wheel, everything. She reached over and took hold of my arm, but she didn't say anything until I'd parked the car and turned it off.

Then she cocked her head and said, They're doing all this for you?

They're doing all this for us, I said.

Just because you sing . . . she said. Just because you're Jim Lewis, the—what do they call you?—the Hillbilly Cat. She liked saying that, and she smiled and said it again: the Hillbilly Cat.

We walked into the park and there was a fellow waiting, a quiet little man in a pair of dungarees. Where should we go? I asked him.

He shrugged. I can run most of them, he said. Except the Tilt-a-Whirl. Can't find the key.

What about it, baby? I said. Want to ride the Tunnel of Love with me?

Jim! she said, and she slapped playfully at my arm. No thank you! She turned to the fellow and said, Can we just walk around? Is that all right? The fellow nodded.

She was wearing a white sweater, and man, she was built, I'm telling you. I met her one night when Dewey brought her by the house, and that's what I noticed, first thing. And then her red hair, and some little freckles on the bridge of her nose. She must have been about seventeen. Dewey brought her in and introduced her, and right away I said to her, Come on over and sit here. Come sit here and talk to Jim. So she came over and we talked all night, just real soft and nice. She left late and she gave me her telephone number.

The next day I went up to New York City to do *The Steve Allen Show*, and I guess I got distracted. I tried to call her from my hotel, but the boys were making so much noise I could hardly hear her. Then we went down to Florida and played some places, then on to New Orleans, and then we came back home. I had a few days off and I called her again. She let me dangle a little, and then we went out for a meal late one night, and that's when I surprised her by taking her to the park.

It was strange, being on the midway when it was empty, with all the lights on, bare and bright, and the sky flat and black up above. I liked the way she held on to me as we went around. The fellow opened up a shooting booth and, man, I really wanted to win her something, a stuffed animal or something, but I was laughing too hard and I kept missing the little thing I was supposed to hit. I could have just bought her everything, but I wanted to win it. Then she started making fun of me, and that ticked me off. But there wasn't anything I could do about it: she was so pretty when she laughed.

She said, Come on. Let's go into the fun house.

I don't know, baby, I said. It's dark in there, it's the middle of the night. —Trying to scare her a little, you see. It must have worked, because she got serious on me all of a sudden.

All right, no, then, she said. I want to go on the roller coaster. And she took me by the hand and led me to it.

We must have ridden that roller coaster about a dozen times, all by ourselves. That's all she wanted to do, was go around and around, flying up into the night so high you could see all of Memphis, right down to the river. At the end the car would come gliding gently down, and she'd let me kiss her, and feel her a little bit, and then she'd make me stop so the fellow running the ride wouldn't see us. And then we'd go around again, screaming and yelling until I was light-headed.

When we'd had enough the fellow started to take us back to the entrance, but we passed by the fun house again, and this time she really wanted to go in. He went around and started it up, and when he came back he said, You two go on. I'll be waiting by the exit.

Inside there was all the usual stuff: scary things jumping out of the walls and all that. She held on to me tight, and every so often I would goose her, just to watch her scream and jump. Then we came to the hall of mirrors. You know what those places are like: mirrors all around, even on the floor and ceiling. Every which way we turned, there we were, her and me. Don't we look good, baby, I said, and we kissed for a while, right there in that room.

Then she did something no girl had ever done to me before. Not like that, anyway. She pulled back out of my arms and slowly sank down to her knees, smiling a little but without saying anything. Then she unzipped my pants, reached in gently, pulled it out, and started to kiss it, like she was kissing me on the mouth. Boy, she surprised me. I mean, I didn't know clean from dirty, I wondered where she'd learned a thing like that. I almost said, Honey, don't put that thing in your mouth—like I was her mama or something. But I didn't say that. Maybe I was a little bit frightened of her, fearless as she was. How mighty is the tenderest thing: maybe she made me weak. Maybe I just liked it. I didn't say a word.

Well, I didn't say a word, and she kept right on doing what she was doing. I looked around and all I could see was myself, standing there, tall and dark, with my curly hair, my long nose, my broad shoulders, and the back of her head right down at my hips. I could hear the sound of her down there, on me, and I could feel every little thing she did. Then I could smell her mouth, and she started doing something with her hand, and I lost it pretty quick after that.

She stood up slowly, and she had a thoughtful look on her face, almost solemn, like she'd just finished reading an important story in the newspaper and didn't want to talk about it. Her lips were all swollen and red, her hair was a little messed up, and she'd got some on the curve of her throat. Her beautiful curved white throat, and some of my stuff right on it. I couldn't let her walk out like that, but I didn't know how to tell her, so I handed her a handkerchief and mumbled something. Thank you, she said, and then she wiped it off, and gave me the handkerchief back. I put it in my pocket. —Now, why did she thank me? I should have been thanking her, but then I couldn't, because she'd done it first.

We started out of the fun house, and I was thinking, This girl, this very girl, what she did. Man, I felt like I was about ten feet tall, but as wobbly as a newborn foal, and I stumbled out the door with her, back into the fairgrounds.

The fellow was waiting for us at the exit, like he said he would be. I wondered if he could tell what we'd been doing. I guess I gave him some money, and he put it in his shirt pocket, turned, and disappeared back into the park.

The sun was coming up when we got in the car. We drove to the gate and the same man who let us in flagged me down. He had a piece of paper and a pen. Mr. Lewis, he said, shy and tentative, like they always are. My daughter talks about you all the time. She plays that record of yours over and over again. She's got your picture in a frame on her desk.

I wanted to say to him, Your daughter? Do you have any idea what this girl here just did? And she's somebody's daughter, too. But I couldn't say that—he was still wearing that big pistol, you know—so I laughed a little and signed the paper. I wrote a note there, and I put down my name.

We got out on Lamar again and she asked me if I ever got tired of that.

Tired of what? —For a second I thought she meant tired of the sort of thing she'd done to me, and I wanted to hear her say it. I wanted to hear how she would describe it.

Signing your name for people, she said.

Not really, I said. Sometimes, if I'm trying to have a private moment somewhere—like if I was with you, and we were talking about something important—I don't like to get interrupted. But mostly I appreciate it.

We drove on in silence for a little while, and then she spoke up again. Sing me something, will you? she asked.

What do you want to hear? I said.

Oh, whatever you like, she said.

I think she expected me to sing something fast and rocking, but I wanted to surprise her, so I did a verse of "Keeper of the Key" instead, while the sun came up on the morning. Cruising slow around the corner to her street, we passed three colored girls walking early on the sidewalk. They waved, and I hit the horn for them.

Do you know them? she asked.

I stopped singing and turned my head around to look at them again. They were doing this dance, the three of them, right there on the sidewalk. Just this beautiful little bumping dance, early on a summer morning, like dark angels with joy to spend. No, I said. I don't know them.

Well, they know you, she said. I suppose everybody knows you.

I dropped her off at her house and I walked her to the gate. At first I didn't want to kiss her good night, you know, unless she'd at least drunk some soda or something first. But I kissed her and it wasn't bad at all, and I told her I'd call her, and then I watched her disappear into her house, a little lamb who swallowed a lion.

:::

I kind of lost touch with her after that. I tried to call her once or twice, but a whole lot of things were happening that summer, and then the years, the records and the movies, and everything. I heard she met a boy who worked in the oil business, and she married him and moved to Corpus. I used to wonder what she told him about me, if she told him what had happened, what she did to Jim Lewis, back when the world was green. I used to wonder what all the things were that she never told me.

Not too long ago I ran into Dewey. She was on my mind, and I asked him whatever happened to her. He said she came down with a cancer. The doctors cut her all up, but she wasted away and died. So I never will see her again, and I never will talk to her. She's out there, wandering in that winter between the stars, where there's no company, and no solace. As pretty as she was.

In church they sing about going home when you die; I wish I could be sure that was true. Because as far as I can tell, any two things just get farther and farther apart in this world, and each moment is colder than the last. I'm not going to see her again. It scares me, I'm telling you, almost more than I can say. I go to bed scared, and I wake up just as scared.

YOU DON'T SEE THE OTHER
PERSON LOOKING BACK

:::
:::

Michael Lowenthal

THEY SAY ANIMALS resemble their masters, so I shouldn't have been surprised that Oscar, Tommy's Seeing Eye dog, the instant he was unharnessed, rose to his hind legs and humped my knee. But you've got to expect a yellow Lab to have some boundary issues, and Oscar was easy enough to distract. A stern "Down, boy!" and a toss of his stinky rawhide chew, and he snuffled off to a different sort of pleasure. His master proved significantly more persistent.

Tommy was my roommate on the Rainbow Bear Valentine's cruise for blind gay men and friends. I had decided to share a room to save on cost, and left the choice of with whom to the trip's planner, a blind gay travel agent; before our sail date, he gave me Tommy's name and number. I called Tommy and we chatted amiably about our hobbies, our hometowns. He was glad to hear my voice, he said, so that when we got to the ship he'd recognize me. His voice herked and jerked with a nasal Mid-Atlantic accent, inflected upward on all the wrong syllables. In the same tone as he'd asked what types of books I tend to read, he inquired, "Do you like massages, Mike?" I answered with a lengthy, equivocating *hmm*, followed by the statement that I wasn't entirely averse to them. Tommy, not indicating if he gauged my apprehension, pushed the broom of small talk once again: Was it as cold in Boston as it was in Pennsylvania?

I didn't hear from him for more than a month. Then, three days before departure, I was greeted by a message on my machine: "Mike, it's Tommy. I was wondering if you'd bring some cream for your skin so

I can massage you. And I like a rectal thermometer, if you could bring one along. I like the feel of one going up my ass, but that's entirely up to you. Anxious to see you on Sunday. Take care."

:::

Months earlier, when a friend, apropos of nothing, asked what I thought it would be like to be gay (as we both are) and blind, my response didn't include rectal thermometers. Not knowing any blind people and never having thought about their sex lives, my immediate reaction was pity: sexual attraction must be so faint within that visual eclipse, without the sparkle of pretty faces, flirty looks. Almost as fast, though, pity mixed with a nervous sort of envy—as though *I* might be the one in the dark. This was the same brand of irrational sexual jealousy I've felt toward women, whose orgasms, unlike men's procreation-intended spurts, seem more purely about pleasure for its own sake. When blind people—*without* the aid of visual inspiration—feel the burn of sexual desire, is that desire, I wondered, deeper, more authentic?

But these musings applied to blind people of any orientation. For a blind person to be openly *gay*, I imagined, must require an even greater intensity of attraction. The recognition of sexual identity is complicated enough for sighted gay people; how much more fraught must it be if you have no visual experience of gender, if all you have to follow is straight society's lead? Right away I wanted to meet someone openly gay and blind, someone who, despite this double disorientation, feels his attractions so keenly as to stake his life on them. Maybe he'd validate the doggedness of my own desires.

I searched the library for information about homosexuality and blindness, but found not a single citation. I contacted Stanley Ducharme, PhD, of Boston University, editor of the journal *Sexuality and Disability*; in his sixteen years in the job, he told me, he hadn't received any submissions on the topic. The most extensive treatment of the issue is a subsection of a chapter of the 1933 text *The Blind in School and Society*, by Thomas Cutsforth. Writing about homosexuality among students at residential schools for the blind, Cutsforth deemed it "a problem of environmental causation . . . a perfectly natural, although unfortunate, result of the conditions under which the children live." This didn't sound much like the sexual stalwarts my imagination had conjured.

Turning finally to the Internet, I came upon a Web site for BFLAG: Blind Friends of Lesbian, Gay, Bisexual, and Transgender People. The group, I learned, was founded in 1996 and counts forty intrepid members. I joined a list-serv to which many of the BFLAGers subscribe. A typical exchange:

<<My name is Alejandro and I live in Mexico. I have an eye problem called keratoconus, and although I am not totally blind I am not very distant from that. I have had a difficult time finding a boyfriend because most gays are mostly concerned about their looks and as I wear very thick glasses most of them think I do not look "attractive.">>

<<My name is Peter and I live in Sydney, Australia. I am 35 years of age and totally blind. I am in exactly the same position when it comes to finding someone. All men think about are looks. I think what's in the heart is more important.>>

If I had sought validation, now I felt accused. Had *I* ever considered dating a blind man? Does my own vision act as a kind of blindness?

When an ad was posted on the list-serv for a blind Valentine's cruise group, I decided that I had to go along. I was hoping that a week among some sightless gay men might make me see something new about desire.

:::

In San Diego I waited two hours in line to board Royal Caribbean's *Vision of the Seas.* Searching the crowd of two thousand passengers for a group of visually impaired men, I scanned a human catalog of failed attempts at beautification: women with penciled eyebrows like appliquéd licorice, face after hypertanned face. And yet everyone appeared ebullient and contentedly coupled; I, who had recently separated from my boyfriend, was the only person identifiably alone.

I found Tommy's and my stateroom on Deck 4. Although the *Vision* was still firmly moored, my stomach queased. I hadn't spoken with Tommy since receiving his phone message but had left a return message on his machine, explaining that while I was looking forward to making new friends on the cruise, I would not be interested in any physical intimacy.

I walked in calling, "Tommy?" but he wasn't in the cabin (which was roughly the size of my kitchen back in Boston). His clothes crowded one half of the closet.

I unpacked my own clothes and set out exploring the ship, telling myself I was searching for my roommate, but hardly looking. I hiked fore and aft through the warren of tight hallways, then upstairs to the Casino Royale and Champagne Bar, to the pool, solarium, and jogging track.

Hopelessly lost, I ended up at the Viking Crown Lounge, where I spied a man at the bar, gulping a margarita, a Seeing Eye dog curled at his feet. I steeled myself and approached, preparing to offer my most neutral, nonsuggestive handshake, then remembered that Tommy's dog, he'd told me, was young and yellow. This one was black, with a light rime of gray around the muzzle, and wearing a rainbow neckerchief.

"So, this guy comes to read the meter," the dog's owner was saying to the man next to him. "And when I show him in, he goes, 'You blind people are just so amazing. You just blow me away, all the things you can manage by yourselves.' And I wanted to say, 'Yeah, that's right, guy. I can even *jerk off* by myself. Don't like to, but I can if I have to.'"

The man waggled the straw in his margarita, basking in the laugh he'd known he would earn. Although he was seated, he radiated the pratfallish energy of a physical comedian. His skin was acne scarred, and his nose was the bulbous knob seen in caricatures of Bill Clinton, but his take-no-prisoners humor was magnetic and sort of sexy.

I introduced myself and asked if he was in the Rainbow Bear group. He turned in the direction of my voice and offered his hand. His name was Howard, and his friend was Dave, a sighted Englishman with close-cropped silvering hair and an affable, snaggletoothed smile. They had met last year on a Caribbean cruise and decided to rendez-vous on this trip and room together.

"And who's this?" I asked, patting the dog's head.

"His name's Harvey," said Howard. He felt for the dog's rainbow neckerchief. "He accessorizes wonderfully, don't you think?"

:::

Was Howard what I had expected, after months of thinking about blind gay men in the abstract?

Blindness has long been associated with sexual deviance. In the Middle Ages, blinding was a common punishment for sexual crimes— a not-so-subtle symbolic castration. In literature, too, characters are often blinded for sins of sexual transgression: think of Oedipus, Tiresias, and even Peeping Tom, who was blinded after sneaking peeks at Lady Godiva. The link persists today in superstition: masturbate too much and you'll go blind. And yet, as much as blind people have been feared and shunned—blindness was often thought to be contagious—they have also been revered. In antiquity, from Greece to China to Ireland, blind people frequently served as bards. There is a long tradition of the blind as seers, soothsayers, and mystics—individuals who, lacking sight, compensate with an abundance of insight and/or foresight.

How similar this is to gay people's situation: oppressed and denigrated, accused of spreading scourge, yet in some ways celebrated and esteemed. In certain Native American tribes, gay members have been honored as shamans. And in even the most repressive cultures, gay people have been disproportionately lauded for their creative (if not procreative) talents: as court jesters, artists, and musicians.

As I had readied myself to meet men who are both blind *and* gay, I imagined them at an enigmatic nexus: where fear meets awe, and hatred meets reverence. They're doubly outcast—but might they also be doubly visionary?

:::

Nearing our assigned dinner table in the Aquarius Dining Room, I came upon a man being tugged by a tawny guide dog, bobbling behind the animal as though it were a child and he the child's wind-tossed kite. His neck was thicker than his mostly bald head, which looked slightly misshapen, like that of an infant, or like a pumpkin left too long on the porch.

"You must be Tommy," I guessed, as he veered perilously close to a waiter balancing a tray of eight salads. He appeared just as off-kilter as his phone message had sounded.

"Mike?" he said. "How'd you recognize me?"

"Your dog," I fudged. "He's just like you described him."

The rest of our group was already at the table, and we introduced ourselves one by one. I sat next to Bill, a natty Philadelphian with more than a passing resemblance to E. Lynn Harris, whose current potboiler, he said, had been his afternoon's guilty-pleasure reading. (He listens to books on tape while on the treadmill.) Next to Bill was Robert, the trip's organizer, a large man (his Yahoo profile mentions a waist of fifty-four inches, leg inseam of thirty) with a whispery bass voice and glaucomatous eyes. Robert's sighted partner, Tim—partner both in their travel agency and in their eight-year relationship—was an avuncular, heavyset man who in comparison to Robert seemed tiny.

Carl was next, at fifty-nine the oldest by a decade, his Mississippi drawl and his clunky corrective glasses both thicker than any I'd previously encountered. Then catlike Doug, whose buzz cut flashed with silver, as did his blank, squinted eyes. And finally Steven, Doug's sighted boyfriend, a Texan with a wry, friendly smile. (Howard and Dave, whom I'd met in the Viking Crown Lounge, were seated at the next table over.)

I struggled to remember each new acquaintance's name, but the blind men didn't seem to have this problem. They called to one another from across the table, carrying on animated conversations while they also read about "tagliatelle gifted with portobello mushrooms" on the special Braille menus and, learning the lay of the land, fingered their intricate place settings (five forks, four spoons, three knives). Our waiter, oblivious to their multitasking expertise, appeared to panic when he realized that most of our group was blind. As if the blind men were children, or invisible, he addressed only me and the other sighted guys. I wanted to feel outraged on the blind men's behalf, but in truth the waiter's gaze, directed squarely at my eyes, helped alleviate my own discomposure.

Tommy's phone call had left me on the lookout for strangeness; I kept waiting for someone to propose a group massage. But the meal was almost eerily run-of-the-mill. Like any couple, Doug and Steven debated sharing their entrees. Carl rated the quality of the ship's potent coffee. Bill, in deference to his figure, declined dessert.

A *Vision of the Seas* crew member, in full eye-patched, tricorned buccaneer regalia, came from nowhere and held a plastic cutlass to Robert's neck, growling, "Argh, matey!" while a photographer snapped pictures. Robert, with no idea what was happening, defended himself against the fake blade, but the pirate was already on to his next victim. "Argh," he repeated, inflicting his punishment on each unsuspecting blind man. When my turn came, I stared at the camera like a hostage.

Dinner stretched until ten thirty, and I was pooped. While Tommy headed to Deck 5 and its row of custom-built mulch boxes where Oscar could relieve himself, I retreated to our room. I stripped to my underwear and climbed into the narrow bunk closest to the door, which we had agreed would be mine. When I turned out the light, our cabin—the ship's cheapest sort, with no windows and a heavy, fireproof door—succumbed to darkness of a degree I'd seen only once, when I toured Alcatraz and got locked in solitary. Lulled by the ship's rocking, I dropped asleep.

It felt like weeks later when I was woken by the hands. They touched my ankle first, through the blanket, then my shin. I heard the approach of heavy breathing.

"This is my bunk," I blurted. "Yours is farther."

The breathing got louder. I couldn't see anything but could sense Tommy kneeling, shuffling closer. His hands were on my face now, and I grabbed hold of his arms. My pulse felt like a choke chain at my throat.

"I just want to see what you look like," he said.

Get away, I wanted to shout, but would Tommy think me scared of blind people? And wasn't I? Shouldn't I get over that? I kept my grip tight on his wrists, but let him rove.

"I haven't shaved in a couple of days," I said self-consciously, then wondered why *I* was apologizing.

He handled my features like a sculptor shaping clay, as if he weren't appraising my face so much as creating it. He lingered at my outsize nose, the feature that most people find unattractive, but that for those few who like it seems to be a fetish. It's what initially drew Scott, my longest-term boyfriend, to me from across a crowded room, and I'll never forget my shock, the first time we were alone, when he put his mouth over the whole huge thing and sucked it.

Might Tommy, too, have a nose fetish? If so, how could he have known my appeal without this grope? I had read about the challenges of sex ed for blind people, whose learning relies so much on tactile exploration (which in the case of strangers' bodies is taboo). In the 1970s, blind-rights activists advocated special sex ed classes making use of live nude human models, and in Scandinavia a few such courses were attempted. Elsewhere, however, the plans were squelched: models, it was worried, would be perceived as enjoying vicarious sexual thrills.

Thrills? I was clammy with discomfort and alarm. How far did I have to let Tommy go to assuage my guilty conscience?

Just as I had reached my breaking point, he abruptly concluded his reconnaissance. He moved over to his own bunk, undressed, called good night, and in seconds fell to high-horsepower snoring.

Even without the noise, I couldn't have slept. I was mad at Tommy for using his blindness to take advantage of me, mad at myself for believing that he had done so, and madder still for not knowing which was true. It was so dark I couldn't see my own hands.

I lay there, as my heartbeat subsided back to calm, and thought about things unseen but alluring. I once got a call from an editor who mentioned another Boston writer. Did I know him? His name was Vestal McIntyre. I didn't know him but I knew instantly—unequivocally—that I would, and that we'd hit it off in more ways than one. *Vestal McIntyre!* I can't explain it except to say that it was love at first name. I looked Vestal up in the white pages, called him, and proposed a date. We met days later and climbed presently into bed. Our fling lasted months. He's still one of my best friends.

Handwriting has given me hard-ons: not the look, but the feel, the stippled loops and slashes on the backside of anything penned by Scott, who writes just as forcefully as he loves. Smells, too: the scent of vetiver, which Scott used to dab on his neck, still drives me wild. But how much are these attraction by association? They turn me on because they remind me of Scott, who hooked me with his looks when we locked eyes across a room.

The phone sex industry relies on people's ability to be turned on by the voice of an unseen partner. But most customers, I think, hear the voice and construct a visual image to go along with it—an image based on someone they *have* seen.

What if you've never seen anything?

:::

Doug was born three months premature and kept in an incubator, where overexposure to oxygen caused a condition known as retinopathy of prematurity and left him completely blind. I sat with Doug on day two of the cruise, at a retirement party for Robert's guide dog, Zeppelin, who suffers from arthritis. It was a festive affair by the pool on Deck 9, complete with a frosted rum cake and reverent testimonials ("Zeppelin knocked me backward, away from the car, and saved my life!").

Doug hadn't yet spoken directly to me, but I sensed that his shyness hid a fierce curiosity, apparent not in his eyes, where we usually think of that trait as being evinced (his were cloudy and often misdirected), but in the alertness of his posture, the tilt of his head toward unfamiliar voices. When I took the initiative, he seemed eager to talk. After years in the computer field, he told me, he works now as a massage therapist. I flinched, recalling Tommy's snooping hands, but Doug, anticipating my reaction, added, "It's tricky. You say 'massage' and people assume it's something sexual." He assured me that his business is legit.

Doug was thrilled just to be sitting casually among a group of blind gay men. Until two or three years ago he didn't know of any others, despite the fact that he's been involved with gay culture since the early 1970s, when, as a senior in high school, he entered a gay bar for the first time. He'd been having sex with boys for a decade before that.

Later, when we met privately, I asked Doug how—with no visual sense of either gender, and knowing that boys were expected to like girls—he realized that he was gay.

"There was never really a question in my mind," he said. "There was always something more appealing when you said 'boy' versus 'girl.' Boys smelled better."

"Like what?"

He thought a second. "Like outside: grass and dirt and sweat."

And boys, it seems, were readily available. Throughout his early teens, Doug had frequent sexual encounters with boys, and his blindness was "not in the least bit" an issue. "In the bathrooms at school we all checked each other out," he recalled—which for him meant with his hands.

In college at Texas Tech in 1972, Doug overheard some rednecks talking about how "the faggots are going to be out in full force tomorrow," and after calling the student center anonymously he found himself at the very first meeting of a gay campus group. "I had to work really hard to become part of that group," he said. "I think it was mostly the blindness. People were a little standoffish."

In the years since, Doug has found most of the gay world—which he feels is overly focused on questions like "Does my butt look good in these shorts?"—similarly skittish about accepting a blind man. But he has enjoyed a number of short- and long-term relationships, all with sighted men. I asked about his current boyfriend, Steven, and in particular if he had any sense of what Steven looks like.

"I know that most of y'all pick people by the way they look," he told me. "And I know that's how I *don't* operate. I couldn't tell you what sort of jawline Steven has, or what sort of nose. I mean, I could tell in comparison to myself—his nose is a bit longer and more squared off. He's told me that his hair is sort of red-blond, but that doesn't really mean anything to me."

If he could, would he want to see Steven?

"As selfish as this sounds," Doug said, "if I could see for just ten minutes, I would want to see what *I* look like. I could be hideous or I could be okay, but I don't know. And there are *things* I'd like to see. The house I used to live in. My cat. I would like to see a giraffe, because the concept is just so bizarre. As far as how people look, it may be kind of important, but not terribly."

:::

"Can you get a photo of me blowing?" Bill asked. "I know it's *personal*, but . . ."

"Of course," I said, and aimed the camera. "I'm sure it won't be the first picture of that!"

We were in Cabo San Lucas, Mexico, our first port of call, at a mom-and-pop glass-blowing factory. The shop boss had offered to let Bill try his hand at the craft, and, after private tittering about long rods and hot, stiff tools, Bill consented. When he drew a deep breath and huffed with all his might, the molten blob at the end of the rod globed. The group cheered. I snapped a photograph.

"Ooh, me too," said Howard. "If it's an oral thing, put me next!"

I'd woken that morning groggy, after another fitful, nervous-about-Tommy night, but now, leaving my roommate to his own devices, I was having a ball. These guys were cracking me up, especially Howard, with his incorrigible ba-dum-bum joking. He had the same raunchy, quick-draw wit as most of my friends at home, and his delivery was impeccable, in a grainy voice that trailed off like Jack Benny's at the ends of phrases.

Howard was also wonderful at guiding me in guiding him. At first I called out every obstacle: *steps coming up, maybe six of them, in about four yards, okay now three yards, you're almost there* . . . After five awkward minutes of this, Howard said, "Listen, if you just let me hold your elbow, I'll feel everything your body does and you won't have to say a thing." Instantly our balance of power improved: Howard was the craftsman, I was just the tool.

At the next stop, a stucco church in San José del Cabo, I whispered descriptions of everything I could see: the plain but beautiful wood-work, the half dozen Mexicans, heads bowed in fervent prayer. When we reached the altar, I noted the statues of Jesus and Mary on the wall.

"What colors are they?" Howard asked.

I chided myself for not having included this information; I was still adjusting to being someone else's eyes. Mary was blue, I told him, and Jesus was pure white.

Howard clucked his tongue. "Now, if Jesus was with twelve men, should he really be wearing white?"

The confessional, I thought, would be a good bet—lots of tactile wooden latticework—so I led Howard and Carl over to it. I described the thronelike priest's seat and the bench for penitents.

Immediately, Howard dropped to his knees. "Do they have glory holes?" he said, hands scanning the wooden booth. "Bless me, Father, for I have sinned *a whole lot.*"

"Yeah, Howard," Carl added, "that's why you're blind!"

:::

Howard is actually blind from retinitis pigmentosa. He was born with 20/200 vision: legally blind but still able to see the blackboard in first grade if the teacher used special thumb-thick chalk and if he sat in the front row. By the end of high school he couldn't read even large-print books up close, and now, at forty-six, he retains only the barest light perception.

Howard's early sexual stirrings were similar to those of most gay men. "You knew the boys in your class that you just wanted to be in the proximity of," he told me. "It wasn't even a sexual thought. But there was an attraction there. You liked the way they talked." In 1970, when he transferred from public junior high to the Western Pennsylvania School for the Blind, he finally had the opportunity to act on his desires. "I appreciated it so much," he said, referring to the school's gender-segregated dormitories. "They put the girls all the way over to one side and kept them there." He had sex with a number of his schoolmates, and by the eleventh grade everybody in the school knew he was gay.

From this point, Howard felt driven to join the larger gay world. "I would walk past the Holiday Bar in Pittsburgh, which I knew was a gay bar. I used a cane to travel in those days. I had to learn which side of the street it was on. I had to ask a stranger where it was"—which should have been scary, but desire trumped fear. Since he wasn't yet of legal drinking age, his goal was not to go inside the bar, but simply "to be near there. That's all I thought of at that time."

After he graduated and moved to Harrisburg, Howard became something of a barfly. It was fun, but more important, it was his strategy for attracting sexual attention. "People would say, 'I know this blind guy who's in Harrisburg, and he has a dog.' *Everybody* in those bars knew me. They wouldn't know a lot of other folks, but they all knew Howard. And they also knew he was a sleaze. And he is!"

Was he worried that people might think: He's blind, he needs to take whatever he can get? "I've heard that," Howard said. "But if I was sighted, and engaged in the same sexual behaviors, it wouldn't be because I need to take anything I can get. They would say I was a slut."

Howard eventually fell in love and began a committed, fifteen-year relationship with a sighted man. They split up four years ago, partly due to the difficulties of maintaining a "mixed marriage."

Howard worked in the blind social-services field for almost twenty years—most recently as the founder of a computer resource center for blind people—but his passion is the gay community. For five years he ran the gay and lesbian switchboard in Harrisburg, and at one time or another he has been involved in "every gay organization" in the city. If he weren't blind, Howard told me, he would be "a sighted *gay* person," meaning that gayness would be his prime identity. He said, "I never wanted to be anything but gay."

:::

After touring the church, our group split up, some hunting the best tacos in Cabo, the half dozen rest of us looking for the Rainbow Bar & Grille, which Howard, searching a gay-travel Web site before the cruise, had identified as the sole gay bar in town. (Like most of the blind men I met, Howard uses screen-reading software and is something of an Internet wiz.)

Our tour guide, Doris, declined to accompany us, but she pointed out the spot we were looking for, a block away. We trooped over, a traffic-blocking procession of men and Seeing Eye dogs. But when we got there we saw no sign and no bar, just a hotel. We turned around our human train with roughly the same ease as we might an actual locomotive and retraced the steps to where Doris had left us. Still nothing.

We reversed the group once more, now beginning to attract attention. I jogged into the hotel lobby and asked in Spanish for the Rainbow Bar & Grille.

"Are you sure?" the desk clerk said in English, clearly thinking I'd gotten my Spanish wrong. He glanced past the open door to where the group of blind men and their dogs patiently waited. "That's a *gay* bar."

I assured him that was precisely what we wanted.

It turned out that the bar was in the next building over, with a half-hidden door marked only by a tiny notice of its hours of operation, which, unfortunately, did not include now. I imagined the hilarious scene our gang would have made barging into such a determinedly concealed bar.

As we chugged off, disappointed, in search of lunch, I considered the hotel clerk's apparent surprise that a group of blind men might be gay. I could have mounted a high horse and convicted him of a multiplicity of isms, but the truth was that the men in our group barely registered on my own gaydar. Sure, both of Doug's ears were pierced, and Howard's dog wore his rainbow neckerchief, but when Doug asked me intently, "Do we blind guys 'read' as gay?" I had to tell him I didn't really think so.

The concept of gaydar is slippery at best, dependent on overgeneralizations and cultural context. (A classic conundrum for gay Americans abroad: "Is he gay or is he just European?") And yet, as much as signals can get scrambled, there seem to be some genuine means of recognition. On one level, it's all in the eyes, the practiced glance that balances dare with fear. Blind men can't receive or send such signals.

There's something else, too: the only term that comes close is "self-consciousness." Growing up with the fear of being unmasked, most gay people develop an early preoccupation with their appearance, and sometimes a delusion of being constantly watched. This self-consciousness manifests in different ways and degrees: mannered, theatrical gestures and gaits; overprimped hair and skin and clothes. The blind gay men I met, although they know they can be watched, never actually see themselves being seen, and don't appear to be as prone to self-consciousness. My sample size was tiny, but none of the men's mannerisms was the slightest bit stylized in the ways that usually trigger gaydar.

But if blind gay men don't "look" or "act" gay, does this really reflect essential differences, or does it say more about the constructed nature of gay culture? Many components of the conventional gay "lifestyle" are inaccessible to blind men: noisy gay bars are tricky to negotiate; gay novels and newspapers are rarely available in Braille or audio, and most gay Web sites are not designed compatibly with screen-reading software; even porn movies, which for legions of gay men have served as sexual primers, are largely useless (try just listening to the dialogue). If much of "gay style" is a marketing contrivance or a result of aped behavior, blind men are less likely to feel its influence. As Doug told me, "I could never pick up a GQ or a *Blueboy* or an *Advocate* and look at pictures and tell what people are wearing." In terms of stereotypically gay gestures, he said, "If you haven't seen it, how would you know how to do it?"

And yet, Doug's experience also suggests a more intrinsic source of gay identification. When he was a boy, not yet in his teens, he accompanied his mother to a shopping mall in Dallas. As they sat in a bakery, sipping sodas, Doug was riveted by the voices of two men at the next table. "I was fascinated by the way they sounded," he said. "I don't know that I knew why. I just knew that they sounded interesting. And when they left, Mom was like, 'Those two men were fairies.'"

:::

Doris had told us we'd need to hire taxis to the dock, but after lunch Bill suggested we walk. "How far can it be?" he said, forging ahead with his dog.

The marina was clogged with vendors hawking cheap souvenirs, but as Bill pointed out, one benefit of being blind is that you can pretend not to notice what you choose. It was typical of Bill to emphasize the good points about blindness. A lawyer specializing in Americans with Disabilities Act litigation, he's acutely aware not only of the difficulties faced by blind people but also of how much those difficulties are imposed, not inherent.

Bill told me about himself as we strolled along the water, speaking with the hyperarticulate, almost homiletic diction that I associate with certain African American newscasters, like Bernard Shaw. He didn't fully lose his vision until he was twenty-one, by which point he'd already come out as gay, so he was able to experience gay visual cruising. "I'm really glad I did that," he said. "I'm really glad I *had* that." And yet he's adamant that his blindness hasn't limited his sexuality. He's had two significant relationships, one for five years and one for seven. Neither boyfriend was blind, but he's "not exclusively into sighted guys, that's just the way it's happened." And although he's open to having another partner, he would insist on maintaining his independence. "I would *never* live with someone I was involved with," he said. "No way."

Bill spoke with relish of influencing the men he dated, teaching them to be more aware of nonvisual sensory input. The idea that sight is necessary for sexual attraction he dismissed as laughable.

What about sex itself: Is it different if you can't see?

Bill bristled. "There's no difference. If anything, being blind is an advantage. If you're prone to feeling uncomfortable, it helps, because you don't see the other person looking back."

Sometimes the best things, he implied, aren't what you see but feel, and I remembered something that had happened at the glass factory. After Bill's triumphant blowing debut, Doris had arrayed glassware on a table. Bill and the other guys inspected the samples, feeling every ridge and swell and turn: margarita glasses, beer steins, a blowfish-shaped candy jar. Everyone's favorite was a tiny tequila shot glass that featured matching dimples on either side: a built-in grip, perfect for thumb and index finger.

The shot glass was passed from hand to hand, and the more expensive, more ornate baubles abandoned. "It just feels right, doesn't it?" Bill said. Doris was dispatched to fetch three sets of four each, with clear instructions to find the indented glasses.

She returned a minute later, empty-handed. "I hate to tell you this, but that glass? It was defective. It wasn't supposed to have those indentations."

And Bill, who'd had his heart set, groaned with disappointment. He knows the difference between defective and just right.

:::

"Down, boy. Down!"

I kicked Oscar's chew toy across the stateroom, trying to keep him occupied while I struggled with my tie. Tommy and I were getting dressed for the captain's reception, to be followed by the formal dinner.

Tommy stood in front of the vanity in just his forty-inch-waist Calvin Klein briefs, dabbing CK 1 on his neck. "So, Mike," he asked, "are you a skinny guy?"

My tie came out wrong, wide end shorter than the thin. "Um, I don't really know," I said. What should I have told him? That my waist is twenty percent smaller than his, or that in the urban gay circles in which I travel I'm probably considered average, with perhaps some flab to lose?

Tommy pulled on his slacks and an oxford shirt. "I might go up later and check out the gym," he said. "It's just in my stomach where I put on weight. I know I don't look near my age. I look much younger."

I wondered who had told him this, and how long ago. His chin sagged. His hair had ebbed to just a horseshoe. To me, he looked his age of forty-five.

I checked my own receding hair in the brightly lit mirror: Am I aging badly? Does it turn people off? I'd bungled my tie again. I tried a third time.

Tommy rifled through a drawer, feeling for his own tie. He asked, "Are you a hairy guy, Mike?"

I stepped away. "Hairier than some. Less than others."

"You sure are evasive!" Tommy said. He knotted his tie: perfect on the first attempt.

I *was* being evasive. Why shouldn't I tell Tommy the basic facts that were he sighted he'd be able to gauge at a glance? I've imparted more intimate details to strangers in bars and dance clubs. In those contexts, the exchange of such personal information is always implicitly seductive; the last thing I wanted was to lead Tommy on. And yet I felt bad for dodging his questions, as though this time I were the one taking advantage of his blindness. Maybe I also wanted to punish him.

"Well, would you look at that," he said, apparently dropping the issue. "Six o'clock and it's still light out!"

He'd told me the day before that he still retains some light perception, but obviously it wasn't much help to him. "You're in front of a vanity," I said. "Our room doesn't have windows."

:::

Gay men are tagged as being obsessed with superficial beauty, and like most stereotypes, this one seems based on some degree of truth. Gay culture—or what passes as such, generated mostly in urban clubs and "lifestyle" magazines—is a conformist cult of the body in which looks are paramount. How do blind men fit into such a world?

In terms of their own appearance, some people's blindness is not readily evident, while others have conditions—cataracts, glaucoma—that make them "look" blind and may cause them to be shunned. But whether or not they appear outwardly different, blind men, simply by the fact of their blindness, call into question the ideal of "perfection" in pursuit of which so many gay men go to extravagant lengths. If sighted gay men's identities, on some fundamental level, are dependent on being *looked at*, blind gay men's presence can be unsettling: Is it really essential to expend such effort on external attractiveness?

But blind gay men are not immune from the concern with how their bodies look. Bill is a regular treadmill user, and more than once I heard Doug—disparaging himself for recently added pounds—recommitting himself to the NordicTrack. Aside from Robert, who is obese and identifies as a "bear" (a category referring to hefty, hairy men), the men I met all seemed conscious of falling short of some body-image ideal.

Weight gain can be a special concern for blind people, often stemming from restricted mobility. Another factor may be blind people's desexualization by the sighted world. Blind people rely on their

sighted acquaintances to help them with outward appearances: to tell
them, for example, if their clothes match, or are stained. But because
sighted people too frequently don't "count" blind people as sexual
beings, they may not think to offer advice about cultivating attractiveness. "That's why there tend to be a lot of overweight blind people,"
Doug suggested. "Nobody says to them, 'Maybe that's not the way you
want to be.'" When I asked Doug about his own self-perception, he
said, "I know other people have much better bodies. But people don't
scream and run away, so that's a good sign."

:::

In certain arenas of the gay world, there are physical attributes more
important than body-fat percentage or 20/20 vision—for example,
in the chat rooms on Gay.com, of which Howard is a fervent devotee.
(It takes two different software packages and a lot of patience for him
to gain access to the site, but he considers it well worth the trouble.)
Howard's online profile is up-front about his blindness, but when he's
in a real-time chat with other horny men looking to hook up, he'll
present himself simply as "46 years old, 5' 10", 195 pounds" and, using
standard gay lingo to describe the length and circumcision of his far-
above-average manhood: "9.5 cut." "I'm going to use that asset to my
advantage," he told me, "because I'm trying to level the playing field.
They don't care then if you're blind."

Howard himself, although he won't be able to see his sexual play-
mates, certainly judges them by superficial attributes; in fact, like any
gay man cruising for casual sex, that's pretty much all he cares about.
"If I'm on the Internet," he said, "and I meet somebody, the first thing
I want to know is height, weight, if there's any facial hair. Then I go
to, 'Are you smooth or hairy?' To actually feel sexually aroused by that
person, the smoothness is such an issue."

I asked Howard how he vets the men he meets in person—say, in a
gay bar. Is he comfortable asking such direct questions out loud?

We were across from each other in my cabin—me on my bunk,
Howard on Tommy's—but Howard stood up now and moved across
and sat next to me. "My little ploy would be that I would sit down," he
said. "I've finally got a bar stool. And I go, 'Boy, beautiful day out there
today. I can't believe the weather!' And if the person doesn't just say,

'Yeah,' if I get a sentence or two, now I realize this person's comfortable talking to me. Plus, now I know there's not an empty chair beside me.

"And if you're continuing to talk to me, then it allows me to go"— Howard patted my thigh—"'Now that's *exactly* it,' or 'I can't believe that, that's awful!' I'm gauging your body language. When a person tenses, I'm already reading that. I'm still trying to get a sense of the person."

What sense was Howard getting of me right now? Was this simulation itself a ploy for sex? (Howard had mentioned earlier that he found my voice intriguing.)

"I may very well say, 'You're really tall, aren't you? Because your voice is coming from way up here. You about six-two?' Then I'm going to make a point like this"—Howard touched my shoulder, a bit more forcefully than he'd felt my leg. "Now I've got stature. I've also got how he carries himself. 'Oh, he's a barfly, he's hunched over, he's in here *every day.*' That just told me a lot.

"Now, they're going to say, 'It's okay if you want to feel my face and see what I look like.' I don't! I mean, *oh yes,* I want to touch their face. But when people say that line? That's like squeaking a Styrofoam cooler. I don't know where that ever started."

I made a mental note to explain this to Tommy.

"But under *my* initiative," Howard continued, "I'm going to find out, so my next move is probably going to be this"—he touched the side of my face. "Okay, now I know he wears glasses. If the conversation is still going on, then I'll find out if he has a mustache. I'm not going to ask how hairy his chest is, but somehow I would find out from this"—he grabbed the back of my neck—"that he's smooth.

"I'm not the one to put the pressure here"—he pressed his leg against mine—"and hold it there to find out if he moves *his* leg over. I don't do that. If we're talking and we're both starting to get touchy-feely, okay, then it becomes just as physical as anybody else, but that's *after* you've already gotten all that positive feedback that the person doesn't mind your attention."

I realized, to my surprise, that I didn't mind Howard's attention, not at all. The utter unabashedness of his scheming had the paradoxical effect of making him seem sweetly guileless. (Whereas Tommy's apparent naïveté came across as creepy.) I found it compellingly sexy

that Howard had thought in such great detail about his erotic machinations. He was a man who could feel his sexual web vibrating at the
slightest touch.

His hand was resting on my thigh again. I put my hand on top of
his and squeezed it.

:::

In his memoir, *Touching the Rock: An Experience of Blindness*, John M. Hull
writes that for sighted people, desire and vision are so closely connected that "it becomes difficult to distinguish between 'I feel hungry'
and 'I want to eat that food which I see there.'" When blindness dis-
rupts this connection, Hull says—referring to hungers both physical
and sexual—desire is often merely "the restlessness of an unformed
longing."

But surely the presence of a sexual partner isn't a prerequisite for
arousal, just as the presence of food isn't a prerequisite for hunger. I
wondered how blind gay men fantasize. Are their longings "unformed"
or sharply shaped? Is desire sparked by images? By abstractions?

"If I was just going to jack off and I was thinking about somebody,"
Howard told me, "it would be me with that person, reliving the stages
from meeting them, from the minute they walked in . . . like seeing
the comic strip beginning to end. It isn't visual. I'm not seeing their
facial expression. I'm not seeing the color of their hair. But I'm seeing
position."

Doug, having been born blind, does not fantasize visually at all.
Sometimes he thinks in terms of touch (like Howard, he seeks "those
thin, young body types, smooth"), but mostly, he told me, it's "scenarios. Lots and lots of scenarios. People with accents. Things outside.
Going to a country where I don't know the language and meeting
somebody and trying to see if we could make a rendezvous happen
without any spoken words." I was astonished by how quickly Doug's
thoughts moved from what's readily accessible to him (sounds, the feel
of skin and sun) to a dream of freedom from the limits imposed by
blindness. But aren't most people's fantasies potent precisely in their
combination of what's possible and what's not?

In Mazatlán, our second port of call, we stopped at a scenic outlook where I described for Doug a swan-diving daredevil. The young
macho scaled a high crag—forty feet up, fifty, to the top—then stood

glistening, preening for the crowd. He looked toward the heavens and crossed himself. Then he spread his arms—a soaring bird—and plunged to the rough-and-tumble surf.

Doug heard the force of my gasp, then, seconds later, my gasp of a different tone when the boy climbed out of the water right beside us. "Tell me what he looks like," Doug whispered.

Like a sportscaster calling the game-winning play, I struggled to find words fast enough: "Brown skin, dark dark brown hair, beading water, twenty-seven-inch waist, just perfect, perfectly ribbed stomach, Champion gym shorts down to his knees, clingy, you can see everything."

"Thank you!" Doug said, matching my breathlessness. "Thank you. My God, that was great." He offered to buy me a margarita.

"Nah, my pleasure," I said—but then wondered about *Doug's* pleasure. What did my description really mean to a man who's never seen brown, who can't hold *soaring* in his hands?

:::

"What's it like rooming with Tommy?" Doug asked. He and Steven had invited me to their stateroom one evening, the first time the three of us were alone.

"Um, it's okay," I said. I still hadn't told anyone about Tommy's phone call or his groping.

"You don't think he's kind of strange?" Steven said.

"I guess he's a little, um . . ."

"Come on," Doug said, "he's obviously got serious developmental issues."

He went on to tell me about a special telephone service that some of the blind men had subscribed to. There was no direct conversation, but individuals could exchange messages of up to a few minutes each. When Tommy joined the network, according to Doug, he had no sense of boundaries. "You'd come home and there would be a dozen messages from Tommy. He wouldn't wait for you to return the first before leaving another. And each one got more and more explicit. I mean, I'm not easily shocked. But hearing those things from someone I'd never met? I couldn't believe it."

"I almost wonder if he's slightly Mongoloid," Steven said.

I was staggered by his use of the term, but also hugely relieved to hear confirmation of my misgivings, especially from a blind man and his boyfriend. I told them that I too had gotten a taste of Tommy's message-leaving.

"Why didn't you say anything earlier?" Doug asked.

"I guess I didn't want to embarrass him," I said, which was true. "And if we were stuck rooming together, I didn't want to make things even more uncomfortable." Also true.

What I didn't add—because as it occurred to me, my throat clenched with shame—was that I'd excused Tommy's behavior because on some level I must have been *expecting* a blind gay man to be perverted.

In a way, wasn't that why I'd signed up for this cruise: to be near to men I'd pegged as lacking inhibitions? If Tommy had conformed to my sexual tastes, might his "depravity" have been just what I wanted?

:::

That night, I couldn't sleep. For one thing there was Oscar, panting away on the floor, liable to accost me, without warning, in puppy love. A bigger problem was Tommy's snoring, a tectonically violent noise. I had a pair of earplugs saved from the courtesy kit on my most recent transatlantic flight, and I stuffed them as deep as they would go, then stuffed my whole head underneath both of my pillows, but still the noise made my brain wobble. It was the sound of an elephant giving birth to a bulldozer.

"Tommy," I called. "You're snoring."

No response.

"Tommy, come on. You're making noise." I clapped my hands twice, I pounded on the wall. "Fuck!" I yelled. "You're driving me insane."

At the last word, Tommy finally stirred, and instantly I realized my mistake, because now that he was awake would come the scratching.

The first night it had happened, the lights were out, and I assumed the noise came from Oscar's corner. In the morning, when the commotion began again, I saw plainly that Tommy was the culprit. Tommy scratched himself constantly in my presence. He lay in his bunk, sometimes in his underwear, sometimes naked, his hand on his abdomen or somewhat lower. Scratch scratch scratch. Pause. Scratch scratch

scratch. It sounded as though he were trying to rescue a man buried alive inside him.

He never acknowledged this or provided an explanation. Crabs, I thought at first. Scabies? But Tommy's clawing was so compulsive that I finally concluded his itch wasn't physical, but existential.

Sure enough, now that I'd roused him, he started up again. Scratch scratch scratch. Pause. Scratch scratch scratch.

Tommy had persisted recently in his advances, copping feels of my leg during dinner and saying, that morning as we were dressing, "I'd really like the chance before the cruise is over to see what *all* of you looks like."

Each evening our cabin steward, as part of the nightly turndown, left us two foil-wrapped Royal Caribbean chocolate mints, along with a sort of terry cloth origami: a bath towel twisted into the shape of a swan or alligator. He deposited these items on my bed, perhaps thinking their presence on Tommy's bunk would confuse him, and so on the trip's first few nights I'd made a point of leading Tommy to my bed and showing him the creations. Tonight, after my conversation with Doug and Steven, I'd decided it was a mistake to bring Tommy near my bunk for any reason. I hadn't mentioned the towel art. And although I'm a chocolate lover, the moment we returned to our stateroom I'd given Tommy my mint as well as his in the hopes that it might, like Oscar's rawhide chew, distract him long enough for me to slip into bed.

Now, well past midnight, I hissed a pointed *shh*. Tommy turned over. The scratching stopped.

:::

In the last port of call, Puerto Vallarta, we finally collided with gay culture—literally. At the Blue Chair Resort, a gay beach in front of a gay hotel, our whole gang galumphed onto the sand, plowing through clusters of bikini-waxed, Corona-sipping men. Attendants nervously arranged chairs for us on the very edge of the resort. Even so, some patrons felt the need to move.

But the blind guys could see neither this self-satisfied slice of gay life, nor the fact that they didn't seem to be embraced by it. So they ordered drinks, propped umbrellas to shade their dogs, and kicked back.

Everyone seemed to have a fine time. Howard and Carl frolicked in the water, then wandered among the klatches of tattooed musclemen, trying to find their way back to our group. If you didn't know they were blind, you'd have thought they were browsing the hustlers.

Later, Carl led Tommy to the surf's edge, and Tommy (who, now that I'd drawn the line more firmly between us, I decided could be almost funny) asked me to hold his oversize sunglasses. He waded into the water, gut drooping over his flower-patterned yellow bathing suit. ("Is this suit blue?" he'd asked that morning in our cabin, and seemed confounded when I told him no, but donned it anyway.) When the first big wave came, it knocked him on his ass. He came up grinning wide, a jackpot winner.

I strolled up to the bar, where Bill and Doug had gone for more beers. They asked me to describe the scene and I did my best—the bright umbrellas, the haughty men, the rising surf—but I left out the part about the slinky Mexican kid two tables over, head shaved to show a dozen sexy scars, who looked at me, looked away, then looked back and finally winked. I returned his wink, ignited by arousal.

"Isn't it nice out here?" Bill said, oblivious to our flirtation. "Just the exact right amount of breeze."

"It's the best place we've gone so far," Doug said.

I looked away from my admirer, my fervor flash-frozen. I should have reveled in our visual dalliance, no longer taking this capacity for granted, but what I felt was profound loneliness—like when you think of something you want to confide to a cherished friend, but then remember that the friend has died.

Why should I have felt lonely? *I* wasn't missing anything; the blind men were. And yet what exactly were they missing? The chance to wink at a Mexican kid whose name I didn't know, whom I'd probably never see again?

My sadness, I realized, wasn't so much for Doug or Bill—they seemed fairly contented in their lives—but for all of us, for the way we seek connection so ardently and so often fail, for the fact that a wink, even if you see it, assures nothing.

:::

The last night, I sat in our stateroom. I'd packed my suitcase and left it with the porters. I'd filled out the customs form. I'd brushed my teeth.

Tommy was up on Deck 5 at the mulch boxes, offering Oscar a last chance to go. One more night, I thought. Just one more.

But as much as he'd made me uncomfortable, I couldn't be mad at Tommy. Howard, who knows him well, had told me that until recently Tommy attended Homosexuals Anonymous, trying to "cure" himself of being gay. And although Tommy had told me he's been in an eight-year relationship with a man, Howard explained that the man is married and only uses Tommy for sex. He said that twice Tommy has picked up strangers who have robbed him.

The door opened and Tommy clunked in. "Hey there, Mike!" he called in a childlike voice.

"Hi, Tommy," I said, and it occurred to me that he might have *given* his valuables to those strangers; he was just that good-natured, just that clueless.

Tommy unharnessed Oscar, and as usual, the Lab frisked up and began humping my leg. I let him thrust a moment before I shoved him off. "I can't believe it," I said, mock-serious. "Tomorrow I'll have to go home to my lonesome life, with no puppy dog to love me."

Tommy plopped heavily on his bunk. "Oh, I imagine there aren't very many times that *you're* lonesome, Mike."

"More than you think," I said honestly.

"Really?" Tommy said. "I always thought it would be different if you had 20/20."

THE ANTHROPOLOGY OF SEX

:::
:::

Martha McPhee

SHE WAS THE AGE I am now when I had an affair with her husband.
I thought of her as all grown up—sagging flesh and a soft middle-aged
body. Her cheeks drooped. There were smile lines about her mouth.
Her age, thirty-seven, seemed impossibly far away and her life like a
disease I didn't worry about catching since it only afflicted the old. I
was nineteen and by the time I was her age I'd have my life figured
out. I'd have children and a husband and a career, money in the bank,
stocks, bonds, and my sister, Serena, living not too far away. I'd have
everything we were promised by growing up American. And that
future floated out there in my distance like an island. I didn't think
about it much but I knew it would be there as surely as I knew that
Bora Bora and Hawaii were out there, somewhere, with their palm
trees and sapphire-blue skies and warm pacific oceans.

I had always wanted to have an affair. When Serena and I were little
we invented a game, which we played with some kids down the street.
The game was a variation on House and we called it Normal Day. In
the make-believe we were all married to each other, leading normal
lives—shopping, charging, drinking, fucking—and at the same time we
were all having affairs. In the world of Normal Day, the trick was not
to get caught. Like any affair there was an exciting period when no one
knew and the secret was hidden tightly by the lovers.

Serena and I adored those words. We'd lie in bed and talk late into
the night about Affairs and Lovers and Rendezvous and Trysts and
Adultery and Betrayal. Any word that implied sexual deception. We
tossed the words into the dark, where they'd hang suspended long

enough for us to muse over them, absorb them, make them ours. My sixth-grade English teacher had always said that if you use a word three times it's yours. Adultery, adultery, adultery.

The psychology was simple: Our mother left our father when I was four and Serena was six. She left him for Another Man (another term we loved—big and strong and tall and sexual). They had an affair and the affair broke our father's heart and the best explanation our mother had was that she had had to. She told us we would understand when we grew up and we wanted to grow up just so that we could understand. She said sex is too important, fundamental, the core. *Sex*, the word grew into enormous proportions. Every time I'd eat an apple to its core I'd think about the word, *sex*. SEX. Our mother left our father for the word. So Serena and I both aspired to affairs—noble aspiration that would lead us to a higher understanding and appreciation.

:::

Her name was Gwen. Gwen, a solid middle-aged name. Her thighs were Jell-O-like. Her belly fleshy. (I look at my own body now and see hers, though of course I don't think of it so negatively anymore.) Thin strands of gray lined her hair. She was on her island, her Bora Bora. Half her life behind her, another half to go. (But the islands of the second half have less to do with perfection than with remedy.) God knows what she imagined her future to hold when she was a child. She was married to a very tall, dark-haired, blue-eyed philosophy professor seeking tenure at a small Maine college. They had a house on a cove filled with lobster boats. They had two cars and plenty of food. They spent their summers in Scandinavia. He provided for her, though she had a job at an art museum in a bigger town not too far away. Her husband's name was Jack and Jack was fucking one of his students. He fucked her in his office. He fucked her in the back of his small car—awkward and uncomfortable because they were both so tall. Outside, a world of blue skies and a beach strewn with driftwood. Lobster boats doing their lobster thing. A few egrets and a few seagulls. He fucked her in cheap hotels and he even took her to Grand Rapids, Cincinnati, and Sioux City to conferences of philosophy professors so he could fuck her there—upstairs in their hotel suite while downstairs a pack of professors discussed Kierkegaard, Nietzsche, Merleau-Ponty,

Freud. They wandered the lobbies importantly in their rumpled tweed jackets. Kierkegaard was Jack's philosopher. He would claim that, "my philosopher," as if he owned the man. She lay on the big king-size bed and waited in silk underwear that he had bought her specially for the occasion.

Her name was Isabelle, spelled the French way because her mother had a fascination with the country and spoke the language fluently and spoke it to Isabelle as an infant so she would have a head start. And Jack liked that, it made him think of Isabelle as French and exotic. Of course, Isabelle am I.

Was this Gwen's Bora Bora, her Hawaii? I met her once, before the affair started, outside a newspaper store on a Sunday. Snow everywhere, so bright you had to squint, and the magnificent bells of the church. My hand slipped into hers as we were introduced. I remember her hand was so small and warm and I could feel the bones. She was shorter than I and her smile so innocent-seeming it was as if a little girl were lost in her face.

On the king-size beds of all the hotel rooms I'd call Serena to tell her about the shabby curtains that actually weren't shabby but which described that way seemed more appropriate for an affair. "What's it like?" she'd ask. She had never had an affair. She had already met Nicholas, the man she would marry. I felt older, wiser, for once, holding an experience that she would have to feed on.

"I've met the wife," I responded, and described her lost face.

"I mean the sex," Serena said with a nonchalance that pretended she was not that interested, though I knew she was.

"He's old," I answered, polishing my nails a bright and alluring red. The smell of the lacquer made me heady. "He's old so it takes a long time."

"*Takes*," she repeated. "Is that a good thing?"

"I think of Gwen," I confessed. "Of her at home missing Jack while I lie beneath him. Of her watching us." Out the windows the cities all looked the same—short buildings with short water towers and smokestacks, dreary gray weather. A cold river flowing between banks of concrete.

"The potential for so much destruction," Serena said. I thought of myself as a mighty bomb, a Daisy Cutter. I could hear her typing.

144 ::: MARTHA McPHEE

She always had to work while talking to me, as if to prove that I was secondary—or at least not central—that she had so much else in her life besides me. She was an aspiring poet in New York City, with a few poems in a few good reviews, all of which made her proud. I could hear sirens racing down Broadway. She always stayed on the phone. Sometimes we could stay on the phone so long we'd have nothing left to say but we'd stay there all the same just so that we could hear each other breathe. "The destruction you would cause if you went downstairs to the conference and introduced yourself," she continued. "Go," she dared. I could see her magnificent eyes pushing me. She was forever lining me up to risk everything, as if it would prove something. Perhaps my love for her or perhaps the simple sister truth: that if I were crushed I'd need her all the more. I was almost tempted to go downstairs because we were just playing with these people's lives.

:::

Serena came to college to visit so that she could meet Jack. He had lunch with us in the student pub, in a dark corner booth. He came late, his big hands nervously working the lettuce in his sandwich because he knew he was being appraised—funny (and endearing) to see such a grown man intimidated by a girl. Serena's laserlike blue eyes held him for a long time in a silent conversation. Of the two of us she's the pretty one—long auburn hair, medium height, a dimple that catches the light each time she smiles, making her whole face sparkle. She cares enormously for her clothes and style—even presses her collars. Ever since I can remember I've been aspiring to her style, but I'm too lazy and never get it quite right so I give up and wear jeans.

I wanted her to approve of Jack, wanted her to want him, wanted her to be jealous, wanted him to fuck her—could imagine us lying in bed together talking about what it was like. I thought of Normal Day, of how she would always find new kids to play the game and when she ran out of new kids she married us off to stars: Steve McQueen, Paul Newman, O. J. Simpson (many years before he killed his wife). Finally Jack blushed and tucked his head in a bashful way and smiled.

"He's too tall," Serena would say later, dismissing him. But now to him she lifted her left eyebrow. She could do that. When we were children she would say that she had double-jointed eyebrows. "Kierkegaard is fabulous on love," she said.

"You would know," he said. The energy was kinetic between us, little jolts ricocheting from her to him to me. "As a poet, that is, of course, you would know about love."

I hadn't understood yet, of course, that Serena and I were playing with each other's lives.

:::

I am Gwen's age now, thirty-seven. This past summer my husband, Lucian, our son, Serena and her husband, Nicholas, and their three girls rented a beach house for the month of July on Popham Beach, not far from where I went to college. I have a fondness for going back to scenes from my past. I don't avoid them. I don't turn them into mythic spots never to be visited again. Instead I return. Returning makes me feel like not too much is gone.

I had been to this beach many times before. It is one of the only beautiful sand beaches in the state of Maine, since a state park preserves most of it. The house we rented was an old Victorian on stilts with a wraparound porch and a turret overlooking dunes thick with dune grass and plovers and the gorgeous expanse of beach. Islands float just offshore, two of them connected to the beach at low tide by sand spits. The north end of the beach curves to meet the mouth of the Kennebeck. It is a pristine mouth, untainted by industry, and wide and deep enough to hold the navy destroyers flowing down to the Atlantic from the ironworks in Bath. The mouth is, I imagine, almost as it was in 1607, when its banks were colonized by the first pilgrims to this country—a history that makes this region noteworthy and thus proud. Here I first kissed Jack, a warm May day with big cottony Maine clouds and the whole world smelling of pine and salt. His lips tentative at first as they found mine, as if asking if this were all right, then finding in my response the authority to be bold, reckless even. Other students lurked about on afternoon strolls, adding to the daring pleasure of that first kiss. Jack had driven me to the beach for a walk and though I knew we would kiss I pretended to know nothing.

Lucian and I had a new Audi. He had a new BIG job as an editor in chief. We were both editors. Serena hoped someday he'd publish her poetry, which so far had not been published by a trade publisher. He did not like her work. He thought it overly emotional and embarrassingly revealing, but he did not tell her that. She also owned a restaurant in New York City, a small restaurant that served just one or two fabulous dishes per night—whatever Serena's fancy chose, since she was also the chef. It was more a hobby than a serious profession, though she was a fine chef—another thing she could do that I could not. Whenever she went on vacation she closed the restaurant down. Even so, when she was in town, it was packed; she was good at making people wait for her.

Our boy, Hunter, was one year old. We had plenty of food and had recently started to acquire stocks. It was a bull market so we thought only of stocks, never bonds, and it seemed our horizon was long. Serena and Nicholas convinced us to buy Intel and AOL and Cisco. We convinced them to buy Sun Microsystems and Qualcomm. We all had Lucent and Amazon. Not much translated rapidly into a whole lot more. The sky was a wonderful pale blue with depth and even when it rained the days were beautiful. We called those days mysteries because each one would be different. It would never simply rain. Rather there'd be a fog so dense you could not see your own feet or thunder and lightning would appear from a clear blue sky. We'd sit on the porch and watch the weather like some people watch a movie—the lightning dancing across the water, then the beach, then the dunes, approaching us. But we were not scared. Not even the girls were scared, though they ran through the house screaming, until Nicholas told them to quiet down.

Serena's daughters are three, five, and seven and they look exactly like each other and exactly like her. Even Lily, the firstborn. "She looks nothing like you," I used to tease Nicholas, because an old wives' tale has it that firstborns always look like the fathers so that the fathers stick around. It's supposed to be a biological trigger that dates back millions of years, an early paternity test. "Lily looks rather like Lucian," he'd say, teasing right back.

"If Lily were Lucian's child she'd be a boy," I responded. Another old wives' tale says that if a woman doesn't have an orgasm she is more likely to have a daughter. (As it turns out, our mother had three boys with her second husband. *Sex is too important, fundamental, the core.* If everyone were having great sex would there only be boys?) Our child looks just like Lucian. Nicholas smiled that half smile of his that sits on his lips full of knowledge and irony. Sometimes it could seem there was a whole world behind Nicholas that we did not know, that had nothing to do with Serena. Sometimes I found myself almost wishing he had another family, some deviant choice. Just a simple wicked thought, of how much she would need me if . . . But for Serena, Nicholas's mystery only added to his appeal.

When I first learned I was pregnant with a boy Serena asked repeatedly what we were going to do—as if the two of us were having the child. She bought books on the subject, poring over the details of how to raise a boy, making the prospect of a boy both frightening and irresistible. "A little penis inside you," she kept saying. "The way I like it," I'd respond. Sometimes it did feel like the children were ours, we spent so much time together. Her daughters wore our clothes, saved by our mother for thirty years in mothballs in the attic of our childhood home—a reckoning of hers with the promise of our future, that it would be brighter than the past she gave us. Serena clipped back her daughters' hair exactly alike with ribbons, the way our mother had done with us. Sometimes as the girls played it was as if Serena and I were seeing ourselves all over again.

We watched the rain, sipping wine on the wraparound porch of our rented summer home. "I suppose we've arrived," Serena said, lifting her glass for a toast. The rain stopped just as suddenly as it started and a full red moon rose over a lighthouse on one of the islands, the beauty making us feel lucky.

"Suppose?" Lucian noted.

"The ship," I said, pointing to it. The ferry from Nova Scotia passed on the horizon, lit up like a miniature Baccarat crystal ship. And though it appeared each evening, seeing it again always seemed like a surprise.

"The crystal ship," Lucian said. He is a small smart handsome man, shorter than I, with a strong jaw and bright brown eyes, thick blond wild hair, and a sense of humor that ripples out of him like heat.

"Suppose," Serena repeated definitively with that coy coolness of hers. "We're all waiting, as they say, for our ship to come in."

"It passes us by beautifully," Lucian said. It was now so quiet that, except for the waves, you could almost hear the ship chugging along, almost see the passengers dancing beneath the dazzling stars.

"Oh Lucian," Serena sighed, tilting her head back and offering him a sort of challenging stare, a stare that asked him now, What's not perfect about your life? She sat on the arm of his chair, her fingers resting lightly on the jeans above his thigh.

But I ignored the way Serena looked at Lucian. She'd been flirting with Lucian since I first met him. In fact, it was part of the initial seduction—a story we always loved to tell, that she even told as part of her toast at our wedding. I loved it because it showed our unity, how we were inextricably woven together like threads of a fine fabric. But I suppose she loved the story because it illustrated her triumph.

I met Lucian at a party on New Year's Eve. He was sitting in a room filled with men. I liked the way he sat in the chair, as if he owned it, feeling quite comfortable there. I liked the wild nature of his hair, how he seemed not to care about it, and even so it made him look dashing; I liked that the people surrounding him laughed because of something he had said. I found Serena and brought her to the room.

"There's one man here that I want. Find him," I said. She did not need to study the room. She walked directly over to Lucian, interrupted his conversation, and began to flirt furiously—all bubbly smiles and enthusiasm, exuding charm and desire. Nicholas was there but he wasn't paying attention. Serena's flirtations were their aphrodisiac. "You've got to have some trick when you've been with the same person twelve years," they'd say. Nicholas was also shorter than I, with short hair and magnificent light blue eyes and long feminine lashes so dark it always seemed he wore mascara, though of course he did not. Though he doesn't look it, he is a conventional type, an investment banker who spends long stretches of his time in Asia merging telephone companies, the reason Serena can afford to shut down the restaurant whenever she chooses.

Serena flirted with Lucian for the rest of the night, but slowly, slowly I inserted myself until I could see that Lucian was quite confused, then hopeful about a pair of sisters. With a kiss at midnight I claimed him unequivocally.

:::

Serena for serene, of course. And she was. A placid face at thirty-nine. No wrinkles. No signs of undue worry. She was my closest friend. My love, my life. "You're the love of my life," I'd say to her. "You're the love of my life," she'd say to me.

Indeed we hated each other's friends, always telling each other why each other's friends were horrible. Nicholas never really loved me, nor I him. He was suspicious of me, always afraid I'd somehow manage to cheat him out of something. For a long time Lucian would insist that Serena was poison—afraid, I suppose, that she'd cheat him out of something. "She's dangerous," he'd say. "You're just jealous," I'd say. Her defense against attack was flirting, and she flirted with Lucian, knitting Lucian into her—her big eyes on him, so intensely interested in every word he uttered. It never occurred to me that she would flirt for another reason, that her flirting could be dangerous, that it could cheat Lucian of me. Friends, for Serena and me, were enemies, capable of annexing the best part of our country.

As children playing Normal Day we sometimes fooled the others by having an affair with each other. We sneaked off and touched tongues. Lightly and quickly at first. Serena's tongue was warm and had texture. A little bland, but soft and deep. At first we touched tongues because she promised me five cents. Then simply because we liked the sensation. I wanted to disappear in her tongue, become her tongue.

:::

The tide came in and out like breathing, revealing the sand spits so quickly the crabs didn't have a chance to hide—those sand spits like arms reaching out from shore to the islands, clutching them. Hawaii? Bora Bora? The gulls swooped down and devoured the crabs. Their carcasses lay strewn about the isthmus.

On one of the two islands stands a mansion in a grove of pines. A wealthy man from Boston built it for his wife. The house is an exact replica of an old colonial house on an island in the mouth of the Kennebeck and that faces the island of the wealthy Bostonian. His wife had liked that house so he had copied it for her so that she could look at the one she admired while being inside its replica. Not long after the house was completed, the wife was killed in a boating accident in the Caribbean. They had one young boy.

We sat in chairs close to the sand and read the paper. Nicholas was in Asia for a two-day deal. "Getting Serious About Adultery: Who Does It and Why They Risk It," I read aloud, holding the paper above my face to shield my eyes from the sun—and as I read the headline of the article somewhere and for some reason I regretted it. Like when you read an article on cancer and then realize you wish you didn't know the details, start to fear you have the symptoms.

"An appropriate article for us," Serena said with that dismissive nonchalance of hers, that what-you're-thinking-isn't-as-important-as-what-I'm-doing attitude of hers.

"Let's go for a swim," Lucian said, and jumped up. "Coming, darling?" he asked, and I thought he meant me, but it was Serena he was speaking to. And then, as if he realized his mistake, his eyes darted to me with a please-come look. Serena jumped up and followed him. They dived into the water as if it were warm. Something ugly was gnawing its way into my mind. I tried to push it out. I have a tendency to destroy happiness with fears of all the terrible things that can go wrong. "An apocalyptic imagination" is how Lucian describes mine—my ability to see the worst-case scenario as a fait accompli.

On his blanket the baby slept, making clucking sounds. Serena's girls were jumping about at the edge of the water, building sand castles and making noise—like a force, some intense weather system—all dressed alike in red bathing suits with white polka dots. Ribbons in their hair. If they were my children I'd yank those ribbons out. I wondered about them, about their being three. They fought all the time with Lily as the leader, and I wondered what their secret world was filled with. Did they think yet about Bora Bora? Sometimes I'd spy them studying the island of the Bostonian, hoping to see his son walking over the bald rocky slope from the ocean to the house—seduced already by wealth and pain.

The thing kept gnawing inside me like those holes the girls were digging in the sand; when they're deep enough the walls cave in, keep caving in until water swamps the hole. Lucian loves me, he loves, he loves, I thought, as if I were trying to convince myself. We had just made love while Serena watched the baby. We said we were going for a walk, but I knew she knew what we were doing. He loves me. My cheeks still flushed. The light lit his hair, turning it golden; their heads bobbed as they swam far out. I could hear the high pitch of their laughter. I was too afraid and cold to swim as far out as they could. I remember understanding just then, at that particular instant, as water brimmed over the surface of my hole, that Serena wanted to have an affair with Lucian—knew it like you just know some things, perhaps something I should have known for a long time now. It seemed my stomach fell a great distance, as on a roller coaster, and I wanted to disappear, become impossibly small. Every nerve alive.

"What's wrong?" Serena asked. She stood above me. The cold salt-water dripped off of her onto me. She was wearing a one-piece black bathing suit—a sort of 1940s style, square across the hips, a little like shorts hugging her butt, a halter at the chest loosely holding her big breasts. Her auburn hair fell in tresses down her chest. She would never show her tummy after the girls were born. It was scarred with ugly purple and black stretch marks ripping across her pale pink flesh—still full and flabby. She had made me rub belly balm, gooey and smelly, on my stomach so that the same would not happen to me. Then like a shot I wondered, Has she succeeded, has Lucian fucked her?

"Nothing," I said.

"I know something's wrong," she said.

If I lose her I'll have nothing, I thought.

"Should something be wrong?" I asked, looking up into her face, behind which was the big bright blasting sun—there to sting my eyes.

Lucian dripped cold water over the girls, making them shriek with delight and run away from him so that he'd chase them. They loved being chased by him. Already, like their mother, they were master flirts. "He's our other daddy," they'd say, because Nicholas was so often on the road.

There are some things you just don't suspect. I filled up with dread. I don't really know why then and not earlier or later or never. It was July 14, 1998. Bastille Day. Sometime in the afternoon. I had just turned thirty-seven. I was sitting on a beach in Maine reading an article on adultery. I put the paper down and watched my husband as he came back from the girls and his swim—tanned, slender body, wild hair, seductive full-lipped mouth. Was he screwing my sister? Because screwing it would be—all the more delightful for them because they were screwing me. I looked at Serena with her dark Italian glasses and stylish black bathing suit—left eyebrow rising over the frame of the glasses. Of the two of us I have the better body. I'm taller, thinner, tighter stomach from so many sit-ups. I stood up briefly, pretending to get something, just to remind myself, to show my body off in the bikini.

But then I felt ridiculous and old and sat down again. "What does the article say?" she asked.

"Why is adultery appropriate for us?" I said, quoting the article, trying to hide snappishness. She could always tell instantly when I went sour.

"My little sister's having fantasies?" she said, dismissing my paranoia before I had a chance to own it fully. She smiled, it seemed a little too triumphantly—as if she understood perfectly what was on my mind and was quite happy to have it there: she in there in my mind, belly dancing across it. She has a large ribbon mouth and when she smiles it breaks open like a dream to reveal her perfect white teeth and the promise of her good humor, that she'll settle it on you. The Maine water rolled bitterly over my toes. "We love that word, *Adultery*," Serena said to Lucian, and winked at me, trying to pull me back in.

"Normal Day," he said, and bent down to kiss me. Our mother had said that sex was the barometer of a relationship; if you weren't having any the relationship was in trouble. Lucian and I had plenty of sex. The idea of their affair was swallowed up momentarily with Lucian's kiss. "I prefer not to think about my wife having affairs," he said. Sometimes I'd tell Lucian that I wanted to be the other woman instead of the wife and mother. Sometimes we'd pretend that I was.

I laughed and everything seemed right again. Serena snatched the paper, skimmed the article, and began to quote from it. "The human animal is built to love more than one person at a time . . . We have the neurocircuitry that can lead us to adultery . . . The big mystery in evolutionary terms is what do women get out of it?" Then she began to laugh, fits of it. She is even beautiful when she laughs, breaking into shards of light like a fountain.

"For men it's about spreading their seed, for women it's about protecting their offspring," I said. "That's the big mystery," I said—and though I was being ironic it occurred to me that ever since I met Lucian I hadn't wanted to have an affair.

"What can women possibly get out of it?" Lucian said, sitting down behind me and pulling me close to him, wrapping his arms around me tightly until I felt thoroughly loved and protected. *In Normal Day the trick was not to let the others know.* Serena watched us, though I tried not to look at her.

"If women didn't get anything out of it, Lucian, there'd be no one for you to have an affair with," Serena said.

"Serena," I said, unable to hide my distaste.

"Oh come on, you two. Monogamy is not natural. Even Canadian geese, long believed to be the only monogamous animals in the animal kingdom, are not actually monogamous." For fifteen years, as far as I knew, Serena had been faithful. "This article is just another ruse to oppress women, using evolution as an excuse." Or had she? "What about pleasure? What about the sheer delight of the touch, the fingers, of someone new? Think of all the fabulously rich men out there whose pretty wives are screwing their riding instructors, Princess Di, for example—those little intrigues are certainly not to protect their offspring."

"Nicholas, for example," I said, referring to a fabulously wealthy man with a pretty wife. She knew what I meant. We always knew what each other meant. We could never escape each other, no privacy in our thoughts. "The inherent high in betraying," I said, and then asked her if she ever thought about Normal Day, holding her with my sharp accusing eyes. I could no longer feel Lucian behind me. Lucian disappeared.

"You had the affair," she snapped, referring to Jack. "I didn't."

:::

I had written a paper on Abel Jeanniere for Jack's class and it had won a national prize. It was about the French priest's radical position on sex, argued in his book *The Anthropology of Sex*. As a theological anthropologist he saw his task as one of "interpreting love beyond the schemas and stereotypes of (male-female) 'natures' in the truth and freedom of personal relations." In essence, he was investigating sexuality in marriage and raising it to heights it had not achieved before in the Catholic Church. He was making sexual intimacy a human requisite, scorning the doctrine that sex is for procreation alone and the belief that conjugal love is the death of the spiritual life. To lay the groundwork for harmony between human sex and spiritual freedom was a major advance. "To be fully oneself," Jeanniere repeats again and again, "is to know that one is for the other." This idea elevated woman to meet man as his equal—one for the other. To flee from woman-as-flesh is like using her as flesh, and subsequent freedom and creativity will not escape the shadow of this negation. Jack led me to Jeanniere and during long office hours we discussed, dissected, and contemplated the priest's intentions and then I wrote my paper and then it won its prize.

Because of the prize (which involved cash and a trip to Asheville, North Carolina, to read the paper) I was, for a short time, famous on campus. My whole life to this point has not been dominated by sex. SEX. I promise. I'm a book editor in New York City. I have one success followed by a run of disappointments and all that has nothing to do with sex. But it was Abel Jeanniere and sex that led me to meet Gwen a second time.

She had wanted to meet me. Jack told me so. She had heard him talk about me and she had heard me discussed among the faculty and she had seen my picture in the school newspaper and the local newspaper. It was odd that a young woman could write such a successful paper on a priest's ideas about sex. In my paper, I was interested above all in the inherent tension between the priest's preference for celibacy and his acute understanding, celebration even, of conjugal love. In the end, of course, he prefers celibacy.

Jeanniere makes express reference to the need he feels to defend celibacy. He sees its justification as a search for "modes of intimacy beyond eroticism" and for "concrete but universal forms of love." The reduction of sexual desire and pleasure to "eroticism," and of eroticism to an animal instinct, serves his defense of celibacy by making room for the possibility of a higher relation than the sexual. Indeed, Jeanniere at times seems to place human sex ontologically apart from man as man. Sex posits itself to me for the sake of the species, and for me as an individual. "This is the exact point where I can affirm the strength of my own autonomous and personal position, or where I can renounce and lose myself in a nature that is mine but outside myself."

:::

And so went my paper—celibacy leading Jeanniere out of the web of sexual complication to a higher state of clarity and perfection. (Note that I don't say *purity*. He would not have said *purity*.)

Jack talked to Gwen about me, told her that I was a gifted student—one of the few women in his class. I came to campus knowing exactly what I wanted to study, French and philosophy. I designed my own major combining the two and in three short years rearranged the entire department. In my sophomore year the man I worked with most closely, my adviser for this thesis that I had designed, died of AIDS. While he was sick and dying I continued to work with him. When he died Jack took over as my adviser and soon thereafter we began to fuck. For these reasons (all but the latter) I thought that Gwen wanted to meet me. I did not think that she wanted to meet me because Jack spoke of me incessantly.

I remember once we were making love on his living room floor. (He would not make love to me in their bed.) Our clothes were all over the place and someone walked through the front door and into the hall and started talking. A woman's voice that we both thought belonged to Gwen. I grabbed what I could of my clothes and raced away from the room, flying up the stairs and into the bathroom. Her bathroom, thick with her supplies. Rouge and tampons and pads and lipsticks and hair clips and her bras hanging from the shower rod and her underwear (big white overused underwear) and her socks and stockings. All the things that she wanted Jack to remove from her body, but there was no mystery left here and for an instant I felt sorry for her. Water dripped slowly in a leaky faucet. My heart raced. The window was too small to climb out of. The cabinet beneath the sink too small to squeeze into. The shower curtain one hundred percent transparent. Then I heard footsteps on the stairs. This was so terribly real. I wondered did I have time to dress. In my hands, I realized just then, of the clothes I was able to collect, I had only my bra and shoes—strappy high heels that I wore to be sexy. I put on my bra and crouched against the tub.

The door crept open slowly. My cheeks burned.

Caught, busted, snagged, as we used to say during Normal Day. Adrenaline rushing through every single one of us. The hunters and the hunted.

It was Jack. His face was serious. He told me to stand up. I stood up. He told me to put my shoes on. I put my shoes on. He told me to stand in front of the mirror and hold on to the sink. And I did. I could see him in the mirror. His chest pressed against my back and his mouth came to my ear. He whispered into it and his hands crept around my back and inside my bra, a lavender push-up bra that caused my breasts to spill from it. "You're going to feel me between your thighs now," he said. He pushed my back toward the sink so that I bent at the waist and then I felt him. He went in a little and then came out, in a little and then out until I pleaded. "That's right, that's right. Keep telling me what you want, kitten." His fingers were on my nipples. I felt like I was begging. I had no idea who was downstairs. I didn't care if it was Gwen. Let her see me like see this. My heart beat against my chest. "I want to hear you sing." I was begging, ready to scream. "Not too fast," he said, and moved away from me entirely. "Please," I said again, Gwen's big underwear staring at me. I wanted her to see me like this, wanted her to walk through that door. There was no stopping this. I was entirely his. He could do anything. "Tell me everything," he whispered, warm wet soft, coming into me again. "Just exactly what she would do to you?"

Were Serena and Lucian involved in this? So magnificent, like being cracked open and offered up to the universe. A life is being sacrificed for your pleasure. SEX. Exquisite, like glass breaking, shattering a thousand fractured parts of me to become completely whole and new again. My mother left my father for sex. I had no one to leave for Jack, but after that encounter, had I had a boyfriend I would certainly have left him for Jack. I almost wished I had someone to leave. "You have me to leave," Serena had said when I told her this story.

I met Gwen the second time at the main entrance to the philosophy department with Jack standing tall nearby. If I had asked Serena then about Gwen she would have said, "But of course Gwen knows. It's obvious. She might not admit it consciously. But she knows. If she didn't she wouldn't be interested in you." Serena loves to say that nothing gets by anyone. She says as well that we all know exactly what is going on. Did I already know about Serena and Lucian? For how long had I known? If we don't see something that is standing right in front of us it is only because we choose not to. We have that ability—to choose not to see.

Gwen and I shook hands. I was sweet. I smiled a big and young and toothy lying smile. I can imagine now what Gwen thought of me as she peered down on me from the wisdom of thirty-seven. A pretty and very young girl with her life in front of her and so much to figure out.

"I've heard so much about you," she said. Her smile was warm and tender, like her hand. She held on to mine for a long time. It felt as though she wanted to keep my hand. She studied me closely. I felt as if she were finding me in that bathroom. She was quite short. I looked her in the eyes. Hers were sympathetic. I was trying to figure out whether she knew. I loved that she kept my hand. I could feel Jack behind us, studying the moment as well. I loved the feeling of my hand clasped within hers as Jack watched on. It was as if our hands were communicating something, we were speaking back and forth to each other. A private conversation that Jack couldn't hear. I'd think about that conversation for years. I believe I was telling her that I did not love Jack. Never would. This was just a game. I'd break his heart—would I? Or was this just the hubris of youth? But at that moment all the destruction I had the potential to cause vanished. It was a long handshake. By the end of it Gwen understood something, that I was just a twerp, a punk. But she had held my hand protectively as well. "You're brave," she said. "Congratulations on your prize."

Later she'd tell Jack that I was lovely, that she felt sorry for me, that I seemed bright. She'd say many things about me. They'd discuss me over dinner. I'd be there at the dinner table, dissected. She couldn't get enough of me. She'd want to know what he thought would happen to me, what my grades were, did I ever talk about my family, did I have a boyfriend. I imagined, sometimes, that they talked about me while making love. She'd tell him that I was cute, pretty, so impossibly young. The fat, swollen cheeks of youth. And Jack would relay this all to me while we were fucking, trying desperately to reignite the wilting sex. Gwen had accomplished her task; she had given her permission.

:::

We fought that night, the night of the adultery article and the swim and the "Coming, darling?" First Lucian and I, then Serena and I, then Serena and Lucian. When Serena is mad at Lucian she simply stops speaking to him. When she is mad at me first she screams and then she gives me the silent treatment. The kids safely asleep, Serena making some elaborate meal for us to feast upon, I wondered ever so fleetingly what life would be like if she lived very far away from me, if our lives were not inextricably intertwined. And the thought blew in a soothing freshness, like that cold Maine water cleansing my toes. I imagined my family, husband, son, and me, in our own world, happily doing our own thing, with no need for Serena. And thus I began a fight. It was easy to make Serena fight. She had many scabs to pick. I brought up her poetry, said, "Oh, Lucian should publish you," knowing well he wouldn't over his dead body, knowing well he thought her a wretched talent—not that extreme, but I was upset. I have a knack for making people feel bad, for picking their worst and most humiliating wound.

"Come on, Lucian. Why not?" I said. We were on our second bottle of wine, the remains of *risotto al funghi porcini* on our plates. The smell of Maine drifting through the windows making us cold. I would not give them my permission.

"Well, perhaps," Lucian said, trying to get out of it, giving me a please-stop look, not understanding fully the depth of my intentions.

"Let's schedule it. Set a date. Which poems would you choose? The one in which she talks about her bloody tampons?" I persisted. My face was red and ugly with the wine and the anger. And so on it went until my scheme worked and Serena declared that Lucian had no intention of publishing her and we were all drunk and fighting and crying.

"You don't like my poetry, do you?" Serena asked Lucian.

"Let's not fall into this, Serena," Lucian said calmly, saying her name with a familiarity as if he had said it to her privately many times. "Don't you see what she's doing?" As if it were the two of them who were the pair.

"Is that true?" she asked.

He was silent.

"Lucian, is that true?" she asked again, saying his name as if she owned it. Everything rotten blossoming before me—one lover questioning the truth of the other. How long had I known? How often was I a part of her orgasm? What did he whisper into her ear? I knew of a man who cheated on his wife, called his wife while he was fucking his lover because hearing her voice in the midst of it all made the orgasm all the more complete.

"Just keep spreading your legs, darling," I said, "and he'll publish you." My gut pulled the rest of me inside out and into it.

Lucian shoved his chair back from the table and stood up and told me with eyes of hatred that I'd gone too far this time. "Why are you doing this?" he said with disgust. He stacked plates impatiently. If he were innocent he'd have laughed this off.

"Why are *you* doing this is what you should be asking," I said. I wanted to go back to the afternoon and do it all over, choose not to read that article, choose to stand up when he asked, "Are you coming, darling?" Yes, yes. I am.

Lily appeared at the foot of the stairs, her little sleepy face like a doll's. We became quiet. "I want my daddy," she said.

"He's in Asia," Serena said, barely noticing the girl.

"When's he coming back?" she demanded. "I want him back now."

"It's all right, dear," Lucian said, approaching her. For Lucian the children always came first. "He'll be back soon."

"I don't want you. I want my daddy," she snapped.

"Lily," Serena said. Lucian went outside and Serena followed him and then so did Lily. Those old wives, they say that children know the truth.

:::

I lie on my bed in the turret. Outside the moon is so full and bright it seems like dusk. Low tide and those arms reaching greedily to the islands, mocking me. Bora Bora? Hawaii? I lie there for a long time before Serena comes. I cry a little, then make a bet with myself about what it means if she comes. If I hurt her she would not come. Then she appears and lies down next to me.

"You win," I say, and then get confused. "Or have you lost?"

"Why are you doing this?" she asks.

"You sound like Lucian," I say.

"I love you," she says. "You're it," she says—I'm all she has. My nose is pinching. I can hear my baby breathing. "You've done this all for nothing," she says.

"Have I?"

We lie there for a long time, listening to the light wind, the waves, the night. The moon continues its march across the sky. I remember an annoying man from college, a boy, really, who had close-set eyes and was unfortunately small; he made himself look even smaller by wearing outsize jackets. He walked around campus with a little notebook, taking notes, always needing to know everything about everyone and somehow finding out the information. He drew me a diagram once, when I thought my affair with Jack was my own big secret. The dia-

gram had the names of dozens of our classmates, an intricate diagram
with many crisscrossing lines leading from one name to another to
another. With a pencil in his hand and his beady eyes lit with enthusiasm he showed me how I had slept unwittingly with a good portion
of my class. He revealed this to me by informing me that Jack had
slept with a girl named Cathy before he started fucking me, and Cathy,
before fucking Jack, had fucked a good many others. His pencil started
zigzagging all across the page and I began to laugh. I laughed hysteri-
cally, almost scaring the pathetic boy. I supposed he had wanted me
to be upset by his revelation. Instead I saw Abel Jeanniere's celibacy
lifting him beautifully above the intricate web of sex creeping through
all our lives—mere mortals making messes of our lives. I laughed for
the priest's endearing insight into our foolish fucking glee—generation after generation after generation. Not long after the births of the
three boys my stepfather left my mother, running off with his young
secretary. And I laugh again now, thinking of all this. I feel Gwen's long
handshake giving me permission—understanding for the first time her
wisdom. The laugh gives Serena permission to speak.

"Do you really think I could hurt you?" she asks, staring at the ceiling.

"Yes," I say, "because you already have. You've wanted me to believe
in your affair."

"A bluff, you mean?"

"Did you want that power—if I wouldn't always love you most then
I'd hate you most and thus still love you most?" A strong breeze comes
through the walls and it seems the whole house moves.

"Where's Lucian?" I ask, getting a notion.

"He's walking," she says, understanding the notion. "He'll be gone
awhile."

Those waves like a breath, like breathing, rolling in out in out tire-
lessly over the course of a day a year a life a millennium—whispering,
brushing cool air over warm skin. Our bare arms barely touch. She
smells like risotto, onions, and porcini, the sweet scent of wine, like you
could eat her. Though it's light outside, it's dark in the room. I close my
eyes. I can hear her breathing. I can feel her twisting toward me. I can
feel her so close to my face, her lips on mine, her tongue on mine.

"Do you want to hear the truth?" she whispers.

"I already know the truth."

THE ROOM IN THE ATTIC

∷

Steven Millhauser

I

WAKERS AND DREAMERS

I first saw Wolf in March of junior year. This isn't his story, but I suppose I ought to begin with him. I had slung myself into my seat with the careful nonchalance of which I was a master, and had opened my ancient brownish-red copy of *The Mayor of Casterbridge*, which held nothing of interest for me except the little threads of unraveling cloth along the bottom of the front cover, when I became aware of someone in the row on my right, two seats up. It was as if he hadn't been there a moment before. I was struck by his light gray suit—no one in our school wore a suit—and by the top of a paperback that I saw tugging down his left jacket pocket. I felt a brief pity for him, the new kid in the wrong clothes, along with a certain contempt for his suit and a curiosity about his book. He seemed to be studying the back of his left hand, though for a moment I saw him look toward the row of tall windows along the side of the room. One of them stood open, on this mild morning in 1959, held up by an upside-down flowerpot, and for some reason I imagined him striding across the room, pushing the window higher, and stepping through. When everyone was seated, Mrs. Bassick asked him to stand up. It was an act he performed with surprising grace—a tall young man, sure of himself, unsmiling but at ease in his light gray suit, his hair curving back above his ears and falling in strands over his forehead, his long hands hanging lightly at his sides, as if it were nothing at all to stand up in a roomful of strangers with all eyes on you, or as if he simply didn't care: John Wolfson, who had moved to our town from somewhere else in Connecticut, welcome to William Harrison High. He sat down, not quickly or clumsily as I would have done, and leaned back in an attitude of polite attention as class began. Five minutes later I saw his left hand slip into his jacket pocket and remove the paperback, which he held open on his lap during the rest of class.

Later that day I passed him in the hall and saw that he had shed his jacket and tie. I imagined them hanging forlornly on a hook in his locker. The next day he appeared in a new set of clothes, which he wore with casual ease: chinos, scuffed black loafers with crushed-looking sides, and a light blue long-sleeved shirt with the cuffs rolled back twice over his forearms. I envied his ease with clothes; girls smiled at him; within a week we were calling him Wolf and feeling that he was part of things, as if he'd always been among us, this stranger with his amused gray eyes. Rumor had it that his father had been transferred suddenly from another part of Connecticut; rumor also had it that Wolf had flunked out of prep school or been thrown out for unknown reasons that seemed vaguely glamorous. He was slow-smiling, amiable, a little reserved. What struck me about him, aside from his easy way with clothes, was the alien paperback I always saw among his schoolbooks. The book marked him: it was as if to say he'd gotten rid of the suit, but refused to go farther. That, and the slight reserve you could feel in him, his air of self-sufficiency, the touch of mockery you sometimes felt in his smile—it all kept him from being simply popular. Sometimes it seemed to me that he had made an effort to look exactly like us, so that he could do what he liked without attracting attention.

We fell into an uneasy friendship. I too was a secret reader, though I kept my books at home, in my room with the wide bookcase and the old living room armchair with a sagging cushion. But that wasn't the main thing. I thought of myself, in those days, as someone in disguise—beneath the obedient son, beneath the straight-A student, the agreeable well-brought-up boy with his friends and his Ping-Pong and his semiofficial girlfriend, there was another being, restless, elusive, mocking, disruptive, imperious, and this shadowy under-self had nothing to do with that other one who laughed with his friends and went to school dances and spent summer afternoons at the beach. In a murky sense I felt that my secret reading was a way of burrowing down to that under-place, where a truer or better version of myself lay waiting for me. But Wolf would have none of it. "A book," he declared, "is a dream machine." He said this one day when we were sitting on the steps of the town library, leaning back against the pillars. "Its purpose," he said, "is to take you out of the world." He jerked his thumb toward the doors of the library, where I worked for two hours a day after school, three days a week. "Welcome to the dream factory." I protested that for me a book was something else, something to get me past whatever was standing in my way, though I didn't know what it was that was in my way or what I wanted to get to on the other side. "What gets in your way," Wolf said, as if he'd thought about it before, "is all this"—he waved vaguely at Main Street. "Stores, houses, classrooms, alarm clocks, dinner at six, a sound mind in a healthy body. The well-ordered life." He shrugged and held up a book. "My ticket out of here." He gave that slow lazy smile of his, which had, I thought, a touch of mockery in it.

:::

He invited me to his house, one warm April day, when all the windows stood open and you could see out past the baseball field to the railroad tracks running behind it. We left together after school, I walking beside my bike as my books jumped in the dented wire basket, Wolf strolling beside me with a nylon jacket flung over one shoulder like a guy in a shirt ad and his books clutched at his hip. I lived in a newish neighborhood of ranch houses not far from the beach, but Wolf lived on the other side of town, out past the thruway, where the houses grew larger, the trees thicker and greener. We entered the shade of the thruway overpass, filled with the roar of eighteen-wheelers rumbling over our heads, then cut across a small park with slatted benches. After a while we found ourselves walking along a winding road, bordered by short brown posts with red reflectors. Here the houses were set far back from the street behind clusters of pine and oak and maple. At a driveway with a high wooden fence along one side and a high hedge on the other, we turned in and climbed a curving slope.

Around the bend, Wolf's house appeared. Massive and shadowy, it seemed to stand too close to me as I bent my neck back to look up at the row of second-floor windows with their black shutters. The house was so dark that I was surprised to notice it was painted white; the sun struck through the high trees onto the clapboards in small bright bursts of white and burned on the black roof shingles.

"Welcome to Wolfland," he said—and raising his right arm, he moved his long hand in a slow, graceful flourish, shaped like a tilde.

He opened the front door with a key and I followed him into a living room so gloomy that it felt as if heavy curtains had been closed across the windows. In fact the curtains were open and the windows held upward-slanted blinds that gave a broken view of sun-mottled branches. In the sunnier kitchen he tossed his books onto a table on which sat a gardening glove and an orange box of Wheaties, picked up a note that he read aloud—"Back later. Love, M"—and led me back into the living room, where a stair post stood at the foot of a carpeted stairway. Upstairs we walked along a dusky hall with closed doors. Wolf stopped at the last one, which he opened by turning the knob and pushing with the toe of his loafer. Repeating his flourish, and adding a little bow, as if he were acting the part of a courtier paying homage to his lord, he waited for me to enter.

I stepped into a dark brown sunless room with drawn shades. One of the shades was torn at the side, letting in a line of light. "Watch out," Wolf said, "don't move," as he crossed the room to an old brass floor lamp with a fringed yellowish shade and pulled the chain. The light, dark as butterscotch, shone on an old armchair that sat in a corner and looked wrong in some way. But what struck me was the book-madness of the place—books lay scattered across the unmade bed and the top of a battered-looking desk, books stood in knee-high piles on the floor, books were crammed sideways and right side up in a narrow bookcase that rose higher than my head and leaned dangerously from the wall, books sat in stacks on top of a dingy dresser. The closet door was propped open by a pile of books, and from beneath the bed a book stuck out beside the toe of a maroon slipper.

"Have a seat," Wolf said, indicating the armchair, which I now saw was without legs. I sat down carefully in the low chair, afraid I might knock over the book piles that lay on the floor against each arm. Wolf pulled back the spread with its load of books, which went tumbling against the wall, and lay down on his back with his head against a pillow, one arm behind his neck and his ankles crossed. That afternoon he told me that the difference between human beings and animals was that human beings were able to dream while awake. He said that the purpose of books was to permit us to exercise that faculty. Art, he said, was a controlled madness, which was why the people who selected books for high school English classes were careful to choose only false books that were discussable, boring, and sane, or else, if they chose a real book by mistake, they presented it in a way that ignored everything great and mad about it. He said that high school was for morons and mediocrities. He said that his mother had agreed never to enter his room so long as he changed his sheets once a week. He said that books weren't made of themes, which you could write essays about, but of images that inserted themselves into your brain and replaced what you were seeing with your eyes. There were two kinds of people, he said, wakers and dreamers. Wakers had once had the ability to dream but had lost it, and so they hated dreamers and persecuted them in every way. He said that teachers were wakers. He spoke of writers I had never heard of, writers such as William Prescott Pearson, A. E. Jacobs, and John Sharp, his favorite, who wrote terrific stories like "The Elevator," about a man who one day enters an elevator in a fifty-six-story office building and never comes out except to use the public bathrooms and the food machines, and "The Infernal Roller Coaster," about a roller coaster that goes up and up and never reaches the top, but whose masterpiece was a five-hundred-page novel that takes place entirely during the blink of an eye. Compared to these works, things like *Silas Marner* and *The Mayor of Disasterbridge* were about as interesting as newspaper supplements advertising vacuum cleaners.

"Care to see the attic?" he said suddenly. In the warm cave of books I had half closed my eyes, but Wolf had risen from the bed and was already standing at the door. I followed him out into the dusky hall, past the top of the stairway, to an unpainted door that looked like the door of a linen closet. It opened to reveal a flight of wooden steps. Up we went into that hot attic, where tawny sunlight streamed through a small round window, fell against bare floorboards and splintery rafters, and weakened into a brown darkness. As we passed along, I made out old couches and bureaus and armchairs, as if we'd broken into the furniture department of a big-city store. Then we came to a big old-fashioned record player, which rose up to my chest; Wolf opened the top to reveal a dim turntable, on which lay a ghostly white bear with outstretched arms. He next led me to a wooden wall with a door; the door opened onto a short hall, with a door on each side. He stopped at the left-hand one, knocked lightly with a single knuckle, and bent forward as if to listen. "My sister's room," he then said, and ushered me in.

When he closed the door behind us I found myself in total darkness. I had the sensation that Wolf was standing close to me, but I could not see him there. Then I felt something on my upper arm and jerked away, but it was only Wolf's hand, guiding me. Slowly he moved me forward through the blackness, as I held an arm before me as if to protect my face from branches in a forest. "Sit here," he whispered. He placed my hand on what seemed to be the high back of an upholstered chair, with a row of metal buttons running across the top.

I felt my way around the chair and sat down while I sensed Wolf settling into another seat nearby. I was sitting in a straight-backed stiff chair with hard, upholstered arms, the sort of chair you might find in the ornate parlor of an aging actress in a black-and-white movie. "Isabel," he said quietly, "are you awake?" I strained my eyes in that thick darkness, but I could see nothing at all. It struck me that it was all a hoax, an audacious joke meant to ridicule me in some way. At the same time I listened for the slightest sound and narrowed my eyes until they trembled with the effort to see. Anything could have been in that room.

"She's asleep," Wolf said, and I thought: Perfect, a perfect trick. I imagined him looking at me with a superior smile.

"Wolf?" a voice whispered, but so lightly that I wondered whether I had imagined it.

"Isabel," Wolf's voice said. "Are you up? I brought a visitor."

Something stirred. I heard a sound as of bedclothes, and what seemed like a faint sigh, and somewhere in that darkness I heard the word "Hello."

"Say hello to Isabel," Wolf said.

"Hello," I said, feeling irritable and absurd.

"Tell her your name," Wolf said quietly, as if I were a shy six-year-old child, and I would have said nothing, but who knew what was going on, there in the dark.

"David," I said. "Dave."

"Two names," the voice said; there was more rustling. "Two are better than one." I wondered whether Wolf had learned the trick of throwing his voice. "Do you like my name, David Dave?"

I hesitated. "Yes," I said. "I do."

"Uh uh uh," she said playfully, and I imagined a finger wagging in the dark. "You had to think about it."

"But I do," I said, thinking quickly. "I was listening to the sound of it, in my mind."

"Oh, that was a good answer, David Dave, a very good answer. I don't believe you, not for a second, but I won't make you pay a penalty, this time. So hey, how do you like my room? No no, don't worry, just kidding. What's Wolfie been telling you about me?"

"Not too much, actually."

"Oh good, then you can make me up. Isabel, or The Mystery of the Haunted Chamber. Hoooo, I'm feeling tired. Will you come back and sit with me again, David Dave?"

"Yes," I said. "I will. Definitely."

I heard a long yawn, and a mumbled phrase that sounded like "See ya later, alligator," and then I felt Wolf's hand on my arm and he was leading me out of the dark room and shutting the door carefully behind him. We walked in silence down the wooden steps and the carpeted steps into the gloom of the living room. Evidently it was time to go. Maybe he didn't want me to question him about that little game of his, up there in the dark. If he wished to be enigmatic, that was fine with me.

"She likes you," he said at the front door, standing with his forearm up against the jamb and his other hand clasping his raised shoulder. He lowered his voice to say, "Don't worry about anything." "Okay," I said, and walked down the front steps to my bike, with its dented wire basket filled with books. Kicking up the stand, I swung my leg over the seat and gave a wave as I started down the winding drive. At the bend I glanced back at the house, rising in a kind of twilight, then swung round to watch the shade-darkened drive as I rushed down between the high fence and the hedge, and when I burst onto the street I had to tighten my eyes in the sudden harsh light of the afternoon sun.

II

ADVENTURES IN THE DARK

All the way home, along hot streets printed with the curved shadows of telephone wires, I saw the high dark house, the cave of books, the black chamber. It all reminded me of something, and as I rode through the shade of the thruway overpass and broke into the sun it came to me: the darkness of the movie theater, the sun-striped lobby, the emergence into the glare of a summer afternoon. I had always liked that moment of confusion, when your mind is possessed by two worlds at once: the hard sidewalk with its anthills and its silver gum wrapper, the sword fight in the high room with the crimson curtain. But soon the grainy sidewalk, the brilliant yellow fire hydrant, the flash of sun on the fender of a passing car, the jewel-green traffic light become so vivid and exact that the other pictures grow dim, and you can hardly summon up the vague dark house, the book piles on the floor, the dim voice in the dark. I had the feeling that if I turned my bike around and rode back I'd find nothing at all—only a winding road lined with trees and a few dark posts with red reflectors.

At home I greeted my mother in the sunny kitchen, where she held up her hands to show me her flour-covered fingers and smoothed back a lock of hair with the back of a wrist. In my room I tossed my books on the bed and slumped down next to them with my neck against the wall and my legs dangling over the side. My wooden bookcase, painted a shiny gray, filled me with irritation. Here and there among the books were spaces given over to other things—old board games, a wooden box of chess pieces with a sliding top, two collections of stamps, a varnished bowl I had made in wood shop in the seventh grade. On top was my display of minerals, each with its label, and then came a globe on a brass stand, an electric clock with a visible cord, and a radiometer with vanes spinning in the light. Even the books exasperated me: they stood in neat rows, held tightly in place by green metal bookends with cork-lined bases.

On the beige wall and part of my bureau, long stripes of sunlight, thrown from the open slats of my blinds, lay tipped at an angle.

That night I woke in the dark. But I saw at once that it wasn't dark: light from a streetlamp glimmered on the globe, on the leather edges of the blotter on my desk, on the metal curve of the shade of the floor lamp beside my reading chair. Suddenly I thought: the attic was empty, no one was there—and I fell asleep.

The next day I saw Wolf in English, French, and American history. I passed him twice in the halls, saw him leaving the cafeteria as I entered, and spoke with him briefly after school, checking my watch as we stood on a plot of brownish grass near the bridge that crossed the railroad tracks and led to the center of town. I had to get over to the library and work my two-hour shift. Wolf stood smoking a cigarette with his thumb hooked in his belt and his eyes narrowed against the updrifting bluish smoke. He said nothing about his house, nothing about Isabel, and as I walked down toward Main Street I felt a ripple of anger, as if something had been taken away from me. I could forgive the deception but not the silence. On the second floor of the library, where I stood removing books from a metal cart and studying the white Dewey decimal numbers on the back before placing the books on the shelves, I recalled his book-mad room and wondered whether I had fallen asleep there, in that stumpy armchair, and dreamed my visit to his invisible sister.

It was like that for the rest of the week: a few meetings in class, a few words after school. It was as if he'd invited me on an adventure and changed his mind. I felt like the victim of an unpleasant joke and vowed to stay out of his way. That weekend I set up my Ping-Pong table in the garage and called up my friends Ray and Dennis. My mother brought out glasses of lemonade heavy with ice cubes and we ate fistfuls of pretzel sticks and ran after the white ball as it rolled down the driveway toward the street, where kids from next door were playing Wiffle ball with a yellow plastic bat and a man with a strap around his waist stood leaning away from the top of a telephone pole. Afterward we sat on the screened back porch and played canasta on the green card table. On Monday I worked again at the library, and on Tuesday, a day off, Wolf invited me to his house.

It was still there at the top of the curving drive, less dark than I had remembered it, the clapboards distinctly white in the broken shade of the pines and Norway maples. As we walked through the living room toward the stairs, a tall handsome woman in khaki Bermuda shorts and a white halter entered from the kitchen, carrying a trowel in one hand

and wearing on the other a grass-stained glove. I saw at once that she was Wolf's mother—saw it by something in the cheekbones, in the eyes, in the air of careless authority with which she inhabited her body. She thrust the trowel into the gardening glove, reached out her long bare hand, and shook hands firmly. "I'm John's mother," she said. For a moment I wondered who John was. "Sorry for the mess. You must be David." "He is, and then again he isn't," Wolf said, and throwing an arm across her shoulders he added, "What mess?" As she turned to him with a look of loving exasperation, she raised the back of her hand to her temple and smoothed away a piece of dark hair—and suddenly I imagined a world of mothers with hands dipped in work, raising their wrists gracefully to smooth back their hair.

In his room with the drawn shades he sat in the legless armchair with his feet up on the bed, while I lay across the bed with my neck against the wall, one foot on the floor and one ankle resting on my knee. He spoke only about Isabel. She was shy, extremely shy—hence the meeting in the dark. Whenever she met someone new—an ordeal she preferred to avoid—she insisted on the condition of absolute darkness. Thick curtains hung over the windows of the attic room. But don't worry—when she got to know me better, when she got used to me, he was sure she'd come out of the dark. Besides, she didn't *only* stay in her room—sometimes she came down for dinner or walked around the house. It was only strangers who made her nervous. He appreciated my willingness to visit her, she needed to see people, God, did she need to see people, though not just any old moronic people. As soon as he'd met me, he'd been sure. Truth was, about a year ago she'd had some kind of—well, they called it a breakdown, though in his opinion her nervous system had discovered a brilliant way of allowing her to do whatever she wanted without having to suffer the boredom of good old high school and all the rest of the famous teenage routine. She hadn't attended school for the last year, but the board of education had allowed her to study at home and take the tests in her room. She was much more studious than he was, always memorizing French irregular verbs and the parts of earthworms. She was a year younger than we were. He himself would love to have a nice little breakdown, to use that word, though frankly he'd prefer to call it a fix-up, but he suffered from an embarrassing case of perfect health, he couldn't even manage to catch a cold, something must be wrong with him.

Wolf reached under his chair, brought up a pack of cigarettes, and held it out to me with raised eyebrows. He shrugged, thrust one into his mouth, and lit up. "It all depends on how you define health," he said. He drew the smoke deep into his lungs and, raising his chin so that his face was nearly horizontal, blew a slow stream of smoke toward the ceiling. When he was done he raised a shade, opened the window, and made little brushing motions with his hands toward the screen. He blew at the screen with short quick bursts of breath. He closed the window, lowered the shade, and turned to face me, leaning back against the window frame with his hands in his pockets and his ankles crossed.

"Do you have a girlfriend?" he asked.

It wasn't a question I was expecting. "Yes and no," I finally said.

"Brilliant answer," he said, with his slow lazy smile. He pushed with his shoulders against the window frame and stood up. "Shall we?" He nodded toward the door.

I followed him up the wooden steps into the sun-streaked dark attic. In the little hall he whispered, "She's expecting you." At the last door he knocked with his hand held sideways, using a single knuckle. He opened the door—in the dim light of the hall I caught sight of the edge of a bureau with a shadowy hairbrush on top—and a moment later I was in utter darkness. He led me to the high-backed chair, and as I sat upright against the stiff back and gripped the chair arms I felt like the wooden carving of a king.

"Welcome, stranger," the voice said. It seemed to be coming from a few feet away, as if from someone sitting up in bed. "What brings you to these parts?" I had the feeling that Wolf was staring at me in the dark.

"I was looking for the post office," I said.

"This here's the 'lectric company, mister," Isabel said.

The black room, the stiff chair, the word "'lectric," the sense that I was being tested in some way, all this made me break into a sharp, nervous laugh.

I could feel Wolf rising from his chair. "I'll be in my room. Just ring if you need anything." I heard his footsteps on the rug. The door opened and closed quickly.

"Did he say 'ring'?"

"I've got a bell."

"Oh—your Isa-bell."

"Do you always make jokes?"

"Only in the dark."

"And when it gets light?"

"Dead serious."

"Lucky it's dark. Let's play a game."

"In the dark?"

"You'll see."

I tried to imagine some mad game of Monopoly in which you had to select your piece by touch, trying to distinguish the ship from the car, then roll the dice across an invisible board and carefully feel their smooth sides to find the slightly recessed dots. I was wondering how I might contrive to move my piece along an unseen board when I felt something soft against my fingers and snatched my hand away.

"Here," Isabel said. "Tell me what it is. You can only use one hand."

I reached out my hand and felt a soft pressure against the palm. I closed my fingers over something furry or fuzzy and roundish, with a hardness under the fur. On one side the fur gave way to a smoothness of cloth. It felt familiar, this roundish furryish thing about the size of my palm, but though I kept turning it over and stroking it with my thumb, I couldn't figure it out.

"Give up?" she said. "Actually, I should have told you—it's part of something."

"Is it part of a stuffed animal?"

"Well, no. Close. Actually—you'll kill me—it's an earmuff. It came off that metal thing that goes over your head."

She next passed me an object that was hard and thin and cool, which immediately shaped itself against my fingers as a teaspoon.

"That was way too easy," I said.

"Well, I felt guilty. Try this one."

It was small and curved, with a clip of some sort attached to it, and suddenly I knew: a barrette. There followed a hard leathery object that was easy—an eyeglass case—and then a mysterious cloth strip with tassels that turned out to be a bookmark, and then a papery spongy object with a string attached that I triumphantly identified as a teabag. Once, as she passed me a small glass object, I felt against the underside of my fingers the light pressure of her fingertips. And once, after a pause in which I heard sounds as of shifting cloth, she let fall into my outstretched hand a longish piece of fabric that she immediately snatched away, saying, "That wasn't fair," bursting into a laugh at my protest, and refusing to identify it, even as I imagined her slipping back into a shirt or pajama top.

After the touching game she asked me to describe my room. I told her about my bookcase, my armchair with the sagging cushion, and my wall lamp that could be pulled out on a fold-up metal contraption, but she kept asking for more details. "I can't see anything," she said, sounding exasperated. I tried to make her see the X-shaped crosspieces of the unfolding wall lamp over my bed, and then I described, with fanatical care, the six-sided quartz crystal, the pale purple fluorite crystal in the shape of a tetrahedron, and the amethyst geode in my mineral collection. When it was her turn, she described a cherrywood box on her desk, with four compartments. One held a small pouch of blue felt tied with leather thongs and containing a silver dollar and an Indian-head penny, the second held a pair of short red-handled scissors, the third a set of tortoiseshell barrettes, and the fourth a small yellowish ivory figurine, a Chinaman seated with his legs crossed and holding an open book in his lap. One of the man's hands was broken off at the wrist, he wore a broad-brimmed conical hat, the ivory pages of the book were wavy—and as she described the ivory Chinaman in the compartment of the cherrywood box, I seemed to see, taking shape in the darkness, a faint and tremulous Chinaman hovering at the height of my head.

We were playing Ghost when I was startled by a knock at the door. Quickly the door opened and closed; I was aware of a momentary change in the quality of blackness but saw nothing. "It's nearly five thirty," Wolf said; he knew I was expected home by six. "See you, stranger," Isabel said as Wolf led me toward the door. Downstairs I greeted his mother, who was standing in the living room with her arms reaching up to the top of a drooping curtain. When she turned to look at me, keeping one hand on the curtain and waving the fingers of her other hand, I saw that her mouth was full of safety pins.

I now began to visit Wolf's house after school on Tuesdays and Thursdays, when I was free of the library, and on weekend afternoons. I would climb the stairs to Wolf's room, where we talked for a while, and then he would rise from the chair or bed very slowly, as if he were being tugged back by a tremendous force, and lead me up to the attic.

At the door of Isabel's room he knocked with one knuckle, lightly, twice. Without waiting for a reply, he held open the door and closed it quickly behind me before returning to his room. If he cared that I was spending less time with him than with his sister, he never showed it. If anything, he seemed eager for me to visit her—it was as if he thought I might cure her in some way. Exactly what it all meant I didn't know, couldn't care. I knew only that I needed to visit Isabel, to be with her in that room. The darkness excited me—I could feel it seize me and draw me in. Everything in me seemed to quicken there.

The darkness, the hidden face, the secret room, the unseeing of Isabel—it all soon came to feel as much a part of her as her voice. If I tried to picture her, I saw a wavering shadowy image that hardened gradually into a tall girl in Bermuda shorts, holding a trowel. Sometimes, before she faded away, I saw gray, amused eyes—Wolf's eyes. She loved games, all sorts of games, and it occurred to me that one thing we were doing in that room was playing the game of darkness. She was like a child who closes her eyes, stretches out her arms, and pretends to be blind. For all I knew, she might really be blind—she might really be anything. Whatever she was, I had to go there, to the dark at the top of the house.

In one of our kitchen drawers, the one to the right of the silverware drawer, there were two flashlights, a regular one and a very small one, the size of a fountain pen. One day not long after my first visit, I slipped the small flashlight into my pocket and carried it with me into the darkness of Isabel's room. My plan was to take it out during one of our games, fiddle with it, and shine it suddenly and briefly, as if by accident, at Isabel. She would spring into existence—at last!—if only for a second, before vanishing into the hidden world. I would apologize and we would continue as before.

As I sat in the stiff chair, holding the little flashlight and listening to Isabel tell me about a new word game she'd invented, I kept waiting for the right moment. I could hear her shifting in the bed—I imagined her moving her arms about as she talked. Then I imagined her sleeves, perhaps pajama sleeves, slipping back along her gesturing forearms. At that instant my desire to see her, to strip her of darkness, became so ferocious that I raised my fingertips to my throat and felt the thudding of my blood. I imagined her startled eyes, brilliant with fear. It seemed to me that to shine the light at Isabel, to expose her to my greedy gaze, would be like tearing off her clothes. With a feeling of shame, of sorrow, and of something that felt like gratitude, I returned the light to my pocket.

On the way home I thought: What attracts you is the darkness, the existence of an unseen, mysterious world. Why do you want to destroy that world?

Meanwhile, in the unmysterious world outside Wolfland, I burst out laughing in the cafeteria, raised my hand in American history, banged my locker shut. I shelved books in the library, drank cherry Cokes at Lucy's Luncheonette, and went miniature golfing on Friday nights with Ray and Dennis, while cars rolled by on the Post Road with their windows open and tough-looking boys with slicked-back hair slapped their hands on car tops to blasts of rock 'n' roll. At every moment I felt haunted by Isabel, but at the same time I had trouble remembering her exactly, in the world outside her room. The sunny world kept threatening to make a ghost of her, or to erase her entirely, and I began to look forward to the coming of night, when she grew more vivid in my mind.

One Saturday morning as I was walking in town, on my way to buy a birthday card for a girl in my French class, I was shocked to see Isabel strolling out of Mancini's drugstore. Her dark hair, cut short, was held back by a glossy barrette, and her short-sleeved white blouse was tucked into her jeans, which were rolled up to midcalf. A navy blue pocketbook, slung over her left shoulder, kept bumping against her right hip. Although I knew that it couldn't possibly be Isabel, that I had allowed a scattering of details, which must have been collecting in my mind, to attach themselves to this stranger strolling out of Mancini's drugstore, still my heart beat hard, my breath came quick, and not until later that afternoon, when I climbed the wooden stairs, did I grow calm in the rich blackness of Isabel's chamber.

Sometimes when I sat with her in the dark I wondered whether she was deformed in some way. I imagined a twisted mouth, a smashed nose, a mulberry birthmark spreading like a stain across her face. As a ghost swarm of ugly Isabels rose in my mind, I felt repelled not so much by the images as by something in myself that was creating them, and as if in protest another kind of Isabel began to appear, blue-eyed

Isabels and smiling Isabels, Isabels in red shorts, Isabels in faded jeans with a dark blue patch in back where a pocket had torn off, Isabels in white bathing suits wiping their glistening arms with beach towels, until my brain was so filled with false Isabels that I pressed my hands against the sides of my head, as if to crush them to death.

One night I thought: The blackness is a poison that soaks into my skin and makes me insane. During these seizures I have delusions that I call Isabel. The thought interested me, excited me, as if I had found the solution to a difficult problem in trigonometry, but as the night wore on, the idea grew less and less interesting until it left me feeling bored and indifferent.

One afternoon as we were playing the game of objects, Isabel said, "Now hold out your hand palm up, this is a tricky one." I was instantly alert; something in her voice betrayed a secret excitement. Holding out my hand as she had instructed, I heard some movement on the bed. A moment later I felt a softly hard, heavyish object lowered slowly onto my palm. A confusion came over me, I began to close my fingers over it, suddenly there was a wild laugh near my ear and she snatched the strange object away, crying, "Couldn't you guess? Couldn't you guess?" but I had already recognized, lying for a moment in the palm of my hand, Isabel's warm forearm.

As the evenings became hotter I found it difficult to sit at my desk doing homework in the light of my twin-bulb fluorescent lamp. I had always found it pleasing and even soothing to complete homework assignments: the carefully numbered answers, the crisp sound of turned pages, the red and yellow and green index tabs, the clean white notebook paper with its orderly rows of blue lines and the pale red line running down the side. Now it all irritated me, as if I were being distracted from the real business of life. Through the screens of my partly open windows I could hear the sounds of my neighborhood at dusk: low voices in a nearby yard, the rising and falling hum of a distant lawn mower, dishes clinking from an open window, the slam of a car door, a girl's high laughter. I began memorizing the sounds and collecting new ones so that I could report them to Isabel: footsteps in another room, which might be my father going into the kitchen for a box of crackers or my mother coming in from the back porch; the sound of a garage door being lowered; the wheels of a passing bicycle rustling in the sand at the side of the street. The sounds pleased me, because I could bring them to Isabel, but at the same time they disturbed me, for it was as if the world that separated me from Isabel were growing thicker and more impenetrable as I listened.

At night I kept waking up and falling asleep, as Isabels tumbled through my mind. In the mornings I felt sluggish and heavy-headed, and sometimes during the day I would catch my mother looking at me in the way she did when I was coming down with something.

One afternoon toward the middle of June, Isabel seemed a little distracted. It was hot in the attic room and the darkness seemed thick and soft, like fur. I could hear her shifting about on the bed, and then I heard another sound, as of fingers stroking cloth, but silkier. "What are you doing, Isabel?" "Oh, brushing my hair." I imagined the brush I had half glimpsed on the bureau as it pulled its way through stretched-out hair that kept changing from dark to blond to reddish brown. I heard the clunk of what I thought must be a brush on a table and suddenly she said, "Would you like to see my room?" My hands clutched the arms of the chair—I imagined a burst of light, like a blow to my forehead. Isabel laughed; her laughter sounded cruel; I knew nothing about this girl in the dark, who was suddenly going to reveal herself to me in some violent way; I could feel an Isabel rising in my mind, but her head was the head of some girl in my English class, which faded away and was replaced by another head; something touched my arm. "Get up," her voice said, very close to me.

Holding my wrist in her hand, she led me through the dark and placed my hand on cool wood surfaces, roundish knobs, soft protuberances, velvety edges. Images of drawers and padded seats and velvet jewel boxes floated in my mind. After a while I felt against my palm the familiar back of my upholstered chair with its row of metal buttons. "Is the tour over, Isabel?" "One more item of interest." She took a step and, still holding my wrist, placed my hand on a rumpled softness that felt like a sheet. "Tour over," she said, and released my wrist. I heard a creak, a rustling, silence.

"So how do you like my room?" she asked, in a voice that came from the other end of the bed.

"It's very—it's very—" I said, searching for the exact word.

"You probably ought to lie down, you know. If you're tired."

I climbed tensely onto the bed, pressing my knees into the mattress, and began crawling across it toward her voice. "Nnnn," I said, snatching my hand away as something moved out of reach. The bed seemed long, longer than the entire room, though I was moving so slowly that I was almost motionless. "Are you there?" I said to the dark. Isabel said nothing. I patted about: a pillow, another pillow, a sheet, a turned-back spread. "Where are you?" I asked the dark. "Here," she whispered, so close that I could feel her breath against my ear. I reached out and felt empty air. "I can't see you, Isabel." Deep in the room I heard a burst of laughter. "Can you fly, Isabel? Is that your secret?" I listened to the room. "Are you anywhere?" Still kneeling on the bed, but raising my upper body like a rearing horse, I swept out both hands, my fingertips fluttering about, stroking the dark. From the pillow and sheets came a fresh, slightly soapy scent. I lay down on my stomach, pressing my cheek into a pillow and inhaling the scent of Isabel. In the darkness I closed my eyes. Somewhere I heard a sound, as of a foot knocking against a piece of furniture. Then I felt a pushing-down in the mattress. Something hard pressed against the side of my arm. I felt the hardness with my fingertips and suddenly understood that I was touching a face. It pulled away. "Isabel," I said. "Isabel, Isabel, Isabel." Nothing was there. In the thick darkness I felt myself dissolving, turning into black mist, spreading into the farthest reaches of the room.

III

REVELATION

On a brilliant afternoon in July, under a sky so blue that it seemed to have weight, the beach towels on the sand reminded me of the rectangles of color in a child's paint box. Here and there a striped beach umbrella partly shaded a blanket, where an open cooler stood among yellow water wings and green sea monsters. On my orange towel, in the fierce sun, I leaned back on both elbows and stared off past my ankle bones at the place where the rippling dry sand changed to flat and wet. Low waves broke slowly in uneven lines. The water moved partway up the beach and slid back, leaving a dark shine that quickly vanished.

People were walking about, running in and out of the water. A tall girl with a blond ponytail and coppery glistening legs came walking along the wet sand. Her bathing suit was so white that it looked freshly painted. Her sticking-out breasts looked hard and sharp, like funnels. A small rubber football flew spinning through the bright blue air. In the sand a gull walked stiffly and half lifted its wings. Down in the shallow water a muscular senior in a tight bathing suit crouched on his hands and knees—suddenly another boy came running down the beach into the water, flung his hands onto the back of his kneeling friend, and flipped into the air, landing in the water with a splash. Tilted bottles of soda gleamed here and there in the sand beside beach towels, a girl in a turquoise-blue two-piece stood by the foot of the lifeguard stand, looking up and laughing, and high in the sky a yellow helicopter seemed stuck in the thick blue heavy summer air.

Laughing, whooping, running their hands through their wet hair, Ray and Dennis came striding toward me, kicking up bursts of sand. They picked up their towels and stood rubbing their chests and arms. Water streamed from their bathing suits.

"So guess who I ran into down by the jetty," Ray said, laying out his towel carefully in the sand. "Joyce. She said Vicky thinks you're mad at her." He threw himself facedown on the towel.

"I'm not mad at her. I just want—I just need—"

"Ah just *want*," Dennis said, holding up his hands as if he were gripping a guitar. "Ah just *need*." He strummed the guitar.

Summer had come, season of sweet loafing. I spent long hours lying on the beach, playing Ping-Pong in my shady garage, and reading on the screened back porch, where thin stripes of sun and shade fell across my book from the bamboo blinds. Even my job at the library seemed a lazy sort of half dreaming, as I wheeled my cart slowly between high dim shelves pierced by spears of sun. But as I lay on the beach running my fingers through the warm sand, as I bent over to retrieve a Ping-Pong ball from a cluster of broken-toothed rakes and smooth badminton poles rusting at the bottom, all the time I was waiting for Isabel. She slept until one or two in the afternoon. No one was allowed to visit her till the middle of the day. Wolf himself never rose before noon and seemed amused at what he called my peculiar habits. "The early bird catches the worm," he said, "but who wants the worm?" I found myself rising later and later in the morning, but there were always hours of sunshine to get through before I arrived in the dark.

"Up so soon?" my father said, glancing at me over the tops of his eyeglasses as he bent over his lunch in the sunny kitchen.

Sometimes, to pass the time, I took long drives with Ray and Dennis, when Dennis could borrow his mother's car. My plan had been to get my license as soon as school was out, but I woke each day feeling tired and kept putting it off. We would drive along the thruway until we saw the name of some little town we didn't know. Then we drove all over that town, passing through the business district with its brick bank trimmed in white and its glass-fronted barbershop with the slow-turning reflection of a striped pole before heading out to the country lanes with their lonely mailboxes and their low stone walls, and ended up having lunch at some diner where you could get twenty-two kinds of pancake and the maple syrup came in glass containers shaped like smiling bears. Dennis wore sunglasses and drove with one wrist resting on the wheel. In his lamp-lit room with the drawn shades, Wolf had told me how he'd taken the written test six months ago without once opening the boring manual. "And?" I asked. He smiled, raised a finger, and drew it across his throat.

And at last I made my way up the wooden stairs and disappeared in the dark. "Isabel," I would say, standing by the chair, "are you awake?" Or: "Isabel, are you there?" Sometimes I felt a touch on my arm and I would reach out, saying, "Isabel? Is that you?" as my hand grasped at air. Then I would hear her laughing quietly from the bed or across the room or just behind me or who knew where. She would say, "Welcome, stranger," or "Lo, the traveler returns," or nothing at all. Then I would make my way over to the bed and pat my way along the side and lie down, hoping for a fleeting touch, hoping she would be there.

I visited her every day. When I wasn't working at the library, I rode to her house at three in the afternoon; in Isabel's room I would forget the other world so completely that sometimes when I came downstairs I was startled to see the lamps in the living room glowing bright yellow. Through the front window I could see the porch light shining on black leaves. Then I would phone my parents with apologies and ride my bike home to a reheated dinner, while my mother looked at me with her worried expression and my father asked if I'd ever happened to hear of a clever little invention called the wristwatch. At night I could hear my mother and father talking about me in low voices, as if there were something wrong with me.

On the three afternoons a week I worked at the library, I would ride over to Wolf's house after dinner and not return until after midnight. Sometimes Wolf's mother, who liked to stay up late watching old movies on a little ten-inch television in the darkened living room, offered to drive me home. I would sit with her on the couch for a while, watching a snippet of black-and-white movie: an unshaven man in a rumpled suit stumbling along a dusty street in a Mexican town, a woman in a phone booth frantically dialing as she looked about in terror. Then I would load my bike into the trunk of the car and sit with Wolf's mother in front. On the way to my house, along dark streets that glowed now and then under the yellow light of a streetlamp, she would talk about Wolf: he'd failed three subjects, he was smart as a whip but had always hated school, she was worried about him, I was a good influence. Then with her long fingers she would light up a cigarette, and in the dark car streaked with passing lights I would see her eyes—Wolf's eyes—narrow against the upstreaming smoke.

At times it seemed to me that I inhabited two worlds: a sunny and boring day world that had nothing to do with Isabel, and a rich night world that was all Isabel. I soon saw that this division was false. The summer night itself, compared to Isabel's world, was a place of light: the yellow windows of houses, the glow of streetlamps, the porch lights, the headlights of passing cars, the ruby taillights, the white summer moon in the deep blue sky. No, the real division was between the visible world and that other world, where Isabel waited for me like a dark dream.

One afternoon as I stood by the chair I felt something press against my foot. "Isabel, is that you?" In the blackness I listened, then bent over the bed. I patted the covers and began crawling across, all the way to the pillows, but Isabel wasn't there. I heard a small laugh, which seemed to come from the floor. Carefully stepping from the bed I kneeled on the carpet, lifted the spread, and peered into blackness, as if I were looking for a cat. "Come on, Isabel," I said, "I know you're there," and reached my hand under. I felt something furry against my fingers and snatched my hand away. I heard a dim sound, the furry thing pressed into my arm—and closing my hand over it, I drew out from under the bed an object that wasn't a kitten. From the top of the bed Isabel said, "Did you find what you were looking for, David Dave?" but ignoring her I pressed the thick, furry slipper against my face.

Sometimes I tried to imagine her in the world of light. She lay next to me on the beach, on her own towel, with a thin line of sand in between—and though I could see, in my mind, that thin line of sand, and the ribbed white towel with a blue eyeglass case in one corner and a bottle of suntan lotion in another, though I could see a depression in the towel where she had kneeled, and a glitter of sand scattered across one corner, though I could see, or almost see, a wavering above the towel, a trembling of air, as if the atmosphere were thickening, I could not see Isabel.

But in the dark there was only Isabel. She would touch me and vanish—a laughing ghost. Sometimes, for an instant, my fingers grazed some part of her. She allowed me to lie down on the bed beside her but not to reach out. I could hear her breathing next to me, and along my side I could feel, like a faint exhalation, her nearby side, so close that my arm hairs bristled. These were the rules of the game, if it was a game—I didn't care, felt only a kind of feverish calm. I needed to be there, needed the dark, the games, the adventure, the kingdom of her room. I needed—I didn't know what. But it was as if I were more myself in that room than anywhere else. Outside, in the light, where everything stood revealed, I was somehow hidden away. In Isabel's dark domain, I lived inside out.

Meanwhile I was getting up later and later. One day after lunch my mother said to me, "You're looking tired, Davy. This friend of yours . . . Wouldn't it be better if you stayed home today?" And looking anxiously at me, she placed on my forehead the cool backs of her fingers.

"Don't," I said, jerking my head away.

One afternoon I found Isabel in the dark. Instead of walking to the right of my chair, as I usually did, I changed my mind at the last moment and walked to the left—and suddenly I stumbled against her, where she'd been crouching or lying, and I fell. I disentangled myself in a great flailing rush, and as I did so I felt for an instant, against my ribs, a slippery silky material that slid over something soft that suddenly vanished.

Because she had asked me about the beach, I began to bring her things: a smooth stone, a mussel shell, the claw of a small crab. I collected impressions for her, too, like the dark shine of the sand as the waves slid back, or the tilted bottles of soda beside the beach towels. The soda itself looked tilted, against the slanted glass, but was actually level with the sand. She always wanted to see more—the exact shape of a wave, the pattern of footprints in a sandbar—and I felt myself becoming a connoisseur of sensations, an artist of the world of light.

But what I longed for was the dark room, the realm, the mystery of Isabel-land. There, the other world dissolved in a solution of black. There, all was pleasure, strangeness, and a kind of sensual promise that drifted in the air like a dark perfume.

"Do you know what this is?" she said. "One hand. Come on. Guess."

In my palm I felt a soft, slinky thing, which filled my hand slowly, as if lowered from a height.

"Is it a scarf?" I said, rubbing it with my thumb as it spilled over the sides of my hand.

"A scarf!" she said, bursting into wild laughter.

One day Dennis said to me, "So what's with you and Vicky?" We were sitting on my front steps, watching people on the way to the beach, with their towels and radios.

"Nothing's with me and Vicky."

"Okay, okay," he said. "Jesus."

Sometimes I had the sense that Isabel was revealing herself to me slowly, like a gradually materializing phantom, according to a plan that eluded me. If I waited patiently, it would all become clear, as if things were moving toward some larger revelation.

"You're so good for me," she said, whispering near my ear. I felt her hand squeeze my hand. In the dark I smelled a faint soapy scent and a more tangy, fleshy odor. When I reached out I felt her pillow beside me, still warm from her head.

On the beach one day as I lay thinking of Isabel, I overheard a girl saying ". . . August already and he hasn't even sent me one single solitary . . ." Something about those words troubled me. As I pressed my chest and stomach against the hard-soft sand under my towel, trying to capture, for Isabel, the precise sensation of hard and soft, it came to me: what troubled me was the knowledge that time was passing, that it was already August—August, the second half of summer, August, the deceitful month. Still the hot days seem to stretch on and on, just as they did in July, but you know that instead of a new summer month shimmering in the distance, there's no longer any protection from September—and you can almost see, far off in the summery haze, the first breath clouds forming in the brisk autumn air.

It was about this time that I noticed a little change in Isabel. She was growing restless—or perhaps she was only searching for a new game. Now when I arrived she was almost never in bed, but was somewhere else in the room, standing or moving about. One afternoon when I entered the dark I could hear her in an unfamiliar place. "Where are you?" I said. "Over here. Be done in a sec." I heard a wooden sliding, a creak, a rustling, a slide and thump, as of a closed drawer. There was a ripply, cloth-y sound, a snap, more rustling. "There!" Isabel said. "You can come over now." I advanced slowly, holding out an arm. "Sorry!" I said, and snatched my hand away. "Fresh!" said Isabel. "So! How do you like it?" She seized my wrist and placed my hand on her upper arm and then for a moment on her hip. "It's a new dress," she said. "Stockings, too. Or scarves, according to *some* people." I heard scritch-scratchy sounds, as if she were rubbing her knees together. "So! Can you dance?" A hand grasped my hand and set it on her waist. On the fingers of my other hand I felt the grope of a closing hand. Fingers seized my waist. "*One* two three *one* two three!" she chanted as she began to waltz in the dark—and I, who had taken dance lessons in the eighth grade, led her round and round as she hummed the Viennese Waltz, till she smacked into something and cried, "Don't stop!"—and as I turned round and round in that room, knocking into things that fell over, I felt her hair tickling my face, I smelled a faint perfume that made me think of oboes and bassoons, I pressed my fingers against the hard, rippling small of her back as she hummed louder and louder and something went rolling across the room and burst against a wall.

Because the bed was almost always empty, I no longer hesitated by the chair. Instead I went straight past it and lay down on my back with my head on a pillow and waited for her to present herself. After a while she would greet me and sit down on the chair with her feet on the bed. Then she would talk to me about her plans for the future—she wanted to be a doctor, she wanted to help people, she wanted to travel—while I lay in the dark and tried to imagine Isabel stepping from an airplane, in some bright airport, somewhere.

It was during one of these afternoons in early August, when she sat in the chair with her bare feet resting near my lower leg, that she told me about an idea she'd been turning over in her mind. She'd been thinking about it, actually, for a long time, though she hadn't been ready to face it, really. But now, thanks to me, she felt she had the courage to do it. Of course, it wasn't the sort of thing you would just go ahead and do without giving it a whole lot of thought—you had to sort of sneak up on it, in your mind. And that's just what she'd been doing, over these last weeks, and it felt right, so right, it really did. And so, to make a long story short, or a short story long, she was going to break out of the dark—let in the light—before the month was over.

A moment later she said, "You're not saying anything."

I said, "Are you really sure you—"

"Absolutely," Isabel said.

Now whenever I entered she was full of plans. At first she'd thought to change things gradually—a dim candle at one end of the room, then on my next visit a lamp on the bed table, and finally the opened curtains—but the more she thought about it, the more she liked the idea of announcing the new era dramatically. A complete break—that was the way to go. And once the darkness was gone, why, she could do anything—anything. She felt it in her bones. She'd always wanted to learn how to play tennis, for example, and had foolishly put it off. She wanted to see people, do things. She missed her aunt in Maine. She and I could go rowing together—there must be lakes around here. We could go swimming at that beach of mine. And as I lay back against the pillows, listening to her as she sat on the chair with her legs on the bed, I could feel her kicking her heels in excitement.

One afternoon as I climbed the carpeted stairs, on my way to the wooden stairs that led to the attic, it struck me that I hadn't seen Wolf for quite some time. I had visited him occasionally, on the way to Isabel's room, but not for the past few weeks or so, and I felt a sudden desire to see him now. I knocked on his door with a single knuckle—two light raps—and after a pause I heard the word "Enter," uttered in a tone of mock solemnity.

I pushed open the door and saw in the mildly sunny room a big new desk against one wall. Wolf was sitting at it with his back to me, bent over a notebook. The shades had been replaced by white blinds, and through the open slats I saw sunstruck green leaves and bits of blue sky. The tall narrow bookcase was still there, fastened upright against the wall, but the stray piles of books were gone, in place of the sunken chair stood a red leather armchair with a red leather hassock, the room had an air of studious neatness.

Wolf turned to glance over his shoulder, and when he saw me he frowned and then slowly began to smile, while his frown gradually lessened without disappearing entirely. With a flourish he indicated the red leather armchair.

As I walked over to it, he jerked his thumb at the desk. "The new dispensation." He shrugged. "It's very interesting. They want me to do well in school, but they think I read too much. Books as the enemy. Hence our new friend here. I call him Fred." He patted the desk as if it were a big, friendly dog. "They think it's good for my—what was that word they used? Oh yes: character."

I sat down in the new chair, placing one leg on the hassock, while Wolf half rose and swung around in his wooden chair so that he straddled it, facing me. His crossed forearms rested on the back. On the bed I noticed a new plaid spread.

"And what have you been up to, David Dave?" he asked, looking at me with his air of amusement.

"Oh, you know. The library. Ping-Pong. Nothing much. You?"

He shrugged a single shoulder. "The salt mines." He nodded toward the desk. "Summer school. Punishment for dereliction of duty. Have I mentioned that I flunked three subjects? A family secret."

I lowered my eyes.

"And look at this neat little number." He swung an arm back to the desk and held up a booklet. "Driver's manual. From the Department of Motor Vehicles, with love." He tossed it back. "My father was very clear. Failure will no longer be tolerated." He shrugged again. "They think I'm a bad influence on myself." Wolf smiled. "They want me to be more like—well, like you."

"Me!"

"Sure, why not? Straight As, the good life, all that jazz. A solid citizen."

"They're wrong," I said quietly, and then: "Don't be like me!" It came out like a cry.

"If you say so," he said, after a pause.

We sat for a while in silence. I looked at the big pale desk, with its shiny black fluorescent light and its green blotter in a dark leatherish frame, at the new plaid bedspread, at the clean bright blinds. "Well then," I said, "I guess—" and rose to go. Wolf said nothing. At the door I turned to look back at him, and he gave me that slow lazy smile, with its little touch of mockery.

In the darkness of Isabel's chamber her plans were taking shape. The great event would take place on the last day of August, three days before the start of school. I lay on the bed remembering the first time I had entered the room; it seemed a long time ago. "Isabel," I said, "do you remember—" "Are you listening?" she said sharply, and for a moment I did not know what she was talking about.

One night I woke and saw Isabel very clearly. She was wearing white shorts and a bright red short-sleeved blouse. She was leaning back on both hands, with her legs stretched out and her face tilted back, her hair bound in a ponytail and her mouth radiantly smiling. Her face was vague, except for the smile, with its perfectly shaped small white teeth and its thin line of glistening pink between the bright teeth and the upper lip. I fell asleep, and when I woke again I saw the same image, sharp and bright, and understood instantly where it had come from: I saw the dentist's waiting room, the sunny glass table with the magazines, the glossy page advertising a special brand of toothpaste that whitened as it cleaned.

In the last days of August I had the sense of a distant brightness advancing, like an ancient army in a movie epic, the sun flashing on the polished helmets and on the tips of the upraised swords.

On the day before the final day, I said to Isabel, "Come over here." My voice startled me with its harshness, its tone of aggrieved authority. There was silence in the dark. Then I felt, in the mattress, the pressure of a form, as she climbed onto the bed and settled down beside me. "It'll be all right," she whispered. "You'll see." I could feel her like a heat along my side. My cheek itched, as if tickled by Isabel's hair or perhaps by ripples in the rumpled spread. My eyes were wide open. Images rose up and drifted away: a Chinaman reading a book, bursts of sunlight on shady clapboards, a gray jacket hanging on a hook.

On the morning of the last day of August I woke unusually early. Even my parents were still asleep. I drank a glass of orange juice in the bright kitchen, tried to read on the back porch, and at last decided to go to the beach. As I stepped onto the sand I was surprised to see a scattering of people standing about or lying on towels, and I wondered whether they were there because they had stayed all night. The tide was in. Over the water the sky was so blue that it reminded me of an expensive shirt I had seen in a department store. I laid out my towel, with my bottle of suntan lotion in one corner and my book in another, and then I set off on a walk along the wet sand by the low waves. Farther out the water solidified into patches of deep purplish blue and streaks of silver. In the shiny dark sand I saw my footprints, which stood out pale for a moment before the dark wetness soaked back. I tried to imagine a second pair of footprints walking beside mine, first pale and then dark, vanishing in the frilly-edged sheets of water thrown forward by the breaking waves. People were arriving at the beach, carrying towels and radios. Far up on the sand, a girl sat up, poured lotion into her hand, and began caressing her arm slowly, stretching it out and turning it back and forth. When I reached the jetty I walked out onto the rocks, sat for a while on the warm stone with my legs in the water, then swam out until I was tired. Back on my towel I lay down and felt the sun burning off the water drops. A girl from my French class waved to me and I waved back. Families with beach umbrellas were coming over the crest of sand by the parking lot. The beach was filling up.

I arrived at Isabel's house toward three in the afternoon. At the door Wolf's mother appeared in green shorts and a yellow halter, with a pocketbook over her shoulder and car keys hanging from her hand. "Go on in," she said, "I'm in a rush," and hurried down the steps. In the driveway she turned and called, "John's out. She's expecting you." I passed through the cool dim living room, climbed the carpeted steps to the second floor, and looked at the familiar hall with its closed doors before climbing into the attic. At the top of the stairs I passed through the sun-striped darkness into the second hall and quietly entered Isabel's chamber.

"Oh there you are," she said, with a mixture of impatience and excitement.

"I went to the beach," I said, looking around at the dark. Parts of it were more familiar than others—the part that held the chair, the part that held the bed—and I wondered if I could memorize the different parts by concentrating my attention.

"I'm very excited!" cried Isabel, and I heard her do a little dance step on the carpet.

Slowly I walked over to the bed and lay down.

"What are you doing, what are you doing?" Isabel said, stamping her foot.

"Doing? Just lying here, Isabel, thinking how peaceful it is. You know, I went for a swim this morning and I'm—"

"You're such a tease!" she cried. "You can't just lie there," she said, much closer, and I felt a tug at my sleeve. "You have to get up."

"Isabel, listen. Do you really—"

"Oh what are you talking about? Come on! Come on!" She tugged again and I followed her into the dark. I could feel her excitement like a wind. She drew me across the room and abruptly stopped. I could hear her patting the curtains, groping for the drawstrings. The curtains sounded thick and softly solid, like the side of an immense animal. I imagined the brilliant light outside, raised like a sword. "There!" Isabel said. I heard her tugging, jerking stubbornly, moving her hand about, like a maddened bird trapped in the folds. Something gave way, the top of the curtains began to pull apart, sunlight burst through like a shout, for an instant I saw the slowly separating dark blue folds, a swirl of glowing golden dust, an edge of raised sleeve, before I flung a hand over my eyes. Thrusting out the other hand, I made my way blindly across the room toward the door as she shouted, "Hey, where're you—" Behind me I heard the curtains scraping back; through my fingers I could feel the room filling with light as if a fire had broken out. I pulled open the door and did not look back. As I fled through the attic and down the first flight of stairs, I saw, beyond the edge of my vision, in that instant before I covered my eyes with my hand, a raised reddish sleeve with a slight sheen to it, slipping down along a ghostly shimmer of sunlit forearm, vague as an agitation of air. At the bottom of the second stairway I waved to Wolf's mother, who turned out to be a jacket on the back of a shadowy chair, hurried through the living room, and escaped through the front door. Only when my bicycle was speeding down the curving drive between the high fence and the hedge did I turn to look back at the house, forgetting that, from this angle, I could see only the pines, the maples, the sunny and shady driveway turning out of sight.

:::

School began three days later. Wolf was in none of my classes and I couldn't find him in the halls. I had never called his house before—somehow our friendship had nothing to do with telephones—but that afternoon I dialed his number. The phone rang fourteen times before I hung up. I imagined the house in ruins, ravaged by sunlight. I looked for Wolf in school the next day, but he wasn't there. No one knew anything about him. That afternoon after school I called in sick at the library and rode over to Wolf's house on my bike. At the top of the curving drive it was still standing there, in shade broken by brilliant points of light. Wolf's mother, wearing jeans and a sweatshirt and holding a pair of pliers in one hand, answered the door. In the darkish living room she sat on the couch and I sat in an armchair, holding a glass of iced tea that I forgot to drink, as she told me that Wolf was attending a special boarding school in Massachusetts. Hadn't he mentioned it? A liberal curriculum—a very liberal curriculum. As for Isabel, she'd gone to live for a while with her aunt in Maine, where she spent her summers and where she was now attending the public high school. Her year off had done her a world of good. Wolf's mother thanked me for being so nice to Isabel during her convalescence. At the front door she looked at me fondly. "Thank you for everything, David," she said, and reached out her hand. She gave my hand a vigorous shake and stood watching me from the doorway as I rode off on my bike.

That fall I threw myself into my classes, but all I could think of was the room in the attic. It was as if I were missing some part of myself that I had to have but couldn't find anywhere. In mid-October I got my driver's license and began driving around on the weekends in my father's car. I took up with my semiofficial girlfriend and went to dances and football games. One Saturday afternoon I drove into Wolf's neighborhood, but though I slowed down at his driveway, with its scattering of yellow leaves, I passed it without going in. Often I wondered what would have happened if I had turned to look at her, the day the curtains parted. And I saw it clearly: the sun-filled air, the dust swirling in shafts of light, the bright empty room. No, far better to have turned away, to have understood that, for me, Isabel existed only in the dark. Like a ghost at dawn—like the princess of a magic realm—she had to vanish at the first touch of light. So I drove around in my father's car, waiting for something that never came. By spring of senior year I was caught up in so many things that I had trouble remembering what had happened, exactly, in that dark room, in that vague house, on that winding road on the other side of town. Only now and then an image would rise up out of nowhere and make me thoughtful for a while—an ivory Chinaman bent over his book, a furry earmuff, and that slow, lazy smile, with its little touch of mockery.

MAKE BELIEVE

...
...

Nicholas Montemarano

THE DOCTOR PUSHED the needle into my hip, and a few minutes later—the tranquilizer already turning my brain soft—I was in a field of high grass I could see and hear breathing. I kept going in and out. The doctor's body seemed tall and skinny, warped as in a fun-house mirror. My girlfriend, next to him, moved her mouth in slow motion, but made no sound. I recognized her as someone other than my girlfriend, someone I'd known in another life, someone who had been important to me—my wife or sister or daughter, or someone I had murdered or who had murdered me—and I wanted to tell her this, it was so clear to me, we'd known each other for eons, but I couldn't speak. I reached out and touched her hand, but when I looked again, my arm was at my side, it hadn't moved. I tried to wiggle my finger but couldn't. I closed my eyes and lay in the field of grass and breathed with it, and this was all I'd have to do for eternity. I woke with my face against a cold cab window, then Alex helped me through the rain and into her bed, where a few hours earlier I had fake-raped her at her request.

When she had come home earlier that evening, I was waiting for her in her bedroom closet. She'd asked me to use a knife, but I was much too afraid of an accident, so I bought a plastic knife and hoped that would be good enough. We hadn't planned when or how—she left that up to me—and so when I came out of her closet and put my arm around her neck, she truly was frightened: she dropped her keys and purse and screamed. I put my hand over her mouth and whispered into her ear that I was going to rape her and would kill her if she didn't do exactly what I told her to do. I said she should nod if she understood, and she did. I knew I would have a tough time going through with this if I had to look at her face, so I made her lie on her stomach. I pushed her face into a pillow to muffle her crying. Eventually she was quiet, but I was afraid she wasn't breathing, so I turned her over. I didn't want her to look at me—she really did seem frightened—so I pressed the knife against her neck and told her to close her eyes. "If you open your eyes, I'll kill you," I said, but I don't know what I would have done had she opened them.

I kept my eyes closed too, except when I pulled her hair or slapped her face—never to hurt but rather to give the impression of hurting—and when it was over I told her not to move until an hour after I was gone, and if she got up to call the police I might be waiting outside her door, and I'd come back in and this time . . . but I couldn't finish this sentence because I was sure I was having a heart attack. I stood beside the bed, trying to breathe deeply and slowly, but my heart was beating so rapidly I thought it was going to seize, and the pressure in the center of my chest was so severe I couldn't speak, but I must have been making some sound, quick shallow breaths, and Alex turned around and saw that I wasn't acting. She gave me one of her Valium, and a few minutes later I asked for another. We waited, me on the floor now, her rubbing my back, telling me it was going to be okay, I didn't do anything wrong, she wasn't hurt, it was all make-believe, but nothing she did or said could slow my heart. She took me downstairs—I think she forgot to put on her underwear, forgot to lock her door—and we took a cab to the emergency room, where they asked me, and then Alex, if I was on drugs.

:::

We had met at work, but not the way most people meet at work. I took a job caring for a man with cerebral palsy—cooking for him, doing his laundry, feeding him, bathing him, helping him use the bathroom, helping him do everything a person needs to do to live. My first day on the job a young woman, tall and thin and with wonderfully crooked teeth, came to the man's house to ask for her final check. She kept touching her nose ring and couldn't stand still—she was shifting her weight from one leg to the other in a kind of rocking motion that lulled me into staring at her. Henry, the man I took care of, told her she had to leave, that there was a restraining order, and that she couldn't have her last check because she had stolen some of his pills. "I need those pills so I don't shake as much," he said, "and you stole them from me."

"We've been through this," she said. "I never touched your pills except to give them to you. I'm very sorry you feel the way you do."

"I don't have any check," he said. "I'm not your boss."

"This is total bullshit," she said.

I followed her out, Henry telling me all the while not to bother with her. "Don't listen to her," he said. "She's trouble."

Outside, I asked her if she was okay, if there was anything I could do, by which I meant: Don't go yet. I want to look at you. You remind me of . . .

"Why are you staring at me like that?"

"I'm sorry."

"I'm very tall for a woman, I know."

"It's not that," I said. "Listen, if you don't mind my asking, why were you fired?"

"I took one of his pills," she said. "But it's not what you think. I have my own prescription, so the way I see it, I wasn't really stealing."

"They just hired me, so I guess I'm your replacement."

"You won't last six months," she said.

"Six months," I said. "I was thinking a few weeks, until I find something else."

"Aren't you going to ask me why I take Valium?"

"I wasn't going to ask," I said. "It's none of my business."

She took out a pen and asked me to write my number on her arm. "I'm going to call you and we're going to become friends," she said. "We're going to have an adventure. Is that okay with you?"

"I'm not the adventurous type," I said.

"But you are," she said. "I can always tell."

:::

She invited me over to her apartment, a large high-ceilinged room divided into sections by shoji screens—a twin bed and dresser in one section, a sofa and two high-backed Victorian chairs in another, a desk and drawing table in another. She made lamb chops, and when I told her I didn't eat meat she tried to bait me into eating some. "Come on," she said, holding the meat near my mouth. "I want to see you have a bite, just a nibble. Just to prove that you're not afraid of anything."

"But I *am* afraid of some things."

"Are you afraid of me?"

"No. You have a scar on your wrist."

"Well," she said. "You have a big nose."

"I'm sorry I said that."

"Don't be," she said. "I was seventeen, it was stupid."

"I'm still sorry."

"Stop saying you're sorry."

"Okay," I said.

"Actually, I lied," she said. "It was last year. But I'm fine now, I want to live. Now it's your job to change the subject."

"How can you afford a place like this, wiping asses for a living?"

"I don't wipe asses for a living, *you* do."

"Seriously," I said.

"My parents died and left me a lot of money."

"I'm sorry."

"You're not supposed to say that."

"Well, I *am*."

"You say 'I'm sorry' way too much," she said. "You must feel guilty about something. Did you run over a dog?"

"How's this?" I said. "I regret the unfortunate passing of your parents."

"Don't," she said. "I'm rich."

"Did you not like them?"

"I stopped liking them for a while," she said, "but by the time they died, I liked them again."

"Did they die together?"

"Nothing dramatic like a car accident or plane crash. Something much more romantic. They both got cancer and died within a few days of each other."

"That's romantic?"

"Of course!" she said. "My God! How can you *not* think that's— Come here," she said, and when I did, she kissed me. She stopped kissing me only to say, "Do you see? Do you see what I mean?"

196 ::: NICHOLAS MONTEMARANO

"I'm not sure," I said, and she kissed me again, then pushed me onto her bed.

"I'm not a slut," she said. "I'm only having sex with you because I have great intuition and I know you're a good egg and would never hurt me."

"Okay," I said.

"Do you know that I'm not a slut?"

"Yes."

"And you wouldn't hurt me, right?"

"Right."

While we were having sex, she kept saying, "Like this," and she would move my hand, or we would switch positions. She had long, delicate toes, and her stomach was so flat, her hip bones so sharp, that I kept touching her there, but gently. "Don't be afraid," she said. "I won't break." At times it felt like she was trying to wrestle with me, and we found ourselves in positions it was impossible to have sex in: me hanging off the side of the bed, my back to her, or me sitting on her back, but facing away from her, so that all I could think to do was lean over and kiss her ankles and the bottoms of her feet. With someone else I might have stopped and laughed and said, "Hold on, hold on, what are we doing? We're not in the circus." But her face, when we faced each other, was serious, and she appeared to be straining more than anything—trying to climb over me or pull me over her, pushing me away when I came close, pulling me back when I moved away. When I was finally inside her it seemed to happen by accident: I was holding her down by her wrists, she was pushing up, and suddenly I felt it, and then we hardly moved at all, our hips grinding into each other in slow, deliberate movements that hurt. Near the end, she put my hand over her mouth and pressed, but eventually it wasn't her pressing, it was me, and the more she seemed to like it, the more I leaned into her, and then I grabbed her hair, and she seemed to like that, and then I pulled her hair, and we both liked this, and as she came close to finishing she began to hyperventilate, and I almost stopped, but didn't, and when it was over, she cried. When I asked her what was wrong, she said, "I knew you wouldn't hurt me."

:::

At work the next day, while I was pulling up his underwear, Henry said, "She's your girlfriend, isn't she?"

"Who?"

"I'm telling you, she's trouble."

I helped Henry put on the rest of his clothes, shaved him, wet and combed his hair, then put him in front of the TV. "If she's your girlfriend," he said, "how can I trust you? How do I know you won't start stealing pills for her?"

"She didn't steal any pills."

"Do you see what I mean? Already you're defending her!"

"You're not my father," I said, and he turned his chair away from me. For the next few hours he spoke only to tell me what to do: Change my shirt, get me some water, take me outside, get the mail, fold the laundry, I need to use the pot, give me a shower.

"She's not my girlfriend," I said.

"I can see it," he said. "It's too late. You're already lost."

"She's just a girl."

"She's very charming when she's not being crazy," he said. "She used to try to sweet-talk me. She'd show up an hour late, then bake me brownies."

"Maybe she was just being nice."

"One night, this guy showed up looking for her. A big guy, big like a football player. I saw him through the window. He was banging on the door, but spoke in a calm voice. 'I know you're in there,' he said. 'Don't make me angry. You're going to be in trouble if you don't come out.' His voice was very calm, it was creepy. I sat in my chair next to the door; she hid in the shower."

"So what," I said. "She had a crazy boyfriend."

"Good luck," he said.

:::

Alex and I spent most nights together at her place, which was fine with me—my studio was half the size of her apartment and didn't have hot water. I'd been showering every three days in cold water, a quick lather and rinse; I'd even shaved my head so my hair wouldn't get as itchy.

"You should walk on your lease," Alex said. "You can move in here and be my houseboy."

"What exactly does a houseboy do?"

"Whatever he's told to do," she said.

"I already have that job."

She cooked for me, and played garage rock, and sang loudly and terribly to me until her downstairs neighbor banged on his ceiling. She said things like "I have to be careful, I could fall in love with you," or "If we had kids, I'd want them to have your nose—it's a substantial nose, but it's beautiful." But every time we had sex she asked me to do or act out something hurtful. When she told me to hit her, I assumed she was asking me to spank her, so I smacked her ass, which was the only fleshy part of her body, but she said, "No, I want you to hit me in the face."

"I don't know," I said. "It doesn't feel right."

"Come on," she said. "It can't be wrong if I'm *asking* you to do it."

"I don't think I have it in me."

"Bullshit," she said. "You have plenty of anger in you. I've seen it."

"When?"

"When do you think?"

"I'm not an angry person."

"Like this," she said, then slapped my face.

"Jesus," I said. "That fucking hurt."

"If you don't slap me, I'll slap you again, next time harder."

"Have you thought about taking up boxing?"

The second time she slapped me, the noise sounded fake, the kind of noise they dub over slaps in movies. My face stung, and I was embarrassed; my instinct was to hit her back, but I didn't. Instead, I got on top of her, held down her arms, and said, "What the *fuck* are you doing?" She tried to kick me, so I put my knees on her thighs. "If you hit me one more time, I swear—"

"You swear what?" she said.

:::

After we had sex, she cried, and after she cried, she made us martinis, which we sipped in bed. She touched my face where she had smacked me, and told me she was sorry. "I don't want you to be afraid," she said.

"I don't want anyone to get hurt."

"Listen," she said. "I only want to feel good. Isn't that what we all want—to feel good, and to make others feel good?"

I put my hand around her wrist, the one with the scar. "I think I pulled out some of your hair."

"It'll grow back."

"I'm not a bad person," I said.

"No," she said. "But you're angry."

"Why do you like it that way?"

"Why do *you*?"

"I don't know."

"That's a beautiful answer," she said. "It's my favorite answer of all time. I don't know, you don't know, no one knows. And it doesn't matter, as long as we're happy." She put her lips against my ear and whispered, "Are you happy?"

I nodded yes.

"Do you love me?" she said.

"I don't know."

"You don't know what?"

"I don't know if I love you."

"You just said 'I love you.' I *knew* you did."

"Very funny," I said.

"I bet if I said 'I love you' into your ear enough times, and just the right way, I could get you to say it back to me."

She started whispering into my ear, so softly at first that I couldn't make out what she was saying, but then I heard "I love you" over and over, then, "Say it, say it, come on, you can say it for me," and then the phone rang.

Her machine picked up, there was a pause, and then a man's voice. Alex kept her lips near my ear, but stopped whispering. The man was crying, or had been. "I know you're there," he said. "Please pick up the phone." His voice was calm, the way Henry had described the voice of Alex's ex-boyfriend the night he came looking for her. He said, "I've been feeling sick. We need to see each other." Alex got out of bed and stood near the phone, and for a moment I thought she was going to pick up. "Alex," he said. "Do you have someone there? If you have someone there, I want you to . . . Please pick up the phone."

A few seconds after he hung up, before either of us had a chance to say anything, the phone rang again. The machine picked up, and the same man said, "I know you're there. Do you think for one second that I don't know you're there. I can see you. Remember, I can always see you. Your hand is on the phone and you're listening to me . . ."

The third time he called, he said, "I'm going to keep calling until you pick up. Your phone is going to ring all night. You can unplug the phone, but as soon as you plug it in again, it's going to ring."

For the next few minutes the phone kept ringing—four rings, a pause, four more rings—but Alex didn't move away from the phone, probably because she was deciding what she wanted to tell me: the truth or a lie or a combination of the two.

"Are you going to unplug the phone?" I said. "Or would you rather your houseboy do it for you?"

"I would rather my houseboy do it."

"Well, the houseboy would rather you do it."

"I don't think I can."

"It's quite easy," I said. "You grab the cord and pull."

The phone rang again, and this time the machine picked up. There was a long silence, and I found myself afraid to speak, as if her ex-boyfriend could hear *us*. I surprised myself by picking up the phone, but as soon as I heard his voice I realized that my bravado was akin to yelling at someone as you drive by in your car. He said, "Alex? Alex? . . . Okay, you don't need to say anything. You've taken the first step, which is picking up the phone. Now, listen carefully. What you're going to do is take a cab to my place. You're going to do this immediately, do you hear me? . . . Do you remember the last time we had to do this—how easy it was? It's going to be that easy. Can you say yes if you understand? . . . Alex, if you're not here within twenty minutes, I'm going to come there, and if I have to come there, I'm going to be very disappointed, and you don't want me—"

I put down the phone, then pulled out the cord. "I'm going to leave now," I said. "If you want to come with me, you're more than welcome. But I'd rather not get involved with something I know nothing about."

"I don't know what to do," she said. "Tell me what to do."

"That's not part of the houseboy's job."

Only after I'd opened the door did she say, "Okay, wait, wait. I'll come with you. Let me leave a note on the door, just so he . . . no, fuck it, okay, this is crazy, I'm coming."

:::

This was the first time anyone had been to my apartment in the year I'd been living there. My sister had lived there before she died, sometimes with two or three people, usually her boyfriend and his friends, all of them so high they mostly sat around staring at the walls, nodding off. My sister didn't use heroin until she realized it was the only way she'd be able to stay in her boyfriend's life. They both OD'd in this apartment on the same night; she died, he almost did, then he found God and became a motivational speaker. I went to one of his seminars about a year after my sister died, prepared to stand up and expose him, but I sat there and listened to what he had to say, most of which made sense, I had to admit, even though I hated him—I'd hated him from the moment I met him—and what would I have exposed anyway that he hadn't already exposed? His entire seminar was built upon his addiction and recovery. He probably would have invited me up onstage; he probably would have hugged me, would have asked my forgiveness, whatever step that is, this guy who killed my sister, now with his Jesus hair and beard, his hemp shoes, beads around his wrists, his neck. But he didn't make my sister do anything—even he said that in his seminar: *No one can make you do anything. You are responsible for your own actions. There's no one else to blame. You have to let the past die. The only moment that exists is the present. In every moment you're born again.* All these maudlin truisms were in fact true—at least he convinced me that they were—but I hated that they came from his mouth, and if my sister *was* to blame, well, then there was hate for her too.

It was unnerving to have another person in such a small space now, especially the room in which my sister had died.

"Wow," Alex said. "You weren't kidding when you called your apartment modest."

I sat on the mattress on the floor, the only piece of furniture in the room, if you consider a mattress furniture, which I suppose it's not. Until a month earlier, I'd had a desk—actually, an old kitchen table I used as a desk—but the legs had broken, and I didn't own a screwdriver or a hammer or any tool one might use to fix anything broken, so I threw out the legs, and for several weeks I'd been sitting on the floor, Indian-style, hunched over the tabletop to write letters to old friends from graduate school, making up excuses about why I'd dropped out. I told them I didn't really want to go into social work, which was only part of the truth. Another part was that my sister had died, which they all knew about. The rest of the truth was that I didn't believe you could help or save certain people, no matter what you did, and when I realized this I had a bit of a breakdown and began to have terrible dreams, and even during my waking hours I found myself imagining the worst kinds of violence: walking down the street, often just to be outside after too many days in, I would imagine strangers punching or stabbing or shooting me, or I'd become certain that something was about to fall on me, a brick or a chunk of ice or a plane or sometimes nothing specific, an invisible weight, the air itself, and I remember my surprise when nothing happened, when people walked past without looking at me, or when I looked up and saw only trees, the sides of buildings, clouds. And so, no longer in school, and with no job, I decided to move into my sister's old apartment on Avenue B—I'd been renting it since she died, even though I was in graduate school in Philadelphia. It was five hundred dollars a month, and my unused student loans covered the first ten months, most of which I don't remember, and when I ran out of money I got the job taking care of Henry. It appealed to me because I wasn't expected to save him—I couldn't make him walk, couldn't make him stop shaking—but, rather, all I had to do was feed him and dress him and keep his ass clean, and if that sounds unduly bitter or cold or dramatic, it's probably all three.

"Why do you live here?" Alex asked me.

"It's cheap," I said. "Besides, I don't know how long I want to stay in New York. I think I want to live in the woods or something. Get a dog, live off berries and grubs."

"You really do need to be my houseboy." She sat next to me on the mattress, then put her head in my lap. She lifted my shirt and started kissing my stomach.

"It would be a gross understatement to say that I'm not in the mood," I said.

"Did you just call me gross?"

"Don't joke," I said. "Nothing's funny right now."

She smiled dumbly and pitter-pattered her fingers against her bucked teeth like a crazy person. I could feel another me beneath the numb me who, once he started laughing, might laugh all the way into a straitjacket, but I didn't want to give Alex the satisfaction—I felt, at that moment, a strange certainty that this woman would take everything from me, that she could get me to do anything for her, so I didn't smile.

"Knock it off," I said.

"Okay," she said. "I'm sorry."

"I'm waiting for you to speak."

"We were living together for about a year," she said. "It was a very volatile relationship—you know, the unhealthy love/hate thing—and eventually I left him, but I went back, then I left him again, then I went back, then my friends came and got me and moved me out."

"So you didn't even leave him on your own?"

"I left him twice on my own."

"Did he hurt you?"

"We hurt each other," she said.

"I mean, did he physically hurt you?"

"Are you hatching a theory?" she said. "Because it sounds like you're trying to hatch a theory."

"My theory is that I don't know you."

"You know me," she said. "You knew me the moment you met me. People are drawn to each other for a reason."

"Are you talking about me and you, or you and him?"

"Both," she said. "I'm talking about everyone. We know what we're doing way more than we'd like to believe. When people get out of fucked-up relationships, they say, 'What was I thinking?' or 'I didn't know what I was doing,' but we always know what we're doing. On some level, I mean. Maybe in that part of our brains or souls we can't access, but we *do* know what we're doing."

"So what are we doing?"

"We're sitting on a mattress in what might be the most depressing apartment I've ever been in," she said. "God, I can't imagine a worse place to die."

"Why do you like it when I hurt you?"

204 ::: NICHOLAS MONTEMARANO

"Why do *you* like it?" she said. "Why are you so angry?"

"I'm not angry," I said.

"Do you hate your mother?"

"My mother's old," I said. "She has arthritis and osteoporosis and is lonely and I feel sorry for her, but I don't hate her."

"What about your sister?"

"I don't have a sister."

"You've mentioned a sister," she said. "You said she was five years older. That's how I remember."

"You're confusing me with someone else."

"I'm sure it was you."

"Well, I'm sorry. I guess you know more about me than I do. Tell me about my sister. What's her name? What's she like?"

"Her name is Imogene, but everyone calls her Gene, except you, you call her Imogene. Growing up, she had a lot of boyfriends, and you were jealous because you were in love with her."

"Great," I said. "That's a lovely story."

"So," she said. "Who did a number on you?"

"Maybe you're right," I said. "We shouldn't talk anymore."

I got under the covers with my clothes on and watched her get undressed. She looked sad the way my sister used to when she'd had a fight with her boyfriend. As far back as I could remember, she was always trying to please boys, always walking behind them or tugging on their shirtsleeves, or else calling them or writing them earnest but sentimental letters, always asking for something, more attention, more love. She was engaged twice, and both times I heard my mother call my father, whom she had divorced when I was five, and ask him to speak with June—that was my sister's name—but my father was on his third wife by then, a girl not that much older than June, and he never stopped by or called, and that was why I felt it was my job to save her, even though I was only thirteen the first time she got engaged, eighteen the second. Both times, the guy backed out, and both times my sister had a new boyfriend within a few weeks—naïve, awkward guys who were crazy about my sister and had no idea she didn't love them.

I watched Alex drink a glass of cloudy tap water, and a protective urge came over me. She was wearing Wonder Woman underwear, and it was difficult not to see her then as a girl, her legs the long, skinny legs of a teenager, her stomach muscles tight like June's had been her last few years.

She stood beside the mattress and looked down at me. "I didn't mean we shouldn't talk at all," I said. "I just meant that we should change the subject."

"Take your jeans off," she said. "It's very uncomfortable to sleep next to denim."

I took off my jeans and shirt and tossed them onto the floor. Alex turned off the light and got into bed, then put one of her legs between mine. "Thanks for being such a great houseboy," she said.

:::

I woke from a dream in which children were jumping from buildings. It was my job to catch them, only they didn't fall, they floated away like helium balloons.

Alex was standing by the door, dressed. A voice inside my head said, "Let her go," but I couldn't stop myself from stopping her. "Are you going to see him?" I said.

"Who?" she said. Then: "No, God, of course not. I can't sleep, and I was afraid I was keeping you up, so I was going to go home."

"I was sleeping just fine."

"You were kicking," she said. "And your breathing was funny, like you were running."

"It was probably a dream," I said. "I used to have a really great dream, but I haven't had it in a few years, where I can dunk a basketball. The rims are about twenty feet in the air, and there are a dozen players on the other team, but I float right past them and dunk, over and over."

"You weren't having that dream," she said.

"Come back to bed."

"I'm restless," she said. "There's nowhere to go in this apartment. I thought of sitting on the toilet and reading a magazine, but that's too depressing."

"I can come with you," I said.

"No," she said. "I want to be alone, if that's okay."

"Sure," I said. "But be careful."

"I'm not going to see him," she said.

"I meant that this neighborhood isn't the safest."

"I'll be fine," she said.

After Alex left, I lay in bed unable to sleep, remembering the last time I tried to stop my sister from going back to her boyfriend. It was a few months before she died, and I could see—everyone could—that she'd been using, that she was in trouble. The previous times I'd tried to talk her out of this relationship, she had nodded her head and agreed with everything I was telling her. She would say, "I know, I know. God, you're right. I really do have to get my shit together. I know he's not good for me." But the last time, she didn't even pretend. It was the drugs now too. "Listen," she said. "I love you, and I know you're trying to help, but I know what makes me happy. I'll be okay," she said. "I'm going to get him to quit, but he can't quit without me. That's why I'm doing this—so we can quit together." When we left her apartment, I watched her walk down the stairs, and I was sure I'd never see her alive again, so I closed my eyes and fell forward and tumbled down the stairs, and I heard something snap on the way down, though I had no idea what—everything hurt—and only when I reached the bottom did I realize it had been my ankle.

June tried to convince me I was okay. She said, "Try walking on it. Maybe it's just a sprain." She tried to pull me to my feet, but I cried out. She kept saying, "Are you sure you can't walk? Maybe if you lean on me."

"It's broken," I said. "I need you to call an ambulance."

"You didn't have to do this!" she said. It was the first time in my life she'd raised her voice to me. "You're not helping me this way!"

She called for an ambulance. Two men came and put an air cast on my ankle, then carried me downstairs on a stretcher. Before they put me into the ambulance, I said to June, "Meet me at the hospital."

"Okay," she said.

The men asked June if she wanted to ride with them, but she said no, she'd get herself to the hospital.

"Do you know where it is?" one of the men said.

"Yes," she said, but I already knew she wouldn't be there.

:::

As I was getting Henry ready for his shower, I asked him about Alex's ex-boyfriend. "What else do you know about him?" I said.

"She's causing trouble already, huh?"

"No," I said. "It's not that. I like her, and I'm concerned."

"Well," he said. "I don't like her."

"You don't have to like her," I said. "I'm asking for me."

"The time I told you about is the only time I saw him. He called here a lot. I could tell it was him because her voice would change. A girl talking to her father."

I picked up Henry and moved him into his shower chair. The water was too cold, he said, so I made it warmer and warmer until he said okay.

"Did she ever say anything about him?"

"Not much," he said. "Only that they were getting married."

I rubbed shampoo into Henry's hair, then rinsed it, then rubbed in conditioner. I washed his face with a washcloth, then his hands and feet, then the rest of his body. "Don't forget my bottom," he said.

"I wash that last for a reason," I said. "Unless you want me to wash your ass, then your face."

I rinsed the conditioner from his hair, then rinsed his body, then started to dry him. He said, "She showed up for work a few times with bruises."

"People get bruises," I said.

"On her face," he said.

"Did you ask her about them?"

"Only the first time," he said. "She told me she got into a bar fight, but I knew she was lying."

:::

Once, when I was eleven and June was sixteen, I undressed her, put her in the tub, and ran cold water over her. My mother was away for the night and June was supposed to be watching me, but instead she went out with a man my mother had forbidden her to see (he was twenty-two and had a mustache), and he must have gotten her drunk or high or both. I remembered what to do from a TV movie I'd seen: when someone drinks too much or takes too many pills, you make them drink coffee and put them in a tub of ice. I didn't know how to make coffee, and we didn't have enough ice to fill a tub, so I ran cold water over my sister. Her breasts looked much smaller naked than they looked under clothes. If she had been wearing a bra, I would have left it on, just as I left on her underwear. Her eyes were closed, and she kept mumbling something incoherent, and I asked her to open her eyes, and when she didn't, I opened them for her, and she weakly slapped my hands away, and we kept playing this game until she got sick in the tub.

But worse was the night a few years later, the summer before June started college, when she didn't come home. My mother sat up all night at the kitchen table, smoking cigarettes from a pack she kept for emergencies. I sat on the stairs, watching her, worried that my sister was dead, that this would kill my mother, that I would be forced to live with my father, who was a stranger to me, or that perhaps my father wouldn't want me. My mother yelled at me to get back in bed and keep my door closed, but every time I heard a car stop outside, or voices on the street, I came out of my room to see if it was June. By morning, my mother had given up, had "washed her hands" of my sister. She didn't scream when June came home, didn't try to shame her, didn't punish her. From the stairs I could see my sister breathing on my mother's face to prove she hadn't been drinking, but my mother turned away and said nothing. When June came upstairs, I hugged her and told her I'd waited up all night too, and she said she was sorry. She closed her eyes and took a deep breath, and I saw then that someone had written the word SLUT in black marker on one of her eyelids. When she opened her eyes, I asked her to close them again, and when she closed her eyes, I smacked her. She stepped back, her mouth open. I don't think I knew what the word *slut* meant, but I knew enough to know that my sister had been lying to my mother, and that any word written on my sister's eyelid could not have been written with kindness. She ran into the bathroom, where she must have looked into the mirror. I heard her crying, and after a few minutes I went in. She was washing her face. She kept turning to me to ask if it was all gone. "It's just my crazy friends," she said. "It's only a joke, it doesn't mean anything."

:::

I had a key to Alex's apartment, and sometimes I was there without her. One afternoon she came home but didn't know I was there. I was in the bathroom, drying after a shower, and didn't hear her. I walked out of the bathroom just as she was about to walk in. She screamed so loudly, as if she were being stabbed, that I was afraid someone would call the police. Even after she knew it was me, she wouldn't let me near her. She sat on the floor, shaking, while from a few feet away I told her I was sorry and tried to reassure her that everything was okay. She took some Valium and breathed deeply. After a few minutes passed—I had moved closer to her, but didn't touch her—she said, "I'm so embarrassed."

"You didn't know I was here," I said. "I was scared too. I'm going to name one of my new gray hairs after you."

"It's not that I was scared," she said. "I was beyond scared. My God, I was a complete wimp."

"You're being too hard on yourself."

"Sometimes, I want to kill him," she said. "I have fantasies about terrible things happening to him."

I waited to see if she would say more, and when she didn't, I said, "Instead of being your houseboy, I can be your hit man. The only problem is, I'm not very tough."

"I bet you could beat someone up if you were angry enough," she said. "Haven't you ever been in a fight?"

"Not really," I said. "The closest I've ever been to a fight was when I used to practice wrestling moves on my sister." I stopped when I saw the expression on her face. She was kind, and didn't say anything, didn't say, "I *knew* you had a sister!"

"When I was in high school," I continued, "I used to get her into submission holds. I would twist her legs, or sit on her back and pull her hair. Once, I picked her up, upside down, and dropped her on her head, and for three weeks she had to wear a neck brace. She pretended to be dead. She kept her eyes open and wouldn't answer when I asked if she was okay. She held her breath and didn't move. I was so scared I actually got a hard-on." I looked at Alex for a reaction, but her expression didn't change.

"During a trip we took for my birthday last year," she said, "he wouldn't stop at a rest stop so I could use the bathroom. I told him I had to go, but he ignored me. He wouldn't get off the highway, and I actually had to—I think you could be a hit man if you wanted to be one."

"If I were given the right assignment," I said.

"He convinced me that he was supernatural," she said. "One of my friends was on to him—she knew he was being cruel to me—and one night she confronted him, and they made a big scene, it was very embarrassing, and on her way home that night she got into a car accident and died, and he said to me, 'Do you see what happens?' He said, 'You have no idea what kind of forces are working for me.' And I believed him! I was certain that if anyone helped me, that if I even asked for anyone's help, that person would die."

"Does that mean I'm going to die?"

"I don't think so."

After a long pause she said, "I'm sorry about your sister."

"What about her?"

"She's gone, isn't she? I mean, she died, right?"

"Yes."

"Poor Imogene," she said.

"June," I said.

:::

After she told me more details—how he made her take a cold shower and then stand in front of an air conditioner for three hours; how he didn't let her sleep for four nights, screaming at her every time she closed her eyes; how he forbade her to speak with anyone but him, forbade her to eat until he had eaten, forbade her to use the same soap he used, to drink from the same glasses he drank from; all his fascist rules she followed—after she told me all this, our sex changed. For the next month, until the night I fake-raped her. We agreed—Alex reluctantly—that I would no longer hit her, or pretend to hit her, would no longer scratch her back or pull her hair or bite her lips or pinch her nipples or push her face into the headboard or wall, would no longer act out any cruelties toward her, whether she asked me to or not, and sometimes she did not have to; I would no longer say the mean things she liked me to say, which I came to like to say, which I will not repeat here. Instead, I said kind things to her, and washed her hair, and rubbed her back and feet, and cooked her dinner, if you consider making grilled cheese sandwiches cooking, and for several weeks became a kind of houseboy, after all, and we might as well have been an old married couple, and the entire time I knew I was losing her.

Two nights in a row, when I started to kiss her, she didn't kiss me back. The second night, she told me she felt anxious: She wanted to scream; she wanted to throw something out her window—the phone, a lamp, a chair.

"As long as you don't throw *me* out the window," I said.

She didn't smile. "Haven't you ever wanted to jump out a window?"

"No," I said. "That wouldn't be my first choice. Quick, sure, but I think pills and booze in a bathtub would be nice."

"Let's do it together."

"Sounds like a great date."

"I'm being a crazy bitch tonight," she said.

"Excuse me," I said. "We don't use the word 'bitch' in this house."

"Not anymore," she said.

"It's nice to be nice to each other."

"We've always been nice to each other."

"Not always," I said.

"You were never really hurting me," she said.

"I don't think I was helping."

"But you *were*," she said. "Without it, I feel like hurting myself." She held out her hands; there was a cut on each palm.

"Great," I said. "You get *me* to hurt you so you won't have to do it."

"You're not really hurting me," she said. "That's the whole point. You act it out so I don't have to actually do it."

"But why me? Why couldn't anyone do this for you? Is it because I'm good at it? I mean, for God's sake, I don't want to be good at this."

"Don't be so dumb," she said. "It's because you're a good egg and I know you'd never really hurt me."

"But someone *did* hurt you."

"Yes," she said, "but he's not you. Listen," she said. "Imagine you had a terrible experience. Let's say you were mugged and beaten on a particular street in a neighborhood you like. One option is never to go back to that street for as long as you live, which is a kind of death, the way I see it. The other option is to go back to that street with someone you trust, to prove to yourself that it's safe. I'm only asking you to take a walk with me."

:::

I have to be careful about how I write the rest of this story. Even when you're writing about what actually happened, you can still write yourself into a corner, and right now I'm in a corner. The problem isn't that I don't know what happens next. I began this story with what happens next: I wait in Alex's closet for her to get home, come up behind her, press a plastic knife against her throat, and pretend to rape her. Then I feel a pain in my chest, she takes me to the emergency room, a doctor gives me a needle to slow my heart, et cetera. One problem is that I don't know how to explain my actions, or, rather, my character's actions. I don't know how to make what he does believable. Why would this guy, given what he knew, pretend to rape his girlfriend? Did he actually believe he was helping her? In an earlier draft of this story, my character didn't know that Alex's ex-boyfriend had abused her; he found out only after he'd fake-raped her. That way, his decision to participate might be justified: well, he didn't *really* know what was behind her request. When I finished writing that draft, I liked my character, but I could not say that I liked myself, and I wanted to. I wanted the reader to like me too, or at least to sympathize with me. But what good would that sympathy be if it were for a fake me? Despite my best intentions, I couldn't help but spin this story, just as I can't help but spin every story that's really about me. I make myself a little better or worse, depending on what the story needs. I have my character do things I almost did, but didn't quite do. Or I leave out things I actually did do—things too embarrassing to name, even though I believe those are precisely the things that should be named. Or I give my character a different name, or no name, as here, or a dead sister named June, when my sister's name was not June but sounded like June. But there's one person out there who knows who the narrator of this story is, who knows what he did and didn't do, what was said, what wasn't said, and I've changed her name too, which is the least I can do. But for her sake, and for mine, I'd like to revise a few things: I used a real knife, not a plastic one, and as I had sex with her, I cut her back by accident, and she really was frightened, more so than she would have been had I not cut her back, and when I was finished I didn't feel a pain in my chest, she didn't have to take me to the emergency room—we had a drink and ate dinner and watched TV—and this wasn't the last time we played these roles for each other: we kept doing this for the rest of our time together, a few more months. We didn't stop until the day I was shaving Henry and he said something about Alex. "I wouldn't be surprised if she turns up dead one of these days," he said. "She's trouble, and I think you should stay away from her." When I finished shaving him, I rubbed aftershave on his face, even though he had told me many times never to use aftershave, especially if I had cut him, and he cried out and nearly fell out of his chair. He asked me what the hell I was doing, was I crazy, was I picking up some of my crazy girlfriend's craziness, and it was then that I felt a pain in my chest, and it stayed with me, a dull ache I tried to rub away, but couldn't, and later that night, as Alex and I were getting ready for bed, my heart was pounding inside my chest, I was certain it was going to seize, and Alex brought me to the emergency room, where a doctor gave me a needle that warped the world as in a fun-house mirror. For the next few days Alex kept asking me what was wrong; I kept saying, "I don't know," or "It's nothing—don't worry about it." She wanted to know why I was afraid to touch her, to come near her; she wanted to know if this was how it was going to end; she wanted me to talk to her, to open my mouth and say something, for God's sake.

"Do you recognize yourself in this?"

"You've written me as a crazy bitch. Crazier than I was."

"I'm sorry."

"I told you not to say that."

"He should be sorry," my mother says. "He makes things up. I never 'washed my hands' of my daughter. I never gave up on her."

"I know you still have my number," Alex says. "Call me. I'm different now. I've been in therapy."

"Call her," my father says.

"Don't call her," Henry says.

"One more revision," my sister says. "You never threw yourself down the stairs."

"I thought about it. I wanted to."

"Listen to me," my sister says. "Even had you done that for me, even had you broken your neck, even had you broken every bone in your body, you couldn't have saved me."

PILGRIM GIRL

:::
:::

Mary Otis

FOR ANOTHER SECOND Allison is safe. She's outside the Wingerts' house, and the front door is still shut. But Janie Wingert is coming down the hallway, her tasteful heels clicking on the terra-cotta tiles, and Allison has dressed up as a traveling saleswoman, though she doesn't know why. She has no products. Why didn't this occur to her before now? It seemed like a great idea when she was in her bedroom, not raking her shag rug, the thing she was supposed to do when she got home from band practice. It seemed like a great idea to root the frosted-blond wig out of her mother's stocking drawer, where her mother hid it after the Lions Club Mardi Gras party. It seemed like a great idea to jam it on her head and walk across the street.

Janie Wingert opens the door, holding her orange cat, Mr. Teddy. Janie is in sales, real sales, important sales that include clients, accounts, quotas, and jumping on planes, and this occurs to Allison, the unreal salesperson, too late. Janie looks at Allison in her band blazer and the black funeral skirt that she filched from her mother's "occasional wear" drawer.

What was Allison thinking? Perhaps she was trying to "get out of herself," something her mother made her write on a piece of paper last Sunday—"I, Allison, will try to get out of myself"—and sign and affix to the refrigerator.

"Hi, Janie," Allison says. "I'm a saleswoman." And she can see the look in Janie's eyes, the kind she would, for example, give a Hare Krishna, the sort of individual that Allison recently heard Janie describe to her mother as a "tangled soul." Though Allison suspects Janie would just as soon kick a Hare Krishna as look at one.

Janie is deft at appearing out of herself. She pries Mr. Teddy from her shoulder, Mr. Teddy of the six toes on each foot and the continually shell-shocked look, and holds him in her arms, as if he were a homecoming queen bouquet.

"What are you selling, Allison?" Janie says as she stares at Allison's white vinyl and yellow-flowered overnight bag, which Allison grabbed at the last minute as a sales prop.

"What you need to buy, Janie." Allison is completely aware of her crummy sales technique. Mr. Teddy, who is generally inactive, suddenly bats one paw in her direction.

Janie squints at Allison and begins to back away from the door. Then she stops and says, "Rick, honey, come here. Allison from across the street is trying to be funny or something."

And then it hits Allison. Rick. Rick. Janie's husband who has a blond beard and works at an insurance company, but seems very outdoorsy nonetheless, the type that she could easily see as a carpenter, for one day Allison hopes to move to California and marry a carpenter. It's Rick. The reason she is pretending to be a traveling saleswoman. Again, this occurs to her too late.

"Hey, Allison, what's shakin'?" Rick always knows just what to say. Once, when Allison was riding her bike home from school, Rick asked her if she was all right and she said she was, and Rick said she seemed totally depressed. That was one of the happiest days of her life, so far.

"What's the good word?" Rick takes a bite from a roll in his hand. It seems more exotic than the rolls at Allison's house. It has seeds. She looks at the bread between his index finger and thumb, how he's squeezing it just a little bit, ever so gently in between each bite.

Suddenly her head is itchy. Sweat runs down the back of her neck.

"What's in that suitcase of yours?" Rick asks. And Allison remembers that she hid her sketch in there, the one she's been working on for two months, entitled "A Woman's Mind." Allison is a terrible artist, but she has taken great nightly comfort in working on this picture of a woman's brain that extends upward like a multilayered parking lot, on each level squeezing in all kinds of subversive thoughts and romantic hopes, each of them encoded in strange symbols that would mean nothing to anyone but her. Still, she hid it. Rick must not see this.

"Products," she whispers.

"Allison," Rick says. "Allison, you're a real laugh riot."

:::

At home, Allison's mother and Aunt Tuley are waiting in the kitchen for her. Tonight is the last night of the Family Fun Expo at the mall, and her mother really, really wants the three of them to go to a costume photo booth called "Old-Fashioned Days" and get their picture taken as pilgrim ladies because they live only two towns away from Plymouth, Massachusetts, because this photo could have Christmas card potential.

"Where have you been, Allison?" says her mother.

"Trying out for the seventh-grade play," Allison says, using the fabulous excuse she cooked up while crossing the street from Janie and Rick's driveway to her own, and already she sees that her mother is fixated on the fact that she's wearing her wig and funeral skirt. But for a moment Allison has special powers. She has been referred to as a laugh riot by a twenty-four-year-old man.

"Well, that's a step in the right direction," says Aunt Tuley. Aunt Tuley is her mother's younger sister. "Much younger," Tuley will always add. Tuley is only eight years older than Allison. She was voted Most Pert in her high school yearbook. "What play?" she says.

"A new play."

"About?" says Allison's mother.

"About salespeople," Allison says. There's a horrible feeling inside the wig, as if there are warm scrambled eggs on top of her head. She'd mushed down her long brown hair with Vaseline, such was her eagerness to get that blond shag wig on her skull.

"I could see you onstage," says Aunt Tuley, lying.

That's not a thing that would come to anyone's mind, Allison thinks. She's too still, for one thing. Actresses move around a lot. She has dead arms.

"Though you are a little static." Aunt Tuley is an English major at Salem State College, and she constantly throws around her "Power People" vocabulary words.

Allison bursts into tears. Aunt Tuley and her mother are both so used to this that neither one reacts, and her mother, not even looking at her, pours her a bowl of Apple Jacks to eat in the car on the way to the mall. Allison watches Tuley and her mother walk out the door, and she stands there, crying in her hot wig with her dead arms. And it's completely out of the question that her mother's going to wait in the car while she changes out of her traveling saleswoman getup. Allison yanks the wig off her head and savagely whips it across the kitchen table. Then she picks up the bowl of Apple Jacks and dumps it in the trash, a pathetically tiny "fuck you," and every bit of her newfound, Rick-induced composure has vanished, as if she never had it at all.

:::

No one is at the "Old-Fashioned Days" booth except Dee Deluca, who works there every year for extra cash. Dee, a professional drill team coach, can often be seen stomping around downtown with a canvas sack of batons over her shoulder. Might as well be a sack of guns.

Dee tells Allison's mother there's only one female pilgrim costume left. There used to be more, being that they were so popular, but people ripped them off.

Aunt Tuley has the brilliant idea that Allison will be the one and only pilgrim girl, and before Allison knows it, she's in a dowdy black dress that smells like K2r spot remover, and Dee presses something that looks like a doily on her head and slowly rotates it as if she's screwing in a lightbulb. Allison remembers that she's heard rumors about Dee, how she'll tie a girl's wrists to her baton with fishing wire if she drops it in practice. And when she hands Allison a fake stone mortar and pestle with its grubby Pier One sticker half-melted off, Allison doesn't want to touch this item that in part reminds her of a tiny stone penis, but she takes it anyway, and when Dee commands her to hold it directly in front of her belly button, she keeps it there. Allison doesn't mention to Dee that the pilgrim costume is basically bogus, that pilgrims actually wore colors. She read that in one of her favorite magazines, *The Young Historian*.

Dee fiddles with the camera and asks, "How tall are you, miss?"

"Five-eight," answers Allison.

"Tall. That's tall for a pilgrim girl," says Dee, as if she's doing them a big favor. Allison closes her eyes, and all around her, she hears the swish of voices.

"Open your eyes," says Aunt Tuley. "Don't be churlish."

How powerful of you to say that, Tuley, and through her closed eyelids Allison sends electric hate beams.

"Open them, Allison, don't be childish," and Allison gets some small satisfaction that her mother has misrepeated Tuley. And she's about to open her eyelids. But just before she does, she has a moment such as she's never had before, and as it happens, the outside of herself completely drops away, and she is suddenly and completely in her own underneath, a quiet place where her hidden softness and wonder are gathered and kept in waiting for someday, somewhere, another person on earth to know.

And then, again, she is Pilgrim Girl. One shot is taken with mortar and pestle and one without. Tuley goes to smoke a cigarette outside the Ross Dress for Less loading dock, and Dee comes in for the big kill now that she has Allison's mother alone. Dee is pushing this horrible faux-wood frame on her mother that costs three times what the pictures themselves did, and Allison can see that Dee is wearing her down. And she feels sad for her mother because she knows she'll buy it.

On the way home, Allison sits in the backseat and looks at the picture, which Tuley said looks austere. "Austere in a good way." Each time they pass a streetlight Allison frantically tilts her photograph and studies it, and each time she hopes to, but does not, see loveliness.

:::

Allison has been working on a campaign to get people to call her Ali, pronounced like the boxer. The extent of her efforts amounts to writing *Ali, Ali,* in Magic Marker on the inside heels of both her sneakers, which she has just done while listening to Janie Wingert call Mr. Teddy into the house before she leaves for work.

Ali looks good. *Ali* has punch. *Allison*—a downward-leaning, collapsed bridge of a name—has nothing to do with her. She saw the school bus come and go, but her shoes haven't dried, and Allison looks out her bedroom window and sees Janie standing in her driveway.

"Come here, Mr. Teddy . . ." calls Janie. "Mr. Teddy? Mr. Teddy WONderful . . ."

Rick walks out the front door and Allison thinks she can see that he's had just about enough. She predicts the demise of Rick and Janie's marriage. Too much cat sweet talk. Husbands and wives need to save their kindest words for each other, even when tired or hungry. She read this in the September *Family Circle*.

Rick opens his car door and puts a bag lunch and a large black organizer on the front seat. Rick is a supervisor. Supervising is sexy. And Allison is sure that with just a few small changes Rick could make that leap to being a carpenter. Carpenters hammer alone, supervisors walk down halls alone. Because it doesn't pay to fraternize in that sort of position. This much she knows from her mother, who, though not a supervisor, works as an office manager in a dentist's office. She is "pleasant" to the patients, but she doesn't fraternize with them.

"Mr. Teddy?" and Allison sees Janie standing there in her gray dress that starts narrow at the top, but circles out at the bottom, and she thinks how very much she looks like a little lighthouse, what with her slender shoulders and her moronic head swinging back and forth like a beacon over the same part of the yard that she just looked at five times.

Then Allison sees Mr. Teddy Wonderful sitting to the side of the house, just out of Janie's view, unmoving, staring at air. And she could knock-knock-knock on the window and help old Janie out. She could.

Janie starts to get in her car, but before she does, she cleverly pulls a sweep of her dress fabric to the side with her thumb and index finger. So dainty, Allison thinks, so unlike the way she sits down first, then hurriedly and sneakily tries to snatch fabric from under her butt. No wonder people buy things from Janie. Allison feels crying coming on. She stops and inhales Magic Marker for distraction and looks to the *Ali* heel markings for reinforcement.

Then she puts her feet in her shoes and thinks of the secret of her new and improved name tucked between her sock and tennis shoe. She does not foresee that by the end of the day, her socks will be stained blue, her *Ali*s mangled and blurred, nothing left but a broken-down *i* in her right shoe, even its dot rolled away.

Allison runs down the stairs and out her front door, because there may be a moment after Janie backs out when Rick goes back into the house for something. It has happened before.

Allison has pictured him striding back into his kitchen, which, still smelling of waffles and coffee, has settled into the hush of a day's wait.

And that's when she imagines herself suddenly appearing in the lovely, quiet kitchen with him, as if she's always lived there, and right away he pulls her into the living room, and lies down on the couch with her and holds her. And this is the thing she thinks of every single day in the time between watching Janie's Jetta pull out of the driveway and flying out the door of her own house, finding most often the gaping emptiness of the Wingerts' driveway and Rick's blue Jeep already at the corner stop sign, stopping not for her.

But today she is lucky. Rick's coffee cup sits on the hood of the engine, and he's searching for something in the front seat. He pulls his head out just as she comes to the end of her driveway.

"Hi, Allison, how's business?" Rick smiles at her, and she gets a little scared because he's wearing a dress shirt, and this throws her off. She scrambles to think of some laugh-riot thing to say about products. All she can think of is a TV commercial about alarm clocks.

"Fine," she says.

"Do you want a lift?" He says this to her as if he gives her lifts all the time. A lift: slick and elegant, unlike what her mother gives her: a ride, with the r wrenched out of her mouth in a specific, exhausted way.

"Do you want me to drive across the street to get you?" And Allison realizes she hasn't answered him, and she is completely aware that this is a joke, but sadly, her mouth has broken.

"Or you can walk. If you need the time alone." No one—no one—has ever suggested that she needs this. Rick turns away, and Allison wants to sob at the sight of his back.

Then suddenly she is across the street and in the Jeep. She'll be unable to recall how she got there when she replays this moment on her continuous brain feed as soon as fifteen minutes from now.

The car rolls out of the driveway, and Allison is in love with this moment, with the way the tires bounce over a bit of uneven pavement, with the way Rick puts his hand on the back of her seat as he turns his head to look at oncoming traffic, with the way the Jeep stalls, and how when Rick shifts, the car shoots forward a little, and Rick laughs. Her life has burst open, and she feels a gush of love for the door handle of the Jeep, which she is clutching.

"Would you like a sip of coffee?" Rick asks Allison.

Her arms feel like swollen water balloons. "Only if it's leaded." Her mother's line.

"Leaded with a little milk and two sugars." Rick hands her his All-state Insurance mug. The mug isn't hot, and she sets it down on her crotch. She doesn't know why. She instantly feels between her legs a small circle of heat begin to spin, and Allison wills it to stop, but the circle only flies tighter in upon itself. She stops breathing.

"I'm sorry," says Rick. "Do you not drink coffee?"

"No, I do. I do." She puts her palm over the top of the mug. Another bad choice. She might as well have put her hand down her pants. Allison is sure he knows everything. She still doesn't think she's breathing.

The two drive in complete silence for nine minutes. Rick stops at the stoplight in front of Cappy's Clam Shack.

"They're closing next week for the season," says Rick, looking out the window. Cappy's is halfway to school, and Allison is aware that already it's almost over, this perfect lift, this holding of a lettered mug, this almost-drinking of coffee.

She lifts the mug to her navel and holds it there, as she did her Pilgrim Girl pestle, and she remembers Dee Deluca telling her to hold it "naturally, as if it was something you touched all the time." She keeps the mug very straight. Still, she does not drink the coffee.

"I love their fried clams, and I surely miss them in the winter," says Rick. To *surely* miss something indicates to Allison great sensitivity. *Now* is the time to drink his coffee to signal her understanding. But she can't. And she doesn't know why. And the space between her legs seems as if it's opened into her lap, which now feels like a tumble of warm socks.

"What do you think, Allison, do their fried clams rate in your book?"

"I've never had them." Her mother calls Cappy's "Crappy's." She isn't allowed to eat there.

Rick pulls into the school yard. Allison desperately tries to think of some impressive food she once ate.

Rick turns his head to look at her, and she sees up close that the middle of one eyebrow is missing. She looks at the little skin road, which zags at a diagonal toward his nose. Belatedly she gets a hit of

Dial soap off his beard. She tries to enjoy it, since she fears she'll never get this close again.

"Did Mr. Teddy cut your eyebrow?" she asks, hoping.

"No, I fell on a dock when I was ten. But Mr. Wonderful *did* do this," and he holds up his right hand and shows her a scratch on his knuckle. "Though Janie doesn't care. That cat's her baby."

The Jeep idles in front of the entrance to Allison's school, and Rick looks at her, waiting, waiting for something. And maybe it's his mug of coffee. But unfortunately, she just rolled down the window and dumped it out, and some of it's dripping down the side of his Jeep, and she can't believe she did that, because when she was little, her mother and Tuley used to drive to New York City in the middle of the night, and they wouldn't stop at a public restroom and they made her pee in a juice can and dump it, and she *never* hit the car.

She weighs the benefits of telling Rick this story.

"Well, I guess that's that," he says as Allison hands him his empty mug.

"I'm sorry," she says and offers to run into the school snack bar to get him an orange juice or chocolate milk.

"Don't sweat it," and Rick pats her thigh, and her lap starts up again, and she feels a deep tugging that makes her think of beach grass, of how you can pull and pull on it, but it never lets go.

"I'll tell you what, though, you *can* buy me a beverage this week when I take you to Cappy's for lunch. How 'bout that?"

"You're going to lunch?" Because Allison thinks she heard what she heard, but maybe she didn't.

"I go to lunch every day, silly." He reaches out and very lightly pretends to slap her face, and she does nothing. Absolutely nothing.

"Oh, Allison . . . such a serious girl." And he takes her hand and brings it to the side of his face, and she feels the pulse in his jaw, a tiny beating heart.

"Well, think about it, and tell me what day would work for you." He abruptly drops her hand.

"Thursday," she says, not thinking about it, because it's the obvious choice. She loves Thursday, which she thinks of as a complex, violet day, unlike the other days of the week, which are primary colored and lack all subtlety.

"Thursday it is. Shall I steal you away at noon?" And again Allison is shocked that he talks to her as if she decides things about her life all the time.

"My class eats at 11:25 AM." She is aware that no sophisticated lunch-taker would say this.

"That can be managed," says Rick, and he shifts in a way that makes the Jeep go back a little before it goes forward, and Allison finds this all incredibly sexy, the supervisor talk, the way the Jeep moves like it has hips.

She walks away whispering, "That can be managed, that can be managed," while simultaneously tapping into the continuous brain feed and rewinding it to the exact spot when Rick offered her a lift. And by the time she reaches the school door she has speed-played every single glittering instant that followed.

:::

That night Allison works on her drawing of "A Woman's Mind." She is stuck on the perfect symbol for this morning's events. She tried a coffee cup, but it looked too rest-stop-sign, too Girl-Scout-badge.

She overhears her mother and Tuley talking downstairs in the kitchen about Tuley's Saturday night date. Allison can't hear everything, but Tuley comes through loud and clear every time she pounces on "gyrational." This may not be a real word. Tuley is greedy and sneaky that way; the more words she knows, the more she pretends to know.

Tuley dates a lot. Allison's mother doesn't, ever. Because her mother loved her father.

Allison's father was killed crossing a street, and her mother says about that, "Don't poke at it." Allison once heard Tuley tell a date that her father was drunk and that he was hit by a car full of drunk Boston College students. She asked Tuley whether the students went to jail. Tuley said, "Don't poke at it."

Allison hears her mother take a pass at the living room's braid rug with the electric broom, and then she begins to snap off lights, and Allison knows that's a signal that she is planning to go to bed. She can hear Tuley in her bedroom, recording words and their meanings into a tape recorder, which she'll play back while she sleeps.

There is a pause between the turning off of the front window light and the pulling of the overhead dining-room chain lamp, and Allison can tell her mother is listening all the way upstairs and hoping she'll come down and talk to her. But she won't.

"Mr. Teddy?" Allison scrambles to the window, because it's Rick's voice, and this is like a magic sign; he never calls the cat, and of course he's doing it just so he can secretly communicate with her. But then she sees that Rick is with Janie. They're in their bathrobes, waving flashlights in tiny circles toward the shrubbery, under the car, under the Jeep. Rick takes Janie's hand, and they call some more.

"Janie said Mr. Teddy has been gone since this morning," says Allison's mother. She has a habit of creeping around in her stocking feet, and already she's halfway across Allison's room. In her hand she carries a blue ceramic coffee cup with pink painted letters that read "Camille." Allison's father made it for her years ago, and it's the only one she ever uses.

It's too late for Allison to hide her sketch, and her mother curls up on the end of the bed and puts out her hand. Her at-work, pleasant, and in-charge face has almost completely given way to her at-home, tired, and wondering face. She leans toward Allison, and Allison can smell her Trésor perfume and the faint office fragrance of Xerox and pens.

"What's this a picture of, Allison?"

"A picture of thinking."

She looks at "A Woman's Mind" and turns the picture sideways, even though to Allison it's obvious the head only goes in one direction.

"Oh." And that's it. That's all her mother says about the entire catalog of her secret life. Allison is equally relieved and furious.

Rick and Janie have moved to the backyard and their calls sound weaker, yet more urgent, as if carried across water.

Allison's mother lies back on her bed. "You put so much time into a cat, and off it runs anyway," she murmurs. She's in her pre-konk-out, depressing-proclamation phase. Allison hates the dental patients on whom all her mother's niceness is spent. Her mother starts to breathe from her throat in a delicate, puzzled way that sounds as if she'll never get enough breath, never get some important question answered.

Rick and Janie stop calling Mr. Teddy, and it occurs to Allison that she was, in fact, the last person to see him. She puts her hand to the cold windowpane, where she holds it until it stings.

Allison puts her comforter over her mother, although she doesn't tuck her in, and goes downstairs to walk the different colored circles in the braid rug until exhausted, to think a Rick thought for every color, beginning with the green circle: cracked eyebrow.

:::

Thursday morning, while Allison waits for the school bus, she sees Janie standing silent and unmoving in the Wingerts' driveway. The bow of her peach silk blouse is tied in a floppy, hasty manner, and already it's slipping loose. Janie doesn't turn her head or look around. She seems preoccupied, carrying out the impossible task of measuring loss.

Just before the bus pulls up, Allison watches Janie walk to the end of the driveway and check the "Lost Cat" sign taped to the telephone pole in front of the Wingerts' house. Janie seems to read the words as if she hadn't written them herself, as if they might instead be directions to where the finding should begin.

:::

There are only a fisherman and a woman with her elderly mother in Cappy's, but Rick takes Allison to the porch that overlooks the water. Strains of "Midnight at the Oasis" float from the kitchen. Allison thinks that she and Rick are a secret, and a secret is like carrying a pitcher of water that almost sloshes over, one she tries to keep from spilling, one she almost hopes does.

Rick removes the food from both lunch trays and sets it on a picnic table. Allison wishes she had done that. Janie would have. She moves her purse next to Rick's big black organizer. Her purse slouches over, looks like an embarrassing lavender kidney.

Allison ordered only a cup of clam chowder. Her mother has always said that when someone other than family feeds you, you wait until a specific food item is offered. But Rick said, "Whatever you want, Allison, whatever."

In the gray afternoon light, the blond in Rick's hair seems turned inside out, a flat shade of brown. He's halfway through his fried clams when he stops to gulp the orange soda he didn't let Allison buy after all. Allison doesn't usually watch grown men eat, and she's surprised at the speed with which he bites and swallows, the concentration. When her mother explained sex to her, she said it involved the man "concentrating very hard."

Rick opens his organizer and Allison gets a whiff of real leather. He turns to a certain page, taps it, continues to eat.

The wind whips her hair into one eye, and she pushes it back only to have it happen again. She takes the little blue comb from inside her purse and tries to fix her hair while staring into her lap, as if this makes the action invisible.

Rick stops eating. Then he says, "You know, Allison, you're the type of girl who will be beautiful someday, but probably not until you're thirty."

Allison looks at her chowder, which has congealed on top. Thirty. Seventeen years to wait. Might as well be nine hundred. The front of her chest feels thinned out, brittle, like a square of cold tin.

Rick says, "Allison? Allison?" He cocks his head like he's talking to a young girl. Not her.

She hears the ocean water slap stupidly, quickly against the porch pilings, as if to say, "What what what what?"

Rick closes his organizer and pushes it with some deliberation to the side of the picnic table and away from Allison's purse, which sits there foolishly, seeming to wait for the next little bit of his attention.

"But I love you now," she says. She is aware that her mouth is slipping around, that she doesn't look joyous, that people should be happy and confident when they say this thing.

"Oh, Allison." And she thinks that she sees in his eyes a certain sort of allowance, an acceptance such as a person who loves you back might have. But then something within Rick immediately pulls to the surface, something that neatly steps over whatever he might feel, and over the fact that she is crying. Her arms have gone extra dead.

"Thank you, Allison." Rick smiles at the picnic table. She is being supervised.

Then Rick asks her if she is going to eat her chowder, or she thinks he did—her listening is spotty at present, and it's not unlike being in the faulty ALM language booth at school, the one that spurts French conversations over a crackling headset. Whole sentences go missing, always the ones you really need.

Rick takes the roll that came with her soup, and he wraps it in a napkin, puts it in her purse, tells her to make sure to eat it later. He asks if she wants a cup of coffee. She shakes her head.

"Shall we, then?" he says. Now they are getting up. Getting up is the thing to do. Allison follows Rick to the wooden porch railing, all the while staring at his back. Embarrassment and longing press equally inside her heart, as if on either side of an equator. Rick puts her Styrofoam cup of chowder on the porch railing, and a gull immediately swoops down, only to stand one inch from it, not eating, not taking.

"Ha-ha," laughs Rick.

"Ha," laughs Allison. And she's grateful, because for a moment they are just two people laughing at a stupid bird.

Then they walk toward the stairs that lead to the parking lot, but just before they get there Rick stops. He seems to consider something. He takes Allison's hand and awkwardly swings it once before he leads her behind Cappy's kitchen to an enclosed, hidden area, where there's nothing but a dumpster and a jumble of wooden crates on the ground. She doesn't understand why he puts her in front of him with his hands on her shoulders. It seems like he's about to calculate her height.

But instead he pulls Allison closer and very gently puts his hands on either side of her face, and he looks at her like a person who long ago resigned himself to a certain measure of life. No more, no less.

Then he kisses her and her insides unfurl, suddenly beautiful, like a lush bolt of fabric thrown out upon a table.

"If you were older, you would possess me," he says, and at that she ventures to touch him, but all she can do is gently, awkwardly, press a spot just above his right hip.

"I bet there's some boy right now who's smitten by you," and the word *smitten* will forever mean the inside of his mouth, the temperature of his tongue, and how he sucks on her upper lip for just an instant, before kissing her for the second and final time of her life.

And suddenly there's light within her and light between them, a generous bestowal that spills everywhere and all at once.

Then they are simply two people, leaving a restaurant and crossing a parking lot stretched beneath plain and unending daylight.

During the drive back to school Rick says, "I have a very important meeting this afternoon." He says this too quickly, too loudly.

"What's it about?" Allison says.

"What's what about?"

"The meeting." And Rick looks puzzled for a moment, as if she'd asked a particularly personal question, and she can see that she's stepped outside a certain domain into one that now doesn't include queries about actual life activities.

"It's about benefit packages." Further questions don't seem to be expected, and Rick checks his watch, although there's a clock on the dashboard. It's 12:11, only eleven minutes past the first time Allison was truly and completely out of herself.

Just before she gets out of the car, Allison asks about Mr. Teddy.

"Still lost." Another narrowing in of all that has gone before. Rick looks down at his steering wheel. Then he looks at her and says, "Allison," and she sees one last glimpse of inexplicable yearning and confusion already corralled by guilt.

"I hope you find him soon," she says.

"I'll pass that on to Janie," says Rick.

:::

It's Saturday morning, and Allison waves goodbye to her mother as she leaves for a half day of work. Her mother thanked her for this, thinking she got up early to see her off.

But Allison has a secret plan, a plan to give Rick Wingert her Pilgrim Girl picture. She stayed awake all night, polishing and rotating her memory of light until now, in remembrance, it's lost all streaming capacity, is caught and hardened like a pearl.

A last push of summer sun falls across the small of Allison's back, but a cold, businesslike wind blows directly at her chest. Her body is a useless wall between two seasons.

She hunches over and stares at the Wingerts' house, willing a curtain to be drawn back, the porch light to go off. The house, unbudging, refuses to reveal anything. She traces her eyes in ever-widening circles around the home, as if it's caught in a bubble against which it threatens to burst.

Then she sees him. Mr. Teddy. He's lying motionless, stretched out on a piece of cardboard near the Wingerts' mailbox. Allison stands up, though she doesn't move, and she watches two, three, four cars drive by. It rained last night, and the road is slightly damp, as if sweating from the effort of being driven upon. She watches the road awhile longer before she looks back to the mailbox. Mr. Teddy is still there, alone.

Allison runs inside to get a towel, and she looks in the bathroom closet, but all that's left are guest towels, which are never to be used, not under any circumstance at all, and she ends up grabbing her own pink towel, which is still wet and smells of her jasmine hair conditioner.

:::

Someone even crossed Mr. Teddy's paws, and Allison sees no visible sign of harm until she stands over him. Then she sees that something is wrong with his mouth, which hangs open crookedly, graceless. There's so little blood for him to be dead. The air around Allison seems to tighten, and her hands feel completely weightless as they throw the towel over Mr. Teddy and bundle him up as if he were a baby.

Allison rings the Wingerts' doorbell over and over. Its triple-tone chime sounds ridiculously, horribly happy.

Janie opens the door just a crack, already suspicious. "What is it, Allison?"

Allison looks at a little clot of face lotion that has dried near Janie's right eye.

"*What*, Allison?" And Janie pulls the collar of her robe tighter.

When she doesn't answer, Janie starts to close the door, saying, "You're not funny, Allison, you're just not funny."

"I've got Mr. Teddy." And then Janie opens the door all the way, and she comes toward her, but Allison can't bear to put him in her arms, so instead she very gently sets him inside the house on the carpet. Janie rushes into the living room, screams for Rick, and Allison hears him running down the stairs.

The door to the Wingert home slams.

Allison turns away and starts to run. She runs like crazy, though there's no place to go. And she won't know exactly when her Pilgrim

Girl picture flew from the pocket of her corduroys. But it must have, because she will never see it again, and she'll assume that it went blowing around the world, like a ticket to a place that has already been visited, of no further use to anyone.

SICK FUCK

:::

Lucia Perillo

I BEGAN THIS by asking Jim if he'd mind being included in something I was planning to write about sex.

"No one wants to read about sex," he said.

"Everyone wants to read about sex!"

"Not about you having sex."

Then I had to admit he had a point. Ungrammatical as his response was.

:::

Not about me, okay, there is nothing singular about me, my contortions are conventional—except that the puppet strings of my nerves have grown corroded with scar tissue. From a subjective perspective, this feels much as it sounds: my legs feel like the antennae of a TV tuned to a channel where no signal is coming in, and the static fuzz is humming loudly. They've also become spastic, lock-kneed at odd moments, my feet like those of Barbie, ready for the high-heeled shoe.

It is not an appealing picture. But if I am going to write about my sex life, you should get a good look, especially at the segue from my legs to waist, where my body starts getting strange. I have had a machine implanted in my belly: it delivers drugs to my spine via a tube. The tube runs under my skin and I can't feel it with my fingers except where it bends to enter one of the interstices of my vertebrae. The bend makes a spongy bubble in my back's lumbar curve, and when I first discovered this rubbery spot I could not keep from poking it.

The machine is about the size of a tuna can. Before it was implanted the surgeon showed me how it looked: gleaming and pseudo-liquidly

232 ::: LUCIA PERILLO

silver, like my high school track team's stopwatch. Its top side is flattened, which creates a point on either side of that flat spot, where the metal feels to be just one cell layer away from breaking through my skin. The surgeon even Jim calls Doctor Dreamboat (tall/handsome/ flies plane/et cetera) made a pocket under my skin and slipped the can into it like a large item zipped into a small coin purse, so that now it rests just forward of the wing bone on my right hip. A three-inch scar runs above it, and because the incision did not close properly there is a dry purple lozenge of scar tissue at the center of the slice, where the incision puckers in, just above the place where the device's arc is flattened.

When I volunteer to show off the machine, men in particular usually turn down the opportunity, though it's a party trick in which I take some glee—if the body has to be defiled, one might as well spread the discomfort around a little. Only after the operation was I struck by the lightning bolt of sexual implications, having changed my frontal view forever. But this is how time iterates itself for everyone, I know, I know, by hacking us to bits—the breast removed, the kidney taken: this is the storyboard of the modern body. Or we are remodeled with added bits, with titanium under our skin or inside our arteries.

The pump and its scar fit exactly in the palm of my hand, with my thumb resting on the flattened spot. When I am trying to give an erotic purpose to my nakedness and do not have an appropriate piece of drapery, I leave my hand there like Napoleon with his wrist curled into a pocket.

Even though the disappearance of one's young body is a tired lament, it is especially galling to me not only because of how I once worshipped at the temple of physical fitness but also because of the extremity of my body's being sacked. When I asked Jim the other day how he could stand making love to such a freak, he said: "That's what eyelids are for." (Of course the word *freak* is somewhat confrontational, somewhat melodramatic in its assessment of the body, and in slang usage it also refers to a person who is willing to defy sexual convention. Which is another form of aggrandizement, this defiant persona used to fill a vacuum caused by the body's losses.)

So we keep our eyes shut, though actually the dropped lid was always my preference—I never wanted to see the face that makes the cry that poet Louise Glück calls "the low, humiliating / premise of union." Before her, the nineteenth-century French poet Charles Baudelaire elaborated in prose, and at greater length, on the subject:

> Do you hear those sighs, those groans, those cries, those rattles in the throat? Who has not uttered them, who has not irresistibly extorted them? These unfocused sleepwalker's eyes, these limbs whose muscles spring up and stiffen as if attached to a galvanic battery: the wildest effects of drunkenness, delirium and opium will certainly not give you such horrible and curious examples. And the human face, which Ovid thought was created to reflect the stars: there it is, bereft of speech, with an expression of wild ferocity, or slackening in a kind of death. For certainly I think it would be sacrilege to apply the word *ecstasy* to this sort of decomposition.

The face is embarrassing and also frightening: the body at its moment of utmost concentration, as if it were in the midst of committing a violent crime. But then also, oddly, the face looks almost bored, as if it is about to drop off into sleep, as if it were a decoy face we concoct to camouflage the oddity of what is going on. This is probably why female praying mantises chew off their mates' heads: so that they never have to see that face again.

Especially maddening is the knowledge that we are being looked at just as we are looking: in order to proceed, I have to make myself forget this, and then I soldier on alone. But when I close my eyes and conjure images, the merest whisper of disease will kill the romantic urge; so my real body must be banished, forgotten, in a fudging of the facts. To do the work of my delusion I call on what I call "the dirigibles," zeppelins made of skin, my surrogate inflatables—(that archetypal taut flesh)—from the planet of their silk bedding. From the journals of Anaïs Nin with their fringed lamp shades and brocade pillows. From the cranial basement's leather chambers with its pneumatic apparatus.

When I was a kid, they were treasure, buried under my father's mattress, where I'd find not just *Playboy* but magazines like *Argosy*—magazines that featured hoity-toity nudes photographed through colored filters. I remember bringing a copy to the storeroom of Mr. Phillips's fourth-grade class, where we girls—and only girls, as the boys did not seem courageous enough to invite—scrutinized the torsos that ultimately yielded none of their secrets despite the intensity of our interrogation. The secret of buttocks' rolling countryside and the nipple's artsy silhouette.

In my imagination, these surrogates are like elephant seals—the male-to-female ratio among their population is low—and possibly this is because of how they entered my childhood brain, as a girlish preoccupation. To my grade-school brain, the bodies called like sirens, and the quest for them took me to my father's nightstand and through his drawers, then to tree houses and crawlspaces crisscrossed by sunlight coming though the lattice that was supposed to beautify the creepy darkness underneath the porch, the place where cats gave up the terrifying screams that accompanied their love. I am brought back to that childhood territory by the better side of the dirigibles' nature. Common earthly life is present in them (in many respects a body is just a body) but its form has been so transformed that it seems they must have swallowed a potion, like Mr. Hyde with all his majestic lawlessness.

But their ability to work spells over us also can seem, at least in adulthood, like a degrading trick—the stack of porno magazines left beside the toilet at the fertility clinic, so insultingly unscientific. Now the flesh arrives daily, whenever I dial in to check my vapor-mail, and it *is* like Mr. Hyde's, if he had set up a drive-thru franchise for his fizzy beverage. Relentlessly this flesh scuttles after novel permutations, having exhausted the more conventional ones. But there are no novel permutations anymore, and I think of a line from John Berryman's *Dream Songs*: "We are using our own skins for wallpaper and we cannot win."

This is the primitive world we've re-created with our electronic wizardry. But way before humans arrived at any sophisticated ideas of commerce, sex in most animals made use of the economies of scale—lots of reproduction, lots of offspring produced with the slim hope that one might make it to adulthood. One of the most cherished books I own is my ninety-nine-cent 1976 copy of Haig H. Najarian's *Sex Lives of Animals without Backbones*, replete with line drawings of protozoa blending and splitting. It contains also a sketch of the various copulating positions of squid. The breaching of various species of ovum, gametes moving like the harlequins of Cirque du Soleil. There is a drawing of hermaphroditic snails who pile orgiastically one on the other, penetrating whatever orifice is most proximate.

Professor Najarian doesn't come right out and state it, but his book is a testimony to the primordial birthright of our desires. We cannot help them, so we are innocents. He dedicates the volume to his mother.

:::

With the combined forces of money and evolution and electronics at work, it seemed bound to happen that naked skin would exhaust itself. This exhaustion sends me back to my pathetic self, the self I have banished—and of course as soon as the mind banishes the actual body then the actual body insists on barging into the Jacuzzi in the Hawaiian isles where one was attempting to build a modern-day diorama modeled after, say, something from a painting by Paul Gauguin.

There is also the problem of the wheelchair, which must be banished from the diorama, whereupon the wheelchair retaliates by barging into the scene too. One wants to camouflage it with garlands, or weeds like what the soldiers in Vietnam wore on their heads, but that would only make it more obvious. I've thought of asking Jim to remove it, but doing so would make my faint-heartedness too blatant. Instead let me look at it steadily and say, *Yes, that is my wheelchair over there.* Oh no, that is too tough, so I close my eyes and enter a darkness where it wreaks havoc nonetheless.

From the first I heard of it, I was eager to see Pedro Almodovar's movie *Talk to Her*, which builds its plot around the erotic potential in the afflicted body. The two female leads occupy slots far from the center of the spectrum of possible incapacitation—they're in comas. And the story makes use of doubles, two couples, two healthy men and two comatose women: one has been in a car accident when the movie commences and the other, a bullfighter, gets gored while we watch. But it is the sight of the inert body being handled that makes the viewer squirm, as the male nurse Benigno rubs it with emollients. He opens her legs like the handles of a pair of pliers so that he can perform the offices of the washrag and the menstrual pad. Her total pliancy is a parody of the pornographic ideal, and we soon grow confused over whether we are seeing acts of charitable love, or courtship, or duty, or perversion.

In the movie the women are, in a strange way, perfected. One good (if predictable) joke—when Benigno voices his intention to marry his Alicia—is that they will get along better than most married couples. The bullfighter's boyfriend, on the other hand, has a normal relation to his lover's comatose body, which means he is estranged from it and helpless in its presence. Benigno's advice: *Talk to her.*

Most of us tend to panic when confronted with the mystery of stricken flesh—we do not know how to fix it, and this is the cause of our estrangement and helplessness. There is also an iota of fear: of contagion, no matter how irrational, no matter how nontransmissible the sickness. As lovers *and* nurses, the men in the movie have a choice only of the perverse relationship or the inadequate one. This is a neat cinematic dichotomy, of course, about which we know one thing for sure: that the body's languishing will somehow be resolved in two hours, whereupon we will once again step out into the true and scary world that has no such finite starts and ends.

Scary because here the languishing can go on for years, and whatever allure the pliant body might have inevitably deteriorates as the caregiver is worn down by his duties. Almodovar's movie does give to one of its women the cinematic cliché of the miracle cure, but coming to terms with my illness has forced me to give up on that possibility, which I think caused the relationship between my psyche and my illness to remain childish, meaning that it was presided over by a child's false sense of immunity to time. While last year's therapist felt that my giving up on hope had darkened my outlook, I think hope shackled me to my body as it dropped like dead weight to the floor of the sea. And surrendering hope has left me feeling unburdened, lighter, strangely giddy as I float.

There is an erotic component to this surrender—it comes from the self relinquishing control, throwing itself away. Then the body is offered to whatever seizes possession of it—whether the seizer be disease or time or a human lover. Or it could be religious ecstasy—as in Bernini's *Saint Theresa and the Angel*, her head tipped back with her eyes closed and her mouth hanging slack, again that half-bored, half-sleeping decoy face, signaling that the attention normally given to the world is being turned inward with all the intensity Theresa can muster.

I'm getting my picture of the sculpture from the cover of the book *Erotism* by Georges Bataille, French philosopher of the sexual appetite whose thinking derives from a blend of Baudelaire and the Marquis de Sade. Bataille takes for his book's premise that *eroticism is assenting to life up to the point of death.* I don't know what this means in pragmatic terms, but my brain drifts in the same direction as the main current of his thought: that we are each so alone in our bodily organism-ness that our spiritual lives, and our sexual lives, act out our desire to achieve communion with something beyond the edges of our own skin. The egg and sperm's smashing together is the version of his thesis writ in miniature; in larger form, there is the example of the human falling down enraptured and speaking in tongues, an Esperanto that links the soul to a mystical race from the beyond.

There is also the larger drama that takes place in the bedroom, more serious than a game, sort of like the living tableaus that women would form at garden parties in the nineteenth century, the Three Graces with their limbs so intertwined they become one sculptured entity. (I know about this only because I had to orchestrate exactly this kind of fused flesh in my role as the mayor's wife in our sixth-grade production of *The Music Man.*)

You can see why these activities would be appealing to a cripple. Joining forces with someone else means a respite from fighting the body's ravages on one's own. Strife loves company, especially strife in which one is bound to go down the loser. Plus it seems that if I can get deep enough into my body maybe all its disturbing symptoms will disappear, the way the storm goes calm at the eye of it. And this *does* happen—a bit of good biology I chalk up to the pain relievers called endorphins that are released by the brain.

There are also practical considerations: sex is usually accomplished lying down, a posture that camouflages frailty. Except of course now the bulge of the pump is always there.

:::

To be partly human and partly a mechanical thing: this is a cyborg, in the parlance of science fiction. Sometimes the cyborg becomes an

238 ::: LUCIA PERILLO

erotic object for her very freakishness: I have seen several *Star Trek* epi-
sodes that hinge on this premise. She has the stamina of the machine,
plus the mystery of who-knows-what carnal apparatus. She has human
beauty, usually manifested in a slightly abstract form, sheathed in silver
skin or with a face partially occluded by a metal superstructure. Part of
me thinks that being a freak is interesting—the great hunt of my youth
was for some distinction that would render me more exotic than the
run-of-the-mill other girls. And one of the most arousing memories of
my recent life is Jim batting my hand away from where I was using it to
anchor the hem of my T-shirt, this when the foreplay was just starting
to take, him saying, *I don't care if I see it.*

All my life, in health and out, I have hunted for communion—drugs,
meditation, mountain climbing, men, a variety of religions; I have
sought dissolution of my physical walls, the body cast off like clothing
stepped out of and kicked across the floor. Lately I've even looked at
the maundering of that newest of Bataille's offspring, the art history
professor in France who supposedly had sex under highway bridges
with street people and stevedores. I understand why she would want to
do it, though I see it as a weakness in her character, this desire to cast
off the body when there is nothing wrong with hers.

As far as poetry goes, the body in extremis has given us Crazy Jane
and Baudelaire—or for a more homegrown example, we could look at
Raymond Carver's "Proposal," a poem that is partly about making love
after his diagnosis of terminal cancer, surely a justifiable circumstance
for self-relinquishment:

> Back home we held on to each other and, without
> embarrassment or caginess, let it all reach full meaning. This
> was it, so any holding back had to be stupid, had to be
> insane and meager. How many ever get to this: I thought
> at the time.

How many ever get to this: see how the diseased want to be an exclusive
club, a Mensa society of fornicators. We think our love takes greater
courage, no matter how limp our secret handshake is.

And it occurs to me that someday I will eat these words I've written
here, because what I know most surely about my erotic life is the fact

that it is provisional. My body will have changed by morning—and, in all likelihood, not for the better. And Cupid is a little guy whose energy seems liable to flag as the body starts grinding through the hard work of decay.

Because decay underlies it all, is both the substance of our graves and the loamy below-porch cat-shit-littered birthplace of the dirigibles (Yeats's Crazy Jane pops their balloonlike forms when she says, "Love has pitched his mansion in / The place of excrement"), I should also mention the second of Bataille's great themes: about how taboos arise in order that the body's interior and exterior not be mixed. Blood and feces are not permitted to present themselves in open air, except under controlled and ritualized circumstances. Civilization simply does not function when one loses control of one's bowels in the big box store (this was not me, by some lucky stroke, though I said to myself, *You coward*, when I did not help the woman whose violating of the taboo I had witnessed in Costco; instead I scuttled away like everyone else, afraid of how wildly, how flagrantly, she had swung an ax at the ice of my human heart.)

Fear of the swampy wilderness in the body's interior is one of the idiosyncrasies of the human species. Wrote the diarist W. N. P. Barbellion in 1915, to show us how contrary the animal kingdom can be on the matter of this taboo:

> The vomits of some Owls are formed into shapely pellets, often of beautiful appearance, when composed of the glittering multi-coloured elytra of Beetles, etc. The common Eland is known to micturate [note: this means pee] on the tuft of hair on the crown of its head, and it does this habitually, when lying down, by bending its head around and down—apparently because of the aroma, perhaps of sexual importance during mating time, as it is a habit of the male alone.

Polite society imagines that the worst part of disability—the real horror of it—comes from how porous disease will make the corporal boundary, and as a result much energy goes into camouflaging the taboo's breakage. So I hide the bulky package of my disposable underwear underneath the bathroom sink. Once, when giving myself an injection of interferon, I hit a vein by accident and a rooster tail of blood sprayed across the stark white kitchen. It was obscene but also thrilling, a phenomenon I was familiar with only because I'd read the novels of Denis Johnson. He sums up the taboo in one of the stories in his book *Jesus' Son*: "There's so much goop inside of us, man . . . and it all wants to get out."

If I examine it calmly, I can see it's a needless waste of emotional voltage, the panic roused around the job of hiding the material leakage of the self. The Costco is full of shit, it will not be harmed by more; my dinner may spray from my mouth and my bladder may shudder around what it impounds, but it is still worth that uncontrollable raucous laughter when the right gang is assembled at the table. Jim has a quick wit and so he is especially familiar with all these leaks. The other day we were alone when my nose dripped on my lettuce leaf, and quickly I popped it back into my mouth for a joke—why can't the fluids return, they've only moved an inch, and they might have gone there in a back-sniffle anyway? *You're sick*, he pronounced—*ha! exactly!* It is easy for an invalid to get exhausted by the vigilance—that foremost among our mortal chores should be this job of keeping the goop inside.

When it comes to sex, though, what we want is leakage: for the essence of self to get through to somebody else somehow. And this applies not just to body, but to mental essence as well: we want to experience the same ecstatic goop that's packed inside the person with whom we're trying to fuse. And we want that essence to be received not in words but in actual *feeling*, a direct body-to-body download—at least I do. I want my faulty neural circuits to be overridden and over-written. I want some mental analog of the copulatory experience of an eland.

The trouble is words, how they remain the barbed-wire fence wrapped around us that we cannot climb: "If someone *says* to me what he has thought," writes the philosopher Wittgenstein, "has he really said: what he *thought*? Would not the actual mental event have to remain undescribed?—Was *it* not the secret thing—of which I give another mere picture in speech?"

Sometimes I too turn into a philosopher when Jim and I go pad-dling on a river slow enough to leave us no real work to do, and on these afternoons deep in the shade of alder trees I will ask him: "Do I really know you? Do I really know what you *think*?" On this question what Wittgenstein has to say is: "'Why does what is going on in him, in his mind, interest me at all, supposing that something is going on?' (The devil take what's going on inside him!)"

The question causes Jim also to turn into a crank: "You've known me for twenty years, for God's sake! Of course you know me!" A man who favors action over deliberation, he thinks I invent inane speculations for the purpose of driving him crazy.

And to clarify Jim's position that started me off—*Nobody wants to read about you having sex*—I think what he meant was: *Why would you speak?* In answer, I can only say that a writer will sometimes deign to consider her audience, and it is my belief that people are generally interested in sex, probably even in me having it.

I, MAGGOT

:::

Mark Jude Poirier

MY MOTHER RARELY SPOKE of my father's family history, but when she did, she spoke in threats: "Ask one more question about that cousin-fucker, and I'll kick the queer right out of you!" or "I'll kill Mr. Maggot if he ever shows his inbred face around here again!" Because I had never heard the terms *cousin-fucker* or *inbred*, I was intrigued. I was ten. I knew what *fucker* meant; a teenage neighbor boy had shown me confusing, shaky videotapes of himself fucking a fat girl from the street over. I couldn't imagine fucking any of my three cousins, not even Bill, whose round shiny biceps stirred me in ways I knew, even at ten, I shouldn't be stirred.

My thirst for knowledge led me first to the dictionary, which didn't fully answer my questions, and then to my mother's closet, where I knew she had hidden a shoe box of old photos, clippings, and letters—important things.

I was more familiar with my mother's closet than my mother was. Her wardrobe was not that extensive, and I had memorized her dresses, blouses, tube tops, shoes, even undergarments. Don't think that I'm a cross-dresser, because I'm not. I never got into that. I was more into organization, so stepping into my mother's closet was both frustrating and exhilarating. I had no siblings, no friends except for the teenager who fucked the fat girl on tape, so I'd often spend hours reorganizing this closet while my mother was at work, xeroxing or doing whatever it was she did in the strip mall office full of agents who rented out other strip malls. I carefully arranged the dresses—only twelve—by season, then subarranged them by color, light to dark. They were equally spaced, hanging three inches apart from one another. I measured with a yardstick, marked the rod with chalk. The shoes: also by season, then by heel height. But, before I organized anything, I took mental pictures of where everything was so I could perfectly restore the messiness after I had my fun. I had to. If my mother knew I had been in her closet, she would have clobbered me.

I found the box right where I had seen it last: behind a pair of scuffed red pumps. (Oh, how I wanted to buff and polish those hideous shoes!) I knew which man in the photos was my father. I had the same nose as he did, a dimpled three-balled proboscis, a nose I would later learn branded me as a cousin-fucking, maggot-loving, meat-wreath-building piece of inbred trash. My favorite photo of him, a photo I was smart enough to later swipe the night before my mother sent me down to UCLA, at age fourteen, to take part in the Feminine Boy Project, shows him washing his car, a bright cerulean sports car—a TR7, I recently determined after extensive Internet research. He's wearing Levi's and a T-shirt with rolled-up sleeves. Butch. Me, except butch. Not forced butch—real butch. Today, the photo is framed in a tastefully basic frame of dark oak, on a crisp, light blue matting. It sits on my desk next to the computer on which I type this.

The other photos, even the other photos of my father, held no interest for me. My mother, graduating from junior business college in a hideous lavender cap and gown; a small home my parents once rented in Nova Scotia; me, minutes after my birth, my foreskin intact. The letters were boring. A few from former boyfriends, one of whom wrote that he missed my mother's "hot titts [*sic*]." There was, however, a ten-page document, handwritten in a loopy script, rolled tightly, and tied with a red ribbon. It was composed in an obscure French dialect—of course, I didn't know that then, when I was ten; I just knew it was a foreign language. I eventually swiped the document as well, and brought it with me to UCLA when I was fourteen.

The Feminine Boy Project: forty boys, ages six to eighteen, prancing, diddling, tickling, wanking, mincing—all under the careful and close supervision of two psychiatrists whom I shall call Dr. X and Dr. Y. We feminine boys lived in a small dormitory that had formerly been used to house visiting football and basketball squads from the PAC-10. The very thought that some big dumb jock from Arizona State or Stanford had once slept in the very bed I was sleeping in, had once sat at the desk where I sat, had once lathered his muscles in the shower where I showered, sent me into a high state of arousal. There were big, clunky early-eighties video cameras mounted on the walls in each room. I'm quite sure now that Dr. X and Dr. Y had once been feminine boys themselves and that their research was nothing more than fodder for their prurience.

The Feminine Boy Project was San Francisco's Castro District in miniature, so it prepared us well for the life that awaited us. The boys who were most masculine, or who had developed the skills necessary to come across as masculine, were the ones we all wanted. None of us wanted a prancing Nellie like ourself. The more masculine boys— MMBs—only wanted boys like themselves. That left a bunch of frustrated young fags, each of us getting bitchier as the days passed.

Dr. X and Dr. Y fawned all over the MMBs, especially the postpubescent ones, granting them special privileges, buying them gifts of body oil and wrestling singlets. We received nothing except three drab meals per day, all of which tasted of musk because, as I later learned, they were laced with testosterone. Yogurt: testosterone; jelly toast: testosterone; cheese pizza: testosterone. The hormones caused several of the boys to develop beer guts, hairy necks, and shrunken testicles but did nothing to help eliminate lisps, expressive hands, or fits of girlish giggling.

After weeks of shoving seminars, basic math and science courses, two hours per day of physical education where we were smacked into learning to throw perfect spirals, I discovered that I could sneak out after dinner for a few hours and stroll about the UCLA campus.

The fourth-floor restroom in the university's main library was where I learned that there are some butch men—mostly closet cases— who prefer the company of girly boys. After a few months of ritualized abuse from strangers in stall three, I explored more of the campus, and eventually found my way to the French department, where I met Emille Gaudette, PhD, the crackpot Canadian dyke who would eventually translate the papers I had stolen from my mother's closet.

Emille was a visiting professor from a small island close to the island from which my father's family hailed. I was a smart kid, if I do say so myself; I knew that I needed someone from the Nova Scotia area to translate the papers, and I asked the secretary, a man I recognized from the fourth-floor restroom scene, if UCLA was home to anyone like that. He directed me to Emille's office.

Emille's door was ajar, and there she sat: a grotesquely obese blob, her blubbery wrist cinched by a man's thick digital watch. She ate pungent sardines from a can. Colette paperbacks were stacked on her desk in precarious towers. She wore a green pantsuit, with a large set of keys affixed to her belt. I had never seen a dyke before, so I was a little taken aback, but the social skills I'd learned at the Feminine Boy Project came in handy, and I introduced myself.

"I have heard about that Project of Feminine Boys," she said in a husky French accent. "I think it is vile, and I have written several letters to the chancellor in complaining."

"It's not that bad," I told her. "Some of the older guys are cute."

We chatted a few more moments, and then I asked her about the papers. She was intrigued, ran her finger along her hairy upper lip. "My childhood was very near to the Island of Prince Robert," she said. "Bring me the papers tomorrow."

I did, and the translation follows:

I, Maggot
By Jean Poirier XII
Translated from the French By Dr. Emílle Gaudette

On the northwest corner of our island, the Island of Prince Robert, where in winter the wind lashes us so hard that our teeth freeze and crack and dislodge from our purpled gums, where the Gulf of Saint Pierre is gray with millions of dead octopuses, where each of us bears the surname Poirier or Gaudette and, responding to some atavistic itch, curls up with his cousin to stay warm and perpetuate the bloodline, the Spring Meat Wreath custom continues—and will continue despite the protestation of my younger brother, Barthelmew.

Throughout winter, each of us in this seaside hamlet of Parmonte dreams of the tinkle of maggot chimes. When the days begin to elongate, we happily prepare by breaking shovels and choosing meats.

Three meats must be used in the braiding: beef, pork, and horse. If no horse is available, as has often been the case, dog can be used, but only if the pork is substituted with lion of the sea. Beef is always available. Pork is not. Moose may be substituted for pork, but not if horse is unobtainable. In this case, snake is used in lieu of horse—which pleases many, as the snakes are easily braided, especially the thin Nova

Scotia ice snake, sometimes called the Saint Pierre ice eel, although it is a reptile, not a fish. Thus there are myriad possibilities for the meat wreaths, each producing its own odor and sound.

Barthelmew drinks soybean milk from boxes emblazoned with Chinese characters. He will not sit at the table with the rest of the family—my father, my sister, and me—if any product of animal is being consumed. He does not eat ice cream, of course. Most cookies are made with eggs, so he avoids them. The colored marshmallows in some American breakfast cereals hold their shapes with the help of gelatin that is made from the hooves of various ungulates. He eats no soup prepared with beef or chicken stock—and what palatable soup is not? Barthelmew rides a ferry every few weeks, even in the darkest and coldest months, across the bay to Newfoundland—a six-hour voyage, sometimes through bergs of ice the size of skyscrapers—to buy his animal-free food products from hippies who escaped to our hemisphere for political reasons. Barthelmew eats in his bedroom with the door shut, which my father and I find disrespectful to my sister, who painstakingly prepares our meals. My sister often cries.

The antics of Barthelmew are especially tiresome now because the Meat Swap is in full swing. I search for the best strips, adhering closely to the rules of combination. There is a surfeit of horse this year! Tough bands of the most sinewy cut hang from hooks above many of the booths. I prefer the traditional beef, pork, and horse wreath, as the dog and lion of the sea tend to fall rather quickly, and the hypersalinity of snake blood causes the snake flesh to cling to the meat frame long into summer. I have seen well-preserved and maggot-free snake meat hanging on family doors in July. Imagine waiting until late summer to hear a round of maggot chimes! The availability of horse this year is a good omen: the summer will be long and wet, and the winter short and dry.

Today Barthelmew marches through the Meat Swap holding a placard: IF YOU ARE GOING TO KILL ANIMALS, AT LEAST EAT THEM. He does not utter a word, just paces by the booths, abiding the jeers from angry meatmongers, hiding his face behind his stringy hair. Someone flings a liver at the back of his head—a wet slap.

I promenade along the cobblestones of Parmonte, my white canvas trousers blotted with the blood of the three animals. I step over hundreds of traditionally broken shovels, playfully kicking a few to the curb. My meat satchel is full and heavy. Cousins wave to me from windows and stoops. Their fingertips are bloodstained, their springtime grins wide and honest. Meat is in the air. It is palpable.

The man—considered a man if he is at least fourteen years of age by the first of January—and his winter cousin braid meat together. They make one wreath. The wreath is officially the property of the male and will hang on the door of his house, on the door of the house of his father, or on the door of the house of his oldest brother. The winter cousin is permitted to stay with the man until they both hear the first tiny peals of the maggot chimes. The man builds the frame of the wreath with branches and nails. The winter cousin is permitted to nail the braided meat to the frame, but traditionally it is the task of the man.

We speak French. Our pallor is like the milk of cows, and our hair color ranges from mahogany to tar black. Our hair is thick. No man balds. There are six nose types among us: coned, hooked, hooked cone, conical upward hook, downward hook, and the dimpled three-balled proboscis. My father, my sister, and I were each blessed with the conical upward hook, that of my sister being the daintiest. Barthelmew has the dimpled three-balled proboscis. He is nineteen and has never taken a winter cousin. I believe he is a homosexual.

My winter cousin Doreen waits for me on the front porch, holding her meat satchel like a newborn, rocking it. She has daubed her full bosom with blood, the conventional gesture to indicate she is willing to be my winter cousin again next year. This makes me happy, as she told me in March of last year that my knob-loving needed improvement. I found the appropriate pamphlets in the office of the town physician, studied the diagrams and photos, and went to work that night, her soft thighs pressing my ears flat against my head. Now, the maroon smudge across her cleavage and her coquettish smile tell me that my knob-loving has improved. Barthelmew has never loved the knob of a winter cousin.

:::

According to lore, the original meat wreath was hung in 1874 by Jean Poirier to win the heart of Geraldine Gaudette, the town beauty. The Gaudettes were poor. The children, including thirteen-year-old Geraldine, were gaunt and often ravaged by impetigo, lice, and Canadian sallet worms. But the beauty of Geraldine shone through her afflictions. When young Jean noticed her, he was smitten. Each night, he sneaked meat morsels over to her window. He exchanged the napkin-wrapped meat for transfenestratory kisses. The father of Geraldine was a proud man, and when he learned of the amatory transactions of his daughter, he forbade her from accepting the meat. He forbade Jean from setting foot on his property and threatened to kill him with a garden shovel.

Jean began to hoard meat scraps under his bed until he had enough to make a silent statement—the original meat wreath. But the meat was not braided; it was nailed to a circular board in clumps. Jean felt the rotting meat was a perfect badge for the hateful restriction—if Mr. Gaudette chose to deprive his daughter of the meat, it should openly rot. Each morning, as the Gaudette children passed the Poirier house on their way to school, they stared at the carrion. They smelled it, too, and when they gagged, they would be reminded of their scornful and hapless father, the man who could not provide them with meat of their own. Geraldine never gagged. She breathed in the sweet rotten stink like ambrosia, and her grubby collar was wet with tears by the time she reached her desk at school.

One afternoon, upon returning from school, Jean noticed a maggot plop from the carrion. A moment later, another fell. They squirmed at his feet as their parents buzzed around his head. The falling maggots gave him an idea: the rotting meat was not enough by itself; he needed something beautiful to represent the love he felt for Geraldine. Beautiful sounds! Chimes!

He first tried a cowbell, built a little wooden frame for it and placed it under the falling maggots. Maggots did hit the bell, but the sound was barely audible. Next he hung many small bells of the type usually reserved for reins on holiday sleighs. When the maggots hit these bells: sweet little pings. But the sounds were unsatisfactory to Jean, not quite loud enough. He went to the toolshed and pounded the cowbell into a flat sheet, the clapper and all. When he put down the hammer, the cowbell was the size of a large dinner plate, and as thin as paper. He sawed small notches around the edge of this flat sheet. To these notches he tied the jingle bells with the laces from his old church boots. Using eight sticks, he rigged his new work under the wreath. The final product looked like a miniature wood and metal trampoline.

He waited for the maggots to fall, and when they did, the sound was beautiful: melodious and rich, a politely tuned gong sound followed by the happy jingle of the holiday bells. When bits of carrion fell, the sound was equally sonorous, but deeper, more pronounced.

That night, Jean tiptoed across the lawn of the Gaudettes, ducking behind trees and bushes. He knocked lightly on the window of Geraldine and told her to meet him on his front porch. There, next to the maggot chime, outside the door, Jean had prepared pillows and blankets. They spent the remainder of the night in the arms of each other, listening to the maggot chimes, every note sending a charge through their intertwined bodies.

As he had done every morning since he learned Jean was interested in his daughter, Mr. Gaudette woke in the darkness with nervous energy coursing through his veins. He stretched, put on his boots, and walked down the hall to check on Geraldine. Her sleeping pad was vacant.

He draped a coat over his wool underclothes, grabbed a shovel, and ran to the house of the Poiriers, where he found his daughter and her paramour.

As the first rays of sun stretched across the dewy spring grass, Mr. Gaudette stomped his boot on the shovel, easily bisecting the esophagus and larynx of Jean. The vertebrae separated with ease. The moist cracking sound woke Geraldine, and she screamed.

Nine months later, she gave birth to the first Poirier-Gaudette, a boy she called Little Jean.

:::

Doreen and I braid the meat in my bedroom after spreading newspaper over the floor. The braiding symbolizes the perpetual union of Jean, Geraldine, and Little Jean. Doreen is a tight braider; her three meats become one. Watching her hands as she tugs the wet tendons fills me with joy. Another winter with her! Our wreath is handsome, and I pull the velvet tarp off the maggot chime. Only one group of

Poirier-Gaudettes makes the chimes. They live behind the tallest hill in Parmonte, in a large barn. The men in the group have bulging forearms on which they tattoo images of their winter cousins. The women in the group are said to have the largest knobs on the island. I have never taken a winter cousin from the chime group, so I cannot verify the knob information. For his fourteenth birthday, a boy is given a maggot chime by his father, who walks over the hill the night before. The boy becomes a man in a brief, secret ceremony. I am not at liberty to divulge the details of the sacrament, but I can say that it is painless and quite pleasing. Barthelmew refused to participate in the ceremony. My father is still disappointed.

I carry the wreaths, and Doreen carries the chime. I hang the wreaths, and Doreen places the chime. We smile. She licks my neck. Her tongue is warm.

Tonight, my sister, who has never been taken as a winter cousin because of her lazy eye and clubfoot, prepares the Spring Meal: pheasant stuffed with sweetly marinated beef cubes, glazed in molasses, served on a bed of raisins, chestnuts, and woven bacon strips. And à la carte, she serves us zesty venison muffins, steamed broccoli, and russet potatoes. While the main course my sister prepares is quite traditional, she strays from the norm for dessert and carries in a large prune and maple pie, still steaming from the oven.

My father watches wistfully as Doreen places her fork on her lap, wipes her face with a napkin, and licks my neck. My sister mimes the procedure, licking the air. We leave a portion from each course of the meal on the windowsill to attract men to my sister. Someday she will be braiding meat with a man, I am sure. Someday a man will love her knob. I tell her this. I remind her that her fine cooking will win over any man. My winter cousin and my father agree. My sister smiles and begins to clear the table when we hear a shriek from out front.

I first see tall flames, then Barthelmew amid them, flailing madly like a caged monkey. Some of the broken shovels are not burning, but the fire is big enough to engulf him. Flames dance from his back and legs. His charred head smokes. His shrieks become louder, more pained, higher in pitch and more infantile. Then they stop. I hear the crackle of the fire. He crumbles. His seared head lies flat against the lawn.

My sister screams. My father screams and stomps his feet. My winter cousin does not scream; she gasps, then begins to breathe quickly.

I smell Barthelmew. The stink of Barthelmew is thick. It gathers in my throat and I taste it. I taste him.

A note is nailed to the door just below the meat wreath. Three words in the jagged scrawl of Barthelmew: A FINAL PROTEST.

Where is my maggot chime?

END

Postscript:

I read the translation in Emille's office a few days later, and was horrified when Jean was murdered and Barthelmew burst into flames. Emille did not try to comfort me directly, only said, "The story of Jean is an excuse for inbreeding in a small gene pool. And it is unclear if Barthelmew actually died. I have read other documents that indicate he constructed a large puppet of meat and burned that in his stead. He made his family think he burned, but he lives happily with his man-lover on a small farm of organic vegetables in Oregon, United States." Not true, I'm sure, but a nice unexpected gesture from a macho woman like Emille.

That night, in the dorm, I gathered several boys from the project, and I read them the translation. Silence followed. Several boys' cheeks were streaked with tears—for Barthelmew, the tragic lovers, or all of them, I don't know, but there was a beautiful solidarity among us until stupid Dennis dramatically flipped the blond bangs from his eyes and asked, "What's 'knob-loving' mean?" I wanted to punch him. Honestly. But I realized that was probably what Dr. X and Dr. Y had been conditioning me to do, so I sat on my hands.

BLOOMS

:::
:::

Peter Rock

I TOOK A JOB no one else wanted, and I learned many things I would never have believed. Here's an easy one, to start with: fungus can bloom inside books. Different kinds of molds, mostly, in dark, damp libraries where the air isn't too good. Fungi cannot make their own food; they take what they can from other organic matter. They start on the fabric and cardboard of the books' covers, then feed on the pulpwood in the pages, the vegetable dyes in the ink—kind of like how moss grows on tree trunks, swings from branches.

Samples are taken, and sent to a laboratory, to check if the bloom is virulent. Usually, it's not—it's only penicillium or aspergillus—and then they send in a team to clean it up. This is no job for librarians. They hire other people, whoever they can get. It's not exactly skilled labor.

An injury had forced me from my previous occupation. I'd been working down the shore, on the boardwalk. I wore a suit with three inches of padding, a hockey mask painted with a fanged smile. I leapt around behind fake trees, in front of a canvas backdrop, and people shot paintball guns at me. Ten shots for three dollars—I had targets on my suit, my helmet, a bull's-eye on my crotch that everyone found hilarious. I wore two cups, with padding between them. Tough-talking boys couldn't touch me, cursing with their cracked voices, slapping their temporary tattoos; it was their girlfriends—bikini tops, slack expressions, baby fat under their arms—who had the deadly aim. At the end of the day, in the shower, I counted the round bruises on my skin.

One day I was recounting a story to a friend of mine, holding the mask in my hand. He had one of the guns, twirling it around his finger like Jesse James. When it went off, it caught me in the face—side-swiped me, actually, not even as hard as a punch. Dark red paint splattered across my temple, into my ear. I was left with this detached retina, where my vision's crooked and everyone I talk to thinks I'm trying to say something else; it's still shadowy on that side, but some days I believe it's clearing. Some days I'm not so sure.

My boss said he couldn't be held accountable for a time I wasn't working. Playing grab-ass—those were his words. And, of course, with my vision wrecked, my depth perception completely gone, I did not make a very challenging target. I was sore all over. We gave away half the stuffed animals in one afternoon.

Fortunately, none of this impaired me for the new job—the blooms did not move so fast. I answered an ad and was hired over the phone, told where to be the next morning.

They said I'd work on a team; what that meant was one other guy, Marco. He was forty, at least, from South Philly, where he still lived. Older than me, and heavier, with gray flecks in his hair, which was thick on the sides but you could see through it on top, his scalp shining. He had a heavy way of walking, almost sliding his feet. His hands would hang down at his sides, opening and closing with each step. My first impression was that he would never surprise me. Nothing he would do, nothing he would say.

We didn't shake hands when we first met, he just started to show me how things worked. Hair pushed out the collar of his T-shirt, both front and back. He'd done this kind of work before, and he told me there were worse jobs.

I've had them, I said.

He told me he was only working long enough to make enough money to get out of town, and I nodded and said that sounded wise.

I have to get out, he said. The reasons are personal.

We went through a side door, on a kind of loading dock, down a flight of stairs. The books we were dealing with were on two floors—a basement, and then another basement beneath that. There was not one window. Marco had already isolated the area with clear plastic sheeting, hung up the warning signs.

He helped me into my suit, that first day. It was white, made of Tyvek, with a long zipper up the front and zippers on the sides of the legs. We wore latex gloves, and baggy paper booties we had to replace every time we went outside. The hoods on our heads had clear plastic face panels; we wore battery packs on our belts; a fan with a tube blew filtered air in front of our faces. It took one morning of breathing my own breath in that hood before I quit smoking. That's one positive thing that came of that job.

The blooms, they were a green fuzzy mold, streaked with black. Fibrous, like nothing you'd want in your lungs. They rested atop books, forced the covers open where they weren't tight in the shelves and squeezing each other. We started out with the vacuums, fitted with HEPA filters that trapped spores. Marco would work one aisle and I'd do the next. The shelves were tall, but sometimes I'd pull out a book and see him there, on the other side, his face close but his expression hidden. We kept moving, slowly and methodically, as if we were underwater.

The days went fluidly, each like the one before it, progress marked only by the bookshelves left behind. Sections of maps, then encyclopedias. Novels, even poetry. It was strange to spend so much time so close to a person without being able to talk with him. We went our separate ways at lunch, and the rest of the time we were inside the suits and ventilators. It was all white noise down there—the fans, the rustle of Tyvek, the sound of pages being flipped under our gloved thumbs.

At least a week passed before we first had lunch together. He asked me to join him. We walked half a block, bought sandwiches from a truck, then headed toward a little park. When the children in the playground saw us coming, they started screaming, Astronauts! We always got a kick out of that.

The wooden bench we sat on had been chewed by pit bulls—the owners train them to do it, to strengthen their jaws. Next to the jungle gym, the plastic swings were so gnawed they looked melted. When we bit into our sandwiches, shredded lettuce fell onto the ground, tangled with cigarette butts.

Marco stood and tried to touch his toes. He stretched his arms and grunted. All that work in the damp library tightened his joints.

I wonder, he asked, if you wouldn't mind rubbing my knee a little.

I'd give it a try, I told him.

Not everyone would, he said.

If it helps, I said.

I kind of kneeled down and tried to get a decent hold, through the slippery Tyvek, using both hands. Marco picked up his sandwich, closed his eyes. He obviously shaved, but there were always these long whiskers along his throat, ones he missed. I rubbed his knee. The sun stayed where it was, straight overhead, stuck there.

You're probably wondering what I'm going to do for you, Marco said.

I told him not really. My knees felt fine.

I live in a row house, Marco said. So I share walls with my neighbors. Thin walls.

A couple lived there, and he'd hear their arguments—threats, recriminations, then the usual coming to terms. Marco would turn up his radio, or go out walking around his neighborhood.

Italians, he said, almost spitting.

I thought you were Italian, I said.

I am, he said.

There was an Indian spice shop near that park, so it always smelled a little foreign. The air was thick. Marco picked his teeth with his fingernail as he spoke.

Pay attention, he said. This won't turn out any way you expect.

I told him I had no expectations.

Sometimes on the mornings after the arguments, Marco would run into the man from next door. You're lucky, the man would say, you were safe—a wall between you and her. Pray for me, these nights! He and Marco would laugh together.

What happened to him? I asked, guessing ahead.

I just stopped hearing him through the wall, Marco said. Stopped seeing him in the front yard. He was gone.

And that was your opening, I said. Don't tell me—she's incredibly beautiful.

Yes, Marco said. But that's not the point.

We took our time in the basements of the library, though we weren't being paid by the hour. It wasn't that I got a lot of thinking done, exactly; it was almost a different plane of some sort, listening to my own breathing, a kind of meditation. Sometimes I even thought of the people who would follow, who would be able to read the books because I'd saved them.

Sometimes people came down the stairs, descended by mistake, and I'd catch glimpses, twice-distorted by my face shield and the clear plastic barriers. The people seemed to have no feet, to move fluidly, as if they were growing their way smoothly upward again, beyond my sight.

Sometimes, on my break, I'd climb those stairs; I'd hold the door slightly open, my ventilator around my neck and the cool air on my sweaty face. I spied into the library, and it was quiet up there, just like it was supposed to be. A green and yellow parakeet hung on to its perch, inside a bamboo cage. I heard the sound of pages turning. If I held the door open a little farther, I could see the desk where the librarian sat. She was about my age, with dark black skin, gold eyeglasses; her hair was braided close to her head in curving lines, the loose ends like ropes whipping her shoulders. Her fingers were thin, her smile wide as she answered someone's question. Whenever I turned away from her and began to descend into the basement, it was as if my body grew heavier with every step. I wanted her to know there were real people underneath her, that I was beneath her every day. I wanted to tell her I'd wiped mold from musical scores and hummed the melody, that I'd read a Russian story about grown men swimming in the rain, another where people could see into the future and still couldn't change it.

If I could tell the librarian one story, it would be this one. And I would tell her only a little at a time, the way Marco told me, until she had to know what would happen next, until she couldn't stand it.

He never used the woman's real name, since he said I was his friend and he was afraid I'd try to track her down, once I'd heard it all, that I'd only get myself in trouble. Louisa—that's the name he chose for her.

Their houses shared a porch, so all Louisa had to do was reach over the railing to ring Marco's doorbell. She wanted to ask him a favor. Groceries. She had the list in her hand, and he took it when she held it out.

It's my eyes, Louisa said. I can't see a thing. She told him that the doctors had found nothing wrong, physically, but that didn't help her.

Marco looked at her eyes, and she didn't seem to see him. Her eyebrows had always been tweezed into a narrow arch; now they were returning, thickening. She stood there, barefoot on the concrete porch, the toenails of her left foot painted red. All the words on the list in Marco's hand tilted, and some stretched off the edge of the paper, cut short. Others were written right on top of each other; he struggled to untangle them.

When he returned from the store, he offered to put the things away for her, and she said she could do it. Stay, she told him. You can talk to me while I do.

She held the door open and then led him, moving deftly around the furniture, hitting the light switch exactly and just for him. Later, he tried it in his own house, his eyes closed. He bruised his shins and tore his fingernails; he cursed and stumbled and wondered if she heard him, if she guessed what he was doing.

In the kitchen, she reached and found the knobs on the cupboards; inside, they were carefully organized, all the cans lined up.

I've got it all figured out, she said. I miss being able to read, but that's about it. I was halfway through a book when it happened.

Marco asked if it had happened all at once, and she told him she had one day where everything went dim—that gave her a chance to prepare—and then the next day that was it.

Is it just pitch-black? he said. Or is it like nothing at all? Marco wasn't sure what he meant, exactly. He couldn't stop watching her hands.

Somewhere in between, she said.

He stayed until all the groceries were put away, and then said he'd be happy to help her again.

I remember what you look like, Louisa said, but do you mind? She reached out, and slowly her soft fingertips moved down his face.

Yes, I said, when he told me that. I knew this was going somewhere.

You know nothing, Marco said.

I learned not to say things like that, eventually; it only made him stop talking—it was as if I'd sullied the way it had been. If I asked, he'd say to wait, to be patient. He could only tell it a little at a time; otherwise, it made him too sad.

The conversation at lunch would turn to other things. We'd walk to the park, stripping off our latex gloves, the sweat between our fingers going cool, the zippers of our suits pulled down and their white arms dragging behind us. The weather turned hot and dark, overcast. Trains came and went, slowly, sat on the tracks behind the playground. We watched the dogs, betting on which owners would pick up after theirs and which would pretend oblivion. Down there they had dogs of all shapes, with their tails lopped off, their ears pinned up. Marco knew the names of all the breeds and what they were for. He'd have his arm across the back of the bench, fingers drumming next to my shoulder. I didn't mind. Once we saw a guy crash his bicycle into a parked car as he tried to look behind him, to check the ass on a girl he'd passed. Marco got a good laugh out of that—a little shift like that would bring him around again.

All right, he'd say, turning toward me. Where did I leave off?

The next time Louisa rang his doorbell, she was holding a book in her hand. She asked what he was doing; when he said nothing, she asked if he wouldn't mind reading to her.

She had already read the first three chapters. It was a novel where all the characters were rabbits, but it was for adults. Thick. Later, he borrowed it, to catch up on the beginning.

Louisa wanted him to read to her in the bedroom, so she could lie down and imagine it all. She set a chair next to the bed, then took off her shoes and stretched out.

This isn't right, she said, after a few pages.

The way I'm reading? Marco said.

She said it was strange, because she couldn't see him. She said that his voice was kind of disembodied, and that distracted her from following what was going on in the story.

Is it all right if I reach out and touch you? she said. While you read?

They tried it for another few pages, but she still couldn't get a sense of him.

What is it? he said.

Your clothes, Louisa said. It might be better if I didn't have to feel you through them. Is this turning too weird? You don't know what it's like, like this; I start to need different things to feel anything, to understand.

At first it seemed it would be enough to take off his shirt, to strip down to his underwear. Part of it was to test her, maybe, to see if she was having him on somehow, and part of it was that it excited him.

Did she know you were all the way naked? I said, afraid to interrupt.

I believe so, he said.

He had never been involved in anything like that, he told me, never
felt that way. He'd been married before, even, and this was different—
he felt it in his heart, he said, knowing how ridiculous that sounded.
And he never even touched Louisa, not once, yet sometimes, as the
weeks passed, he'd wake up in the middle of the night because he'd
been laughing in his sleep. He'd just lie there, smiling in the darkness.

Are you happy? Louisa asked him, a little later, that first night.

I guess so, he said.

She told him it seemed like an uneven trade.

Well, he said. I can see. I can read. I can see you.

Are the lights on? she said. Can you see well enough?

Yes, he said, except you're wearing clothes. As soon as he said that,
he was sorry, and he wanted to take it back. He wanted to say it was a
joke, but it was too late for that. Louisa had already begun to answer.

One piece at a time, she took off her clothing, folded it, and stacked
it at the foot of the bed. She lay back, her hand on his leg again. He
knew he was not allowed to touch her, just as she could not see him.

Now, read, she said.

And that's how it always was, after that. There was nothing showy
about it, as if she were alone, unlacing her shoes, unbuttoning her shirt
as he began to read. He turned the lamp up high and moved it closer
to her; her shadow twisted low across the opposite wall, attached to his
by her hand, checking that he was there. He flexed his bare toes on the
cool floorboards.

Louisa's skin was dark and smooth, solid, hiding her bones. She
wasn't skinny. Her thighs were heavy, a scar above one knee. Stretching
and turning over, she'd laugh and hold a smile, showing her teeth, listening. She had a faded tattoo of a rose on her right hip, and a smaller,
clearer one over her right nipple. Perfume rose from her skin as Marco
read; sometimes he'd look up into the full-length mirror on the wall
and see her thin waist angling out to her rounded hips, and himself, the
book in one hand and a glass of water in the other.

He drank between chapters, rested his voice. He counted the few
hairs that circled her nipples, watched how her breasts slid across each
other when she turned, enough space between them to hide a flattened

hand. The hair under her arms matched that between her legs, where the edges, unshaven, were growing back. Her eyes stared and stared, shining.

Are you happy? she asked him.

He told me that she wore no jewelry at all, that there was nothing on her. Nothing. She and Marco hardly spoke, except for his reading, or deciding on the time they'd next meet. He never asked about her husband, and Louisa never brought it up. He felt there were many silent understandings between them.

Of course it took him weeks to tell me all this, and even in pieces the information was not easy for me to process. It was difficult to shake. Sometimes, even now, I set a glass of water beside me and I hold a book in one hand. I read aloud, my voice echoing off the tight walls of the room I rent, not letting my eyes wander from the page, and I imagine my other hand belongs to Louisa, and that she is listening to me, and that she can't see a thing.

Marco's story was far-fetched, but I had never known him to lie. Still, I'd sometimes watch him at work, pausing with a book open in front of him, and I'd wonder if he was coming up with stories to tell me, or searching for something for her, or if he was just staring into the words without reading them, trying to think.

We both slowed as the weeks went on; he slacked off worse than I did, but I didn't mind. Mostly, we spent our time reading. We were using the rubber sponges then, so there was no longer the vacuums' roar. The reflection of the face shields made it difficult to read; sometimes we let the hoods slump over our backs and wore only the ventilator masks with the HEPA filters, our eyes clear and uncovered. In the books where the fungus had really taken hold, it bled down into the pages in red and purple stains, blurring letters, eating words that we could not recover.

Louisa and Marco did not always meet at the same time. Once she'd called him at three in the morning, saying she couldn't sleep, saying she could hear his footsteps and wouldn't he like to come read? They finished the first novel, then went through another, and another. She liked books about animals, others where women took charge.

One of their understandings was that she had to come for him, and not the other way around; after all, he was doing her a favor. It was on a night when he waited—listening for the doorbell, the phone, her knock on the wall—that he heard the man's voice. Next door, and it was not the voice of Louisa's husband.

Marco was jealous, partly, but he also feared something was wrong. He took a can of corn from his own cupboard so he could use it as an excuse, say he forgot to give it to her.

He tried the doorknob before the bell, and the door swung open. He stepped inside, the can of corn in his fist, ready to hit someone with it. In the dim living room he moved around the furniture as easily as she had that first day. He'd come to know her house that well.

In the hallway, closer to the bedroom, he listened; something about the man's voice seemed strange, the rhythm too regular and Louisa never interrupting. He stepped to the doorway and looked inside.

She was stretched out on the bed, wearing a long flannel nightgown, her face turned to the ceiling. On the bedside table, a tape recorder was playing, and the man's voice looped out from it, a hiss behind his words.

Marco took another step, into the room, and waited there, silently. He could tell she sensed him, that she knew he was in the room, and the fact that she said nothing made it all worse. As the taped voice looped around, Marco turned and walked back down the hall. He locked the front door and gently pulled it closed.

The next day, she told him the news. Her vision was returning; it was clearer each day. And the reading couldn't be the same if she could see the shape of him, his slumped shadow and the words coming out. Closing her eyes wouldn't work, when she knew she could open them. Awkward—that's the word she used. Soon she'd be able to read, once again, on her own.

When he told me that, I couldn't stop thinking about it. He'd been right—something in me wanted to find her, to hold her down until she saw some sense.

Marco never read to her again. He did find a place, though, where they made those tapes; he went there and volunteered, read a whole book into a microphone. He hoped Louisa might hear his voice, and remember, and have second thoughts. The sadness I felt, hearing this, was like I'd breathed in the spores and they'd thickened in my throat, blooming darkly through my organs, cold, one at a time like the way a blackout spills over sections of a city.

There was a time I believed and hoped that job could continue indefinitely, that I might persuade Marco to stay on, but those blooms are seasonal, mostly. Nothing stands still.

We were finishing up, just wiping down the shelves with the Clorox solution, when he told me the end of the story. In fact, Marco left before the job was finished, without any warning, and I handled the last few days—tearing down the plastic barriers, taking down the signs—by myself. He left that way, I believe, so he wouldn't have to say goodbye.

It wasn't as if he thought things between him and Louisa could have continued—he knew the balance had changed, that they couldn't return—but he expected it all had to go somewhere, that it couldn't just trail off into nothing.

She refused to speak about it. She was cool, not quite unfriendly. She turned down the simplest favors. She said that had been a different time, that they had been different people who needed different things.

He felt that they were the same, inside the changes. He needed her, and he couldn't stand the way she looked at him, every day, watching him with those same eyes as he came home from work with his hood and ventilator bouncing along his back, the arms of the Tyvek suit tied off around his waist. Her gaze rested cold on him, settling so he felt it even after he was inside his house. He sat alone, shivering; it was very, very quiet on the other side of the wall.

If I ever see Marco again, I'll tell him that I know what happened, even if she was ungrateful, even if she never understood.

He healed her.

NO SMALL FEAT

:::
:::

Robin Romm

MY MOTHER DIED a year and a half ago. It seems that if I write the truth, that it was cancer, no one will publish this story—cancer being a little too ubiquitous. So, for this story, let's call it consumption. It's a romantic idea, anyway—the lungs, the air hunger, the weakness.

My boyfriend, Kierny, is a writer too. He claims to be a novelist, though apparently he also wrote a few stories while I was back in Idaho, adjusting my mom's meds, switching her oxygen tubes around. I found out about Kierny's story writing by accident. It was Saturday and I sat at my kitchen table, trying to write. I was in a bad patch, working and reworking the same fragments. A goose flying out of a woman's mouth. A child hit by a bus. Nothing was going anywhere.

"Why didn't you *tell* me?" Olivia demanded. I'd picked up the phone on the first ring, assuming it would be Kierny.

"What? What didn't I tell you?" Olivia was a friend from graduate school. Everything excited her. Her own ears seemed to make her shrill with joy, but in spite of myself I felt a surge of hope. I'd spent most of the past two years traveling back and forth to care for my mom, then, when she died, dealing with her wreck of an estate. I'd been floundering around, teaching a class here or there, falling into debt. So I welcomed this—whatever it was Olivia was about to impart.

"God, it's like the best one in the anthology, Sarah. You must be so fucking proud."

I had four stories published the year before my mom died—a few in really good places. I'd been on a roll. The magazines came to me in shrink-wrap, my name shining out in glossy black or blue or pink. Did an editor somewhere forget to tell me she'd submitted one for a prize? Could recognition be this delayed?

"It's an incredible rendering of your mother. Just amazing. There's even the way she did that thing when she ate—that thing with her teeth—just a sec, you must know the scene—here it is—page 239—"

"Olivia, what are you talking about?" I asked.

"What do you *mean?*" she said. "Kierny's story in *Best American*," she said, "'Consumed.'" It wasn't April Fools'. No, it was October. The tree outside was bare as a broomstick.

"Sarah?"

"I didn't know about it," I said.

"Oh God," Olivia said. "Whoops."

:::

Kierny didn't pick up his cell phone, which was just as well; I couldn't formulate a thought. I got in my car and drove to the bookstore.

It was probably a mix-up. Another Kierny. Another mother. Kierny had a competitive streak. Every time I had a story accepted, he locked himself away for weeks, working to catch up. But we were honest. We'd been through such hell together. Those midnight phone calls I made after I finally wrestled my mother into bed—my anger the only thing available to me. He lay in bed those awful winter nights, listening to me berate everyone—from the doctors to my closest friends; he didn't try to reason with me. When she finally died, he drove all night from California to make the funeral—showed up in a wrinkled gray shirt and borrowed slacks. He greeted extended family. He cried when I cried. He shoveled dirt into her grave. Had all of this just been research?

I could see the dust floating in the air of the bookstore. Huge skylights cut through the roof and the glossy paperbacks shone. There it was—on the wooden display table with the latest by Eggers, Chabon. *Best American*—its bright orange cover beckoning. I opened it. A few big names and then: Kierny McAllister . . . "Consumed."

Why hadn't he told me about this? I flipped to his bio. "Kierny McAllister is a Louisiana native living in Berkeley, California. 'Consumed' is his first published story."

"The fucker," I said aloud. A woman with a toddler in tow shot me a look. I shot one back.

The fucker.

:::

I brought the book to the cashier and slapped it on the table. I couldn't even read the first line. I threw the book in the trunk and went to find Kierny. He was probably at his studio writing more stories about my life, more stories about my dead mother. For God's sake, Kierny, get your own death. Get your own pain.

Kierny's studio belonged to the McDonald's of art studios. A company bought up vacant lots around California and erected these cheaply constructed corrugated-metal buildings. Kierny had a spot on the ground floor next to a woman who made custom tarot cards and animal-shaped soap. Outside his open door sat a bench and a bunch of happy-looking poppies.

He'd left his door ajar.

"So were you ever going to tell me?" I said.

Some kind of grease had worked its way across his glasses. Papers scattered around him on the floor. He looked annoyed.

"Hi, Sarah," he said.

I went to hold up the book, but I didn't have it, so I ran back to the car, unlocked the trunk, got it out, and ran back. I held it up like a little orange picket sign.

"Look what I found! Someone named Kierny McAllister is writing stories about my mom!"

"Sarah, Jesus," he said.

Kierny turned back to his lit-up screen and saved his document. Then he calmly closed his laptop. It made a soft click.

"So you read it?" he asked.

My arm skin prickled.

"No, not exactly, not yet."

"You haven't read it and you're this mad?" He raised his thick eyebrows.

"I can't believe you'd write a story about my mom dying, send it out, get it published—and never run it by me."

He pushed his dark hair off his forehead. "I was afraid you'd have a bad reaction," he said. "Which, may I add, you are." Kierny took a breath and held it, gazed past me at the poppies. I moved my foot back to squish one.

"It's about death, Sarah, and—I didn't want to bring up more death stuff for you."

"You didn't want to bring up more death stuff for me? Are you kidding? This is *my mom* you wrote about. For you this was a story, but for me it was *real*."

"Shhh. Sarah, there are people working here."

I'd always thought Kierny was adorable—his bright blue eyes and blackish hair. His way of leaning when he walked, as if it would make him less tall. He had an excellent sense of style, too. It was one of the first things I'd noticed about him. He wore these old-fashioned blue cotton shirts and painter's pants. He had lean, strong arms.

Now, Kierny looked a little anemic. I could see his wormy temple veins. And he had a cold. He looked plugged up.

I turned around, went back to my car, drove home.

With a tall glass of whiskey, I tried to settle myself long enough to read the story.

:::

I couldn't do it. It was the middle of the day, too hard to read. I shut the blinds to approximate night. I turned on all the lights. I fed my cat. I washed the dishes. I felt dirty. I felt like crying. I turned on the shower and stood under it.

All the stories I had written about my mom's death had come back with little slips of paper. *We just get so many stories about cancer* (oops, I mean consumption)*, it's impossible to publish another! We do admire your writing, though, so keep sending us work!* Or, *The grief is palpable—you've allowed us to see it in a new way. No small feat! But we're afraid grief isn't enough for us. We need a larger worldview. Maybe submit to our next theme issue, CLASH: Ugandan Politics and the New Urban Male . . .* One editor suggested I wait until I was in the next phase of my life before sending another story. It got so obnoxious that I stopped sending the stories out. No one wants to hear about mortality, I figured. Dead moms, dead dads—they're a dime a dozen.

I took a Xanax.

I opened the book to his story.

I kept imagining what it would feel like to get closer to her—to hold her, undress her, run my hands over the strange rubber of her skin. Even if she was my girlfriend's mother—my girlfriend's dying mother—in that state—so near to death—she was magnetic.

:::

Okay, fine. She didn't die of consumption, she died of cancer. And like most cancer deaths, it wasn't pretty. Her breast turned purple, then black, then it ate itself. Her skin grew tough and red. Sores opened on her lips and forehead. The tumor grew so big it was like a globe pressing out of her chest. She smelled like fish and sweat and unflushed pee. She was delirious for weeks, coming in and out of the world.

My mother had once been a dancer. She stood erect and held her head high. Before she got sick, she used to coil her thick hair in a bun at the nape of her neck. Men smiled at her in grocery stores. Students filled every dance class she offered.

She was sick for eleven years before she died. The treatments and steroids made her hair change texture. It fell out and came back wiry, streaked with a dark, flat gray. Then it fell out again and came back in patches. Her skin took on a chemical glow. She gained weight. She wasn't magnetic in her death state. Kierny could barely stand to be in the same room with her. When she was in the final stages, moaning, balling her fists, rolling back her eyes, he wouldn't even visit. He stayed in California, apparently imagining all this, working extra hours at his magazine job.

I was alone when she died. Her friends from the dance school were helping out during the day, and we'd hired a couple of night helpers. But all this time—as her body morphed, swelled, and rotted—I held her hands. I wiped the oozing. I don't have any siblings. And my father, he's not around.

I'm straying. I'm writing about death again. Damn it. It's become a habit. Is the key to insert sex?

GRATUITOUS SEX SCENE #1

The night after my mom died, Kierny arrived in Boise. I don't remember very much about that evening. There was whiskey and beer and lots of casserole. Some of my mom's friends had arrived and were answering the phone. Dinnertime passed, then it was night. We went upstairs to my childhood bedroom.

He held me and I tried to relax. My body wouldn't stay still, wouldn't calm. I felt a little bit violent. I wanted to throw the little porcelain box off my bureau and watch it shatter, hurl books through the window, leave bloody scratches up my own arms. And so, I pulled away from him, pushed him down on the bed, undid the button of his jeans.

It wasn't sex I wanted, not really. I wanted to watch him under a spell. I wanted to control him.

"Are you sure?" he asked. I untied his shoes, pulled off his boxers, looked at his pink penis lying a little lopsided across his stomach. I took it in my hands, then in my mouth. It pulsed and quivered. Finally he started panting. I went faster, pulled at the base—and then he came all over my quilt.

"Oh wow," he said.

"Yeah," I said.

But I still felt violent.

:::

Kierny, you might be interested to know, has both of his parents. He's from New Orleans. His dad is a physicist. His mom is a pediatrician. He has a sister named Wendy who is happily married to a veterinarian. His younger brother, Anton, is at Yale.

Kierny is a well-adjusted person. In fact, Grover Edgar, a student in our graduate workshop, once said you could tell from Kierny's prose that he hadn't felt a whole lot of pain in his life. "It's like what an alien might imagine human pain would feel like," he'd said.

At the time, I'd thought Grover was kind of an asshole. His dad had killed himself and it was all he could write about.

"Red rover, red rover, help Grover get over it," Kierny had joked.

. . . in that state—so near to death—she was magnetic.

You want more of Kierny's story? Well, go buy it. It's copyrighted. I'm only providing a synopsis.

The story takes some funny turns, Kierny being a funny guy. He's with Terri (the fictional me) and Lucinda (my fictional mom) while Lucinda is dying. In the story, Terri is having a lot of trouble managing the daily tasks—administering meds and doing laundry—because Terri is obsessed with yoga and detox diets. (I am most certainly *not* obsessed with yoga or detox diets.) Terri watches yoga videos on the television in the basement, leaving the male character, Theo, with plenty of time for monkey business.

Of course, Lucinda and Theo never actually have an affair. But they do have numerous meaningful conversations on the nature of life and death. Pithy ones, even. But a particularly stunning scene involves Lucinda fantasizing about having a one-night stand.

"I was too well behaved in my life," she says to him. "I wish I'd broken a few more rules." In this scene, she's just been bathed by a nurse. She reclines in the bed, her hair wrapped in a turban. (A turban? Hair?) She won't tell him the details of her wishes, but in her eyes he sees a filmstrip: a dark house, white linens, soft light, and the deep line down a woman's spine.

He feels a powerful pull and says, "I think I need to get a beer." Lucinda rubs her dry feet together suggestively.

At the bar, which he goes to alone in Terri's truck, he meets a young undergrad, Fiora. Fiora's a biology major. She's got dark skin, long, dark hair, and a small diamond in her nostril. She's nothing like poor Terri (who's milk-and-honey pretty, but who's turned a little stringy and dour during these hard months). Fiora's eyes are coy, her lashes shine. She laughs at Theo's jokes and her fingers travel up the inseam of his painter's pants.

Outside, on the gravel of the parking lot, he bites at her jaw. *She smelled like oatmeal and coal*, Kierny wrote. (Kierny once told me about a girlfriend he'd had at summer camp when he was fifteen. She smelled like oatmeal, he'd said. And when I said that was kind of a dumpy thing to smell like, he disagreed vehemently, saying oatmeal was about as earthy as you could get.)

What do you think happens? Yes! They sleep together! At her dorm. Beneath a large tapestry with camels on it.

Terri doesn't find out, but strangely, Theo doesn't feel guilty. He feels more in love with Terri and more alive than he's ever felt. Tenderness overwhelms him, and so, a week later, he tries it again. Only this time, it's much more dangerous—it's with Diego, the nurse.

(Caretakers are not a sexy lot. In Idaho, we got a lot of women with dyed red hair and smoker's coughs who chattered endlessly about their cats and car payments. Some of them were expert crocheters, cross-word puzzlers, or card sharks, but sex object, now that was simply not on the list.)

Diego is a svelte biracial man, paying his way through a graduate degree in English by working nights caring for hospice patients. He's got—these are not my words—"skin the color of burned butter" and "eyes one shade paler than teal." Theo is not gay—he had one "experimental" experience in college during a spin-the-bottle game when he was trying to impress a bisexual coed. But Diego is flaming gay—and unmistakably sexual. He has a gay man's flair for fashion. Even while making house calls to dump commodes and wipe sores, he's wearing tight T-shirts and formfitting pants.

At one point Theo almost tells Lucinda what he's done, he wants her to see him in a new light: a man with free will, able to live out her fantasies for her. He wants them to have a virtual affair. But before he says anything, she takes his hands and holds them and he feels an opening in his body, as if she already knows, blah blah blah.

Eventually, Lucinda dies (she just closes her weary eyes and—kaput—she fades), Theo realizes that he'll never get any closer to her—that she is gone, but her spirit is everywhere, lives inside of them all, and this gives him a kind of peace and a renewed zest for love and life.

It's an annoying story, isn't it?

So palpable! So felt! I imagine the editors said. *You've helped us to see death in a new way! No small feat!*

I don't get it. I truly don't. Which is why I'm going to write this story, call it fiction, and then apply to law school.

:::

I didn't sleep the night I read that story. Instead, I sat up with a photograph of my mother, taken three weeks before she died. In it, the two of us are sitting on the brown overstuffed sofa. My arm is around her shoulders. Her face is gray and the oxygen tubes drape over her chest. One of her eyes is drifting. My face is close to her ear, like I am whispering something to her.

Don't die, I'm saying—you can see it in the way I'm clutching her nightgown with my hand. *You are all I have, my family, my mother. You can't just leave me here.*

GRATUITOUS SEX SCENE #2
(Or, "A Brief Story of My Conception, August 1977")

It's New York—SoHo. And this is the night my mother will meet my father. My mother, Brenda Oberlin, has just turned twenty-three. She's long and thin and wears tight jeans and flowing tunics, her dark hair curls loosely down her back.

She doesn't know it, yet—that this night will be fateful. She knows this: she is not a lesbian, as much as she likes Alice, as pretty as Alice is with that sly face, shiny lips, and that shocking black hair. She's been sleeping with Alice for three weeks, trying to feel the energy. They're roommates above a Greek restaurant in Queens. They've come to this art opening because Alice is a painter. She's friends with a friend of the artist and wants to get into a gallery he's showing in. It's a large room and it smells like dust with something sweet mixed in—nail polish or turning meat. Sage bundles burn on little metal altars in the corners.

The artist is a skinny, dark-eyed man with a grin that makes him look like he's got food in his mouth. He's less handsome than Brenda's usual boyfriends—less handsome but more talented. She likes the strange birds he paints, their beaks menacing but their eyes patient and all-knowing. He's wearing a strand of purple beads over a linen shirt. He's drinking beer with a straw.

Brenda stands near Alice in the corner, eyeing him as he greets guests. And then when he backs out of the room for a cigarette, she follows.

She says, "I just love your work," and then feels stupid. She's young and it's summer. Her body is light and airy, no different than the heat off the building, the eggy air coming out of the vent they stand over, the white East Coast sky. She bums a cigarette and imagines that his hand doesn't stop at hers, but reaches past her, grabs her behind her ribs, pulls her in. She thinks of his body—so much more substantial than Alice's—his dick hard against her thigh, and the heat of the sky, the heat of the vents, and the warmth of her own blood conspire to make her look too deeply at him, woozily almost, as if they have already crawled in and out of bed a hundred times.

They talk about the neighborhood, a Russian diner. They leave together, despite the guests inside, the paintings lit by expensive lights that shine down from the windows to the dark pavement. They buy a bag of M&M's and a fifth of whiskey and start kissing beneath his apartment.

Keys, a heavy door, a room with exposed brick, and a ratty sofa. His hands are large and they slide around her, hoist her up against the wall.

"You smell good," he says. She's wearing Chanel—but under that she smells like an athlete.

He carries her over to his sofa—the bed's lofted, too hard to get to—and he slides off her moccasins, her jeans. She's drunk. He's drunk. It's quick and sloppy but it feels good—slippery and exciting—no talking, no negotiating. They slide off the sofa onto his shag rug. "I'm leaving next week," he tells her before he drifts off. He's got a hand in her hair. "A fellowship. I'll be gone a long time." She shrugs. He sticks his fingers inside her to feel his wetness there. Again she is heat—heat and headiness and the feel of her wet skin on a soft shag rug.

:::

For two days after I read the story, I didn't hear from Kierny. It seemed to me that he was too much of a coward to call, but that's not his version. His version is that he was giving me time to recover. When he finally did call, his voice sounded locked up.

"How're you doing?" he said. Was it guilt making him sound that way? Because in his tone I heard deep annoyance, as if I'd read that story against his will.

"I'm all right," I said.

"I had to process it," Kierny said. "What you were going through was hard on me too. You know it's fiction, it's a fantasy—and I didn't tell you because, well, I just kept putting it off. I didn't want to hurt you. I'm sorry."

I looked at the crack in my ceiling.

I don't have a patent on death. I wouldn't want one. Really, he can have the subject—the whole big feat of it. I'd love to write stories about surfing teenagers, international spies, funny grandmothers, dogs that fly. But death is my map, the thing I've been living next to for years. There hasn't been another phase of my life to look to, just one long strand of a mother fading out, then being gone. She lasted eleven years dying. Shades of lonely, lonely, then alone.

"Look, it would be easier to talk this over in person," Kierny said.

He arrived with a bag of groceries. A bottle of wine.

For a moment, seeing him sheepish in the doorway, I caught a glimpse outside of my own anger. One time Kierny and I hiked to a lake in the Sierras, both of us singing Beatles and Springsteen until our voices cracked, still singing while we swam naked in the lake. Then some teenagers came out of the woods and pelted us with pistachios. Another time I crashed his car into a pole in the parking garage and he flipped out and looked like a moose and I told him and he yelled at me and then we both started laughing and Kierny spilled his Coke.

The baguette stuck out of the bag and he looked confused, like he wasn't sure whether to challenge or console me.

"I brought salami," he said.

:::

She says, "You're on your own now, kiddo."

"I know," I say.

"I'm gone."

"I know."

"You don't believe it."

"No, how can I? You were just here."

"I'm not speaking to you. You're imagining this."

"Why am I failing at everything, Mom? Why is it all falling away?"

She's not in the sky, in my body. She's not in her bones in the pine box in the grave. She is simply gone. My father—I used to try to look for him by attempting to track down old paintings, but he never became big, someone else probably painted his birds more successfully. I imagined them, the two of them, the feelings they once had—feelings that must have seemed consuming: they were hungry or tired or angry or ashamed. I imagined that night between them, the heat on their skin, the dizziness, the longing. And I reached for Kierny then, as he was eating a piece of salami. I pulled him in close, my hands behind his ribs.

I would leave him the next day and write this story. There was time for that. But now there was pressure on my cheeks and nose, like the beginning of drunkenness or grief.

"Are you sure?" Kierny asked, leaning in, his damp hands traveling up my back.

His breath was meaty, spicy.

I unbuttoned my shirt and let it fall away as I climbed on top of the table.

"I'm sure," I said.

SEX AND THE SINGLE SQUIRREL

∴

Elissa Schappell

I HAVE BEEN A LOT of very different people in my life—a cheerleader and a coke fiend, a good daughter and a bad girl, an exhibitionist and a shut-in, a religious seeker and a nihilist. It is my sickness that I can imagine doing, or being, just about anything. This is complicated by a desire to inhabit the lives of people much unlike myself, to see how they really live. How else to explain why I would willfully dress up in a raccoon suit and let strangers grope me?

Unlike a true "furrie," I don't feel that my best and truest self can only be expressed through an animal alter ego, or through sexual or nonsexual role-playing online or in person, or through the adoption of furry ears, or a tail, or a full fur suit. I don't possess an intense spiritual connection to the animal kingdom, and despite an erotic fondness in my girlhood for a sheepskin rug, I have never had a carnal urge to *possess* a stuffed animal—or, not yet.

For the Anthrocon Furries of Myth and Legend convention in the King of Prussia Hilton, located just miles from the scenic battlefields of Gettysburg, I have chosen to make my debut into the "furrie fandom" as Miss Trixie, enchantress of the night. I am fabulous in my rented raccoon fur suit, which appears to have been crafted out of a 1970s midpile brown-and-black-striped shag carpet.

Furrie fans have come from all over the United States, as well as Canada and Australia, to rub shoulders and noses with other lovers of Sierra Club calendars and Sonic the Hedgehog video games, not to mention their online furrie sex partners and chat room confidantes. They've come for the furrie workshops like "fur suit dancing" and "fur suit sewing," roundtables on "furrie spirituality," furrie drawing classes, an erotic furrie art auction, and more. The furrie universe is vast, encompassing many worlds: there are also sci-fi aficionados, computer wizards, Renaissance folk, gaylaxians, nerds, cat people, dog people, erotic-art fans, born-again Christians, lovers of parade balloons, shamans, healers, animal rights activists, bikers, and curiosity seekers.

I have chosen Trixie, or Trixie has chosen me, because we share certain personality quirks. Like the Kinko's employee I met who was a wolf—loyal, dangerous, a loner—or the substitute teacher who was a panther—sleek, brave, and feared—I, like raccoons, have a fondness for the dark and for dramatic eye makeup, plus a jones for spying on the neighbors, inciting the kind of commotion that causes people to throw on their robe and grab a flashlight. Trixie, masked and mysterious, like desire itself, plays to all my worst voyeuristic tendencies. Hidden behind her face, in the darkness of my suit I can move undetected in and out of the action around me. It is hot in my head, and my breathing is heavy, echoing disconcertingly in my ears. It's the same sound you hear in slasher movies, the frantic panting of the stalked ingenue hiding in a closet watching the killer, chain saw slung across his back, sniff her panties. Or maybe it's the other way around. Indeed, aren't I the crazed maniac hidden in the shadows, just waiting for my moment to pounce?

Certainly I do not look scary. Sadly, I am not regulation human-raccoon size, so the suit hangs on my shoulders and bags around my ankles, giving me a kind of hip-hop rodent look. My head is a huge plaster cast, fitted inside with what looks like a welder's helmet. All breathing is done through a narrow slit scarcely big enough to accommodate a cocktail straw and through my big, sexy, heavily lashed eyes, which are made of mesh. Trixie's wide-spaced eyes are cute, but render me walleyed. I keep bumping into people and furniture, paws out feeling for the walls, like a drunk out of a Beatrix Potter book. I catch glimpses of people in bunny and tiger ears, and others wearing bear, iguana, and fox tails. But I have yet to see another fur suit.

:::

The mood in the hotel lounge is that of a homecoming reunion. Clearly, judging from all the snuggling and canoodling going on in the lounge, the delighted yips and coos of recognition, most haven't laid eyes or paws on one another in months. And, unlike at home, where no one suspects that the junior lawyer likes to dress up like a wolf and crash through the forests with other guys dressed as wolves, here they can be out. *We're here, we're deer, get used to it.*

For others, it's the first time they've met snout to snout, and so there is the requisite uneasiness at discovering Big Big Ben is a petite Jewish woman who wears glasses, and that Kitten with a Whip is not a bossy dominatrix but an obese and meek manager of a health-food store who endured twenty hours on a bus to be here. It intrigues me that there is so much psychic fallout when you find out that the online partner with whom you are engaging in frisky fun isn't the gender you imagined them to be. That a person doesn't mind having virtual sex with another species but doesn't want that person to *not* be of their gender, or to *be* of their gender, seems odd. Oh, the slippery machinations of lust.

In the lounge there is a bulletin board on which people leave messages searching for furrie friends, offering hugs, or noting who gives the best back rubs in Canada. Stuffed animals are in abundance. I recognize some men I saw in the lobby earlier, middle-aged, solid industrious types, buttoned-down Republicans, I'd guess. The Willie Lomans of the animal kingdom, here they are talking animatedly about hikes they've recently taken and books they've read, petting the stuffed badgers and otters they hold in their laps like children.

While many furries carry and love stuffed animals, most are quick to distance themselves from the "plushies," also referred to as "Gundies," "plushisexuals," or "stuffies," whom they consider a subspecies of furrie. Plushies are folks whose primary preference for sexual satisfaction is *boinking* stuffed animals. Their motto: *In Plush We Thrust.*

Not unlike other feared or misunderstood minorities, plushies have developed a vernacular all their own. See if you can follow: You're feeling *yiffy*, so you've lit the musk-scented candles and put *The Chipmunks Do Barry White* on the stereo, because tonight is the night you and Paddington are finally going to *boink*. Tonight, Paddington gets *baptized*. Paddington is a *talented plushie*, meaning you won't have to open up a seam to create either an *SPH* (*strategically placed hole*), in which one could insert an *SPA* (*strategically placed appendage*). Paddington can pose with its legs spread and its ass in the air, *begging*. All day at the office you can't stop fantasizing about Paddington's *boink-space*, the place on the plushie that is the most rewarding and enjoyable to *poke*. One of the great things about plush sex partners is you never have to send them flowers or call them the next day! Which is good, because this morning, walking past FAO, you got a *plush-rush* just seeing the new plump Gund bunnies—tomorrow after your lunch hour two saucy Flopsy bunnies will be yours. Can you say *plushgasm? Buy pairs for spares.* Did I mention *plush lovers* never get jealous? Your biggest concern is the carpet burns on your crotch.

Later that night, after Paddington is asleep, sweet dear, you feel *yiffy* again. It's only nine so you drag Piglet out of the closet. Piglet, the old whore, is *plushphile gray*. While *plushplunging* Piglet you grab his *handle bars*, meaning you are gripping his arms or legs in order to *give a meal* or a *gift* to Piglet. Soon Piglet will have to be *retired*, seeing as he's almost too worn and soiled with *spooge* to be a regular partner. Give Me Gundies or Give Me Death!

Okay, weird, but is it any weirder than what "mundanes" (nonfurries) do? What furries disdainfully refer to as *meat sex*?

:::

A downside to wearing the fur suit is the fact that I have to keep drinking water to keep hydrated, and thus have to keep taking off my suit to go to the bathroom. Washing my hands in the sink, I happen to find myself sink to sink with a dominatrix skunk in fishnets, high heels, a black bodysuit provocatively pinned together with safety pins, and the coup de grace: a black thong *over* the bodysuit.

"Great outfit," I say, taking in her ensemble, the gloves, the whip.

"I have to have someone feed me my french fries," the sex skunk says, reapplying red lipstick. "Not that it's a problem."

"Of course," I say, drying my hands. She looks like a real pro. I'd read about a furrie convention in Los Angeles where they sold animal dildos, horses, cows, and—best of all—the corkscrewed meat muscle of a pig. I wonder if she might know about such a thing. That would be something to see. I wonder what it would be called: *The Porker? The Happy Hambone?*

"Hey," I say, as offhandedly as possible. "You look like you might know the answer to a question—um, do you know where—*if*—they sell sex toys here?"

She looks annoyed. "I am a pissed-off skunk, low on money."

"Oh, I'm sorry," I say. Then, "See, what I am looking for is a kind of dildo." She stares at me like I am an idiot. "Um," I say, "a pig dildo—do you know if they even exist?"

The skunk just looks at me and shakes her head with disgust. "Here? I don't think so." *She* looks at *me*, Miss Trixie, with disdain. Her? The polecat slut! Then it occurs to me that she thinks I am one of those despised zoophiles, who actually engage in intercourse with animals. A minuscule and dark subculture of furries I hesitate to even mention.

Before I can explain or offer some obviously spurious excuse—*It's not for me, it's for a friend*—she bolts. I suppose I should be thankful the bitch can't spray.

Outside I walk slowly and gingerly. I could take off my head and see just fine, but I cannot. If the fur suits could be said to have a philosophy, it would be: *Don't take off your head.* Don't take off your head or you will scare the crap out of some kid. Mindful of the innocent, furrie is about fantasy, trust, and play. In truth, no one wants to see my face. *I* am not important; what matters is my animal other—my own best self, the most me part of me—*Trixie.* The fun-loving, happy-go-lucky little troublemaker. The furries want to *know* Trixie, they want to *play* with Trixie. But mostly, it seems, they want to *hug* Trixie.

I hear them before I see them. "Ohhh, how cute!" they cry, and then appear like a pack before me. "Do you like hugs?" someone says.

I freeze, as if in the headlights of a barreling school bus.

At first I can't tell how many there are. But I think I make out four, perhaps five large, docile, flour-white strangers wearing soft-soled shoes, with plushy teddy bears snuggled inside their overalls. I panic as they move in for the hug, a giant squeeze. I can see polar bear key chains girdling a man's waist, pins that announce: I ♥ BEAR HUGS and EVERY TIME A MUNDANE DIES A FURRY GETS ITS WINGS. Off balance, I'm overwhelmed by claustrophobia. My breathing echoes in my ears, like in 2001. *Open the pod bay doors, HAL . . .* and my head rises up off my shoulders. I can't even run—my ankle is still tender from slipping in my mother's garage last night during my practice run. I am close to shrieking when, as quickly as they appeared, the gang of huggers tucks off with a kindly wave.

I rush to my "fur suit walking" class. My brothers in furs are already lined up against the wall as if at an obedience school mixer. While I am grateful to see my fellow fur suits, I am also a little alarmed. It isn't the big red dog who earlier was posing for a drawing class, or the uncostumed French boy with winged-back hair chatting up a man who is a dead ringer for the guy who slices cheese in our deli. It's the hyenas.

Instead of wearing a huge plaster head like me, the hyenas (I think they are cousins) have affixed long latex snouts to their faces, wear fangs, and have painted their faces with red, orange, and black face paint. They've also glued realistic brown and orangey fur to their arms and legs. Their feet, in Birkenstocks, flaunt their black toenails. Their necks strain against their leather collars. They remind me of the ubiquitous tubby guy at football games who has painted his torso in his team's colors, the logo scrawled across his poochy man breasts.

They look me over hungrily; my heart beats fast. They are predators, right? The worst kind, they even eat dead things! In costume or out of costume, you can just tell.

I am thrilled and repulsed at the same time. I don't think I'd like to be ravaged by dogs, or at least not these dogs.

Our teacher, a tall lithe man in black ballet shoes, calls us into four lines and sends us across the floor in pairs. Our first walk is a rocking side-to-side march where we swing our arms like jolly teddy bears. I try not to look at my fellow furries, to just stay in my "Trixie head," but I can't help it. I'm embarrassed and uptight. I'm not a gamboling teddy bear, I am a spaz. My hands fly up to steady my rocking head at least once every pass, as though I have a toothache or am reeling in a state of perpetual shock. All these pups for me?!

Nevertheless, those in costume seem to do much better than those in their street clothes. The orthodontists and optometrists, Cub Scout leaders and college debate kings aren't as loose as those of us in character. Some blush, others actually duck out of class while we fur suits ham it up, wiggling our heinies and flapping our arms, giggling out of a mix of freedom and silly embarrassment.

After the regal walk, the hyenas converge on me, just as I feared they would. I press myself flat against the wall. What if they have rabies or, worse, herpes? I catch myself. I have to be cool, *think furrie*. They begin stroking me, petting my arms, and scratching my back. When one of them starts to enthusiastically massage my right breast—advertently or inadvertently—I yip and sort of wave my paw menacingly at them, baring my teeth. Miraculously, they back away. Despite more than a decade of bumping hips on the New York subway, I find I am squeamish—no, scared—about being touched by strangers. My heart is beating in my mouth, and I can't breathe. They sniff at me curiously. I fight to stay still, reminding myself, *I am Trixie, Trixie, dammit. Trixie is fun-loving, Trixie is playful.* They peer through my eye holes (truly the windows of the soul) to scope me out. Do they think I am a man or a woman? Does it matter? In desperation, I growl. They growl in return, and snarl, rubbing my ears and nuzzling at my neck with their snouts. I want to scream, but instead growl louder, and they stop and cock their heads with suspicion. My mother's admonition to never pet a strange dog runs through my head. Obviously animals have different personal-space issues—strange dogs pile up together and lick each other's balls; squirrels cram into hollow trees like frat boys in a telephone booth. I am just waiting for someone to actually bite me.

Which might not be so terrible. I have to confess, I've always been a biter. Always. Even now, I occasionally want to bite people, out of anger, desire, fondness. Sometimes I do. Years ago, when I heard that Sylvia Plath had, the first time she met Ted Hughes, bit him, I took it as evidence that biting was a sign of genius—not just lunacy. I saw a wolf in the lobby earlier. I think I'd like him to bite me. I know, though, that I do not wish to bite or be bitten by these foul hyenas.

:::

The highlight of the "fur suit dancing" class comes when our teacher, Coco, the portly mascot of the Hershey, Pennsylvania, hockey team, announces, "A time may come when you want to go to a furrie dance, or a furrie rave, or at some time you might wish to slow dance with your heart's desire."

Absolutely. While I've adopted the Pogo as the official dance of raccoons, if tonight at the furrie ball the opportunity to get down with a sulky wolf-boy or a buff gargoyle arose, would I not want to be ready? Or what about my "fur suit walking" teacher, who has, for this class, slipped into his tiger suit?

"Everybody find a partner," Coco says.

Everyone pairs up quickly, leaving me, the only girl, alone. Spurned, I am forced to ask Le Tigre to dance with me. He nods his assent though it is clear that dancing with a raccoon, and worse yet a girl, is beneath his station. It's all so *Jane Eyre*!

Despite being a decent dancer, I plod all over Tiger's big, expensive padded feet. "Dip me," I whisper. "Dip me." After all, I *am* a lady. Reluctantly, halfheartedly, he does so, which is good, as I have to grab my head to keep it from rolling across the floor. For our last dance Coco calls us all into the middle of the floor and instructs us to hold hands in a circle around him. "Know your limits," he warns us. "It's hard to dance with big feet and get funky."

As the song "I'm Too Sexy" begins to shake the room, we set off in a manic ring-around-the-rosy around Coco as he spins, grinds his hips, does the Travolta point, and whirls, then he tags one of the boys. "This is your chance," he yells over the music, "to just go wild and crazy. No one is going to judge you here!"

Indeed, we cavort wildly. Like a bunch of schoolgirls hopped up on Baby Ruths and RC, we circle fast, fast, faster, while shrieking, *I'm too sexy for my shirt, too sexy!!!* When I am finally tagged for the solo (last, of course) I don't care, I go wild in the center. I am the masked mistress in the cage. I am go-go coon.

:::

The Furrie Ball is the highlight of the first day. By day's end I am starting to get used to people grinning at me, looking me up and down, and taking my picture. I pose like a Vargas girl, waving as coquettishly as the calendar girl sexpot I once dreamed of being. I *am special*, after all; I am a living plush toy. Probably never in my whole life have so many people wanted to get into my pants and had no idea, or even cared particularly, who I was, literally, inside.

I spot a couple who'd taken my picture earlier. They seem to be furrie connoisseurs of some kind, although they don't wear costumes themselves. Instead, with their longish, frowsy hair, purple-and-turquoise natural-fiber scarves, and hemp clothing, they look like people who run a candle shoppe and make their own cheese.

"Hi," the man of the couple says.

"Mrow," I say. I go back and forth between making what I can only imagine to be raccoon noises and actually speaking.

"Ooh, what happened to your tail?" the man says, turning me around so he can ogle my butchered bottom. I had hoped no one would notice that my tail was missing. But perhaps it's a turn-on.

All day long no one has mentioned it, and now, suddenly, right before the dance, it's all about the look. I knew it.

"Farmer cut it off with a shovel," I say. They seem nice enough.

The man winces, then laughs. "Uh-huh," he says.

"Must have hurt," the woman says, moving her dark hair away from her face. She licks her lips and laughs.

"Terribly," I say. Not to flatter myself, but I think they're flirting with me. They're both looking at me in the way people do just before they kiss.

"Want to come sit with us?" the man says, gesturing at a recently vacated couch. I wonder how much animal hair is in that upholstery. The girlfriend leans in to me and begins caressing my shoulder. I let her.

"It'd be fun," the woman says, dropping her head onto my shoulder.

"Maybe later," I say, suddenly nervous. "I am looking for a friend, a mouse, or maybe he's more of a mole. Have you seen him?"

They both shrug, it's all casual. Why can't I be more casual?

"We'll look for you," the woman calls out as I scurry away. I'm embarrassed at how flustered I am, then later, am miffed that my first real invitation to join a threesome has come while I am in Trixie. After they leave, I think, *I could have a threesome in a raccoon suit, right?* It's a titillating idea. For me, the whole add-a-lover dynamic has always seemed overwhelming and vaguely hilarious; an orgy is just one step away from hairy naked people building human pyramids. I know I would laugh, but in Trixie, as Trixie, wouldn't that all be okay?

When the ballroom doors open, eager furries pour through the doors. Inside it's dark and rainbows bounce off a large disco ball. A friendly coyote hands out Cyalume sticks, and I am thankful to have something to do with my hands. No one smokes. No one drinks, unless of course they've poured rum into the Coke cans. It's murder. A cheery, older, bland-looking British gentleman I imagine to be a podiatrist or a vicar nods to me. Poking out of the top of his Sansabelt trousers is an unnervingly worn-looking Elmo doll. Elmo appears to be in either ecstasy or great distress, or both. I can see it now, the gotta-have Christmas gifts of 2003—*Come on My Face Elmo* and his pal *Bend Over Grover*.

I cannot tolerate the strobe lights, so close my eyes to dance. I think perhaps this is a good thing, perhaps I will be more graceful undistracted by undulating furries. I enter the throng, and manage a jaunty, lead-footed Rex Harrison sort of jig. I attempt the jolly Winnie-the-Pooh-style fanny shake we practiced in class today but lose my footing, staggering blindly into the crowd. I scan the crowd for Coco. *Oh, Coco, where are you? Rescue me from Old MacDonald's mosh pit!*

Suddenly I am so tired I am staggering under the weight of my head and I have to go to bed.

I share the elevator upstairs with a guy who is wearing parachute pants engorged with Beanie Babies. In fact, his pants are so weighted down with Beanie Babies he is in danger of losing them. I recall a chat board where people swapped stories of wearing Swampy and Mystic in their underwear like furry ben-wa balls when they went to work.

Back in my room I shuck off Trixie and lay her carefully across an armchair, her head facing me. I brush her fur and examine her for spills, stains, gum. I am starting to feel attached to her. I fall asleep that night counting Beanie Babies struggling over a fence. Good night, Cuddles; good night, Sparky.

:::

I start my morning in the Dealer's Den, a treasure trove of furrie collectibles and goodies, comics, art, and toys. At first glance it looks like any convention, with your average-looking joes in Coke-bottle glasses hunched over cases of classic comics, the occasional dude in camouflage selling war medals and postcards. Upon closer inspection you notice that almost all the comics feature animals or stuffed animals—even the erotic art and porn. Whether it's *Oui*, or *Blueboy*, whether one prepares for a date by gluing faux fur to one's body and slipping on a dog collar, or splashing on Canoe and slipping into a pinstriped suit, clearly humans are keyed to react to the same kind of stimuli. We are pretty consistent in what turns us on—the only real difference I see between furrie porn and human porn is that furrie porn has more of a sense of humor. Witness a *Gulliver's Travels* gang bang: a chained lion overwhelmed by an army of sadistic Beanie Babies wielding studded dildos. In another pictorial a teddy bear is exploded by the force of a fox's jism.

Of course, there is the traditional locker room fantasy featuring a huge killer whale with a killer hard-on, preparing to snap a towel at the ass of a smaller, but equally endowed, baby beluga whale fairly dripping with innocence. Then there are the ubiquitous soft-core spreads—the sort of layouts celebrities do in *Playboy*. There are rabbits in naughty negligees. There is a slinky, pink-nippled mouse bathing in a martini glass—very forties—and besotted squids and octopuses doing things only eight-armed creatures versed in the Kama Sutra can do. There's Rudolph in the midst of a seven-reindeer orgy; a wide-eyed reindeer lass in bells being taken from behind by a creature who appears part lion, part wolf, the gift tag around her neck reads *Don't Wait Until Christmas*, while another reindeer, alone on a tropical beach, looks shocked as wild dogs go down on her. Don't you hate it when that happens? There are foxes with pierced nipples chained to walls, and a mouse engaging in autoerotic asphyxiation with a giant boa constrictor—a little something for everyone.

The implications of interspecies sex are amazing. Forget a utopian society where every human marries someone of another race—imagine dogs and cats living together in sin. In fact, not surprisingly, there are also domestic-bliss shots, drawings fit for a close-mated couple's Christmas card, such as the portrait of two middle-aged male huskies sharing a pizza and a six-pack. It might just as well read *Seasons Greetings, Larry and Carl.*

:::

I peek my head into the Diversity in Fandom meeting long enough to get the gist of the antimundane patter. The discussion is being led by Trickster, a twenty-something guy whose long dark hair hangs down to the middle of his back. I recognize him as the wolf boy I was lusting after earlier in the lobby. He's all in black, including, of course, a black dog collar.

"I see people in the fandom who are not dealing with mundanes," says a man in a tie-dyed T-shirt and a studded collar. Some people nod.

"Fuck that, we should isolate ourselves from the outside world," quips one of the men who earlier established himself as being particularly well versed in the human-genome-trans-humanism business; part of the fandom clings to the dream that one day the DNA of animals will be successfully grafted to that of humans, allowing the creation of a true race of lizardmen.

There are murmurs of agreement.

"Hey, on the whole, we are more accepting than the general population," he reminds us. Which seems true, overall—maybe this is why I like them.

In closing, Trickster reminds everyone, "When you talk to mundanes, be nice. After all, mundanes are the future furries."

:::

I am so hungry I could eat an entire can of garbage. On my way to the snack bar I stop into a meeting of "The Herd," which is being led by two cowboys, one outfitted with sinister-looking gold incisors. Some of the men in the group hold homemade or mail-order hooves in their laps, or stroke a horse tail, silently nodding as the cowboy talks as if to a bunch of reluctant alcoholics at their first meeting.

"I don't wear tack and stuff," says the cowboy they call Whitehorse. "I'm not that tacky. I think it's a fetish. And, I get my manes from a Hitching Post. I don't want to think where it comes from," he says, "but isn't it better for the horse to be another new horse instead?"

The men nod.

"Listen, guys, this is all about building friendships," Whitehorse reminds the Herd. "After all, we're all horses."

I am getting better at walking and balancing my head. On my way to the lounge I can even lower my arms almost completely to my sides. I still can't turn my head, or really ascertain where my body is in space, but I can walk confidently in a straight line. I am forced to stop and turn my head, though, when I hear the loud, coarse peal of a woman's laughter nearby. Sitting at a table are three people. On one side is a nervous and emaciated little man with a sad frizz of coppery red hair and a lion T-shirt. Across the table is one of those classically cute nice guys whom girls only want to be friends with. Beside him, in his lap really, is a big-boned blonde in a white tiger suit. She nuzzles and nips at the guy beside her in a way that is unabashedly, desperately carnal. No one in the lounge can keep their eyes off her; it's like seeing parents hitting their children in public or watching a minor fender bender that could at any moment escalate into someone pulling a gun.

She is dangerous, and because I am not me I stride right over and say, "You are so beautiful, you could make Siegfried and Roy weep."

The tigress turns her attention away from the man and onto me.

"Well, hello," she says, sitting up straight. "I'm Tigress."

"You're gorgeous," I say. The red-haired man nods in agreement, beaming at Tigress, and then it dawns on me that in fact she is his wife.

"Sit down," she says, pointing to the spot beside her husband. I sit down carefully.

Both of them are wearing wedding bands, and while the lion husband is trying to seem nonchalant that his wife is nibbling this other man's ear, he fidgets, swallowing and stammering, and trying on occasion to get her attention by reaching out and stroking her arm—which she ignores.

"Male lions have sex like two hundred times," she says with a laugh. "Twice a month, and then nothing." She rolls her eyes. "Nothing." Her little lion husband attempts a faint smile and shrugs. "What do you expect?"

The taking of many sexual partners—having sex whenever you feel like it and with whomever you feel like it, regardless of species—is, for some furries, the most appealing feature of the furrie lifestyle. After all, most animals aren't monogamous. Sure, swans and scarlet macaws and some apes may mate for life, but as for remaining sexually true? Ha. Not to imply that all furries are horndogs—no, many are happily *close-mated*, but neither is necessarily the only one the other will mount.

Suddenly, I look up and lock eyes with another raccoon. The first I've seen! And it's a boy! Ranger Rick is dark and pretty in a tight, striped top and black shorts, and he, he has a tail! A big long bushy one. I swoon. Instinctively I reach my hand back to touch my stumpy rear, ashamed, thinking, for a moment, that I feel a tingle in the spot.

I excuse myself and stride right over to him and introduce myself. "Hello," I say in my most chipper Miss Trixie lilt and lay a paw on his shoulder as though we'd been kits together, nestling in a log, not so very long ago.

"Hi," he says politely. "Can I take your picture?"

"Sure," I say and pose like Betty Page. I can suddenly imagine Polaroids of me as Miss Trixie at the center of a furrie circle jerk, and I shudder with a mix of horror and delight.

"So, you want to get together?" I ask. I am Miss Trixie, I am bewitched by her magic.

Ranger Rick looks surprised. "I'm sorry?" he says.

"I mean, you want to go outside run around," I say. "Do some crimes? Maybe tip over some garbage cans? Play chicken on the highway . . ."

He laughs uncomfortably. "Maybe, uh, later."

I feel so ridiculous standing there in my little rented suit. Maybe if I had a nice suit, a good suit, he'd like me more. He just has to get to know me.

"Sure, later," I say, my face burning red. "Of course, okay."

As I walk away I think, Thank God he couldn't see my face! Then I start to feel aggrieved, for Trixie's sake. I wish I'd said, *Listen, pal, there are plenty of people here who'd kill for some Trixie loving! How many people have come on to you?*

Well, I suppose he could sort of count me.

I'm starting to feel depressed, and it's hot and stuffy in my head, so I head outside to get some air. It's clear and dark, but not too dark to spot a gang of previously meek-looking furries furiously beating a pile of beanbags with sticks, as though the beanbags have enraged them. Later I learn that these "beanbag rats" are created solely for this sort of abuse. I think I could do with a few of them, if only to defuse sexual energy.

When I return, the Costume Ball has begun. It isn't really a ball, in that there is no dancing, only a show and a photo op with the entertainers (furries love a photo op).

It quickly becomes clear that the appeal of most of the skits—dogs joyously, awkwardly rocking out to "Let's Hear It for the Boy"—is of spying on someone gleefully boogying down in her rec room. *Kick out the jams, Curious George!* The crowd erupts when the belly-dancing cats—about as exotic as hummus—begin their sweet gyrations, then grows silent when a dour warthog in green army fatigues skulks on stage, the scene darkens, and he goes into a creepy lip-synced rendition of The Doors' "The End." Afterward, I am actually happy to watch a pair of spunky foxes in spandex and headbands aerobicize to "Let's Get Physical."

The audience members are enjoying themselves, clapping or singing along, two-stepping with their stuffed animals, just living it up. The chemistry changes as soon as the cowboys from the Herd group appear onstage. The cowboy with the golden teeth leads out his buddy Whitehorse and chews out the horse for losing a race, calling him terrible things. When the cowboy turns his back, Whitehorse steals his lariat and lassos him, or rather, attempts to lasso him—it must have worked in practice a hundred times, but this time the lariat has gotten caught on the cowboy's ear. After a terrible second, the crowd begins laughing, and you can just feel the man inside the suit seething. After he finally manages to disentangle the rope from his head, he attacks his buddy, knocks him down, and in ten seconds flat has him hog-tied. The room is silent, the rage and humiliation scarily acute.

For the finale, a drag queen, Lola Bunny, appears like a cartoon Venus. She is a vision in her purple microminiskirt, tight pink sweater (balloons pinned on for tits), and black fishnets. Lola would bring down the house regardless of whom she followed, but the release of tension from the cowboy's masochistic miniplay makes her act the perfect climax for the conference. If I could remove my panties and fling them on the stage, I would happily surrender them.

As Lola begins to croon "Fever," her hips all a-swivel, the crowd becomes unhinged, standing on their chairs, waving their stuffed animal pals, some screaming, "I love you!" I feel gleeful. After the show, people swarm around me taking pictures, and then the music comes on again, and we all start to dance. I dance the way you can only when no one you know is watching. I dance like I shall never dance again, for this is the last time I shall ever dance as Trixie.

:::

This is what I remember when I am back at the costume shop with Trixie lying limp in my arms like a swooning lover. I have put off returning her for two weeks, and now have no choice but to either rent her again for a month or say goodbye. I don't completely understand my reaction. It isn't that I have a profound desire to zip her skin up over mine and become her: I don't. There is just something—the freedom the suit gives me, the idea that I will never be Trixie again—that strikes me as so sad, and I think, as I hand over her skin, that I just might cry.

EROS 101

...
...

Elizabeth Tallent

Question one: Examine the proposition that for each of us, however despairing over past erotic experience, there exists a soul mate.

Answer: Soul? In some fluorescent lab an egg's embryonic smear cradles a lozenge of eponymous silicon, the vampiric chip electromagnetically quickened by a heartbeat, faux alive, while in a Bauhaus bunker on the far side of campus, a researcher wheedles Chopin from a virtual violin, concluding with a bow to her audience of venture capitalists, but for real despair, please turn to Prof. Clio Mitsak, at a dinner party in her honor, lasting late this rainy winter night, nine women at the table, women only, for the evening's covert (and mistaken: you'll see) premise is that the newly hired Woolf scholar will, from her angelic professional height and as homage to VW, scheme to advance all female futures, and the prevailing mood has been one of preemptive gratitude, gratitude as yet unencumbered by actual debt and therefore flirtatious, unirksome even to Clio, its object. Clio, who, hours ago, hit the button for auto-charm, safely absenting her soul (*there*) from the ordeal of civility. Gone, virtually, until dessert. Set down before her, the wedge of cake, lushly black as creekbed mud, parting under the tines of the fork, brings her to her senses, but then she's sorry, because the whipped cream is an airy petrochemical quotation of real cream, and the aftertaste of licked-tire-tread provokes an abrupt tumble into depression. It is an attribute of the profoundest despair not to realize it *is* despair. Kierkegaard. Mitsak. She's vanished down that rabbit hole known as California and her cell never cries *text me*. Her past, rare for a lesbian, has gone dead quiet; her exes have adopted Chinese infants abandoned in train stations. Desire's deserted the professor (she is the deserted train station), and this candlelit table strewn with cigarettes ashed in saucers and wineglasses kissed in retro red makes her want to cry out a warning. Nine innocents commencing the long romance with academe's rejections: Well, she has everything they long for, and look at her. Old! Old! Old! Old! Old! Alone! Alone! Alone! Alone! It's not really there, is it, such stupidity, on the tip of her tongue? Yes it is—(she's drunk)—but look, she's saved, struck dumb by a voice.

The voice can't be described as *honeyed*. It doesn't intend to flatter. Neither gratitude nor the least career-driven taint of ingratiation figures in its tone. The voice belongs to the woman at Clio's left, whom Clio has succeeded, since seating was reshuffled for dessert, in not noticing at all. Such gaps or rifts in social obligation are the prerogative of charisma, with its sexy, butterfly-alighting attentiveness, its abrupt, invigorating rudeness, the masochistically satisfying cold shoulder turned toward any less than stellar presence. Regretfully, Clio concedes (as perhaps the voice, fractionally wounded, implies) that she has managed to ignore beauty.

Q: Briefly explicate Rilke's lines "All of you undisturbed cities / haven't you ever yearned for the Enemy?"

A: When that beautiful voice says, "Selfish us, we've kept you up too late. You're tired," Clio, not yet ready to confront the source, steadies the bowl of her wineglass between two fingers and a thumb, observing the quake of her pulse in the concentric wine rings. The voice qualifies, thoughtfully: "No, *sad*," italicizing with the pleasure of nailing emotion to its right name, and at this ventured naming, Clio feels the startled relief of the very lonely, whose emotions, unless they trouble to name them to themselves, run around nameless. Immediately following relief comes panic, not at all an unusual progression, for there's no panic quite like the panic of having found something you'd hate to lose. Now we come to that asocial moment when the inkblot of private gesture, proof of exigent emotion, stains the unfolding social contract: Clio can't look at this woman. Not yet. Realizing it can only seem strange, she closes her eyes. A person whose composure is not only a professional asset but an actual cast of mind may become a connoisseur

of her own panic, just as, for a Japanese gardener, the random scattera-
tion of cherry petals on raked gravel possesses an inimitable beauty: so
behind her closed eyes Clio experiences, as counterpart to dismay, a
sneaky delight at her own downfall. The Enemy!

Q: *The absurd and the erotic are mutually exclusive modes of perception. That is, no
love object can be both ridiculous and beautiful. True or false?*

A: The voice's owner, perceiving an invitation in Clio's empty glass,
leans in with the bottle, startling Clio, whose closed eyes have pre-
vented awareness of her proximity. Clio jumps, diverting the airborne
artery of wine, which leaps about, bathing her wrist, spattering her dessert plate, splashing from the table's edge onto her black silk lap. The
voice's owner fails to right the bottle until wine rains from the table's
edge, pattering into flexing amoeba shapes on the polished floor, the
voice's owner apologizing manically—yet as if she anticipated some
need for apology?—and setting the bottle down with a thump. *I'm so so
sorrrrry.* It is Clio's lap that the voice's owner bends toward, still uttering wild *sorrys*, so that Clio's first image of her happens to be of the
parting of her hair, a line of skin as naked as if a fresh-peeled twig had
just been unearthed. As for her hair, it is red and in torment, copious,
strenuous, anarchic hair, writhing, heavy, ardent, gorgeous hair tricked
into confinement, knotted at the nape of a neck so smooth and white
its single mole seems to cast a tiny shadow. The tip of Clio's tongue so
covets the mole, which stands out like one of the beads of Beaujolais
on Clio's own wrist, that Clio scarcely experiences the swabbing of the
napkin at her lap—thus, for the sake of the imagined, missing out on
the erotic thrill of the actual, and immediately repenting this, the first
loss within the kingdom of true love.

   "This is *so* not working," says the woman, trying to blot at Clio's
wrist while Clio memorizes every detail of the profile of her future.
Too much forehead, baldish and exposed-looking, as is often true of
redheads, a long nose with a bump at its tip, the smart arch of the lifted
eyebrow, thick eyelashes dark at their roots, fair to invisibility at their
tips. A fine chin. A neat and somehow boyish ear, exposed by the ferocious tension of the trammeled hair. Why boyish? Unearringed, Clio
notes, not even pierced, just a sexy virgin petal of lobe. Under the fine

chin, the hint of a double, a softening in a line that should ideally run tensely along the jaw to the down curve of the throat. This is true of redheads as well, Clio thinks, this appearance of fattiness or laxness in certain secret places, as if the body, where it can, resists the severity of the contrast between pale skin and vivid hair and asserts a passivity, a private entropy, counter to the flamey energy of red. Clio is forty-two to the other's twentysomething: fact. Fearful fact.

"Don't worry, we can get you cleaned up," says the younger woman, "so come on," standing to seize Clio's wrist, leading Clio down a long and shadowed hall, the din of apologies—everyone's, chorused yet random, like Apache war cries—fading behind the two of them, then gone entirely, Clio surrendering to the sexiness of being *led*, for the other hasn't released her wrist and hasn't turned around, Clio Eurydice, prisoner, or child, intently reading the text of this most unexpected of persons, the Beloved. Under Clio's hot gaze the knot of passionate hair at the Beloved's nape, screwed so tight in its coil, releases red-gold strands flaring with electricity.

Q: *The following quotation is taken from* Wittgenstein's Philosophical Investigations:

A face which inspires fear or delight (the object of fear or delight) is not on that account its cause, but—one might say—its target.

Discuss.

A: Prof. Mitsak's new condominium comes with its own scrap of California, backyard enough for two spindly fruit trees, a lumpy futon of gopher-harrowed turf, and an inherited compost heap. It's still winter, the trees' tracery of bare branches unguessable as to kind, but Prof. Mitsak thinks of them as plum trees because sex, for her, was born with a theft: of her grandmother's plum jam, the old woman watching, from the corner of an eye, the child's fingers crooking over the jar's rim, sliding into the lumpish, yielding sweetness, the old woman giving the harsh little laugh peculiar to that kind of vicarious delight, witnessing a pleasure one essentially disapproves of, which costs one something—in her grandmother's case, a steely domestic rigor and a wicked Methodist conviction about the virtue of self-deprivation were both held in check for the duration of Clio's self-pleasuring. The child must have trusted the old woman would tolerate this display of sensuousness, but how could she have known? It will be spring by the time the trees, if their blossoming proves they're not plum, can disappoint Clio, and by spring she hopes to be eating and sleeping again, done with writing and rewriting letters, real, insane, ink-and-paper letters she never sends, through twisting herself into yoga asanas meant to impress the younger, suppler Beloved, who will never observe these contortions. In Clio's previous experience of heartbreak, she's been its cause. All this is new to Clio, and as she says to herself, she's not good at it. She's a bad sufferer, graceless, tactless, wincing, vindictive, a forgetter of goddaughters' birthdays, a serial umbrella-loser. Winter rains down on her head, pelting her with the icy spite of finality: she will never tilt a bottle toward the mouth of a Mei or Ming, or click wedding ring against steering wheel in time to Mozart. Her most parodied gesture becomes the quick, convulsive shake of the head with which she assumes the lectern, flicking rain-drops across her notes, rousing the microphone to a squalling tantrum as water pings against electronics. In each lecture Clio seems to be trailing after some earlier, smarter, more competent Clio, even as she had followed the Beloved, she of the Sturm und Drang hair, down the fatal hallway. How can love do this, divorce one from oneself? One's old, reliable, necessary self? All winter, this is the single relief built into every pitiless week: white-knuckling it at the podium, Clio suffers the loss of something other than the Beloved.

Fridays can be very bad. Those Fridays when faculty meetings are held, Clio must, as often as not, encounter the Beloved—as junior faculty, her attendance isn't always required, but there is this pain, certain Fridays, of having to sit on the far side of a slab of exotic wood from some plundered rain forest, studying the span of the Beloved's cheekbone, a revelation of human perfection. Like human perfection, shadowed. The corner of the Beloved's mouth has an unwarranted tendency to break Clio's heart. That is, the corner of this mouth now and then deepens into a near smile. Suppose everyone were capable of disarming everyone else thus, by the merest turn of a head, by the flicker of an eyelid or the premonition of a smile, then all relations would be grounded in wonder, then everyone would be taken hostage by the immensity of what it is possible to feel.

Q: *True or false: In narrative, desire is scarcely born before it encounters an obstacle; neither can exist without the other.*

A: Following the Beloved down that dim hallway, *you*, in your Questioner's detachment, would have kept your wits about you, and would have observed, on the fourth finger of the Beloved's left hand, the diamond whose mean-spirited glint was hidden by the wonder veiling Clio's mind. Well: she is only a character, much of her own story is lost on her.

In that Ladies' designed for blissful immersion in one's own reflection, the professor stripped bare, the Beloved rinses her trousers under a golden faucet. She twists and wrings out the trousers, then carries them to a dryer on the wall, tapping its round silver button, dangling Clio's black legs in the sirocco, so they weave happily, gusting into the Beloved's own body, then fainting away.

"Really, you don't have to do this. You should be out with the others."

"*I* spilled the wine all over you."

This washerwomanly penance is cute, they both think.

"Why did you say, before, 'sad'?" Clio asks.

"Maybe everyone is, when a dinner party lags on and on. If we had a reason to leave, we'd leave. If we don't have a reason, that's sad. You don't seem to have a reason. Or"—she catches herself—"is it rude to say that?"

When she turns the professor makes a fig leaf of her hands. "It's honest."

"And I was surprised, you know? One always thinks of famous people as having everything figured out. Here. You can try these now."

Q: *Susan Stewart writes: "The face becomes a text, a space which must be 'read' and interpreted in order to exist. The body of a woman, particularly constituted by a mirror and thus particularly subject to an existence constrained by the nexus of external images, is spoken by her face, by the articulation of another's reading. Apprehending the face's image becomes a mode of possession. . . . The face is what belongs to the other. It is unavailable to the woman herself."*

A: What was the question?

Q: *What do you make of that?*

A: Clio, done hiking her trousers up, finds the Beloved in a lazy stretch, the real and mirrored Beloved's arms lifted, fingers interlaced, palms ceilingward, fox-red tufts of underarm hair bristling, little black dress hiked midthigh-high: flirtatiousness or ravishing unself-consciousness, and for Clio, no knowing which. So deep is her confusion that she cracks her knuckles and then remembers how she had hated it when her *mother* did that. Several small wildfires of desire are adroitly stamped out, Mother's is so derisive a shade, and Clio was never out to her. It is the perfect antidote to desire, skinny Mother materializing, upright backbone and the witty incision of her neat, ungiving Methodist smile. Just *try* thinking back through this woman.

It's then that two blazing wings of sensation touch down on Clio's nape, and the Beloved's palms begin to move in soft circles, massaging, worrying at the tension they find, digging in, the Beloved's thumbs closing in on the axial vertebra, so that Clio feels the three-dimensional puzzle-piece of bone click as if newly wedged in place, her entire skull balanced most vulnerably upon the knife's point of sexual alertness, Clio afraid to move or make a sound for fear of dislodging the hands, startling them into flight, so appalling would their loss be. She is aware that savage loss is the counterpart and shadow of this raw arousal and yearning, which she can scarcely trust even as she leans into it, wondering what this means, this sensual charity, and unable to ask, such is the din of sensation, so wholly grateful is she for the cleverness of the Beloved's hands.

"Shiatsu."

"Shiatsu," echoes Clio.

"Mmm. Good for what ails you."

The Beloved's reflection squints at the real-world Clio over her shoulder, to which she administers a comradely slap. Dismissed.

What ails me? Clio wonders. *Loss. Aging. Remorse. You are good for that.*

So this is the dark side of Eros. Always before it was Clio who inflicted the first reality check. The pangs foreshadowing abandonment, the subtly poisonous forewarning: Clio dealt those out.

Now we come, though it doesn't look like it, to our epiphany, for Clio, academe's androgynous roué, contriver of seductions, far-flung affairs, and prolonged breakdowns—here and now, Clio encounters a possibility never before entertained: she's been unkind. Careless with others' hearts. A waster of time and a despoiler of affection. As of this moment, that Prof. Mitsak is dead. Just ask Clio, absorbed in this mirror's vision, herself and her one true love, the radiant-haired object of all future dreams, now rubbing a finger across a front tooth. Clio puts her hands on those shoulders and turns the slender black-sheathed body around. She thinks *heart-stopping* of the weird seizure, like an appalling inward death, of her own breath in her throat, and then all self-narration, even the faint stabs at description that accompany the worst emergencies, stops. Though the red mouth tilts toward her, lips parting, the eyes remain open. Dazzling, desirous, repelled, unreadable.

Q: *Compare/contrast the roles of "body" and "soul" in the act of kissing.*

A: This eyes-open kiss is clumsy: neither body nor soul can readily forgive that. Seduction, it turns out, requires an almost Questioner-like detachment to insure grace. To become a character in the story is to fall from grace. It's as if Clio, in her previous affairs, was always narrator, never simply down in the story, at the mucky, hapless level where she knew only as much as anyone else. Or less. It could be the Beloved needs a narrator, not simply a floundering fellow character. Her teeth grate against the Beloved's, a terrible, nails-on-blackboard sound from which they both recoil.

Q: *Comment briefly on the following quotation.*

Perhaps it was to that hour of anguish that there must be attributed the importance which Odette had since assumed in his life. Other people are, as a rule, so immaterial to us that, when we have entrusted to any one of them the power to cause so much suffering or happiness to ourselves, that person seems at once to belong to a different universe, is surrounded with poetry, makes of our lives a vast expanse, quick with sensation, on which that person and ourselves are ever more or less in contact.

A: Nadia is her name, Nadia Nadia Nadia Nadia Nnnnnnn—*ahhhhh*—deeeeee—uh.

All that drear winter of La Niña, it feels to Clio as if she's trying to keep a wine cork submerged in a bathtub using only one thumb, so dodgy and haywire is this love. Tamped-down love offers not sublimated energy but an exhausting impatience: before long, she's sick of obsession's two-lane Nebraska highway. She welcomes any distraction, even this folder, plunked down on her desk by a junior colleague, untenured, younger even than the Beloved. Fading back toward the doorway, this colleague announces in an injured tone: "We really need to know what you think." *We*, the women. Not that the junior women will be voting on this appointment, but they will have the chance to voice their opinions. Renee, though standing—on the far side of Clio's desk—crosses her legs, a habit of hers. When sitting down she hangs one leg over the other, hooks a toe behind a calf, and strains for ease, a gauche, brain-driven woman whose particular mix of ethnicity baffles Clio. African American? Vietnamese? And Czech? Irish? Dutch? Some unprecedented cat's cradle of deoxyribonucleic acid granted her that shapely mouth, pugilist's menacing nose with flaring nostrils, oily fawn skin marred across the cheekbones by an orange-peel stippling of adolescent acne. That acne, severe and untreated, suggests a raisin-in-the-sun, down-home poverty, valiantly tackled and, at this point in her young career, deeply repudiated. If Renee ever had an accent, it's gone. Not quite gone: some suggestion of backwater lulls and daydreamy delta vowels remains, despite the reign of that impressive will. To suggest a chic she's far from possessing, Renee's left ear is multiply pierced and, adorned with wires and rings, seems more alert than the other, more attuned to signals and nuances. It is to this ear that Clio says, "Calm down. I'll read it. Just calm yourself, Renee."

"You don't seem to get it. You were our only chance."

In this chilly pause, Clio, love's insomniac, fails to suppress a yawn. Renee, fervent with insult, closes in, hurling herself into Clio's office's only unoccupied seat, a meanly proportioned straight-backed chair designed to discommode students who would otherwise linger in Clio's aura of disdainful indifference. Throwing one leg over the other, leaning in, slapping the folder, Renee begins, "We expected so—"

Clio says, "'So'?"

What the hell is the expression stamped on the fine, ethnically inscrutable features. "So much of you, when you came. That you would, not *mother* exactly, at least *care* about our careers. *Open doors* for us. Use your influence with the men, whose basic wish, it can't be lost on you, is that we'd all just go away. What kind of life is this? Helena's bulimia's *a lot worse*, Trish chain-smokes unfiltered Camels, Ellie must be running ten miles a day, Nadia—Nadia's a weird shadow of her former self."

"A shadow?"

"Me, I fantasize obsessively about burning down this building."

"But Nadia? You were about to say why she's a shadow?"

"Even to confess this fantasy probably gets me on about five different lists right now."

"I haven't noticed anything wrong with Nadia."

"Well: you seem to be avoiding her."

"No. No no. Not avoiding her. Why would I avoid Nadia? No."

"Avoiding all of us, then."

"You seem to have found me."

"Right at home in this building I burn down, in my dreams, ten or eleven times a day."

"If you burn it down what will you do?"

"Ha! Even in daydreams I blow out the match. Even in my head, where you'd think I'd have no fear, I can't touch the flame to the shitty carpet. This place! Can't you get a little more involved? Without some input soon, things around here are gonna go in a truly ugly direction. Word here in River City has it that sentiment's running against Nadia's tenure. Why, you wonder? Why? Would you like the figures on just how many junior female faculty this place has ever tenured? Because I'd like to give you that figure. I like that figure for its impressiveness. It's a very round number. Big fat succinct zero. And against that zero is pitted the one person who can conceivably intervene without risking her entire future, except that person, you, refuses to be pitted."

"I will," Clio says.

"You will?"

Down the hallway, a door opens, closes, and is locked, the home-ward-bound deconstructionist whistling merrily, the melody trailing down the floor before vanishing into the elevator, not without lodging itself in Clio's mind. *Miss my clean white linen, and my fancy French perfume.*

"I will start paying attention," Clio says distractedly. "I will pit myself."

"Because I fear the consequences for Nadia if that zero's allowed to rule. Look, did I—?"

"Did you?"

"Offend you."

"There's truth in what you said." Gently, but sick of gentleness, dis-liking the baiting way this woman hangs her sentences in the air.

"Sorry." A pause while this antagonist wonders how far she can push her luck. "But we *really need you*, is the thing."

"Don't be."

"I would open a florist shop," Renee says. "After I burned this build-ing down. If you must know."

"You know what I think of?" Clio says—not, in the moment, even faintly surprised, though in lucid retrospection she will marvel at this question, at having done, next, something so unlike herself, telling a truth, and why, when no good comes of such slips? "A bookstore on a downtown corner in some small town. Rare books, first editions."

"But you're famous. You're fine. You're not at their mercy." *You have everything I want.*

"There are days, lately, when I don't love books."

"You're losing your soul."

Clio reflects on the justness of this observation, and is struck to find herself agreeing. "People open bookstores because they want their souls back."

"Yes they do. I know bookstores where people have *gotten* them back."

They laugh, and then don't know what to do.

"Why did you come in now? About my pitting myself? Why never before?"

"Nadia. She just seems a little *off.* Girl's spending all her time schem-ing ways to persuade men who don't even know she exists that they owe her a *yes.* The vote's next week."

"Right. Of course." Clio knew, but had forgotten, that this was looming, perhaps because, in the cool scholarly part of her soul, and inadmissable though it is, she doesn't much like Nadia's work. Trusting this secret assessment, with the rest of her soul so compromised, would be unwise, she knows, and she's intended, all along, to vote yes, venturing arguments that will make it hard for her male colleagues to vote no. Clio's meant, in short, to do the right thing, or at least the least *wrong* thing. Whichever way it goes, this meeting can cause pain: the pain of Nadia's being granted tenure and remaining near but unpossessable, the pain of Nadia's being refused tenure, thus vanishing forever from Clio's life. If not even a starry glimpse of the object of fear and desire is possible, what will become of that life?

And yet, freed on this, the first afternoon in our story that can safely be called *spring*, lugging her laden briefcase, Clio surrenders to bliss hidden within each Friday, taking the stairs in long-legged, traipsing descent, her voice pitching *up!* and *up!* precariously, caroming off cinder block as if the stairwell were a gigantic cement shower stall, quick with resonance, echoing and amplifying:

"Oh I

"Could drink

"A case

"Of you!"

You! flung into the rainy outer world as Joni Mitchell, trailing rags of her ethereal voice, charges across the asphalt only to find, wading in a slow circle around a rusted-out, tail-finned wreck of a car in the flooding parking lot, Nadia, head bent under the assault of the rain, carrying a sodden shoe box, now and then pausing to hammer with her fist at the car's Bondo-dappled hood. Clio suffers a curious twist of emotion she can't at first recognize, which then comes dismayingly clear. Before, encountering Nadia unexpectedly, she's experienced a number of emotions—shame of a particularly rich, basking intensity, or a pitiless, wired kind of happiness—but never before has any response to Nadia been as mild and lucid as this: disappointment. Dismaying, because while shame and happiness can be explained, in regard to Nadia, what can disappointment mean? An emotion so small and—ordinary.

"This is all I can *fuck. Ing.* Take." *Fuck* and *ing* are blows.

It's been two months since they have exchanged more than cautious *hi*'s, passing in the hall. "Keep hitting like that, you'll hurt your hand."

"I locked myself out. Do you *fucking* believe it?"

"Come get in my car. You can use my cell."

"This had to happen in front of you." Nadia begins to cry. "When all I want—"

"When all you want?" More baiting sentences? Did the junior women catch this from each other?

"Is to be like you, you know. So *together*. So far above the shit and disarray."

Nadia wants not to *have* but to *be* Clio, it seems. *Not at their mercy.* Not at anyone's: a girl's dream. "I lose keys," she says, and tries to catch Nadia's wrist before she can bang on the old car again, but too late: a ruckus of reverberating metal, and the rain drumming steadily on the Chevy's roof and hood, Clio sheltering Nadia's head, now, under an impromptu roof of briefcase.

"Get in my car and we'll figure out what you should do."

"I can't get in your car, I'm soaking."

"You're shivering. Come on."

In Clio's BMW, with its kid-glove leather and customized quiet, German meticulousness exerts its power to heal the psyche, and Nadia grows calmer. Ducking into the passenger side after Clio unlocked its door, she absently relinquished the old shoe box with bulging sides, wound around with duct tape and curiously heavy. Covertly, Clio tries shaking the box.

"Hey!" Nadia cries, and snatches the box away, giving Clio a wild look—accusation and darkening sorrow are in the look, leading her to confess, "This box has my heart in it."

"Your *heart*?"

Nadia leans forward in her seat and rests her forehead against the lid of the box, communing with whatever's inside. After a moment she says clearly, "My little cat." Droplets chase down the spiraling madrone twigs of wet red hair to patter onto the box's cardboard, where they appear as fuzzy, swiftly dilating dots. Her face hidden, she says, "Who loved me for *me*."

There is nothing to say to this, and nothing to dry either of them with, Clio the bad, the negligent mother in the quasidomesticity of the car's interior. Wanting to help but unable to think of anything, Clio sets the wipers going. Fans of visibility flash open and swipe shut, melodically. Around them, the drenched and shining asphalt reveals streaks of rare brilliance, as if light is drilling down into a medium infinitely soft and black, and the other cars stranded here and there across the lot possess the sharp-edged perfection of abandoned houses—of houses where you can see in one window and all the way through, out another window. Clio turns on the heat, not just because Nadia's still shivering; suddenly it seems important that they not be fogged in by breath, and she's worried about the strangeness of Nadia's behavior. "The cat is," Clio says delicately, "*in* the box?"

"Dead," Nadia says to the box.

"Nadia, I'm sorry."

"Fuck, what a word," Nadia says. "*Dead.* Onomatopoetic."

"I'm so sorry."

At last, to Clio's relief, Nadia sits up. "I knew something was wrong all night and I took her in first thing this morning. To the vet, I mean. It was an okay experience, really. They give her this shot and she goes all soft in my hands. This little velvet sack from which all fear just, *sssst*, leaks away. I'm holding her, I'm stroking her, they give her the other shot then. The death shot."

Q: *In the light of your answers to the previous questions, formulate a definition of "beauty."*

A: "I'm sorry," Clio says again, meaning to convey an anxious, electric empathy, though she can't help it: such grief seems faintly ridiculous to her, and even diminishes the younger woman. Is there a fugitive whiff—carnal, catlike?—of decay in the car? She hadn't known Nadia had a cat, but in her experience cats, belonging to lovers or exes or lovers' exes' exes, come with relationships—never before sealed in a box, though. Clio wants to apply the balm of her cool hand to Nadia's forehead, to the temple, where the growth of new hair forms a minute clockwise whorl, like the illustration of the birth of a star, the tiny hairs strung with impossibly fine condensation. For no reason a phrase of Woolf's comes to Clio: "'Reality' . . . beside which nothing matters." Reality for Clio seems born of that fine, nearly invisible star on the

Beloved's temple, and if she wants more than anything to touch it, for the sake of what the other must be feeling, she resists.

Q: *"At the center of each person,"* D. W. *Winnicott writes, "is an incommunicado element and this is sacred and most worthy of preservation." Can this belief be reconciled with erotic love, and if so, how?*

A: She resists. "Where can I take you?" she asks, hating to interrupt this silence, the easiest intimacy they are ever likely to achieve.

Provoked by sympathy, her instinct to redeem herself warring with the haywire wretchedness of grief, Nadia begins to cry again. "Hey, hey come on, it's all right, it really is," Clio says. "I can take you wherever you need to go."

Still Nadia weeps into her hands, not with her hands clasped to her face but rubbing and swiping at it compulsively, as if her hands wanted to *work* on grief, to knead and knuckle it out. This at least—the loss or death of cats being a staple of lesbian discourse—*is* familiar.

"The trouble is I don't know where to go. Or what to do with her." Nadia's voice has a rasp in it, deprivation meeting and marrying remorse, the tone of the truly, bitterly disconsolate. The dead cat smell is stronger now. Nadia says, "I live in this *box*, this apartment, seventh floor, I don't own any of the ground. There's no place to put her." She clears her throat. "I thought of stealthily burying her on campus, maybe in one of those old eucalyptus groves. That's why I brought her. I was actually walking around with her under my arm, looking. But I thought, What if the campus police find me burying this little box of cat? Won't it be ludicrous, won't it get me in trouble, won't they just anyway stop me? Plus, what can I dig with? It's not like I own a shovel. What a fucked-up *life*. I hate my *life*. I can't even call someone and say, 'My cat died,' because everyone I know would feel some kind of irony about the situation, like they would never be caught driving around with their cat in a box, like it could never happen to them. Even Billy. He wouldn't mean to, but he'd convey his—I'm sorry, I'm ruining your beautiful leather."

Billy, Clio remembers, is the boyfriend, who teaches at Columbia, and seems to be mostly a phone presence in Nadia's existence, but as such, sufficient to prevent other entanglements. For example, with Clio.

"He would convey his what?" She can't help this little viper of voyeurism, uncoiling.

"He never liked the cat. So—his relief."

"Oh, no."

"He's going to try not to show it but he's going to be *glad*."

"Surely not, Nadia."

"He's going to think, ah, now we can live together, no impediments."

"The cat can't have been much of an impediment."

"He can be *fussy*. The cat, for some reason, liked peeing in his shoes."

"Listen, I think we should go to my place. I have a backyard. Maybe you'd like to bury your cat there. It's a nice backyard. Shady in summer, when the trees leaf out." Clio promises "plum trees" even as she wonders whether the silken gentleness she's always managed to spin from the straw of her soul for Nadia would vanish at the first scent of cat piss arising from a Manolo Blahnik. Well: not a problem for this lifetime.

"You'd want my cat in your backyard? Why?"

"You need to get her into the ground, right? I don't mind if you use a little of my backyard. I think it's a good use for it."

"How can we bury her in rain like this?"

"Under umbrellas?"

Umbrellas are what they use, taking turns digging and sheltering, Clio glad to break in her Smith & Hawken spade, the soil yielding pebbles of asphalt and shards of glass but mostly giving way easily enough, not difficult to dig a fair-sized hole in, though the bottom has begun to seep before Nadia lowers the sodden box, and because Nadia begins to cry again, it's Clio who shucks the first spadeful onto the darkening coffin, petals falling in a sudden gust and sticking to the cardboard, Nadia crying harder, Clio's lower back beginning to ache and her own eyes to brim. Why is she crying? Suddenly the sadness is a volatile force, impersonal but owning Clio completely, a howl lodged, just barely contained, in her throat. In the virgin spade, the muck glistens like cake.

When Clio is done tamping the earth over the grave, she asks Nadia if she'd like to come in, and Nadia assents. Barefoot, she prowls past the floor-to-ceiling bookshelves with scarcely a sideways glance. Clio can't help registering her failure to read titles or pull out a single one of the Woolf firsts with their fragile, charming Vanessa Bell jackets. In the kitchen Nadia pauses at the refrigerator door. "Wow. All these Chinese babies."

"My godchildren." Each morning, with her first cup of coffee, she stands before the collage of fat-cheeked faces, snowsuits and tutus, try- ing to make sure she's not forgetting another birthday.

"All girls?"

"In China girls get abandoned, so the parents can try for a boy."

"Do you like kids?"

"Only those."

"I can't imagine what it would feel like, abandoning your baby." She imagines: "Like ripping your heart out with your bare hands." She taps several pictures. "These are cute, these tiny violins."

"Suzuki method."

"I want kids."

"Why don't you get out the wine? But let me pour."

"Ha."

Bringing two wineglasses filled to the brim, she sets one by Clio and sits in the nearer of two cubes of chrome and black leather.

Clio says, "I'll make a fire. Get you warmed up." She busies herself with crumpling newspaper and arranging kindling into a tipsy pyra- mid—for some reason thinking, as the lit match wavers, of Renee— she's in luck, the fire catches nicely, and Nadia comes to sit cross-legged beside her, the bath towel now slung over her shoulders boxer style. She rubs the back of a freckled hand across her cheekbone, leaving a streak of wet grittiness. Clio looks away so she won't be tempted to take the towel's corner and erase that streak. She doesn't want to ask if she can, but simply for things to unfold, or not, as Nadia wishes. Nadia hugs her shins, fire-gazing, and says, "I was crazy. You saved me."

"I want something for you."

"Something *for* me? What?"

"You might not understand this, or think it has anything to do with me—and probably it doesn't—but what I want is your happiness. However you want to go about obtaining it. Whatever shape it takes in your imagination. The funny thing is I can want this without knowing anything about it. How you'd even define happiness. Whether you even think it exists."

"What about your happiness?" Nadia says. "Say something happened. Would you be all right if it happened only once?" So, when it comes down to it, she's someone who likes to know what she's getting into. Clio had believed, wrongly, she would prefer not-knowing, risk, improvisation. Perhaps her hair improvises so ardently she feels she must insist on control, elsewhere.

"I don't know." She rues her honesty. "Yes."

"You would? Even if we can't see each other after this?"

"Yes."

"Because this can't turn into a *thing*." Nadia sticks to interrogation: unwillingly, Clio realizes she might be good at it. "I don't want you to get hurt, do you see that?"

"I'm fine."

"Because I'm straight."

"You know I love you," Clio says, "that I loved you the moment I saw you," and then she says, "and you know that's true," and hugs her own shins, the two of them fire-gazing in parallel universes, waiting for what will come next.

Q: *Tell me.*

A: The Beloved's nipples are terra-cotta, her vagina is coral, her hair, floating as it dries, a torrent freed from gravity, roams the air around her face with an unruly will of its own, her high forehead serene in spite of this changeling hair, her little breasts swinging and bumping her whippet rib cage, the mole on her neck vivid, her kneecaps flushed bright pink by the fire's heat as she crouches above the professor, and if Clio wants to think this night the most beautiful she will ever live through, who can disagree? All conspires to ensure the Beloved's tenure: Why would Clio dissent? Let us say that the *yes* she scrawls on a slip of paper, one of several dozen slips collected by the chair, was inevitable. Let's agree that no love should be judged by its duration, and that what Clio learns this isolated night is of rare worth in what Keats calls the school for souls. In Eros 101. But there is another vantage point, the future, which finds Clio dreaming she's lost something and can't find it no matter how she searches. She wakes to find she's bitten her lip until it bleeds. Amoebas of blood stain the pillow slip, and when, later that day, Clio discovers the wedding invitation lurking in her departmental mailbox, she bangs her forehead against the wall of her office in sorrow urgent as autism. Nadia's bridegroom is handsome in his tux—maybe there is, in fact, a slight fussiness in the meticulous shine of his shoes and the primly satisfied set of his mouth; of the two of them, bride and groom, his is the more conventional prettiness. After a boomingly musical interval all heads turn to follow the (newly tenured) bride's progress down the aisle, getting farther and farther away, and the only thing Clio wants to do, there in her pew, is scratch at her own arms, smear ashes across her face, maul and mark her body forever, but a hand clasps hers. This clasp conveys restraint, tolerance, calm. It's Renee's hand, for not long after Clio sat down, Renee slid into the pew beside her, craning her neck to take in the fanciness of the flowers at the altar, concluding, "Swanky." Then, in a whisper: "Mimosa. Interesting choice."

The two trees in Clio's yard prove to be not plum but cherry, merely ravishing. Even the inexhaustible Woolf, in the following days and weeks, holds no interest for the professor. Much, much later it will occur to Clio that though the box seemed to her to possess sufficient weight, and in handling the box she'd seemed to sense inside it something both lolling and stiff, she never actually saw the cat. In fact, the lid had been taped down, the box had been defensively wound around and around again with duct tape. Does it matter that she might have been cheated into *yes*? If it wasn't the cat in the box, what can it have been? Something with the density of the once-alive, with a certain compactness, the weight of dark muscle—say, Clio's heart. It might as well have been her heart, she parted with it so completely that night, and it's so long—so bitterly long—before she will see *that* again.

Q: Does she ever see it again?

A: Sweet Questioner, you care. Clio doesn't really see it again until two years later when, rolling over in bed, lifting herself on an elbow to gaze down her pugilist's nose at Clio, Renee reels off the ingredients of her fawn skin, handsome mouth, and eerie green eyes. Black, Lakota Sioux, Welsh, a little Norwegian. One mystery solved, at least. And look, beyond the ken of this exam they never run out of things to say to each other, though one spends her days leafing through old books, the other up to her elbows in sweet peas and tuberose, cattleya and quince.

Q: *Read the following quotation from Simone Weil's* On Human Personality.

If a child is doing a sum and does it wrong, this mistake bears the stamp of his personality. If he does the sum exactly right, his personality does not enter into it at all.

Argue that this does, or does not, have implications for love.

FROGS

:::
:::

Robert Travieso

EVERYONE WAS DISCOVERING all at once that the Gallaghers'
pool—so elegantly uncared for and appealingly unchlorinated and
so discreetly bunkered in the sloped-down edge of the family's lake-
house property—was filled with *frogs*.

Possibly.

Jeremiah had spotted five so far. None had been moving. Three had
been deceased, bobbing along the surface in a kind of dead-frog's float,
but two had been alive—he'd felt and then seen them brushing insen-
sibly against his leg, suspended in a full-bodied pause between the last
and the next link in the chain of their frog kicks. But five didn't seem
like that many, in the context of this particular pool, which was enormous, and rock-bordered, and fed straight from a stream, so maybe
filled, Jeremiah thought, wasn't exactly the right word. If this were the
YMCA, sure, filled. But perhaps here, among these people, in this
remarkably lakelike body of water, the most lakelike body of water Jeremiah had ever been in, surpassing, in fact, several actual lakes from his
past, there was an expected and accepted level of naturalness, regardless of how heebie-jeebifying it might be. No one, after all, had gotten
out. After the initial discovery—which had been dramatic, which had
involved a scream, two hands clapped fast around a mouth, some shivering, and a still-ongoing cooling-off period in the pool house—things
had calmed down quite a bit. There were still some uncontrollable,
frog-induced yelps here and there, but these were mostly of a hello-
there-didn't-see-you-coming variety, and people had stopped reporting each new sighting. The consensus among the group seemed to
be, even as they shooed the next crop of bobbing frogs farther along

toward the drain with little backhanded splashes—*shoo frog, shoo*—that this was not a freak-out-able offense. The pool was not *filled* with frogs, was the new thinking among the group. Because that would be gross. This was more like *shared*. Or slightly inhabited, or, at worst, mildly invaded, like little harmless moths at the bottom of a cereal box.

Lydia, the discoverer, the screamer, the squeamish, still calming down in the pool house, had been not merely dramatic, but overdramatic. Let's not obsess, let's not get in a huff about a couple or, okay, a few frogs bopping around in our midst, was the new thinking among the group.

But Jeremiah, despite his wish to accept the naturalness of the situation, to see the pool as not *filled*, per se, was, in the end, not really among the group, and so not privy to the new thinking, and so not taking it all in stride quite as easily as the others. Although, truth be told, even if he had gotten the memo, he still might have been a bit hesitant to get with the program, because there was and had been for some time now an enormous inky tadpole galaxy slowly wrapping itself into the shape of a single frothing doughnut around the crotch-close part of his thigh.

Struck still with a mixture of fear, approbation (tadpoles are *amazing*!), and the intrigue of what would come next, Jeremiah began to imagine, from his sheltered spot by the shallow-end steps, that each tadpole was like a proton or a neutron or some other tiny, whirring elemental thing in its individual cloud-contained hyperactivity—a neutron probably—and that each cloud cluster was like an atom, a throbbing whole. Or something like that, something along those lines, something to do with small, spastic components equaling some relatively solid sum—he hadn't taken chemistry yet, and couldn't really get into the proper specifics. But he was in a bad mood, all frogs exempted, and his imagination was working in a reparative overdrive of sorts, grabbing at anything that seized his attention, lulling him with focus, analogizing wildly, calling to him, whispering, *Look, look at the interesting things that have nothing to do with you, look and be amazed and concentrate in a way that removes all else, take the small and make it large, take the large and make it small*, entrancing him, weaving around him a cocoon of concentration.

But could his mind weave fast enough, and tight enough, and with enough opacity to block out, for instance, the sun? He didn't think so. And in not thinking so, in thinking *no*, his thought became a prophesy, or a penknife stabbing his shell, and the whole thing, the whole cocoon, popped like a poked balloon, and the sun poured in and refracted within the pool water and shone deep like a beacon upon the rest of the group—who were frolicking with their own found frogs in cascading intervals of stifled terror and fortified glee, and who were excluding him.

At the center of it all was Daphne Gallagher: smiling, shining, beautiful, dangling.

Jeremiah felt a childish, bed-beating, fist-bashing rage well up inside him, a swallowed stone. On the car ride up he'd been assigned a seat in the "way back," crammed in with the beer and the admittedly good-smelling grocery bags, as far away from Daphne—who had driven—as possible. He'd earned the seat by being the first loser at a one-potato-, two-potato-type hand game that he'd never played or seen before. Dan, the organizer of the game, had won, earning the passenger's front seat. At the time it had seemed like pure unfortunate chance. Now, insanely, after two awkward hours in the lake house, during which he'd watched the rest of the group play a complicated drinking game (that no one had offered to explain to him) involving a banjo, three quarters, four porcelain mugs, and a pitcher of beer, and after five dramatic minutes in the pool, during which he'd first missed out somehow on the initial howling hand-in-hand procession off the diving board (the line had formed quickly, the links had quickly closed) and then drifted silently and under no protest into the cloistered calm of the shallow end, it seemed (that silly seat in the "way back," his elbows resting attentively between the headrests, his desperate voice calling, "What? What?" at all the jokes and stories retold along the way that were not for him, the bumps in the road that sent him to the ceiling, the calls from the front to "watch the beer, dude," the humiliation repressed, the stone swallowed, then suppressed) like the first sign of a conspiracy.

:::

Daphne dangled under the diving board by her fingertips, her body drawn up out of the water and dripping, the tied tips of her pale blue bikini bottoms dipping slightly under the surface—a thimble's depth—and then out into the sun again, in and then out again, in concert with the vibrations of the board. Her neck craned back over her freckled shoulders and rested. Her hips jutted out and framed her oval navel, creating blinks of dark space between her suit and skin. She saw everything upside down. Her long, blond hair hung down and splayed like a paused splash against the water beneath her. She looked out across the length of the pool, took a deep breath, and wondered what Jeremiah was thinking. He was standing alone in the shallow end, staring at the water. She wondered if this was a part of his strategy. But what would be the strategy? Either it was something so highly advanced that she couldn't fully grasp it, or he didn't know what he was supposed to be doing. She narrowed her eyes, examining him upside down. He was foolishly tall, a skinny stalactite, and everything around him seemed to fall under his shadow. His shoulders were caved in, and it looked like they were trying to reach out for each other across his bony chest. He was shivering slightly. His hair was so black it reflected the sun, and it was smushed down in a row of curls across his forehead that made her think of her own terrible childhood drawings, of waves drawn in profile with a black Magic Marker. He had a fuzzy trail that traveled from the wedge at the base of his throat down past the waist of his swimsuit. He was still staring at the water, still not moving. Okay, she thought. It's clear now that he doesn't know what he's supposed to be doing.

But she still wanted to know what he did when he thought of her. This was the selling point. She tried to imagine it. She knew he thought of her, he'd told her at the cafeteria. (But how had they begun their conversation? How had they ended up next to each other? She couldn't remember.) He told her he'd thought of her many times, and he'd said it just like that, in a way that made it clear what he meant, a bold thing to mean, and he looked her in the eyes, and when he said it she shivered and grew warm and thought of his young, ridiculously young, see-through-skinny body on a mattress somewhere and she sucked air and said, softly, "I'm flattered," and she was flattered, or she had been, but she also was turned on, and she let herself begin to think, and in the pause that came next, not knowing what else to do, she ruffled his hair and invited him up to her lake house for the weekend. And now here he was.

:::

"Just show her your nuts," Nick had said when Jeremiah told him about the weekend. They were watching TV in Nick's dad's basement, sitting half smothered in beanbag chairs, tossing a tennis ball back and forth.

"What?" Jeremiah said.

"You know, just show her your nuts," Nick repeated, riffling his hands in simultaneous circles as if what he was saying were very routine. "Just be natural, be yourself, act calm—show her your nuts."

"*What?*" Jeremiah said again. But it seemed possible that Nick was being serious, and his seriousness made his suggestion seem less bizarre. He began to picture himself with a beer, by the fridge, alone with Daphne, engaging her first in some intimate conversation, then slowly, slyly lifting his T-shirt to reveal his testicles poking discreetly out through his unzipped fly, or maybe up through his waistband—or should he just whip them out and lay them in his hand like a gift, and let her do with them what she would? It seemed plausible; it was starting to make sense. Older women knew what they wanted. Or so he'd heard. Or he'd heard, at least, that women in their mid-thirties become ravenous sexual beasts—and Daphne was eighteen, so it only stood to reason . . . He worked out a quick reverse extrapolation of the curve: ravenous sexual beast at, say, thirty-five, back five years, plot, back five years, plot, back five years, plot, yes, show her his nuts. Crazy as it sounded, it was probably the right thing to do, God, but it seemed insane, and what would come next? Would she reach out and stroke him? He began to imagine scenarios that would lend themselves well to his exposing himself—the pool, Daphne had said there was a pool, and a lake, maybe he'd not wear underwear and do leg bends and things around her, make it seem like an accident but give her a wink . . .

"I'm just telling you to be yourself," Nick responded, breaking Jeremiah's line of thought. "I'm just saying, don't try to be all suave and everything. Just show her how nuts you are, how crazy you can be—I think she might actually go for that, you know? I mean, maybe that's why she asked you out."

"Oh," Jeremiah said. "Right. No, yeah, that makes sense. Do you have any Fresca, by the way? Or, like, a grape soda or something?"

"Is it hot in here?"

"Are you hot? I'm, like, incredibly hot—are you hot?"

:::

Crouched now in the water up to his neck, poised rock-still on the balls of his feet, Jeremiah could feel himself reweaving the cocoon. A new order of some sort was brewing within his accelerated mind, but he couldn't yet discern it. The frogs and the tadpoles were certainly involved, as how could they not be, but he couldn't tell what role they were to play. Like everyone else, he could observe, could see with his own eyes, only those frogs that happened to be bobbing in relative stillness around him—the dead, the paused, the poised—but he knew with more certainty than before that for every still frog in the pool there had to be many more in motion, partly because it made simple sense and partly (mostly) because in addition to the now mostly dissipated tadpole doughnut encircling his thigh there was a full-grown and fully motile frog crammed somehow inside the white mesh undercradle of his swim trunks, dashing frantically around in a shroud of disorienting darkness. He felt for it sudden, great sorrow and something that felt like but obviously could not be empathy. He could feel it dallying provocatively with his buoyant genitals, tickling him, struggling to wade through his bushy curls, nudging insistently against his most prominent orifice, searching desperately for some passage or canal that would lead out of his shorts and back toward home. He closed his eyes and hoped it found it as soon as was froggily possible.

:::

"Who the fuck is Jeremiah?" Dan had said when Daphne told him about the weekend. They were lying naked under the covers in Dan's bed, letting their sweat dry, basking and gloating in the glow and steam of their gymnastically articulated vigor, looking up at the ceiling, passing a thin joint back and forth, watching the smoke bunch up above them.

"He's a sophomore," Daphne said. "He's really tall, and sort of weird, and, like, pre-hot. He's in my history class. He's smart. I like him."

"You *like* him?" Dan said. "Like him like how?"

"Like I like him," Daphne said. "Like I want to get to know him better. He did this presentation for class the other day on George Washington Carver—"

"The peanut guy?"

"Yeah, the peanut guy," she said. "And I mean it was really sort of incredible—he lived an unbelievably sordid life, you know."

"Who? George Washington Carver?"

"Yeah—that was what Jeremiah's whole presentation was about, George Washington Carver and his gross sexual proclivities, that and their relation to his genius. It was like a you-can't-have-one-with-out-the-other-type thing, according to Jeremiah. And he tied it all together with a historical perspective and everything and it was really pretty amazing. I mean, that's supposedly how peanut butter and everything got started."

"Do you want to fuck him?" Dan asked after a long period of silence.

"Yeah," she said, blowing out smoke. "I probably do."

:::

Daphne curled her toes over the edge of the diving board now, pressed her butt almost flat against its underside, and wondered, frankly, what Jeremiah's penis looked like, what it looked like at rest, dangling against his thighs. She wondered what his thighs looked like, whether they tensed when he began to grow firm, what he looked like when he was firm, as it firmed. She imagined her hand traveling along the fuzz down into his shorts, grasping him, feeling him grow, hearing him gasp, watching through the water as his growth made his shorts distort. She wondered if he was a virgin. She wondered what his mother and father looked like, if they were still together, if he got along with them, what they talked about at dinner, whether he had any siblings, whether he read before he went to sleep, whether he got a glass of water and put it on his bedside table, whether he was happy, whether he whistled, what his friends were like, what his face looked like when he came. She'd never been with a virgin.

:::

Jeremiah fervently wanted the frog to no longer be inside his swim trunks but found himself unable to scoop it out; unable, even, to open up his drawstring and have a look inside; still unable, really, to move at all, until, in a flash, the solution came to him—an image of his thumbs tucked under his waistband—and he followed what he saw without thinking. The easiest way to free the frog, and the best way for it not to get trapped again, was to remove his bathing suit, to pull the thing down and let it float gently away. He knew it was an eccentric thing to do, absent as it was of any hilarity or skinny-dip sensuality, but a new development within his mind had made it impossible for him to care. He tried not to look over at Daphne, who was still dangling from the diving board. But he did look, and what he saw was that she'd been looking at him, and as she turned away, his hopes returned, and the night loomed inevitably.

:::

The reason Daphne was dangling from the diving board, not quite touching the water, was because she was afraid. Not of the frogs, but of the *amount* of frogs, or of what she imagined to be the amount of frogs—like Jeremiah, she'd been unable to fully get behind the plan to move on, to not obsess—and of their sameness, and the fact of their being so close together, crammed together, really, and uncountable, and in such a small space. It was a phobia, others had it too, her mother for one, her babysitter from childhood, Roxanne (who, she suddenly remembered, used to play "Why Don't We Do It in the Road?" for her on her bedside Fisher-Price record player before she went to sleep, the green apple revolving in a black gloss whirlpool beside her pillow-pressed cheek), for another. She couldn't say, even to herself, quite what the phobia was of exactly, and that only added to the fear. Lots of small, same-looking things all in one place was what it was of, basically. But what was it *of*? What did it signify?

Fear of snakes, fear of bananas, fear of any of nature's shaftlike objects, she could understand. Fear of sharks, she could understand. They come from below and bite your legs off. Fear of caves, or of wells, she could understand. The cold, the wet, the dead-ended. Fine. But what did it mean that a big bag of wasabi-encrusted peas dumped into a bowl gave her the same spooked-out feeling as a sequined dress, or a poppy seed bagel? Or the paint dabs in certain sections of the pointillistic paintings she'd seen on a field trip? Or the thought that the beach was just a bunch of big boulders ground up into billions and billions of little tiny pieces? Or Skittles scattered on a countertop? Or even sometimes an especially starry sky? Her mother's psychiatrist had said that it might have to do with fractals, or with a fear of elemental parts, or complicated wholes, and that was possible, but it still didn't really explain anything. The sameness was mostly the problem. She stopped looking at Jeremiah—who had begun now to look back at her, making it necessary for her to turn away—and began focusing on her finger-nails, examining her cuticles, trying to think of ways in which the frogs in the pool were not, in fact, all basically the same.

It was true, she thought, that they were all green. In that way they were all exactly alike. And it was true that they all jumped extremely high and over distances that were incredibly far in relation to their size, and that they all did the bellowing-from-the-throat thing at dusk—or maybe that was toads, but if it were toads then it was true that frogs in general, as a species, all had this problem where they were constantly getting mistaken for toads, and in that way they were all exactly alike. And they all seemed sort of cute when you looked at them head on, in exactly the same way, in a way that made cuteness not really something to shoot for anymore, and they all seemed mind-blowingly promiscu-ous and focused on that kind of thing nearly all the time—but weren't all these things maybe just a part of what it meant to be a frog?

Daphne wanted very badly to let her fingers go slack and fall into the water, she was cramping up a little bit, and sore, but something was holding her back, keeping the fear there. She looked at the rest of the gang—who were in the deep end all around her, who for a long time now had been hollering for her to get off the damn diving board and come join the fun—and watched for a while as they continued to form a sort of agreed-upon response to the pool's surprise.

Led by Dan, as usual, made basically a lot louder and more obnox-ious by Trevor, made bold by Ben, crude by Polly, giddy by Lydia (who had finally gotten ahold of herself, and who had subsequently made a triumphant, cannonballing return to the good graces of the group), and drunk again by her sister, Maggie, who'd run back into the house and returned with a mostly full bottle of their parents' bourbon, which floated now in offering among them, they were doing an admirable job of it, crafting exactly the right sort of response to the situation, accept-ing the oddity of it, embracing it, creating in the moment of it a banded memory of their really great reaction to be savored in the future; fear-ing the frogs the right amount, splashing them away the right amount, liking them the right amount; allowing the sexuality of the situation to seep in, allowing the boys to pantomime chivalry for the benefit of the girls and the girls to pantomime squeamishness for the benefit of the boys; using it to come together, in clinches, in each other's arms, as a segue, as an excuse, in pairs and as a throbbing cluster in anticipation of the night—making a big deal out of it, Daphne thought, but not making a big deal out of making a big deal out of it.

She wished she could release, fall in, and join them, but the frogs' green sameness echoed inside her mind. She had an image of row after row after neat row of them, perhaps one thousand or two thousand or twenty-seven thousand to a row and more rows than she could imagine, all of them sitting blankly, waiting for instruction, staring at nothing, ribbiting in unison.

And then it occurred to her that though they were all essentially the same unit repeated, without complicated inner lives or theological opinions or whatever, it didn't mean that they weren't all separate creatures with their own specific wants and needs and strategies and deficiencies and regrets and agendas. Maybe not regrets, that was probably stretching it, but certainly something like that. It stood to reason that down there in the water, with all the frogs making love to all the other frogs, and chasing after frogs, and fending off frogs, and succumbing to frogs, and giving birth to frogs, that in some cases there'd be settling, a girl frog settling for a guy frog, or a guy frog losing out on his dream frog to a slightly bigger stud-type frog and then getting together with the next frog that happened across his way. And it stood to reason that there'd be some frogs that through some series of terrible coincidences or near misses, or maybe just because they weren't very personable or strong or fast or pleasing to look at while swimming or leaping or whatever, it stood to reason that there were some frogs that didn't get to make love to any other frogs at all, ever, and that for the rest of their lives had to just swim around looking for food, avoiding eye contact with the thousands of other frogs who'd rejected them. And it also stood to reason that even some of the frogs that did have someone were pining away for someone else, and that even the frogs that were being made love to sometimes weren't perfectly in the moment, or were hoping the whole time that they wouldn't get pregnant, or were even thinking maybe about some other, sexier frog during the whole entire thing.

Or if none of it necessarily stood to reason, then all of it was at least possible, and it seemed to Daphne that while the frogs in her pool, the whole village of frogs—probably something like six thousand generations, or six billion, she didn't really know—were all essentially stupid, that didn't mean that they didn't have decisions to make, and that didn't mean that some decisions weren't simply out of their hands or not up to them, and that didn't mean—maybe?—that they didn't sometimes get really upset and fed up about it, about the whole thing, about all the decisions and occurrences in their lives that they couldn't control, no matter how hard they tried, compared to the really sort of minor ones that they could, and it seemed now to her, as she turned it all around in her mind—though she knew she was being sort of silly and hopeful—it seemed to her that the fact of their greenness and their great jumpingness and their bellowing and their looking so very much like toads didn't have a lot to do with what was going on with each frog individually, which must be something like, or a primitive version of, or a very basic blueprint for, real feelings—because how else could they move and act and do what they did? She'd convinced herself now that it was *feelings*, however simple or small, that drove every frog below her, and it was this understanding that eventually made it possible for her, finally, to let go.

:::

Jeremiah's cocoon, meanwhile, had woven itself fully. He was pretending—no, it was more than that—his body *had become* a landmass in the isolated heart of a shoreless sea, and he was scaring himself almost with the perfection of the model. It felt wonderful to be this thing, this gigantic island deep in the heart of the ocean, crawling with life. This was where the frogs came into the mix; they were rising from the deep, or from wherever they came from, and attaching themselves to his body; they were like sea monsters that no one had discovered, and the tadpoles were like normal-size fish, fluttering around the monsters in commensal harmony. It felt mysterious and epochal and beautiful—the twin peaks of his shoulders breaching and going back under again—and fun, and he was enjoying himself very much.

At first, for the model to work, Jeremiah had had to eliminate, or at least ignore, the existence of his own head—it was simply too grand, it threw the scale all out of whack, it rose too high. But after a few moments, as he became more involved—trapped, basically—in his reverie, he came to think of it as an albatross scanning for food, and then as a hot-air balloon hung high in the sky, and then as the atmosphere itself, curving over and around everything like a vast turned-down bowl or a contact lens, and then as the sun, glowing over everything and everyone, but it still wasn't enough. Nothing seemed enough, he couldn't account for the presence of his own obtrusive dome, it ruined the perspective and made everything seem a little bit fake, until finally, in a turn that immediately seemed obvious, Jeremiah looked down and saw what he'd wrought and felt simple love, and smiled at what he saw, and saw that it was good, and realized at last that his head and all it contained could, in fact, if he wanted it to, be the voice and eyes and reason of God.

:::

Having conquered her fear, Daphne swam over to Jeremiah, discovering along the way that the red thing floating next to him was indeed his bathing suit.

"Jeremiah?" she said, drawing closer. He didn't answer. He appeared to be entranced by something on his body, or by his body in general. As she got closer still, she saw that there were paused frogs and tadpole clouds all over his legs and chest. She could see his pale thing swaying underwater, but she didn't look close. It didn't seem right somehow, despite her earlier imaginations. Everything felt sterile and overenunciated and clumsy between them, even though she hadn't paid a scrap of attention to him all day. She'd been unable to coax herself into making the first foray toward the easy, joshing sort of rapport she'd imagined she'd have with him, or into any rapport at all so far, and he seemed to her to be getting younger and younger with each passing moment, if only because he hadn't made a pass at her yet, or chewed her out for being cold, as any older boy undoubtedly would have. "Jeremiah!" she said again. Again he didn't answer.

"Jeremiah!" she shouted. "Hey, Jeremiah! Are you sulking?" He still didn't answer. She swam around him underwater and came to him from behind. Jeremiah saw a flash of something impossibly huge, then realized, of course, that it was Daphne, and snapped out of it. He'd forgotten where he was. She put her arms lightly on his shoulders. "Hey, Jeremiah," she whispered into his ear, "what are you doing? Are you sulking?"

"No," Jeremiah said, twisting gently out of her grip. He was, in fact, sulking.

"Then what are you doing?" she asked.

"I'm pretending to be a landmass in the middle of the ocean, if you must know. Also, I'm imagining that my head, or maybe my brain, is God, even though I'm an atheist. Or maybe because I'm an atheist. What happened to everyone else?"

"They all went inside," she said. "They're getting ready to go out. We should go in too. We're going to go to this bar called The Schmeiler House, or Der Schmeiler Haus, or The Schmeiler Haus, or something. It's this crusty old place where all the locals hang out. It'll be fun. Do you have ID?"

"Um," he began, not knowing whether she was asking if he had any identification at all or if he had something that indicated he was of legal drinking age. If it was the second, he didn't have it.

"Don't worry," she said, saving him. "We'll figure something out."

"Okay," he said. And then, to fill the pause, "Why have you been ignoring me?" The question came through ventriloquist's lips, and Jeremiah turned sharply away as soon as he'd spoken the words, as if denying his part in their creation, in the manner of a point guard delivering a no-look pass.

"Ignoring you? I haven't been ignoring you," Daphne said, sounding slightly put-upon but mostly bemused, swimming around him in a little smiling circle. A backbone, she thought. He has one.

"Yes," Jeremiah replied, "you have."

"No, I haven't. *Really?*"

"Yeah," he said, biting his thumbnail, turning to face her. "Really."

"Like how?" she asked in a voice that said, *Prove it*, though she knew exactly like how, if not exactly like why. She swam over to face him, entering his little rippling world, getting close, feeling his heat. He didn't seem to realize he wasn't wearing a bathing suit. Or maybe he didn't care. His eyes held her image in their reflections.

"Like this is the first time you've talked to me all day," Jeremiah said, his voice breaking halfway through the word *talked*. He was falling for

her, into her, again, in his mind. God, he thought. She makes me want
to whistle.

"That's not true. Is it? I talked to you on the car ride up—didn't I?"
She put a look on her face meant to connote mental backtracking.

"I don't think so," he said.

"I'm sure I did. Really? I didn't? Not at *all*?" she asked, tilting her
head to the side and scrunching up her nose, a pantomime.

"Not that I can remember," Jeremiah said.

"What about inside? During Sink the Bismarck?" He'd only watched,
Daphne remembered. He'd hovered over their fun like a school-dance
chaperone.

"I didn't play. I didn't know the rules and no one offered to explain
them to me. And I don't really drink. And I think you know I didn't
play."

"Why would I know you didn't play?" she said. Even as he did the
thing she wanted him to do, he annoyed her. He was being petulant,
not angry, and there was a big difference between the two. "Are you
accusing me of pretending not to know that you didn't play Sink the
Bismarck? Do you think I'm, like, playing hard to get?" She began
floating on her back. The sun was almost all the way down.

"Why are you yelling at me?" Jeremiah asked.

"I'm not *yelling* at you," Daphne said, yelling at him. "What am I,
your mother?" She wondered why she was being so mean. "Why are
you being so sulky?" she said.

"I'm not. I'm not being sulky. I promise," Jeremiah said. She was
hurting him. He wondered why. "I wasn't over here trying to get you to
notice me, you know—I just didn't feel like treading water. And plus I
think Trevor wants to kill me."

"Well, Jeremiah, you did grab his balls."

"But he grabbed mine first! He swam up to me from behind and
reached down and grabbed my balls. I thought it was like a greeting
or a code or a thing your guy friends do to each other or something! I
didn't know what else to do! So I grabbed his too!" The whole thing
had been extremely awkward—the two of them standing there in the
water, holding each other's testicles through the thin material of their
respective swim trunks. But it really had seemed like the correct move
at the time.

"He thought you were Dan," Daphne said.

"So it *is* something they do!" Jeremiah shouted back, as if discovering a secret.

"*What?*" she said.

"They grab each other's balls."

"*What?* No—he was just kidding around. And it's no big deal, okay? So don't worry about it. Just, I don't know, Jeremiah, just be more cool or something. Just be more relaxed, okay?" She was standing beside him now, resting her hands on his shoulders in intimate lecture, looking into his eyes. Maybe, she thought. It's still a possibility. His bottom lip was quivering slightly.

He said: "Daphne. This is so, I mean it's like—first of all, why are you denying that you've been ignoring me?" He was incredibly nervous, he was shaking, he felt he had to let it all out or go away forever. "And, like, you *invited* me here, I thought you wanted—I don't even know what you wanted! But you invited me here. You called to make sure I was coming! And now you're, you're treating me like a kid, you know? I mean, what did I do that was so bad? That made you so uncomfortable?" Daphne's hands were still resting on his shoulders, his chest heaved. "I'm not being cool enough? How can I control that? All I've done so far is ride up in the way back with all the beer and food and stuff and not say anything and then watch you guys play drinking games for like three hours and then go swimming with everybody, and deal with the frogs and everything, oh, and that was, like, so *crazy* and so much *fun*, it's like your friends, I'm sorry, I don't even know them but it seems like they're so, they seem like they think everything is, like, *designed* for their enjoyment, and with me it's been like, 'What the fuck is he doing here,' you know? And you barely even introduce me, and it's like I tagged along or something—when you invited me! And I know—Daphne, I don't know if this, I don't know, I don't know what I'm trying to say, it's just that, shit, *I know you like me.*" He looked her in the eyes and did not turn away. "Right? You *like* me. I know it. And I'm here because you want me to be. Because you want to be with me. And I just wish you would treat me like you're supposed to—like a guest, like an *honored* guest. Because I know that that's what the truth is, that that's the way you really feel. Or I hope it is. Or maybe it was and it's not anymore, and it happened on the car ride up or while you

326 ::: ROBERT TRAVIESO

were playing cards or in the pool or when you first saw me this morning, and you just haven't gotten around to telling me yet, but—God,
I'm spazzing out, aren't I?—I just, I'm sorry, I don't want to be telling
you what your feelings are, and I know I'm making a huge deal out of
nothing, I'm, like, shaking here, but I just wish maybe—and maybe
this is too forward—but I want to get close to you, you know? And I
want you to want to get close to me too, and I think maybe you do, and
I hope you're not holding back because you think it's too awkward or
because I blew it somehow or because I'm not what you thought I was
or because you think your friends are going to make fun of you, or for
any other reason that doesn't really or won't really matter in the long
run—you know?"

"Hey, Jeremiah," Daphne said, gripping him, shaking him slightly
as if to make him come to, snapping his head back gently in a languid
version of whiplash.

"Yeah?" he said. He'd said his piece.

"You're sweet. Do you realize you're not wearing a bathing suit?"

"Uh, yeah. Could you do me a favor, though?"

"Sure," she said.

"Could you, like, not look at me? Or if you already have, could you
just, like, erase it from your mind? Or maybe just not tell everybody?
Or just not make fun of me about it?"

"Jeremiah?" Daphne said.

"Yeah?" he said.

"Come here," she said. But he was already there, and she grabbed
him around the neck and pulled him in, hard, and her forehead pressed
against his, hard, and they paused, listening to themselves breathe, and
her breaths began to match his, and his breathing was hard, his chest
was going in and out and he was trembling all over. They were looking
not at each other but at the space they were making, at the shadowy
water between their bodies, and at the drips that were dropping from
their chins, making quiet little ripples in the dark. He was hard, and
she reached down and held him there and said, "Jeremiah, I'm about
to kiss you," and he said, "Okay, okay, okay," and she said, "Don't freak
out," and he said, "Okay, okay, I'm trying," and he was so nervous, but
she caught his chin in her hands and brought his lips to hers and their
mouths came together and their legs wrapped around and the space

went away and they slammed together, smacked together, and pushed hard together with everything they had as hard as they could. Daphne's mind wobbled into one and Jeremiah pressed against her more and more, and she was surprised by how much and how hard she wanted it and how fast it had all come on and how much her legs were shaking and how hard it was for her to stop. She was getting closer and closer to taking him in, and it was getting to the point where he was right there and urgent and poised on his toes above her, and she was taking her hand and sliding her bikini bottoms aside, and for a moment she was pausing and considering the tadpoles and considering the pool water, and it was almost enough to make her stop but it was about to happen, it was almost happening, and then it was happening, they were rocking hard against each other, and then all of a sudden she was pulling away fast and sliding her bottoms back in place and swimming to the ladder and climbing out, going inside and drying off, and Jeremiah was left standing there shivering in the shallow end, alone with the frogs, waiting for himself to go soft.

:::

"So . . ." Dan began, trying to fill up the space between when they'd ordered their drinks and when they were due to receive them, "George Washington Carver, huh?"

The bar turned out to be called Der Schmeiler House. Jeremiah had gotten in using Dan's backup fake ID and had asked everyone in the group to please call him Oliver Sakalidis for the evening, a request everyone so far had consistently refused to honor. All in all, however, things were much, much better than before, even if he did feel at the moment a little bit disembodied from himself. He was in a bar. Ordering drinks, several at a time. Impossible.

Before they left for the bar, Daphne had brought everyone together in a loose huddle in the living room—with the two of them in the center—and had said, simply, "Gang, this is Jeremiah." She then put her arm around him and said, "I'm sorry if I didn't introduce him the right way this morning. I'm sorry if I put anybody in a weird spot. But today was today, and tonight is tonight, and I want all you guys to please make him feel welcome." She then ruffled his hair. "We're on a date, for the whole weekend. I think he's cute and really sweet. Look at

328 ::: ROBERT TRAVIESO

how incredibly long his eyelashes are. Look at how he blushes. Look at his ears, guys—they're like little elf ears! We made out in the pool for a while there, while you guys were inside supposedly getting dressed, and I'm betting some of you were probably checking us out."

She then smiled at Jeremiah, and fixed his hair a little bit, and patted down the collar of his T-shirt, which concealed a hickey, and said, "And that is, of course, okay."

She then swept her arm across the room, gave him a nice little kiss on the cheek as if he were going somewhere, and said, "Jeremiah—meet the gang."

That had been about three and a half hours ago. They'd all been incredibly nice to him ever since.

And now he was incredibly drunk.

"Hey Dan, man," he shouted, even though they were right next to each other. "*How did I get so drunk?*" It was a question Jeremiah had been asking himself for over an hour now, though he'd not in that time stopped drinking. "Also, before you answer that, could you, like, please call me Oliver Sakalidis from now on? Because that is my real name."

"Sure," Dan said. "Here, do this shot with me."

"What's in it?" Jeremiah asked.

"Jägermeister?" Dan said ambivalently.

"Is that the one," Jeremiah said, "that has the Viking woman in the fur bikini riding the white lion, holding on to a giant sword?"

"*What?*"

"Is that the one! I said! That has the Viking woman in the fur bikini! Riding the white lion! I said! Holding on to a giant sword!" Jeremiah was fairly well shouting at the top of his lungs, and pronouncing the word *sword* with a hard and dramatic *w*, and gripping the bar and growing giddy from both the ritualistic release and the lack of oxygen getting to his brain.

"Jeremiah, can we change the subject?" Dan shouted.

"It's Oliver!" Jeremiah shouted back.

"Okay!" Dan shouted. "Oliver! Tell me about George Washington Carver!"

"Wait! Is this grape-flavored?" Jeremiah shouted, staring intently into the shot.

"Forget the shot for a second, Jeremiah!" Dan shouted, turning serious but no less drunk. "Just tell me, because I really want to know—*what*, exactly, was George Washington Carver into? Was he really a pervert?"

"Hey, Dan!" Jeremiah shouted. "Who the fuck is Jeremiah?"

:::

From a booth in the corner Daphne watched Dan and Jeremiah getting along so well and wondered if it was necessarily the greatest or most healthy thing in the world for them to be doing. A few hours earlier Dan had cornered her in the bar bathroom and declared that he did not now nor would he ever in the future accept the fact of their no longer driving to his house after school and having sex, though he'd referred to it as "going out."

"Whatever you're about to have with this kid is just going to be a phase that you and I are going through," he said, and it would have been a good line too, Daphne thought, if it hadn't been word for word exactly what Derrick Waldman had said to her two and a half years ago, when she'd started seeing Dan. They must have exchanged notes.

Boys were sad. Sometimes they were incredibly sad. Sometimes they were pitiful, sometimes they were embarrassing, sometimes they were infuriating, but most of the time they were just little dinky assholes. But what could you do? She realized that Derrick was about eight years older than Jeremiah, and the information seemed interesting and maybe depressing, but not much else.

She started to get up to go talk to Jeremiah, maybe tell him to stop taking so many shots, maybe remind him about their plan to leave early and finish what they'd started, but right as she rose from her seat, he vanished.

No. A false alarm. He'd only fallen, she could see his fingers still hanging desperately to the bar's brass railing. About an hour after she'd had her talk with Dan, Jeremiah had pulled her into the small, dark storage space behind the women's bathroom and sat her down next to him on a case of Lowenbräu. He told her that the number one thing she needed to know about him was that he was a good person, and that he'd never do anything to intentionally hurt her feelings or put her down or make her feel bad about something she didn't do.

"Why," Daphne asked, "would you ever make me feel bad about something I didn't do?"

"*No*," he said, shaking his drooping head violently, "*No*. I *wouldn't*, is what I'm saying." He'd then zipped down his fly and attempted to display for her his testicles, but she stopped him.

"I'm already fairly drunk," he said. "So if this is in any way inappropriate, then please don't hold it against me."

Daphne looked at Jeremiah's gripping fingers now and thought, I still want this to happen. *Why*? What is *wrong* with me?

"Jeremiah!" Someone was calling him from somewhere else.

"What!" Jeremiah shouted, from the floor, to the ceiling.

"Where are you? Come do a shot with me!" He pulled himself up with the help of some sausagey fingers he could not immediately—or ever, in fact—identify. A very, very good song was playing on a jukebox that was attached to the back of his head. The sound was incredibly clear and seemed to resonate all around the room. It was like a kind of country-rock-type song. It was so great!

"C'mon!" the voice that had called out to him in the first place called out again. It was Lydia, smiling, leaning against the bar, beckoning him with her index finger. Her cleavage was extremely apparent.

"C'mon!" she shouted.

"I can't!" he shouted back. "I have to do this purple-grape shot with Dan first!"

Someone is playing the honky-tonk piano, Jeremiah thought, and that is no goddamn jukebox. He turned toward the noise, saw the enormous country-rock band and everyone dancing, and said, softly, "Oh."

"No!" Lydia shouted. "Do this one with me!"

"What's in it?"

"Sugar and lemons! And vodka!"

Daphne made her way over to Jeremiah. "Daphne," he whispered, reaching for her, holding her by the waist, "I want to *kiss* you again! Am I acting too retarded right now for you to want to *kiss* me?"

"I don't know," she said. "We'll see. Can we take a walk? Can we get out of here?" She grabbed him by the belt buckle and pressed gently against his chest.

"Why?" Jeremiah whispered loudly, leaning with dangerous speed toward her face. "You're not having any fun? Can't we just stay? Trevor and Ben and Maggie said they were going to teach me how to play Sink the Bismarck later, and also I have to tell Dan about this enormous lie I told everyone recently."

"Jeremiah!" Lydia shouted. "What are we toasting to?"

"Daphne," Jeremiah said, catching her by the arm as she tried to walk away, "what are we toasting to?"

"Will you ever want to go home with me tonight?" she asked.

"What do you mean?" he said. "Of course, I mean, eventually, but—"

"Jeremiah," she whispered, taking his head in her hands, "*c'mon. Let's go.* Don't—*don't be a little boy.* I want this to happen. Don't you want this to happen?"

He couldn't look at her. He looked at the ceiling, and then at the floor, and then in the mirror that wrapped around the back of the bar, and then back down at the floor again.

He was scared. He was so scared.

"*But, baby,*" he whispered, his mouthed pressed sloppily close to her ear, his hands covering the hands that held his head, his own knife dragging gently across his throat, "*it already happened.*"

"What are we toasting to?" Lydia shouted again, insistently, from somewhere else.

"To sugar and lemons and vodka!" Jeremiah shouted back, hoarsely, without lifting his head. "To the sweet, the tart, and the tasteless!" Daphne began to back away, into the scrum of the bar. She turned to him and said, "That's a Jäger shot you're holding, Jeremiah. It's not gonna taste like grape, or lemons, or sugar, or anything nice. It's gonna taste like shit." He let her go.

"Hey, Dan," he said, turning away, "what's this shot going to taste like?"

"It's gonna taste like fennel. Is that something you're okay with?"

"You bet it is, Dan. And I don't even know what fennel tastes like. I never had fennel before. My mom never made it. We had leeks a fair amount, though. And by the way, you're the man." He was overcome temporarily with perfect, inane delight—reprieve, relief. The band in the background started into a song that absolutely everyone in the bar knew by heart, including Jeremiah. It was a song he sort of hated. People were getting out of their seats, smiling, high-fiving. His head felt stuffed with gauze. The lack of Daphne made him happy. What

332 ::: ROBERT TRAVIESO

would he have done anyway with a girl—no, a woman—like her? What would he have done? What would he have done? Ha. And besides, it wasn't like—*Wait*. Where was Dan? Dan had gotten up at some point without his noticing it, and now he was nowhere to be found, which seemed sort of abrupt—had everyone left without him? Noooo, there was Trevor, and there was Maggie, and there, in the corner, by the wall-mounted set of old alpine skis, was Ben, making out with Polly, and there was Lydia, coming swiftly toward him, and—oh, there, there was Dan, there he was, at the other end of the bar, paying his tab, riffling through a neat stack of bills. "HEY, DAN!" Jeremiah called out, waving his arms in the universal signal for hey-over-here, but Dan didn't seem to see or hear him, and now he was collecting his things and apparently heading for the door. "HEY, DAN!" Jeremiah tried again, but Dan wasn't turning around, wasn't going to say goodbye, wasn't waving to any of his friends, he was just going to sneak out, and that seemed weird to Jeremiah and even a little bit rude until, in his hands, he saw her flip-flops, and suddenly, oh it hurt, like—bam—here is the way things work, suddenly he knew, could almost see, that Daphne was waiting for him on the other side of the door.

Someone called his name, but it was only Lydia, coming toward him. Goddamnit, he thought. Lydia doesn't have a goddamn thing to do with anything or anyone. She's a minor character. Why is she here, with me, at the end?

"Hi," she said. "Come with me. I have to show you something."

He followed her, letting himself be led by the hand. She took him over to where the band was. She led him through the dancing people. They made their way to the very front of the crowd and she grabbed him roughly by the shoulders and turned him around and said, "Look," and he looked, and he saw people moving together, he saw an interconnected mass; he saw people holding each other, keeping each other aloft, touching each other, grabbing each other, putting little bits of themselves into each other and taking little pieces out, he saw people kissing each other, and people bobbing on the toes of their feet, staring across the room, wanting to be kissed. Then Lydia put her hands over his eyes and said, "Now listen," and he listened, and he heard people singing, and he heard people's hands clapping, and he heard the band play, and in between their notes he heard the exertions they made in order to create those notes, and in the crowd he heard the throats of the people at rest in the space between their singing, and he heard the sound of the throats as they began to open, and he heard their breathing and the sound of their giddy feet against the floor and the sweat of their bodies together—he felt he could hear that too—and the band was coming around the bend and heading for the chorus, and the people seemed happy, regardless, and Lydia gently let her hands drop free and walked into the crowd, dancing now too in a kind of circular fashion, hands curling in the air and not even waving goodbye, and Jeremiah stood alone there and everything paused for a moment.

Outside the green door of Der Schmeiler House, Daphne let Dan slide his arm around her waist and slip his hand into the back pocket of her shorts, and as they walked off together the music she heard got fainter and fainter and a thought ran around in her mind in time and tune with the beating in her chest, and it bored her, and the thought was, *That is that.* That is that, she thought, as they walked away. So that is that. So that is that. So that is that. So that is that. So that is that is that is that, Daphne thought, and never looked back, as they got farther and farther and farther away and eventually disappeared.

Back in the bar the crowd was reckless and jubilant, and when the chorus came around everyone put their arms around everyone else and swayed in the rhythm and looked into each other's eyes and all together took a very deep breath and then let it all out and sang the words of a song Jeremiah had known all his life. The song went

> *Joy to the world*
> *All the boys and girls now*
> *Joy to the fishes in the deep blue sea*
> *Joy to you and me*

And eventually, because it was a simple, stupid sort of song, Jeremiah got together and sang it too.

TWO WOMEN

...
...

Matthew Vollmer

1.

Two white women and a black baby stood on the shore of the river, watching the churning water where the keys had gone in. The younger woman had been holding the baby and spinning the keys on her finger, and the baby had been laughing, which, as always, caused the two women to laugh, and then, inexplicably, the key ring—which held keys to the Jeep, the A-frame, the shed, and the older woman's post office box—flew into the air, flashed in the light, and fell to the water.

The older woman, who planned on leaving that night with the baby to meet her husband, the poet, slid off her shoes and peeled off her shirt. Her bra was white. She pulled off her pants. Her panties were black. Her skin was tan and freckled. She replaced her sneakers. "I need goggles," she said, and went in.

"Do you want help?" the younger woman asked.

The older woman said nothing. She took a deep breath and slid deeper into the froth. She went in up to her chest. Her nipples hardened. She went under. The baby, thinking it a game, shrieked when she came up. She dove. She rose up. The baby squealed. She dove. Soon it was too dark to see. The older woman kept diving.

2.

The younger woman and her boyfriend had come from the city to the mountains for the summer. They had come to hike, fish, drink beer, and cook over a fire: to live in the woods in a tent. The younger woman's boyfriend had grown up in these mountains. He knew them. With a machete, he sliced paths to caves and waterfalls. He started fires without matches. He recognized the tracks of various animals and identified distant birds. Sometimes, when they were hiking, he'd pause to pluck the petal of a flower, or the leaf of a tree, and chew it thoughtfully, as though it provided him some message only his tongue could translate.

The boyfriend knew people. He talked a guy into giving him a job manning a ski lift, which, in summer, lifted not skiers but lazy hikers and the aged, both of whom brought sack lunches and cameras in backpacks. At the top, visitors marveled at the view: white sailboats winking on the blue lake, miles of mountains spreading out like folds in a great piney quilt.

Far below, the younger woman spent her days at a grassy lakeside park, reading books in flickering light beneath tall trees. Tourists arrived and videoed the lake; swimmers sunned themselves on the beach. Groups of local preteens, toting rusty skateboards, whistled at her, their mushroom-legged jeans scuffing the grass, their hair gelled into the shapes of flames.

3.

The day she met the older woman, she'd been lying on a towel in the grass, staring at the lifeguard—a woman her boyfriend had dated in high school. The previous evening, the younger woman had been introduced to the lifeguard, at a party with paper lanterns and hollowed-out melons filled with punch and chunks of fresh fruit—a party thrown by the lifeguard's parents. The lifeguard, hair streaked with gold, wore a white sundress. She was so dark and willowy that when the younger woman, who'd just swallowed four lime Jell-O shots, stood next to her, she felt like a drunk, pudgy ghost. The lifeguard hugged her and grinned and told the boyfriend that oh boy, had he had picked a good one this time, they were perfect together, absolutely perfect, et cetera. The lifeguard was the kind of girl, the younger woman realized, that required attention. Unfortunately, no amount of attention could satiate her need for it, and the younger woman's boyfriend, who was someone who enjoyed giving attention indiscriminately, provided it.

"How do you make a tissue dance?" the boyfriend asked the life-guard.

"Put a little boogie on it!" she exclaimed. She wrinkled her nose. She howled. The lifeguard wrapped her arms around the younger woman's boyfriend and squeezed him.

4.

Now the younger woman watched the lifeguard blow her whistle at a fat kid whose butterfly stroke had accidentally splashed an old lady in a bathing cap, watched as the lifeguard flirted with a tall, tanned boy with a rippling stomach. As she watched, she wondered if she could ever come to like the lifeguard. She wondered if she could, somehow, seduce her. She wondered if, given the right circumstances, in self-defense maybe, she could kill her.

"Hey," a voice said. "You're reading my book." An older woman with shoulder-length hair, curls still wet from a shower, stood above her. She wore khaki shorts, a blue T-shirt that said MONTANA, a silver bracelet, and earrings in the shape of butterflies. Her legs, which were very tan, suggested she could run great distances. In her arms, a black baby wore nothing but a diaper. He studied one of his dime-size nipples, as though it were something he could peel away.

"Neepo," he said.

"You wrote this?" the younger woman asked, holding up the book.

"I wish. I just owned it. I sold it back."

The baby squirmed. The woman dangled the baby by his feet. She lowered him to the ground. The baby squealed.

The woman explained that she and the baby lived here in the sum-mer. In the winter, she taught at a university out West. Her husband was a poet, with a residency in the desert. She was supposed to be writ-ing, but looking after the baby was a full-time job.

The younger woman explained that she had come here with her boyfriend, who worked at the lift, and that they lived in a tent at the outskirts of town. The older woman tilted her head and frowned. The younger woman assured her it wasn't bad. The tent was made out of space-age material. There was a yellow glow inside. When the wind came through it rippled. The older woman wondered where they showered. The younger woman, aware of the dirt lining the ridges of her toes, the musk of her unwashed armpits, and the smudges of charcoal on her hands from putting out the campfire, explained that they took water from the river. Sometimes they showered in a motel down the road.

"Oh to be young," the older woman said. They stared out across the green grass. The lifeguard had crawled upon the tanned boy's shoulders.

"Do you think she's pretty?" the younger woman asked.

"Pretty? Yes." She paused. "Smart? No."

"You know her?"

"I've heard her talk. How can you not?"

The younger woman laughed. "Sometimes I wonder," she said, "and I don't mean this in a bad way . . . but what it would be like to be that . . . I don't know . . . unaware of yourself."

"Life would be easier," the older woman said.

"You could rule the beach with a whistle."

They laughed.

"Listen," the older woman said. "Would you like to earn some money?"

5.

"What's she doing?" the boyfriend asked. He squinted across the park, through the slanting light, at the lifeguard, who, still in her bathing suit, cartwheeled across the beach. "She's crazy," he chuckled. He looked in the rearview and rubbed his teeth with a finger. "How was your day?" he asked.

"Fine," the younger woman said. She watched her boyfriend watching the lifeguard. She said nothing about the older woman and her baby.

"She has so much energy," the boyfriend said. The lifeguard, who'd spotted their van, was now jogging toward them, her ponytail swinging behind her.

"Yes," the younger woman said, tearing a triangle of skin from a thumb with her teeth. "She sure does."

6.

They'd been asleep for two hours when the boyfriend's cell phone rang. The younger woman kicked him awake. The tent shivered as he fumbled for the phone.

"*Okay, just calm down,*" he said. The younger woman knew, maybe by the tone of his voice, that it was the lifeguard. The boyfriend unzipped the curved tent fly and stepped outside. He laced up his boots. He stirred the coals in the fire. "Oh my God," he said. "You're kidding. Nononononononono. Of course." The boyfriend beeped off the phone and poked his head through the fly. "Her boyfriend," he said. The younger woman pretended to be asleep. "He was in an accident. She needs a ride. Hey," he said. "I know you're not asleep. You're mad. *Listen.* Her boyfriend almost killed himself. I gotta go. You'll be okay?"

She nodded. He said, "I love you," and departed. The younger woman frowned. Her mouth dropped open. She listened to the van sputter away. She punched his sleeping bag. She cursed. Then, when she realized how far away from everything she was, and that she was alone, and that if her boyfriend, for some reason, became detained, or had a wreck himself, she'd be stuck here, she lay very still. She could hear something. Wind in the leaves? No. A rustling, just outside the tent. A beast? A thief? A pine tree. A muscle in her jaw began to spasm. Then a muscle in her leg. She held her finger up to the light coming through the space-age tent. The finger twitched.

Twitching, she knew, from surfing Webs sites, was the first stage. In a few years, if the disease she thought she might have took hold, her body would be quaking—uncontrollably. She closed her eyes. The older woman and the baby appeared. The older woman's house, which she had not seen, also appeared. She saw herself entering it. She saw herself showering with the older woman's soap and shampoo, drying off with fluffy towels. She saw herself snitching a swig of whatever the older woman kept to drink, and saw herself kissing the baby all over his face. Then she saw herself fixing lunch: vegetable omelets and salad, bananas sliced into discs for the baby.

7.

When she fell asleep, she dreamed. Her mother, in a white bathrobe, a green towel around her head, stood in her kitchen, the way it'd been before they remodeled, smoking a cigarette. She did not say that she was sick or that she was going to have to die again, yet the younger woman could see this would happen: her mother had no hair. The younger woman tried to hug her, but she was deep in thought and did not respond.

8.

"I can't pay you right away," the older woman said.

"That's fine," the younger woman said. She'd not considered money.

The older woman led the younger woman through the rooms of the A-frame. She and her husband had built it ten years before with their very own hands. There were skylights and plants and wood floors and rugs. A white futon. A black recliner. A stereo. "These are his books," she said. "He loves to read. And these are his toys. Does he have enough? He doesn't like clothes but he understands a diaper is necessary."

The black baby burbled. He beat his sippy cup against his chest. He blew milk bubbles.

"He's not ours," the older woman said, stooping down to peel a sticker off his foot. She wiped his mouth with her T-shirt. "I mean, he's ours, but we didn't, you know, make him. We—I—can't. We looked for a long time. Then we were on this list—forever. They finally called us one night. They said they had someone, a boy. He was only two weeks old. But both his arms were broken. He wouldn't stop crying. He'd been thrown to the floor. When I first saw him, I cried. It was the only thing you could do. We took him home and for three weeks we were up all night every night with him." The older woman paused to squeeze his cheeks. "But you're fine now, aren't you? You're a big strong boy now, aren't you? Yes. Yes. That's my baby!"

9.

He was, the younger woman decided, a perfect baby. He came when you called him. He laughed when you squeezed his fat baby cheeks. He put the dead bug down when you said to. He did not eat the green booger on the tip of his finger but instead presented it to be taken away. He stayed very quiet when you read him *The Giving Tree*. He cooed quietly when you carried him around the living room, peering into drawers, opening cabinets, studying the books in the bookcase.

Though the younger woman found no books by the older woman, she counted ten books by the husband-poet. The books wanted her to think of the husband-poet as a rugged, untamed, unstable man. Each author photo was the same. In the photo, he had a grizzled beard and wide eyes and a flannel shirt. Apparently, during ten books' time, the husband's appearance had not changed.

"Will you take a nap?" she asked the baby. The baby smiled, lay down, and stuck his thumb in his mouth. The younger woman kissed him all over his face. She could eat him up, she said. He giggled, and fell asleep.

Outside, it began to rain. The young woman chose a record—*Pink Moon*—and placed it on the turntable. She cracked eggs into a blue bowl. She tossed a salad with wooden tongs. It was good to cook. At the campsite, they had been living out of a leaky, stained cooler that a bear had recently smashed. The inside of the older woman's refrigerator gleamed white, and everything inside—imported cheese, wine, a jar of artichoke hearts, Greek olives, baby spinach, minced garlic, fresh cilantro—had come from far, far away.

"Jesus Christ!" the older woman screamed from the guest bedroom, which she now used as a studio. "Are you fucking crazy?" It took a moment for the younger woman to realize that the older woman was talking not to her but to her husband.

10.

"We can do this," the older woman said, stabbing a triangle of omelet and shutting her eyes. "We have this thing where we go away and go mad and return to each other." The younger woman nodded, as though she understood. "Forget it," the older woman said. "You. Tell me about your boyfriend."

"There's not much to tell," she said. Then, the whole story poured out. The lifeguard. The party. The phone call. The accident.

The older woman lay down her fork and frowned. "What's his problem?"

"I know he's just being nice. I mean, he's nice to people."

The older woman shook her head. She said it sounded to her like the younger woman could do better.

11.

When it was time to go the older woman offered to drive her. The younger woman said she could walk. "Oh," the older woman said, her eyes growing wide. She jogged to the tilting shed behind the A-frame and rolled out a bicycle. Cobwebs floated from the handlebars. It clattered and rattled and squeaked but it was still good. The younger woman took it. She rode it all the way back to the campsite, where she covered the bicycle with branches and leaves.

12.

"Uh, weren't we supposed to meet at the lake?" the boyfriend asked, as he got out of the van. A paper bag was bursting in his arms. He'd brought sausages and rice from the market.

"I got a ride," she said, dropping a load of branches she'd gathered onto the fire pit. He built a fire. She cooked. They drank beer and watched the fire die.

In the tent, when her boyfriend tried to reach into her sleeping bag, the younger woman scooched away. The boyfriend sighed. She asked how the lifeguard's boyfriend was and the boyfriend said not so good. His truck had flipped four times. He would probably walk with a limp. The younger woman waited for her boyfriend to ask how her day had been, but he kept talking about the lifeguard and her boyfriend until she fell asleep, her calf twitching to the rhythms of his voice.

13.

Days passed. Each morning, after the boyfriend went to work, the younger woman uncovered the bicycle and rode to the A-frame. She ate breakfast with the older woman and the baby. She cleaned up after them. The mornings were spent with the baby, while the older woman typed. At noon, they all ate lunch together. Then the baby fell asleep on a blanket on the floor, and the two women drank coffee or smoked a joint or drank a beer. They talked. They held conversations.

Sun streamed through the windows. Clouds descended and erased the trees. Rain lashed against the panes.

14.

It was hard sometimes not to stare at the older woman. The older woman could never be mistaken for a younger woman. In fact, there were too many lines in her face for her age. There were streaks in her hair and her teeth had grown yellow from cigarettes. Her body, however, had kept its shape. Her eyes, which bulged a little, had kept their blue. She was tall and slender and dark. She had soft-looking golden hairs on her legs. However, the raw material of the older woman's body—while unforgettable—was not why the younger woman liked her. It was the way the younger woman heard herself speak, as if her real voice—the one she kept hidden—had given birth to itself.

15.

Sometimes the older woman wrote things down on scraps of paper, folded them up, and slid them into her pocket. When the younger woman told her that she was afraid she might have something inside her that would make her die, the older woman wrote this down on a subscription card for a magazine.

"See," the younger woman said.

"What?"

"My finger."

"Yes," the older woman said, taking it into her own. "You have nice hands. Do you play the piano?" She stroked the hand with her thumb.

"No, I mean *look*. It's twitching."

The woman shrugged. "Mine does that."

"You're making it do that."

"Whatever."

"Have you ever taken ecstasy?"

"I've taken plenty of other things." The older woman smiled.

16.

When the boyfriend found the bicycle, he asked what it was. "A bicycle," the younger woman said. He said he knew that but what was it doing in the leaves and everything. She said she'd found it. The boyfriend was quiet. They looked for branches. He built a fire and cooked eggs. The younger woman, who was not hungry, refused to eat.

The boyfriend ate in silence. As he chewed, he placed his hand on the younger woman's leg. She moved her leg. He sighed.

"What?" she asked.

"Do you realize . . ." He clenched his jaw. "Never mind."

"What?"

"Can you even remember the last time we had sex?" He gestured with his fork. Egg flew into her lap.

"I don't keep track," the younger woman lied, flicking it away.

17.

That night, after a few beers, the younger woman allowed the boyfriend to go down on her. She tried to imagine the older woman. It was hard. The older woman would not have whiskers. The older woman would be gentle. The older woman would not be in a rush; she would not slide a penis inside her. Afterward, the older woman would say something to make them laugh. That, and the older woman would sing.

18.

"Look!" the older woman called.

The younger woman ran into the studio. She watched a muscle spasm in the older woman's arm. The older woman smiled. The younger woman wondered if she was faking. She didn't care. She was entranced.

The phone rang. The older woman took the phone and left the room.

She had never been in the studio. The door was always shut. A desk. A photo of a seacoast. Another of the baby. Another of the same picture of the husband-poet—the same that was inside his books. The younger woman considered the possibility that the husband-poet was a figment of the older woman's imagination. She looked at the screen of the computer. There was nothing there. A cursor blinked, a lone stripe bobbing in the whiteness.

19.

"One of his fucking students," the older woman whispered. "Young enough to be his daughter," she said.

"Oh my God," the younger woman said. She tried to act surprised.

"It's okay," the older woman said, sipping from a glass of tremulous water.

"Would you mind watching the baby?" the older woman asked. The younger woman said of course. She didn't ask why the older woman didn't stay right here so she could take care of her. The older woman took off all her clothes and stood in front of her closet. The younger woman tried not to stare. "That looks good," she said, when the older woman held up a blouse and pants, and the older woman put them on. She grabbed her keys and some lipstick, and ran out the door.

When the older woman's Jeep lurched out of sight, the baby began to cry.

20.

When the older woman returned, it was dark. The baby was asleep. "I had some drinks," the older woman said, slinging her keys onto the couch. "They didn't do a fucking thing." She lit a cigarette, took a drag, placed it in the sink. She wobbled.

"Who did you see?" the younger woman asked.

"An old friend," she said, lighting another cigarette. The younger woman sensed this was a lie—perhaps she had simply gone to a bar and asked for a bottle.

The older woman grabbed the younger woman by the arm. She had something to tell her, she said, something *important*: She'd seen the lifeguard and the boyfriend together. When she left the bar, she'd taken a walk. They were down by the lake, on the swings. The younger woman frowned.

"It's true," the older woman said, releasing the younger woman's arm and taking a drag on her cigarette. The lifeguard, she said, had unbuttoned her shirt. The older woman exhaled a plume of smoke, and described what had happened. She described it with a smile.

The younger woman laughed. She laughed because it could not be true. She laughed because the older woman was laughing.

"I'm sorry," the older woman said, kneeling before the younger woman. Then she threw up.

21.

The younger woman cleaned the older woman's face. She helped her out of her clothes. She washed the older woman's vomit from their hands, and put her to bed. Then she lay down beside her, in the sheets she had changed earlier that morning, and tried not to think about her boyfriend or the lifeguard. She was here now with the older woman, who obviously needed her help. After the older woman closed her eyes, after she began to breathe deeply, the younger woman pressed her nose against the older woman's neck. The fragrance filled up her head. The older woman woke and kneaded the back of the younger woman's neck with her hands. The younger woman cried a little, then fell asleep in the arms of the older woman, who whispered into her ear and stroked her hair.

22.

The younger woman dreamed of her mother. As in previous dreams where she'd come back to life, though she'd become sick again, she refused to hug. She lit a cigarette. "This place is a wreck," she said, and flip-flopped away.

23.

When the younger woman woke, her arms were wrapped around the older woman, their bodies two spoons. She did not move. She was aware of pulsations—her own heartbeat. Her lips were pressed against the older woman's ear, and she feared her breathing might wake her. She touched her tongue to her ear. She moved it slowly. The older woman flinched. The younger woman closed her eyes.

24.

The younger woman was by herself, at the campsite, trying to take off her clothes. Sweaters, socks, boots, long underwear, pants—layers and layers. Her boyfriend drove up in the van. The younger woman asked the boyfriend where he had been. He said, "Looking for you."

He hugged her. She wanted to ask about the lifeguard but she knew if she asked she would cry. She would cry because he had once been her best friend and now he might have forgotten her. She realized that she was hugging the lifeguard, who wore only her bathing suit. The lifeguard blew her whistle at the younger woman.

25.

The younger woman woke. She was alone in the bed.

The older woman was folding clothes and laying them inside a suitcase. "I'm going to find him," she said. "And when I do he will know."

"Know what?"

"He'll just know."

As the younger woman helped her pack, the older woman said nothing of the previous night. Perhaps nothing had happened. They spent the rest of the day placing things into boxes and bags and suitcases and tying knots with rope and filling up the Jeep. The older woman had the radio on as they worked. When the older woman wasn't looking, the younger woman sneaked some things that didn't belong to her into her backpack: a roll of undeveloped film, the T-shirt the older woman had slept in, and a page of the older woman's manuscript she'd thrown into the trash.

The roll of film, once developed, would be blank. The manuscript page, unfolded, would contain a partially decipherable description of a dream the younger woman had dreamed. The T-shirt, unwadded, would be mashed against her face—a filter, sometimes, through which she would breathe.

26.

It took most of the day to pack the Jeep. When they were finished, the older woman announced she was taking the younger woman out to dinner. As they drove to the restaurant, they passed the younger woman's boyfriend. He was alone. He was driving fast. He squinted through the glass, his ashen face hovering over the wheel. The younger woman wondered whether he was looking for her.

At a lakefront restaurant, a moose head watched them eat. The younger woman told herself it might be a scene from the future. This is what it would look like if they lived in the mountains at the edge of a lake. Once a week they would go out to eat, where they would sit, like this, in the dim lamplight and stare at each other. They would love each other and they wouldn't care who saw them. They would, as they did now, take turns feeding the baby. They would laugh, as they did now, when the baby slung spaghetti, when a broccoli spear tumbled into the younger woman's lap.

The older woman reached across the table. She touched the younger woman's hand. She grasped it. She smiled. Rings gleamed on her fingers. A bracelet glinted in the light. She did not say, "I love you" or "I will miss you." She did not say, "You can't stay here! You're coming with me." She did not say, "We could take care of one another, and of the baby, who, now that he's been abandoned by two fathers, is ours."

She said, "You've been so good to us." When the younger woman's mouth trembled, the older woman smiled. "We'll write," she said. "We'll stay in touch."

27.

Diving. Diving. Diving. Diving. It was as if the younger woman didn't know anything about the older woman until she saw her diving in the river that ran beside the place where they'd eaten. Plunging underwater, holding her breath, looking for the keys—it was simply another task that had to be completed before she left. The younger woman could see, though, that she'd already gone. Already, she was driving toward the husband-poet, refusing to acknowledge the possibility that he might not even exist.

Even after it was too dark to see, the older woman—slippery, goose-pimpled, drowning—refused to give up. The younger woman decided she would wait, patiently, until the older woman came to her senses. She would wait until she crawled out of the stream: shivering, hair tangled, skin blue with cold. The younger woman would go find a towel, but then she would not know what to do.

As she waited, the younger woman told herself everything was fine. The keys were sleeping peacefully underwater. Her boyfriend was somewhere, driving, running, yelling out her name, looking for her. The baby, his head against her shoulder, cooed in her arms. Muscles all over her body were twitching—something dark, something light, trying to burst through, trying, without success, to open her up. As the river kept running, kept pouring more of itself into itself, the younger woman, who could see the blur of the older woman's body beneath the surface, the whiteness of her arms as she searched among the rocks, began to count. She didn't know what she was counting, but she knew she wanted numbers. She liked the way they led so naturally from one to the other, the way they appeared to give order. She liked the feel of them in her mouth, as she whispered them—a secret—into the baby's ear. As the older woman surfaced and, growing weary, went under again.

CONTRIBUTORS

CAROL ANSHAW has been the recipient of the Carl Sandburg, the Society of Midland Authors, and the Ferro-Grumley awards for fiction. Her novels include *Lucky in the Corner, Seven Moves,* and *Aquamarine*. Her stories "Hammam" and "Elvis Has Left the Building" were chosen for inclusion in *The Best American Short Stories of 1994* and *1998*, and her short fiction has been published in various periodicals, including *VLS* and *Story*. She currently teaches in the MFA in Writing program at the School of the Art Institute of Chicago, and she is finishing a new novel, *Afternoon on the Milky Way*.

SARAH SHUN-LIEN BYNUM's short fiction has appeared in the *Georgia Review, Alaska Quarterly Review,* and *The Best American Short Stories 2004*. Her first novel, *Madeleine Is Sleeping*, was a 2004 National Book Award finalist. She lives in Los Angeles.

BILL GASTON is the author of *Sointula, Mount Appetite, Gargoyles, The Good Body,* and the memoir *Midnight Hockey*, among others. His work has been nominated for Canada's prestigious Giller and Governor General's awards, and he won both the CBC Prize for Fiction and the inaugural Timothy Findley Award for a body of work. Gaston teaches at the University of Victoria.

ALISON GRILLO is a writer and stand-up comic living in New York City. She holds degrees from Drew University, Emerson College, and the University of Wisconsin-Milwaukee, and has published in such places as *New Letters* and *Washington Square*. Drop her a line at alisongrillo@sbcglobal.net.

DENIS JOHNSON is the author of five novels, a collection of poetry, and one book of reportage. He is the recipient of a Lannan Literary Fellowship and a Whiting Writers' Award, among many other honors. He lives in northern Idaho.

MIRANDA JULY is a performing artist, filmmaker, and writer. Her fiction has been printed in the *Paris Review, Harper's,* and the *New Yorker*. She is the author of the story collection *No One Belongs Here More Than You* and the collaborative art book *Learning to Love You More*. She also wrote, directed, and starred in the 2005 film *You and Me and Everyone We Know*. July is currently working on her second movie. She lives in Los Angeles.

DYLAN LANDIS's short fiction has appeared in *Tin House, Bomb, Best American Nonrequired Reading,* and *Bestial Noise: A Tin House Fiction Reader*. Her story collection, *Normal People Don't Live Like This*, is forthcoming from Persea Press. She lives in Washington DC.

VICTOR LaVALLE's works include a collection of short stories titled *Slapboxing with Jesus* and his novel, *The Ecstatic*. LaValle is the winner of the 1999 PEN/Open Book Award and was a finalist for the 2002 PEN/Faulkner Award.

JIM LEWIS is the author of three novels: *Sister*, *Why the Tree Loves the Ax*, and *The King Is Dead*. He lives in Austin, Texas.

MICHAEL LOWENTHAL is the author of the novels *Charity Girl*, *Avoidance*, and *The Same Embrace*. His short stories have appeared in the *Southern Review*, the *Kenyon Review*, and *Witness*. Lowenthal has also written nonfiction for the *New York Times Magazine*, *Boston Magazine*, the *Washington Post*, the *Boston Globe*, and *Out*. He lives in Boston and teaches in the low-residency MFA program at Lesley University. For more information, please visit www.MichaelLowenthal.com.

MARTHA McPHEE received her MFA from Columbia University. She is the author of *Bright Angel Time*, *Gorgeous Lies*, and *L'America*. McPhee is the recipient of fellowships from the National Endowment for the Arts and the John Simon Guggenheim Memorial Foundation. In 2002 she was a finalist for the National Book Award.

STEVEN MILLHAUSER won the 1997 Pulitzer Prize for fiction for his novel *Martin Dressler: The Tale of an American Dreamer*. His other published works include *The Barnum Museum*, *The Knife Thrower*, *Enchanted Night*, and *The King in the Tree*. His short stories have been published in both the *New Yorker* and *Harper's*. He lives in Saratoga Springs, New York, and teaches at Skidmore College.

NICHOLAS MONTEMARANO is the author of *A Fine Place* and *If the Sky Falls: Stories*. His short stories have been published in *Esquire*, *Zoetrope*, the *Southern Review*, the *Antioch Review*, the *Gettysburg Review*, and *Fence*. His fiction has also been reprinted in *The Pushcart Prize 2003* and cited as distinguished stories of the year in *The Best American Short Stories* for 2001, 2002, 2005, and 2006.

MARY OTIS's short story collection, *Yes, Yes, Cherries*, was published this past May by Tin House Books. She has had stories published in *Best New American Voices*, the *Los Angeles Times*, the *Cincinnati Review*, *Berkeley Literary Journal*, the *Santa Monica Review*, *Tin House*, and *Alaska Quarterly Review*. Her story "Pilgrim Girl" received an honorable mention for a Pushcart Prize, and her story "Unstruck" was cited in "100 Distinguished Stories" in *The Best American Short Stories 2006*. A 2007 Walter Dakin Fellow, Otis currently lives in Los Angeles. www.maryotis.com

LUCIA PERILLO's fourth book of poems, *Luck Is Luck*, was a finalist for the Los Angeles Times Book Prize and was awarded the Kingsley Tufts Prize from Claremont University. Her poetry and prose also earned her a MacArthur Fellowship in 2000. A book of her essays, *I've Heard the Vultures Singing*, was published by Trinity University Press in 2007.

MARK JUDE POIRIER is the author of the novels *Goats* and *Modern Ranch Living* and the story collections *Naked Pueblo* and *Unsung Heroes of American History*. Most recently, he edited the short fiction anthology *The Worst Years of Your Life*. His first film, *Smart People*, will be released by Miramax in 2008.

PETER ROCK is the author of four novels, most recently *The Bewildered*, and a story collection, *The Unsettling*. His novel *My Abandonment* will be published by Harcourt in fall 2008.

ROBIN ROMM is the author of the story collection *The Mother Garden*. Stories in this collection originally appeared in many journals, including *One Story* and the *Threepenny Review*. A former MacDowell Fellow, she lives and teaches in Santa Fe, New Mexico.

ELISSA SCHAPPELL is the author of *Use Me*, a finalist for the PEN/Hemingway award, and coeditor with Jenny Offill of two anthologies, *The Friend Who Got Away* and *Money Changes Everything*. She is currently a contributing editor of *Vanity Fair*, a cofounder and now editor-at-large of *Tin House*, a regular contributor to the *New York Times Book Review*, and formerly senior editor of the *Paris Review*. Her fiction/essays/articles have appeared in *The Bitch in the House*, *The Mrs. Dalloway Reader*, *The KGB Bar Reader*, *SPIN*, and *Vogue*, among other places. She teaches in the low-residency MFA program at Queens University in North Carolina.

ELIZABETH TALLENT is the author of *Time with Children*, *Honey*, *In Constant Flight*, and the novel *Museum Pieces*. Her work has appeared in the *New Yorker*, *Harper's*, *Grand Street*, the *Paris Review*, *Esquire*, *ZYZZYVA*, and in *The Best American Short Stories* collections. She currently teaches at Stanford's creative writing program.

ROBERT TRAVIESO grew up in Baltimore, Maryland, and now lives in Brooklyn. He received an MFA from Brooklyn College. His work has been featured in *SmokeLong Quarterly* and in *Tin House*.

MATTHEW VOLLMER's work has appeared in magazines such as the *Paris Review*, *Virginia Quarterly Review*, *Colorado Review*, *Gulf Coast*, *PRISM International*, *New Letters*, *Salt Hill*, and *Confrontation*. He lives in Blacksburg, Virginia, where he teaches writing at Virginia Tech University.

COPYRIGHT NOTES